A Wave of Breath

A WAVE OF BREATH

ISBN: 978-1-937356-49-1 (Hardback Edition)
ISBN: 978-1-937356-50-7 (Paperback Edition)
ISBN: 978-1-937356-51-4 (Ebook Edition)

Library of Congress Control Number: 2025926457

Publisher's Cataloging-in-Publication Data

Collins, Theresa.
A wave of breath / Tess Collins.
pages ; cm
ISBN: 978-1-937356-49-1 (hardback)
ISBN: 978-1-937356-50-7 (trade)
ISBN: 978-1-937356-51-4 (ebook)
1. Quantum theory—Fiction. 2. Quests (Expeditions)—Fiction. 3. Resurrection—Fiction. 4. Conspiracies—Fiction. 5. Artificial intelligence—Fiction. 6. Mythological fiction. 7. Speculative fiction. 8. Romance fiction. I. Title.
PS3603.O4559 W38 2025
813.6—dc23
2025926457

Published by BearCat Press: www.BearCatPress.com/
Book Design by: Integrative Ink
Book Cover Illustrated by: Sang Oh

BOOKS BY TESS COLLINS

FICTION

The Appalachian Trilogy:
The Law of Revenge
The Law of the Dead
The Law of Betrayal

The Midnight Valley Quartet:
Notown
The Hunter of Hertha

Shadow Mountain Saga:
Shadow Mountain

Other Fiction:
Helen of Troy
A Wave of Breath

Non-Fiction:
How Theater Managers Manage

This book is dedicated to my brother-in-law, Nick Code, because he told me it was the only kind of book that he would read. ;) ;) ;)

A Wave of Breath

Tess Collins

San Francisco

Book Sections

~ San Francisco ~

There were no words for how afraid I was. I, a tiller of words, *generous of heart and bold of vision*, a rival columnist had once called me; *authentic and sassy with a hint of evil genius*, another had said. I knew words. I knew stories. I knew endings like an apocalyptic sermon. But this city now—broken, sorrowful, savage—words would not serve as I watched our Mayor and what was left of our board of supervisors burn on the steps of City Hall. No one had the patience for the words of politicians any longer. They wanted water, and they wanted it now.

"Brooklyn, we gotta get out of here." My neighbor, Jamie Alverez, tugged my sleeve as we scooted toward the crowd's edge. My knees threatened to buckle. The stink of burning bodies curled into my nostrils, and I gagged, stomach lurching as I stumbled backward, away from the flames that had once been people. Some turned away, others ran, hands covering their mouths. A faction angrily pounded their fists skyward, joining the call for vengeance. This wasn't supposed to happen. We all came to talk, work things out, and get resources to those who needed them. A few months into this mess, and one group already had other plans.

At the corner of Polk and McAllister, I glanced back at the chaos. A burning man flailed in a circle. The bulk of the crowd scattered, halted mid-run to look back like me, ran again, stopped again, looked again as if they couldn't accept what they witnessed. Was there anything they could do? What should they do? Minds unable to calculate the meaning. The crash of breaking glass. Wild whooping and hollering to *burn it all down!* I coughed, hand across my mouth, fighting a stomach heave from the nauseous smell of burning flesh. There was nothing I could do.

Paule Oliver's Mid-Market Street group had started this. I watched a pack of about five hundred stream into City Hall, looking for the treasure of bottled water they were sure was hidden there. They'd argued it before it all went wrong, accusing the Mayor of hoarding for the elite. Well, there were very few wealthy people in San Francisco these days. Most'd gone weeks ago. Where, I wasn't sure. Islands, sanctuaries, Disney World for all I knew.

A numbness spread through my limbs as I watched the tide of humanity surge through the shattered glass doors. I wondered if I'd ever written about any of them—mothers, former teachers, artists turned revolutionaries. Now, with bats in hand, they trampled over the line I thought none of us would cross. My faith in negotiation, in decency, in systems built by flawed but hopeful humans—crumbled.

Caravans of buses had come to the city a while back, giving out flyers for people to go live in Central Valley and work on the farms for a guarantee of shelter and food. Rumor was those buses left full, but I doubt that's where the rich had gone. Jamie pulled me, and we trotted up Polk Street, sticking close to the buildings to avoid being seen. Even though all the neighborhoods had agreed on the representative's safe passage, you could never be too sure of a lone wolf looking to rob someone on the blocks that still needed to be organized.

"This wasn't supposed to happen," I rasped, as we sheltered in the side exit of the deserted strip club against its wall-size mural of whales, dolphins, sharks, and other colorful sea creatures. "Look," I pointed. "Sweet butter for the masses." Across the street, a make-shift altar of candles, flowers, and assorted rosaries cascaded around a chalk drawing of the Virgin Mary on the side of a building. A local news anchor, Brace Benton, had been reporting about the various apparitions around the country. A dinghy for terrified people.

"Come on," Jamie urged. "Won't be safe until we get behind our barricade."

We were the Nob Hill group, about three thousand of us to start. We were now down to around three hundred scattered among five buildings on three blocks at the top of the hill. Most of us were the working middle-class. Money in the bank, but not rich. Some had moved into these apartments twenty years prior when rent was affordable. Moving away and abandoning what they had was unthinkable. Now, no one paid rent, nor was anyone calling to collect it. We kept our buildings safe, our streets blocked behind barricades of cars, furniture, and armed protectors or what passed for them. That's what San Francisco had become in these last few weeks—a collection of tribes trying to hold on until this emergency passed. And it had to pass. We had to believe that. Yet, intermittent supplies from FEMA, no National Guard or army of any kind, Red Cross, and churches giving what they could, less and less, until we were this. But we weren't any different than anyone else in what was left of the city.

Jamie and I crawled between abandoned trolley cars at Polk and California, stopping long enough to tell the mid-Polk coalition's sentry what had happened.

"What's this mean?" he asked.

"Nothing good." I wet my lips. "Your committee ought to be back soon. I don't think many followed Paule's lead, but he had weapons, machetes, and baseball bats mostly."

From there, a straight shot up the hill. The streets in between could be treacherous, but the Polk Street crew watched our backs until Caleb Yu motioned that he saw us, and we scrambled over our blockade of cars, furniture, and garbage containers to safety. Safety, I thought. A fragile word—gossamer-thin. It meant nothing in a world where neighbors could turn to wolves overnight, prayers were whispered over candles, and weapons were handed out with the morning coffee. Safety had become more of a wish than a condition.

Jamie and I went down our three blocks and told our street security guards what had happened. We asked representatives from each building to meet the next morning to reassess where things stood and what we needed to do next.

Once in my apartment, I fastened all the locks and braced a piece of lumber into metal slots across the door. It was the only way I could sleep, and who knew how long that would keep me safe. Pulling a chair to the window, I let my forehead lean against the cool glass. Smoke from the Civic Center drifted northward, and I tried not to think of the vacant expression on the Mayor's face when Paule Oliver came down on him with a baseball bat. I closed my eyes and wished for the time no one fought over water.

"Hey, baby." Martin's tongue brushed against mine as the rain shower streamed over us. He held me against a marble wall, his soapy hand on my breast. "Sulis," he whispered, his pet name for me. "My beautiful girl."

"I am not a girl," I replied, smirking mischievously. "Let me show you why."

"Shhh." He leaned into me, his thighs nudging my legs apart, water gushing over us, breath in gasps and liquid heat. He kissed my neck, and my legs encircled him as he pushed inside of me.

"Yes," I murmured, clasping his hips and riding him with the dance of the pelting shower. "Stop!"

His head jerked back, confused. Then, he saw it and we both shifted out of scarlet water cascading around us like a fountain of blood. "Red," he said, staring beyond me, his eyes blinking rapidly. "Red Water. I, I, I have to go."

"What is it?"

He didn't answer. Holding me, he stared at me intently, lips parted, his expression crestfallen as he cupped my cheek. "Go to the store. Buy every bottle of liquid you can carry, and tell no one what you have. Lock yourself in your apartment until I come for you."

I jerked upright. Someone yelling. Blocks away. Probably someone trying to get into a safe zone. I don't know how secure they really were. Mostly, our safety depended on what others thought we had, not what we actually possessed. Surely Paule Oliver wouldn't come this far up. Not yet, anyway. I was beyond thinking someone would arrest him for what he did today. There was no doubt this had changed everything. There was no longer a command structure to... to what? Lie to us? It was hard not to wonder if there had been hidden resources in city hall. My hands were trembling. I shook them out and pulled a can of water from a box marked *Good For Twenty-five Years.* San Francisco was earthquake country, and I was a prepared type of individual.

Sipping the tinny-tasting liquid like the finest of wines. Savoring the sensation like the satisfying intoxication of a lover's touch. Save half for later. Keep the body hydrated. That was truth. Another truth: Martin had never come back for me.

It was Martin's apartment where I'd eventually barricaded myself. He'd rushed out without his keys that day, and there was no way to lock his door but to take the set hanging on his refrigerator. I texted him that I'd walk up the hill and give them to him when he was ready to come home. Only a few blocks down on Bush Street, my studio on the ninth floor of a worn-out redbrick quadrangle had been built after the 1906 earthquake. Days passed with no word from Martin. I went to the store daily, buying as much as possible and filling mine and his apartments with canned food, bottled water, pantry supplies, and toilet paper. It took less than a week for me to notice that other people were inconspicuously doing the same. On the news, Brace Benton explained away the red water as a harmless computer glitch that state officials were investigating. That was the day I stopped trusting the news.

Still trying to understand what was going on or what would happen, I waited for Martin, sure he would return. The only person who noticed me was Mrs. Houseman, an elderly woman with brilliant blue eyes who walked up and down the

Taylor Street steps for exercise. The twenty-five percent grade between California and Pine Streets was popular with exercise enthusiasts or sadists like me who were too cheap to pay for a cab ride three blocks uphill, even if I was carrying forty pounds of supplies. "You again," she called out on one of my many treks up to Martin's apartment. "And carrying that heavy load. Let me help."

"You've got to be the strongest person I know," I chuckled with her. "I'm out of breath halfway up and you jog these steps."

She reached out to take one of the bags that I would not give her. Her tattooed forearm always caught my eye. She must have noticed me looking, but never said anything. It was a faded tattooed number from a World War II concentration camp. "It's a smart girl who prepares." She wagged a finger at me, noticing the supplies were more than groceries. She was quiet, glancing at a scar on the side of my face as we continued up the steps.

I paused at the top of the hill, catching my breath and shifting the bag to my other shoulder. "Mrs. Houseman, do you get the feeling something is about to happen?"

"The wind does seem to shift, doesn't it?" Her eyes narrowed, not looking into mine but at my neck, where the scar traveled to its end. "An ominous feeling. Eerily familiar."

"If you need me to do any shopping for you, I can."

"No, my son lives with me. We're good." She stared at the corner of Huntington Park across the street from us where a group of people watched their dogs romp on the block-long lawn. "I wonder if they'll have to eat them," she said.

My breath caught in my throat, and I couldn't look at her.

She patted my arm, again staring at my jaw. "Let's not make it rain before there are clouds. But," she paused, holding my shoulder. "There are clouds, dark ones."

Her words sliced through the sunshine like icy wind. I looked at the dogs again—golden fur glinting in the sun, tails wagging in ecstasy. I'd laughed at them a few weeks ago, envied their oblivion. Now I saw meat. My chest tightened. I wanted to believe Mrs. Houseman was being macabre, but I couldn't unsee it. There were clouds, she'd said—and I suddenly felt the shadow.

I went to work as if nothing had changed. Life continued. I wrote for the *San Francisco Calendar*, starting as an astrology/obit writer. I'd worked my way up to cub reporter covering city hall. They'd given me my own column five years ago, and I had a growing audience from profiling ordinary working folk along with the occasional celebrity. I aimed to be the next Herb Caen, an icon of San Francisco journalism that, in his day, some had called the *Voice of San Francisco*.

Slowly, staff called in sick. Some turned in resignations. I had trouble getting interviews. No one important wanted to talk about what was happening. Then, there was no water for two days. It returned on the third day, a thin yellowish stream with little pressure. News reports called it the "Water Event" and kept the moniker when the electricity went out, just for a few hours. Media announced that the city had been broken into districts, and each district had been assigned twelve hours a day service. Water went out again for another two days. Rumors of a foreign virus shutting down utility company's computers all over the country competed with ones that terrorists had poisoned the water supply, and the government was not admitting how dire the situation was.

None of my contacts would return phone calls—when the phones worked. The day I was told to stay home, I packed up all I'd bought and took it one backpack at a time to Martin's better-equipped apartment at the top of Nob Hill, a safer neighborhood if only by a few blocks. Nope, I wasn't a rich person. I just dated one.

With the news of nationwide rolling blackouts in all three electrical grids, people panicked. Services were cut to a few hours a day. Businesses shut down, including the *Calendar*. Runs were made on banks, and store shelves emptied. The city instituted food trucks. Every Monday, a Red Cross truck came to Huntington Park, and we were given a bag of food after standing in line for hours. I always took it, even though I was pretty well stocked. When Martin returned, we'd need food for two, and who knew how long this would last.

What I'd thought would last several days turned into weeks. I counted cans instead of days. Inventory became my new ritual. I lined them up, labeled them, touched each one as if its solidity could anchor me to reality. Sometimes I pretended Martin was in the other room, just reading or showering. I'd talk aloud to him, then laugh at myself, then cry. The line between sane and not had become too thin to trace.

After a month, fewer in the community showed up for the giveaways. There was scattered violence. People were killed in the street, and bodies were left lying where they'd dropped. Emergency services couldn't keep up. That's when I realized the populace was leaving the city. Was there more safety in the suburbs? Maybe they had gone to the rural areas of California and lived like hippies in a commune? The National Guard left, to where I didn't know. And now, there was no government. Martin had a house in Bolinas. I wondered if he was there?

I worried whether the electricity would continue. Tap water came out cloudy, and Brace Benton told us to boil it before drinking. He also blamed the Water Event on inept bureaucrats and made a case for a change of administration in the next election. Curious and bizarre rumors floated out on the internet and when we had TV, they reported as if nothing unusual was happening. One day, Benton's co-anchor burst into tears while reporting a slag of feel-good stories, the latest craziness being sightings of the Virgin Mary across the country, even on some Texan's toast. Any bread we came by, we ate, so we'd have to forego religious miracles. Most of us popped as much popcorn as we could during the electrical period since that food lasted well, flushed our toilets when we had water and filled our bathtubs to the rim. Thus, was life in the big city.

Early the following day, I knocked on Jamie's door and was met by his husband, Dan, and houseguest, Julio. Julio, a high school friend of Jamie's, had lived in New York for the last ten years and gotten stuck here during his annual visit. As far as we could tell, nothing was flying in and out of any airport. Unable to return home, they'd kept him. "I'm the entertainment," he often claimed, flamboyantly. He was a funny guy until he realized he couldn't get his heroin fix. After a week of fever, shivering, hallucinations, and dry heaving, he was only now starting to regain his strength. "Welcome to the city of perks and fleas." He bowed and gestured me to enter.

"What does that even mean?" I bopped him on the nose with a manicured finger, the nail coated with Black Phoenix sparkly green called The Intangibles.

He sighed at my hand enviously. "When I worked as a drag queen at Madame Vanilla's School of Vice and Virtue, I had polish that put a spotlight to shame," he said, voice laced with nostalgia, a bittersweet reminder of better days.

"Be good to me, and I'll leave you in my will." I air-kissed him and hurried Jamie and Dan to the morning meeting. "Be a dear, bring tea." I waved my polished fingers in Julio's face on the way out the door. He returned a smartass smirk.

Sitting down at a card table at the Clay/Jones intersection, the view of downtown was the most stunning in the city. The iconic Transamerica Pyramid knifed the sky, flawless and aloof against the fifty-two-story Bank of America monolith and Salesforce Tower, famous for its Eye of Sauron crown on Halloween. The Bay Bridge, now empty of traffic, soared like an arm across to Oakland and Berkeley, and on clear days, Mount Diablo peaked into view. The famous cityscape lured many a tourist and wanderer alike to the bohemian city by the bay. A few months back, I'd have paid thirty bucks for a cocktail with this view. Now I couldn't even cry for what we'd lost.

"You smell like baby wipes," Carl Houseman said, sniffing in my direction.

"Down to my last pack," I snarked. "I'll be smelling like the rest of you soon." His mother sat beside him and smiled at me. They lived in a building opposite Huntington Park, outside our area, but they attended the community meetings even though we didn't protect that block. Carl was a former marine who'd given us self-defense and shooting lessons and lent handguns for our barricade guards. He once called my front kick "an embarrassment to the human anatomy," but when I dropped Julio with a leg sweep, he clapped me on the back and named me "Badass of the Day." It was probably the closest thing to affection he knew how to show.

We waited a few minutes until Bill Mulvey, Sandra Wu, and Janet Billings arrived. Jamie cleared his throat and confirmed what had happened to the Mayor and board of supervisors. He stood, the city skyline behind him, the morning sun reflecting on high-rise windows. Jamie was a natural leader and held our group together almost through the force of his personality. I wished I could comfort people as well as he did; making them feel like help was a wish away. With each passing day, I feared even we would turn on each other for resources.

"Because of this," Jamie continued. "I think we should double up on the night guards at the Jones/California Street blockade and start building more secure relations with Chinatown and Russian Hill."

"Urg," Bill moaned. "That's one more person having to stay awake all night and—"

"It's not forever. Just until we're sure Paule isn't making a run up the hill."

"Everybody hates these shifts," he said. "And Paule's crew is too lazy to climb up the hill."

The awkward silence gave way to everyone looking in different directions. "I'll take the shift this week," Mrs. Houseman said.

"Mom!" Carl said. "Don't start with me."

"I'm well trained," she argued, her elegant hands waving like gliding birds. "I did my time with the Israeli army and am perfectly capable of a throw-down."

"I can do this week's shift," I volunteered. "What Mrs. Houseman can do is watch from your window, which has a pretty good view of Huntington Park. Paule comes up the hill, he'll likely come that way. She'll see him and can alert me."

That calmed Carl and gave his mother something to do in a safe location.

"I've told you to call me Miriam, dear," she said, tapping her cell phone. "Got you on speed dial." Our phones didn't always work, but they were all we had until we could trade for more walkie-talkie sets.

"Okay," Jamie continued. He gave an account of where we were in our food stores, a trade we made with Chinatown, and a mutual aid pack with North Beach for security to the docks when Chinese and South American food ships came in every couple of weeks. We'd broken into every empty apartment except for the top floors of a nineteen-story high-rise, gathered valuables the owner would never need again, and traded with ship owners for fresh food. Yes, we contemplated that we might be charged with breaking and entering someday. I kept the registry of everything taken, expecting we'd pay the owner back. One day. When life returned to normal. "Water," Jamie said, "Water is our biggest issue."

"It always is," Miriam said, her eyes unfocused on a memory I was glad she didn't share.

"I know where," I said, too fast, spitting out the words. Faces turned toward me like sunflowers to the light. "There's water," I whispered. "Tons of it. Stacked floor to ceiling. Only..." I hesitated. Martin's name ghosted across my lips, the memory of his voice a raw blade. "Only one problem. We need Paule Oliver's help." The room groaned, like a collective stomach turning. "The Siriso Building. It's my boyfriend's law office. One time, the security guard was on break, and I saw him accept a bottled water delivery. The storage rooms are huge, and they're on all five floors."

"You've no idea where Martin is, dear?" Miriam asked.

The softness of her voice made mine catch, and my nose burned as I fought back emotions I didn't want to show. "He—He..." I swallowed and cleared my throat. "I've got to believe he's alive." I coughed, working to regain my composure. "Doesn't matter now. We need those supplies. The building has Javon batteries running essential systems if the electricity goes off.

Martin told me about it. Those are directly connected to the security system and will run for years on those hocus-pocus batteries."

"Can we get those too?" Sandra Wu asked.

"The systems work on proprietary connections, so they won't do any good outside the building."

"How does Paule fit into this?" Dan asked.

"The front of the building is in his territory."

"That's just not going to happen," Jamie said.

"We can't trust him," Carl agreed.

"Somebody's probably already taken those supplies," Jamie surmised.

"I don't think so. Martin is the last of his family. He locked up that building every night. Always insisted his employees be gone by six so they'd have a life outside the law. We'll have to put up with Paule's malarkey to safely cross to that area."

"It's too risky," Bill Mulvey said loudly over the overlapping whines of it not being a good idea. "Paule's a criminal."

"We don't have a choice," Miriam interrupted, silencing the group. "I'm waiting for somebody else to have a big idea because I am sick of this yellow piss we struggle to boil."

"The Red Cross will be back," Carl argued. "This can't last forever."

"I used to think that," Dan said, looking directly at Jamie. "We're drawing down on our liquid storage. Last count—"

"Exactly five hundred gallons of bottled water, six hundred fruit juice packets, twenty-five boxes of sparkling water, and forty cases of various sodas," I said, as they all bluntly stopped and stared at me. "I helped with the inventory. Got a good memory is all."

"It's scary how you do that." Sandra Wu crossed herself.

Dan tapped his hand on the table. "The point is when that's gone—what do you think will happen? Polk Street will share, the Tenderloin will gallop in on a white horse? Not likely. We can't count on the Red Cross coming back."

"Well, we'll just keep boiling what comes from the tap," Sandra Wu said.

"Are you serious!" Jamie interrupted. "I watched the Mayor get his brains splattered all over city hall steps. I don't know that we'll have water in the pipes for much longer."

"The Feds will come in soon," someone said. "They won't let this continue."

"They're useless. We're on our own!"

"I get it!" Carl yelled. "Everybody has bigger problems, but why wouldn't Paule take that baseball bat to your head? Anybody come to arrest him? Seen a mention of it on the news? No one cares."

"Because we have something he'll want," Miriam said. "He's got to be wanting clean water as much as anybody else."

"He's got all the drug stores on mid-Market. He's doing better than all of us."

"Oh, and he just beat the mayor to death for no reason," Jamie pointed out. "Come on, he's out of water too."

A pause in the din. The sad and terrifying fear that none of us wanted to acknowledge was that we had a society because we agreed to it. The minute one neighborhood decided not to play, no one was sure what would happen. Water. It was what everyone wanted. A yearning lover too far away to touch. The thought of it inspired. It was survival. It was life.

"Okay," Jamie said. "How do we go about getting a meeting with him?"

Julio cleared his throat as he sat Tenmokus teacups before us. Dressed in a Japanese kimono, he'd pulled his long locks into a geisha's bun and repeated each meeting: *I serve to remind you fools that civilization is sacrosanct.* "I can get you a meeting with Paule Oliver," he said instead.

We all looked at him, flabbergasted.

Julio bowed, mugging in his ridiculous white pancake makeup. "Excuse my bluntness," he said toward Miriam, then toward the rest of us. "But he used to be my drug dealer back in the day."

I had a history with Paule Oliver as well. Not a good one. He wasn't my drug dealer, but he was a pain in my ass when I was a young reporter covering a story on the Tenderloin drug trade. He'd harassed me, yelling to his fellow drug dealers to spit at the narc. After a heated argument, he told me I'd better watch my back. We traded girl-pushes that amounted to nothing. In those days, he was a young teenager, riding a bike in and out of traffic, switching to a skateboard, and putting white chalk in his hair to gray it up if the police were chasing him. He had survival skills that had served him well even though he'd disappeared for a couple of years, presumably in prison. I was a twenty-something trying to write my way into a more respectable gig by taking on tough stories. I hadn't realized an undercover police detail had been following me, and Paule got arrested right after my first major article went to print.

We sent word via Chinatown that Julio wanted to talk to Paule, trading a Fabergé egg for protection, a meeting place, and the chance not to die stupidly. My fingers had trembled as I handed it over—something beautiful for something brutal. Chinatown was armed like a fortress, their AR-15s polished and gleaming. In a city of baseball bats, machetes, and handguns, they were kings. And Paule didn't mess with kings.

After four fuck-offs, Paule agreed to a meeting on the condition that it lasted no longer than fifteen minutes. He didn't like staying in one place longer than that. Waiting at the Dragon Gate on the corner of Grant and California, he was still a no-show after an hour.

"Hold on," Julio said. "He's here. He's just making me wait, little bitch." He perched himself on top of a dragon statue. In times past, tourists would snap their photos here. "Oh, Paauuulleeee! I'm a-waitin' for you, sweetie-pie."

I put a hand to my head and looked at Jamie, Carl, and Miriam, who'd insisted on coming. This wasn't going to work.

"Call me that again, I'll blow your stupid head off." Paule's voice boomed from the shadows of a boarded-up coffee shop.

"We all know what you're capable of, Mr. Oliver," I called out. "We have an offer that will benefit all of us."

"Wait a minute." He kicked out a window board and stepped through it, surrounded by five men holding guns pointed toward the ground. Our five from Chinatown stepped forward, weapons ready.

"Hold on everybody," I called out, "Julio, do something." I said under my breath.

"Paule, have I ever done you wrong? I was a good customer, always paid cash, except that one time I gave you a check, but it cleared." He stepped into the street, making a little turn to show off the pink Chanel suit he had taken from some apartment. "You lay down those bad boys, baby."

Paule glared, and I expected that was the end of it. I should never have brought Julio. I fought not to flinch. My palms prickled. I hoped he wouldn't recognize me.

Then, Paule signaled to his men to move back into the darkness of the coffee shop. I expected him to bail because of Julio's sassing. Instead, he pointed at me. "You're that white bitch wrote for the *Calendar*, used to bust my balls. I was kinda hoping you was dead." He grinned, not a friendly smile but a familiar one, older, meaner, eyes narrowing as if to say he held my fate between his fingertips like a match. "Yeah. Scarface, we called you on the corner."

"Mr. Oliver," Miriam said, stepping around me. "Let's not trifle about a past we can't change," Miriam said, and then—God help her—she slid off her wedding ring. The metal caught the faint light like it was still warm with memory. "A token of trust," she said. "Let my friend here speak, and I think you'll see we have a mutual goal." She placed the ring in his palm, and I watched the moment stretch as she held his hand longer than he was comfortable, but he didn't step back, and Paule shot her a nod after she complimented his Golf Wang jacket. Something shifted. The crackle of violence gave way to something rarer: hesitation.

I felt like I was about to talk to the wall, but given what we'd already invested, I had to try to make this happen. "I'm here to talk about the Siriso building. Am I correct that neither you nor

Dixie Roman has been able to get into it? Don't answer that; I already know you haven't."

"Still a know-it-all," he said.

"The front of the Siriso building faces areas you control. Both sides and the rear are in Dixie's area."

"Which basically means it's Dixie's building," he snarked.

"It's my boyfriend's building. His family built it. It has steel gates that come down over the doors and state-of-the-art security still running on Javon batteries."

"Whoopie-doo."

"Here's the play." I said, voice steady even as my stomach flipped. "You scout out Dixie's security, get the shift changes. Then we go in fast—water, candy, whatever's there, we grab it. Chinatown covers the truck, takes their twenty percent cut. We split the rest." I paused, waiting.

He gazed sideways, thinking, but he didn't turn away. "What the hell are you providing?"

I held up a plastic card. "The master key."

"See, honey," Julio said. "I came bearing gifts."

Yeah, there actually was someone worse than Paule Oliver, and his name sent a chill through me. Dixie Roman. A retired MMA fighter, who had run for mayor, governor, senator, representative, and probably dogcatcher, always lost spectacularly and wore his failures like badges of honor. He sold himself as law-and-order with a slice of wild punch on the side.

After the Water Event, he became a specter of violence, known for setting fires to the homes of anyone who dared oppose him. He never came to the organizing meetings held in the beginning, ignored city and state government, and didn't hesitate to deliver the first blow. The thought of him made my heart race. He was too comfortable in the chaos, almost like he'd known it was going to happen, and I couldn't help wondering if he did. Controlling lower Market Street and the southern waterfront through Bayview, some said he had all of San Francisco to the airport, which meant he would control what everyone got once planes were flying in and out again.

Dixie and Paule had fought over a few blocks in the financial district. No one had won, and both claimed it, mainly because it had several drugstores and a Trader Joe's grocery store. I think both scavenged whatever was there and now the empty blocks stood in technical dispute. I didn't want trouble with Dixie. He was a different sort of bad. Before the fiasco at city hall, I'd never known Paule to kill anyone. That he came out of city hall with thirty pallets of bottled water that he gave to a church to distribute made people less judgmental of him. Dixie would kill you and throw in a dose of torture first. We had to get in and out of the Siriso building without his group ever knowing. I was sure we could as long as Paule held up his part of the work.

The night came. At midnight, cloaked in shadows, we gathered at Grant and California. Twenty of us stood there, hearts pounding in unison, while Paule's crew mirrored our anxiety. The air was thick with unspoken fears, the kind that clung to your skin like a second layer. I could feel the weight of every decision pressing down on me, the stakes rising with each passing moment. The night felt alive, a predator lurking just out of sight, and I was acutely aware that one wrong move could shatter our fragile plan.

It took some doing, but Chinatown agreed to have four armed security people accompany the truck Jamie would drive once we had the supplies in the lobby. Hugging the buildings, we jogged to the Siriso building through several unclaimed blocks in the financial district. I'd watched Martin tap out the security codes many times—not that I'm a voyeur, but I do possess excellent eyesight and a photographic memory. I put the card key into the electronic gate, and it slid up like butter. The code, 9459. Odd numbers that didn't match anything I was aware of. Martin was a person who liked birthdays, special dates, holidays, and as long as I'd known him, never forgot them. He even gave me a lava lamp on the anniversary of our first date. "To light your way to me always," he'd said. Couldn't imagine what 9459 meant. The beeping alarm shut off, and I covered an elephant-sized sigh of relief. "Crowbar," I said, indicating at a desk drawer on the security guard's desk. One of Paule's guys, the one with the crowbar, was eyeing the fire extinguisher. "Hey!" I yelled out, "Over here!"

Paule's glare had been a constant since we sprinted the three blocks from Grant to Battery Street, a storm brewing behind his eyes. I could feel the tension crackling in the air, a volatile mix of frustration and fear. I figured it was just a matter of time before he started complaining.

"Nobody put you in charge," he spit.

"Keys to the vending machines will be in here," I said, much more politely.

After getting the keys, I sent three people to go floor to floor, emptying vending machines into plastic bins we'd brought. I took the rest of the group to the second floor to show them the vending storage rooms. "There'll be one on each floor. Younger folk, I'm sorry, but you'll have to start on the fifth floor and work down. Our elders will start here and go up. Take everything to the lobby, then I'll call in the truck."

I got a glare from Paule, but he didn't say anything. After opening the storage doors on all five building floors, I stopped at Martin's corner office on the third floor. This building would have made an excellent safe house except for all the trouble surrounding it. I hated admitting it, but part of me wondered if Martin might be here, hoped he might be here. I sat in his oversized leather chair and looked at the world from his perspective. His Harvard law degree hung on the right wall and his undergrad from Stanford on the left. A picture of him and Phillip Javon at a Giants game sat on a side table along with one of a past mayor giving him an award. Martin represented the wunderkind whose Javon batteries and other inventions were going to save the world. Back when the world didn't think it needed saving. I wrote our initials in the dust on his desk and circled them with a heart. Silly gesture, I know. *Where could he be?* The truth that was clear to me hurt. That day in the shower. The red water was a signal. He knew what it meant.

The storage rooms were filled with cases of bottled water, as well as toilet paper, towels, and boxes of emergency rations. I looked the other way as Paule's people pushed the fire extinguishers into the supplies. I suppose we did have to be ready. Sweaty, sore, and out of breath, it took us until three a.m. to strip the building. "Unicorn," I said into my walkie-talkie, the code for Jamie to bring the truck to the front of the building. I looked at Paule. "You're sure Dixie's security won't be walking this far north this time of night?"

"I'm sure," he said. " 'Cause I got 'im." From behind the security desk, one of his guys jerked up a handcuffed man with duct tape across his mouth.

"What the fuck!"

"No, no, no, no, no," Julio said, looking from Paule to the man.

"He knows what we look like, Paule," I said, a hand going to my forehead.

"He knows what you look like," Paule sneered. "I'm already famous."

"I don't want a war with Dixie."

"That's your narcissistic personality disorder talking. No one gives a shit about you, white girl."

Julio leaned down beside the man and took the tape off his mouth. The man sucked in air. "You people don't realize what you've done. Dixie'll—"

Paule shot him in the head. The crack of the gun echoed in my ears, a sound that shattered the fragile reality I had been clinging to. Julio fell backward, his grip tightening around my leg as if I were his only anchor in a storm. I think I might have let out a little scream, a raw, instinctive reaction to the horror unfolding before me. My heart raced, pounding against my ribcage like a caged animal desperate to escape.

In that instant, time seemed to stretch, the world narrowing down to the lifeless body on the floor and the blood pooling around it. I felt a wave of nausea wash over me, a mix of shock and guilt. How had we come to this? I was supposed to be a part of the solution, yet here I was, standing in the aftermath of a senseless act, paralyzed by the weight of what had just happened.

The still silence that followed was deafening, a heavy blanket that smothered any hope of rational thought. I could see the faces of the Nob Hill people, their expressions frozen in disbelief, mirroring my own horror. I wanted to scream, to run, to do anything but stand there and witness the brutality that had become our reality. But instead, I felt a cold dread settle in my stomach.

"Truck's here," one of Paule's men called out.

I looked toward the glass doors. It wasn't our truck.

"I don't know what you think you're doing," I said to Paule. "But this—"

He taunted us with his gun. "I'm taking half, bitches," he said. "You can pay Chinatown's twenty percent out of what's left."

Part of me wanted to say *that's not fair*, but how stupid would that have sounded. His crew opened the door and started moving the supplies. Fuming, I waited until he looked away, then shoved Julio into him. The gun scattered across the marble floor, and I jumped behind the security desk and hit an emergency button. A steel gate shot down in front of the elevators where most supplies were stacked.

"The fuck!" Paule yelled.

"Yeah, the fuck," I yelled back. "What you've taken, you got. That's it. Now get out of here Paule, because my truck is coming down that street with Chinatown security guards and their sweet AK-15s."

Julio picked up the gun. I motioned to him to point it. Incredibly, he turned it around and handed it back to Paule. "You got to get out of here, baby."

Paule's lips quivered, his anger stressing every muscle in his face. Lights from our truck hit the side of his. He stuck the gun into the back of his pants, his eyes never leaving Julio's. He turned to leave but paused at the door. "This ain't finished," he pointed at me.

Their truck pulled away and ours pulled up. I reset the security gate, and we had the majority of the supplies.

I looked at the dead man. A man Dixie's people would be looking for. What would be the consequence of finding him in Martin's building if he ever figured out how to gain access. Couldn't let that happen. I grabbed Julio's arm. "You did this!"

"He didn't mean to."

"Wrap this man's head in *your* coat so his blood doesn't spread or leave a trail, then drag him around the corner onto Dixie's side."

"Ugh,"

Then, I slapped him, hard. Julio didn't react. He took off his coat and did the job assigned to him.

As the sun rose, casting a soft golden light over Huntington Park, I rested on a bench, a fragile oasis of calm. I'd learned that those up to no good rarely sought trouble at dawn, but the tranquility around me felt like a cruel joke. The park, once a vibrant tapestry of people sunbathing, kids on the swings, the occasional tourist throwing a coin into the Fountain of the Tortoises, now felt like a ghost of its former self, echoing with memories of a time when joy was still possible.

My insides churned with the remnants of the night's violence, a visceral reminder of how quickly everything could unravel. I inhaled deeply, trying to calm the storm of anxiety swirling within me, but Paule's threat played like a loop in my mind, a dark cloud overshadowing the morning light.

If only Martin was here. The thought pierced through my heart like a dagger, a longing so profound it nearly took my breath away. If I could just touch him, I might feel safe again. The weekend before the Water Event, we'd sat, drinking coffee, on this very bench.

"I think we should get a dog," Martin proclaimed, watching a Golden Retriever play tug-a-rope with its owner.

The word "We" tumbled in my mind as I noted this date as the first time he'd ever called us a We. "You need stronger coffee to wake yourself up." I offered my own cup toward him.

"No, really. Think of all the tricks we could teach the little rascal."

Second time, we're a We. "You work crazy hours. When would you have time?" I couldn't help but beam at him, watching his eyes light up, and his hands animatedly emphasizing his points. Seeing this unexpected glimpse of what was important to him warmed me. He seldom spoke of his dreams or what kind of life he envisioned for the two of us. Hearing him now, I knew we'd come to a threshold. One I'd cross with him to anywhere. I leaned over and kissed his cheek. A beagle puppy tumbled in the grass and yipped while terriers, spaniels, a couple of Irish setters, and a poodle galloped like miniature ponies over and around each other, their owners casually observing, chatting, and sipping coffee.

He melted when a Havanese planted its paws on his tennis shoes and looked up at him for a treat with soulful, adoring eyes. "Next Saturday," he said, squeezing my arm. "We head to the pound."

"A rescue?"

"Best kind."

We never made it to the pound. We were in the shower, blood-red water cascading around us. Someone touched my shoulder, and I jerked aside. Miriam sat down beside me. "I saw you from my window."

"You shouldn't have had to give Paule your wedding ring."

She looked at her left hand, a slight impression on the fourth finger from the years of wearing the ring. "I watched a German soldier take my mother's wedding ring. He dropped it in a bucket filled with other people's jewelry."

"I don't know what to say."

"Say nothing, dear." She rubbed her right hand over her left. "When we reached our assigned building, Mother pulled two pearl earrings from her mouth. Handing them to me, she told me to keep them safe so we'd have a start when we were freed. My father had given them to her as a wedding gift, passed down from his mother. At the time, I thought they meant more to her than the ring, but I think she did it to give me a mission and distract me from the horror surrounding us."

"I can't even imagine," I said, shaking my head.

"I lost one of them. I don't know where, sometime in the aftermath. Some country, some building, some transport. My mother was dead by then. I felt so guilty for so long until I learned to let go and live life and not place value on things but on people." She shifted toward me, touched the skin behind my ear, and traced it onto my jaw and neck. "It's faded now, but this scar—what is it from?"

A shivering cry broke through me. I pressed a hand to my mouth and nose, unable to stop the sob. "My mother," I said, through my fingers. "My mother gave me that scar." I couldn't contain my tears any longer. Missing Martin. Holding place for all those scared and hurting in my world. Crowding memories of a life I left long ago. Trying to keep going despite the uselessness of it all, and yet, none of it compared to what Miriam had endured. How weak and worthless we vulnerable humans had become. I felt like a failure.

Miriam put her arms around me and let me cry. "There's this thing about mothers," she whispered. "Sometimes the great harm they do is meant for good."

The rising sun lit up the stained-glass windows of Grace Cathedral across the street from the park. Gleaming like a fantasy world, the building's gothic beauty stood like a bulwark carrying the world. I sat up, holding onto Miriam's hand, wishing I could take away her profound pain, and here she was, washing mine in her infinite grace.

Two weeks passed like they were being dragged through tar. We made ourselves climb the nineteen stories of the high-rise and emptied the top apartments. Mr. Yu took several children's slides from Huntington Park, placing them over the emergency staircase so we could slide plastic boxes of whatever useful items we found. It took a week, but we netted food for at least a year, valuables to trade with the ships, and enough bottled liquid to keep us hydrated for a very long time. The top apartments were always useful to see what was around us. Chinatown often came up with boxes of food to trade for access. I took them up several times and noticed that it was Dixie's area they watched.

Our cloudy water continued to flow now and then. We left the taps in the on position and called each other when one of us heard it running. We filled every bathtub, every pot, and every bottle we could get until only drops came from the spigots. I managed all the empty apartments on my floor, using the one across from me to soak in its tub once a week, then used the bathwater to flush the toilet.

Electricity flickered through our building for a few hours a day. I wondered who still tended the tangled veins of this struggling city. Some invisible saint in coveralls, stubbornly refusing to let the lights die. I imagined them alone in a control room somewhere, drinking lukewarm coffee, still believing in civilization. I whispered thank you to no one. Whoever they were, God bless them.

I checked email daily for something from Martin. Only the same unanswered messages—digital ghosts I reread like love letters. I'd known him eight years, and we'd been lovers the last two. He was older than me by twelve years, but this was no daddy complex. He was brilliant and beautiful and a renegade powerhouse. We bonded like swans for life. There had to be a reason why he never came back, and I fought the thought of him being dead. When my email dinged, I nearly dropped the phone. *Martin!*

No. *Stella34@ravenmail.com.* My stomach turned as if I'd swallowed a mouthful of dirt. My mother. A woman whose name felt like a bruise. Why would a woman I ran away from when I was sixteen bother with me after all these years? I set the phone aside without opening the email. How did she find me? Stella Tremain was a selfish, hateful, self-aggrandizing bitch that I hoped never to set eyes on for the rest of my life. A rage rose in my throat, and I shook it off with a sardonic laugh. What was she going to do? Ask for money, see how I was getting on in the world, tell me about her latest money-making con. Cradling the phone, I resisted. But I tapped. Of course I did.

The great harm I did, I meant for good.

Miriam's very words. On her lips, those words were sacred. From my mother, they were a trick wrapped in guilt. My vision tunneled. I hit delete so hard I could've sworn the screen cracked.

Later that week, I awoke to someone banging on my door. Someone trying to break in? I hunkered down in the kitchen, holding my breath and Martin's .380 pistol in trembling hands.

"Brooklyn!" Carl Houseman called out. "It's my mother!"

It was then I learned Miriam was a diabetic, and she was nearly out of the long-acting insulin that she needed once a day. After waking Janice Wu, the only doctor left in our group, I hurried to his apartment.

Carl didn't think Janice was necessary. "It's time," he said. "She asked for you."

Miriam lay in bed, so still, I feared she'd already slipped past us. Her skin, paper-thin and porcelain pale, looked breakable. I'd never seen her hair out of place, yet Carl had combed it back with tenderness that gutted me. She didn't stir when we entered. I wanted to believe she was asleep—just asleep—but fear threaded tight through my ribs.

Janice bent to check her vitals, and I realized how quiet it was. No machines. No beeping. Just our shallow breath and the soft rustle of her blanket. We weren't doctors, not really. Just witnesses, fumbling toward mercy.

"I can leave you a bottle of sedatives," Janet said. "It won't help with diabetes, but it'll keep her relaxed and calm. She'll drift off eventually."

"Have you checked around?" I asked. "Somebody's got to have that drug."

"We've checked," Carl said. "Everybody but Dixie and Paule."

"Let's ask them."

I saw Janice shiver and look away. "Someone from the Sunset district went to Dixie for some Imitrex. The family was short on paying him. He had the mother raped and beat her husband and teenage son to a pulp. Not that he cared about the money; he just needed to send a message."

Carl motioned for us to come into his living room. I could see why they didn't move up to our block. He had a triple deadbolt lock and iron bars across the door. The large kitchen was stacked with boxes of supplies, and there was a rifle and three handguns on the mantle above the TV set. He saw me looking at them. Around the gun case were several ribbons for marksmanship and a picture frame with three long bullets. "It's how he takes over neighborhoods," Carl said of Dixie. "He's now got most of San Jose under his thumb, which gives him access directly to the Salinas Valley and—"

"All the food," Janice and I said simultaneously.

The Salinas Valley served as a crucial breadbasket for California, primarily cultivating vegetables and fruits. They had a cooperative agreement with cattle farms further south to supply meat. Drivers would park at a ballpark south of the city, selling their goods from the beds of their trucks. It appeared that farmers were among the few still able to access gasoline. I suspected they also received a significant portion of the water supply. We hadn't relied heavily on trading with them, as we sourced our supplies directly from Chinatown and foreign freighters, occasionally purchasing from farmers north of San Francisco who operated under a similar arrangement at the Golden Gate Bridge. If anything were to happen to those sources, Dixie would become the sole food provider—if he managed to seize control of the region.

"I'm sorry she wasn't conscious," Carl said, breaking my revelry at what we might be facing. "She was insistent on speaking with you."

"I've grown so fond of her," I said, biting back a hurt. "And I'm not ready to lose her."

Janice stared out the window onto Huntington Park, her expression pensive as we silenced our chitchat. "Carl," she said reflexively, as a doctor who knows the patient. "Have you been cutting her dosage?"

"A couple weeks now. I've stretched it as far as I could." He handed her the near empty box of insulin, eyes were teary, accepting what he hated. "How long?" he asked.

"If she were my mother, I'd give her the full dose. Have a few good days before it's time." Janice's voice trembled, and she wiped her nose with the back of her hand.

We stood silently, looking in different directions. All of us had lost people—some to death, some who left seeking safe shelter elsewhere, some who disappeared with fates unknown. We'd accustomed ourselves to chaos. It lived as our neighbor, always ready to move closer than we wanted. We hated it, frustrated with our inability to do anything about what should be so fixable. Chaos, a hard word that lived deep in the throat.

"Give me the box," I said, my voice flatter than I meant. But inside, I burned. I wasn't losing Miriam. Not when I could still fight. I'd seen too much death already—people, systems, beliefs. I wasn't letting her be next. If I had to bargain with monsters, so be it.

I hurried to Jamie's apartment. Something about how Julio and Paule looked at each other had bothered me since we'd looted the Siriso building. It needed an answer, and I would use it if it was what I suspected.

Dan opened the door with a sleepy but annoyed expression. "What's wrong?"

"Where's Julio?"

"On the couch, asleep, like pretty much everybody."

I stormed into their living room and yanked Julio by the hair. I was furious, yes, but under that was raw, shapeless terror. If he cost Miriam her life, I didn't know what I'd do. "Wake up!" I shouted, my voice cracking under the weight of everything I hadn't let myself feel.

His hands raised in defense, reacting in fear of not knowing what was happening, eyes wide and mouth agape. "Who died?"

I jerked him up and pushed the empty medicine box into his face. "You're going to Paule, and you're going to have him get this for me. He's scavenged every drugstore on Market Street, so I know he's got it."

Jamie ambled into the living room, tying his robe as he shuffled. "Brooklyn, don't treat him like that."

"Tell them," I said.

Julio looked to the floor.

"Tell them or I will."

"I got no clue of what you speak, Missy." He crossed his arms, lips bared in a grimace.

I hooked a hand on my hip, looking down on him as he piled himself in the corner of the couch and pulled a blanket around him. "Julio's getting drugs from Paule."

"I. Am. Not!"

Jamie and Dan looked at each other, the disappointment on Dan's face palatable with hurt. "You don't know that," Jamie defended him. "And I don't like you coming in here accusing him."

Dan put a hand on his partner's shoulder. "Julio, is it true?"

Julio couldn't look at them. He inhaled, whimpered out a breath, and whined. "Why you take her side?"

" 'Cause I see what my husband can't," Dan said softly.

Julio let out a huffing cry. "Not the hard stuff," he hiccupped, hands spreading in front of him. "Just a Quaalude now and then, some Oxy sometimes."

Jamie turned away from him and put a hand on his forehead. "I told you the only way you could stay was if you stopped."

"We're living in hell, people," Julio cried. "Don't you plebs see there's no way out of this? We're all just play-acting like we're going to survive, but we're not. We're all dying. Dying of separation and hurt and loneliness, and soon enough, we'll be starving. What's wrong with going to heaven on earth for a few hours?"

"Stop it!" I growled and stomped my foot at the same time. "I don't care what drugs you do or your apocalyptic vision of the future, but you are going to get Paule to find me some insulin, and I don't care if you die trying."

"How are you paying him?" Dan asked, his lips pressed tightly.

Julio wouldn't answer.

"Fuck!" Jamie said. "You realize he's using you for information about us."

"Get up and get dressed. I need this insulin yesterday."

Julio had a signal he called on a walkie-talkie frequency that we didn't use. I really could have strangled him. He'd given Paule a place to meet him, one of the most vulnerable ways into our block, through Grace Cathedral's courtyard. We didn't have the manpower to watch all of it, as the church took up the entire block. It was an accessible entrance into our area without being seen.

We hid behind a car on Sacramento Street, watching the fountain in the center of the church courtyard. When Paule showed up, he sat on the edge of the empty fountain, a package beside him. "Go get it," I said to Julio. "I'll stay here." I waited, watched them kiss, and then Julio dropped to his knees. Unexpectedly, Paule shoved Julio backward, causing him to fall on his backside.

"Tell that bitch to get out here 'cause I know it's not you needin' this shit." He shook the package he'd brought, threatening to bash the medicine into the ground.

I shot up and ran across the street. "Wait! Wait!" I pulled a thousand dollars of Martin's money from my pocket and held my hands up as I approached them. Julio balled up into a fetal position, whimpering the words *I'm sorry*. Paule kicked his backside. "Paule, I'll pay you!"

"What good is that shit to me?" He pulled a gun from his waistband and pointed it at my head.

I stood like a statue, holding my breath, anticipating a blast.

Julio bounced up and shot in front of me. "No, baby, please," he sobbed. "No, don't, please, for me, please don't."

"She saw us, you fool!" he screamed at Julio. "She's laughing her ass off at me right now!"

"Paule, whatever you want," I said, my voice barely holding together. My fingers twitched around the edges of Martin's money. I could smell the sweat on my own skin, and the metallic odor of gun pointed at my face.

I didn't blink. If I moved, I'd die. If I cried, I'd die. If I begged too well—maybe he'd shoot me anyway, just to prove he could.

Julio was sobbing now, and Paule looked like he might unravel at the seams. His face contorted with shame and fury—both aimed at me. I was witnessing a war he fought inside himself, one where love was treason.

"Maybe I want you to suck my cock!" He shook the gun, his arm straining.

I realized the mistake I'd made, squeezing my eyes shut. Paule couldn't afford for anyone to find out about their relationship. He built his street reputation on being the worst of the badasses. Any sign of weakness would demote him in his follower's eyes. And loving someone… that was weakness in his world.

"I can get you another thousand. I'll look and see if we have any jewelry." Paule's face strained against his desire to shoot me, and my anger surged. "For god's sake, you took her wedding ring. Can't you just give her the drug that will keep her alive!"

Paule looked aside. "It's for the old lady?" he asked, letting his arm fall to the side, but his hand quivered, making the gun jerk against his leg. He turned in a circle, a hand on his hip and biting his lower lip. "Julio, I'm disappointed in you. I don't know what this means for us, but I ever see this woman again, both of you are dead!" He turned and stomped off, leaving Julio sobbing. I picked up the package and ran to Carl's apartment.

Janice was still there, and she squealed her amazement that I'd gotten what looked like a good three-month supply of two kinds of insulin Miriam could use. Carl grabbed me and hugged my neck. After giving Miriam a full dose, she roused and asked to go to the bathroom. What a welcome relief, a request so mundane that we all three smothered her to help.

I stayed with her the rest of the night and into the morning. She slept and woke, and once, when I'd dozed off, I jerked awake to find her staring at me. She smiled, licked her lips, and drank some water. "You were talking in your sleep," she said. "I think you should go back to where your mother is. She's waiting for you. She knows her mother wisdom now."

I looked to the floor and fiddled with my hands. "We have a very complicated... oh, who am I fooling. We have a very violent history." I picked at the fray of my sleeve, unable to meet her gaze. Miriam didn't press. She just nodded like she understood something I hadn't said.

Her eyes closed again, and I sat with the silence, not knowing whether to feel grateful or cursed. The thought of my mother's name in this room felt sacrilegious. But somehow, Miriam had touched something I didn't know was still raw.

We never spoke about my mother again, and I doubt she remembered or knew the meaning of the strange words she'd said to me. One thing was for sure—going home where I had a mother who could have cared less about me was never on my bingo card. But why not placate a woman who didn't have long to live? Like Julio said, what's wrong with a little heaven on earth.

Miriam died three weeks later. It wasn't from the lack or culling the dosage of her drugs—it was something softer, more mysterious. Acceptance had settled over her like a shawl, and in those final days, her room lit with the serenity of letting go. I think she chose it, in the end. Willed her heart to slow. Her face that last day was impossibly calm, except for the single pearl earring she wore, a quiet announcement. I sat beside her bed and stared at that earring, knowing though I tried to deny it.

She passed in the night.

We took her body to a North Beach mortuary for cremation. The cart creaked as we pulled her through the streets. People came out of buildings and leaned from windows, solemn and still. They nodded as we passed, as if their eyes alone could offer protection. This was the ritual now. We couldn't offer dignity in life, but we guarded each other in death.

Later that day, Janice sent word out to all the districts in San Francisco to see if anyone needed the leftover insulin. No one did. That broke my heart. It meant there were no sick people. It meant they had all died. What was left… the strong, the lucky, or those waiting to be neither.

Later that week, I found Julio sitting on the cold steps of the high-rise, his knees pulled to his chest like a child's.

"I always wanted to live in a building like this," he said.

"Well, dammit, Janet." I lifted my arm, indicating the nineteen stories. "You got your pick."

"Naw, I went to the penthouse. It's like living at the top of a Ferris wheel. I got dizzy."

We sat quietly, the chill of the night pushing us closer together. "I'm sorry about what happened with Paule."

He waved it off, but the way he hugged his arms closer told me it still stung. "Paule is mean when he's scared. He'll come around."

"Thank you for saving my life."

He didn't look at me. Just nodded, sadness around us like a smoky room. "Paule had good drugs, back in the day," he said softly, a memory and a mourning.

I handed him a sack of twelve half-filled bottles of Black Phoenix nail polish. He eyes went wide as if I'd handed him the Hope Diamond. "You're joking," he whispered, hugging it to his chest. "This is enough to get married in."

Back in the apartment, I laid everything out: the backpack I'd kept ready since the beginning, the letter I'd rewritten a dozen times, the gear I'd told myself was for emergencies only. But Miriam's death broke that lie open. It wasn't about earthquakes or fires. It had taken some time for me to get there. I hadn't been ready to admit what I was really chasing.

Martin.

I'd trace him from memory, from scraps of conversation and offhand comments, the way you track something untouchable and maybe already lost. I'd start with his house in Bolinas, deducing the location from nips of our conversations.

Just before dawn, I stepped out into the fog-blanketed street, layered in oversized and multi-pocketed vests, hoodies, and gear, every pocket filled. The parka and crossbody bag had once belonged to Martin—his scent still lingered faintly in the hood. It felt like armor, like memory I could wear.

Down at our roadblock, a cigarette's burning tip glowed in the dark. Two men faced each other. Carl and Jamie turned as I approached, faces etched with sleeplessness. I handed Jamie an envelope. "What are you two doing out here?"

"Please," Jamie said. "You give Julio all your Black Phoenix nail polish and you're not leaving?"

I chuckled and looked down California Street. A chilly wind blew a fast-racing fog past us, giving the street a haunted look. "Martin's key is in there." I indicated the envelope. "There's some water and food leftover, but I'd appreciate you waiting a few months before adding it to the stockpile—in case I don't find him in Bolinas."

Jamie hugged me, tight. I nearly cried into his shoulder but swallowed it down like a pill. Carl and I hugged too, and then he handed me a magazine of bullets for Martin's pistol and a velvet pouch. "A little of Miriam," he said, squeezing my hand. "I think she'd want to go where you're going. Just make sure you put her somewhere beautiful."

I nodded as I accepted both. "Won't you need these?" I asked, looking at the bullets.

"I've got three jacketed flat noses left for the rifle and a box of handgun bullets," he said. "Things go bad, a handful of ammunition isn't going to make any difference. Those last three. One was for whoever was at the door, one was for my mother, and the final one was for me. Now I got two for the door. I've made my peace with it."

We stood in stillness, all the shared experiences and memories wove together into the bond that makes people family. Then, I journeyed off into the rolling fog small as a breath, heading toward the Golden Gate Bridge with the weight of memory on my back.

~ BOLINAS ~

The first time my mother slapped me, I didn't cry. I tasted blood and confusion, both metallic in my mouth. As I stood at the bathroom sink, clutching a wad of toilet paper to my nose, I stared at her reflection in the mirror—stone-eyed, lips set in a thin, unmoving line. "Say that malarkey again, and I'll knock you backward," she said, like I'd summoned the devil with a science fair project.

I hadn't meant to provoke anything. I was proud—glowing, even—quoting Latin to a bunch of trick-or-treaters, offering Tootsie Rolls and a little mystery. "Visibilia ex invisibilibus," I'd said, hoping to spook them. *The visible is born of the invisible.* I'd won a contest for those words. Tomorrow, my picture was supposed to be in the paper.

But one kid laughed and called my mom a witch. Another asked if I was casting spells. The next moment, Stella flew out the door like a banshee, flung the candy bucket, and the slap— I hadn't registered the slap until I saw blood dripping onto my blouse. My mother pulled me out of high school the next day, ending my borrowed wit and life as an existential philosopher. I buried my words after that, tucked them behind my teeth. If she feared them, maybe the world did too. Words, at least for that time of my life, homed themselves in silence.

I let *Visibilia ex invisibilibus* be my code as I wandered the length of the stalls at a farmer's market on the south side of the Golden Gate Bridge. My backpack bit into one shoulder, and the smell of grilled meat tangling with diesel. The visible was that a dozen trucks from farms north of San Francisco had managed to get gas, suggesting some sort of support—government or something else? The Invisible—superheroes were suspect until proven friendly, as not a car in the city had a gallon in its tank.

A few National Guard types patrolled the perimeter, trying to look effective. I hoped that meant state government was still operating, but the security could as easily be stooges for Dixie Roman if he wanted to expand territory. Goodwill always seemed to be the first step toward annexing neighborhoods. I texted Jamie and told him what I saw. Best they be ready for what was not apparent.

I chatted up farmers, bought a few carrots and a couple of potatoes for my trip, and tried to assess who might give me a lift to the Shoreline Highway exit. I offered money or one of my extra cell phones for trade. No takers but lots of cautious glances at those soldiers. Their unmarked fatigues made me wary of drawing their attention. I decided to sit down at the end of the row of trucks, resting my aching feet, and resolved to find a way to avoid the thirty-mile walk to Bolinas.

Across from me, a twenty-something blond woman stacked up vegetable crates against the wheel of a truck with the words *Jesus Mary & Joseph* red-lettered on the side. She glanced over and smiled at me. "Looking for a lift North, eh?"

"I'll pay to get to Highway One exit. Cash or a spare cell phone."

She looked aside and grimaced when a Mexican woman in the next stall screamed at her.

"¡Son ladrones!"

It appeared neither woman could understand what the other said as an obscenity-fueled rant continued until the Mexican woman stomped away.

"What's that about?" I asked.

Reaching toward me, the blond shook my hand. "No idea what I did, but I think our truck might be an inch into their space. Whatever."

"The way of the world," I said, as she rolled her eyes.

"I have to run it past my ole man, but one-fifty should do it. Leave your bag in our truck and get yourself a bite if you want. That smoky aroma from whatever they're grilling in the meat tent smells divine." She held out her hand, wanting the money now.

I might have hesitated, but barring no other offers, peeled off one-fifty from money kept in my front pocket, making sure she saw only sixty dollars left. I had other money secreted all over my layered clothes, but after that exorbitant ask, I'd rather she think I was down to the last of my cash. And that grilled meat did smell like heaven.

"I'll go check with Joseph. Meet me back here in a half-hour." She smiled and bobbed her head. "By the way, I'm Mary."

I latched and padlocked my backpack to a rail in the rear of the truck so it couldn't be opened or moved. Martin's backpack actually, made of some sort of super-duper material and a zippered lock that opened by my fingerprint. After covering it with my parka, I jumped out of the truck bed, landing in front of a Mexican kid and his mother. I hoped the woman wouldn't scream at me.

"Mamma says don't go with them," he said. "They're pendejos." The woman said something I couldn't understand.

I nodded, unsure if their hatred of the blond fueled the warning or if I should heed it. I'd already forked over the money, so there wasn't much choice in taking that ride. All the same, I decided to be back in fifteen minutes and moved a tactical knife to the front pocket of my hoodie while shifting my cross-body bag closer to my right hand in case I needed the gun. The exit was a twenty-minute ride at most, and I felt confident I could get to one of the weapons if I needed to.

The beef was spicy, salty, and sweet all at the same time, and I wolfed down two portions and bought an extra serving to go. Carrots and potatoes would last well enough on the road, but this bit of meat would be a treat. Back at the stall, the truck was gone. My backpack. My coat. Martin's gear. Gone. For a moment, I just stood there, the meat packet in my hand leaking juices into my sleeve.

"¡Ladrones!" The Mexican woman stepped toward me, her eyes fierce, shaking a fist in the air then pointing in the direction the truck drove.

I didn't move. The world caught in my throat.

It wasn't just stuff. It was *his* stuff. The backpack design he once showed me in blueprints, laughing about how the military didn't know innovation if it bit them. He'd coded it to open with our fingerprints. I pressed a hand to my chest, fingers curling against the fabric, trying to shove the panic back down.

I knew better. I always knew better. But some soft part of me—the girl who quoted Latin, who won contests, who loved Halloween—still thought maybe not *everyone* was lying.

"Ladrones—thieves—that's what they do," the kid said, coming up to his mother's side. "Pendejos," he repeated helpfully, like he was handing me a sword.

"Pendejos," I echoed, swallowing the burn. I wouldn't cry. There was no time for that. It was my own fault. I should've seen it in the shine of Mary's smile. Should've heard my mother's voice: *Think about what you do. Our lives depend on it.*

The Mexican family gave me a ride to the Shoreline exit without asking for a thing. I tried to give them money, but Jose and his mother, Marina, waved it away. I could have kicked myself for falling for such a ruse with the pendejos—which their father, Jesus, pronounced Hey-suz, embarrassingly explained was a derogatory term for the rear-end nether-regions.

"Everybody on the road knows them," Jesus said. "Best start learning what passes for flimflam out here."

"Flimflam," Marina repeated with a bob of her head. "Pendejos."

Pendejos, a new word for me that I meant to memorize and scream out if I ever ran into Jesus, Mary, or Joseph again.

I didn't have that much worth anything in the backpack. Wearing three-layered vests underneath a hoodie, all with hidden pockets, kept my working cell phone, various weapons, solar chargers, and all the cash in Martin's apartment well hidden. I'd lost a solar radio, two good filtering straws in case I had to drink stream water, a tin canteen, a dozen cell phones for trade, clothes, toilet paper, tuna packets, a can opener, and an inflatable sleeping pad.

I was pissed, but it'd been my fault for trusting a smile and not seeing through the obvious scam. That'd be the last time. "Think about what you do. Our lives depend on it," my mother had said as she put me to work stuffing donation envelopes for her flimflam church. "Eye-catching shine is for stupid pieces of nothing, for losers." No time for a pity party, I told myself, pulled tight my equally pocketed hoodie, and entered Tamalpais Valley.

Most businesses in the small town of Corte Madera had their windows boarded like eyes squeezed shut. The Water Event had hit them hard—just like everywhere else—but here, the silence felt tighter. Curtains twitched. A glint from a rooftop told me I was being watched through binoculars. People weren't just surviving; they were bracing for war. A few homes had started gardens in the side yards with hand-painted signs: *Keep Out, Trespassers Shot, No Mercy*. A twisted sort of beauty... survival as art. Good that they were organized. This close to the freeway made this area prey for much worse than pendejos.

As darkness set in, I started looking for a place to sleep. Shrill giggles brought my attention to two children playing on a swing set. For a second, I thought maybe I'd stumbled into a pocket of something normal. A tall man pushed them higher and higher, like he could launch them into a sky that didn't hurt. But the moment I stepped into their reality, it shattered.

"Hey," I called out. The children bolted, shrieking like I was the monster under their bed. I might as well have been. The man pulled a shotgun like a reflex, not even angry, just... resolved. I waved, a slow motion of surrender, and he watched me leave like he'd stare down a storm. What broke my heart wasn't the fear—it was how practiced it was. How ready they all were to run, to arm, to expect the worst.

"Okay," I said under my breath. "Cold night on the side of the road it is." I gestured to him that I was moving along. Sad, this. Children who were only allowed to play after dark. People who no longer trusted. The man would likely sit up all night in case I returned. No one knew who was good or bad.

I did better than the side of the road, finding a house with an overgrown lawn. I watched it for half an hour. Windows dark, only the sound of owls in the tree above me, so I climbed up the chicken-wire fenced porch. I peeked through the windows at a blue sectional couch, throw carpets, and a smashed case where a TV or computer had probably been torn from the sockets. I thought about knocking out a window and sleeping inside but decided against it. If they came back, why add to their fear? I covered myself with a tarp hung over the porch rail and settled between two oversized terracotta planters. I kept warm enough as I listened to coyotes howl late into the night. The bleak, lonely wails sent a chill through my bones. Lamentation without sorrow, only prowess as if to say you journey into my world now. Beware.

The bear's shadow hit first—an eclipse of everything. Then came the roar, raw and primal, vibrating through the soles of my feet and straight into my bones. I dropped my water bottle, my heart jackhammered against my ribs, every breath sliced by fear. Every instinct screamed to run, even though I knew it was the wrong move. Behind me, an arm encircled my waist; Martin held me firm, positioning his body protectively in front of mine. The bear slammed its paws onto the dirt, shaking me to my core.

Martin stepped back, pulling me with him. Without his support, I would have collapsed. My breath came in quick pants, sweat dripped into my eyes, blurring my vision. I focused on Martin, not the bear; he remained locked on the creature, gradually moving us away. My panic distorted reality, making everything feel surreal.

Just then, two small cubs darted out from the underbrush, their tiny bodies bounding across the forest floor. The mother bear shifted as she spotted them, her fierce gaze momentarily leaving us. As the bear lowered itself onto all fours and turned away, a wave of relief washed over me, mingling with disbelief. Martin still held me tight, his eyes fixed on the bear, ensuring our path was safe.

"Let's get back to the hotel," he said gently.

We never spoke of that day but that image of his body shielding mine, branded itself onto me: Martin's stony expression, unwavering and fierce, facing down a stronger opponent. It wouldn't be the last time he put himself between me and something vicious.

Waking as the sun rose, a flicker of orange passed my nose. Then...another. Then...dozens. Monarch butterflies—rippling like firelight across the morning air as they made their yearly pass-thru to warmer weather. I sat up to a spectacular carpet of orange. They moved like they had purpose, like some secret we'd all forgotten was guiding them. I watched them longer than I should have, letting the beauty hollow me out. Martin would've loved this. He would've named them all, told me some weird fact about their migration. I reached for his hand out of habit—and found empty space. The silence behind me was louder than the wings in front of me.

It took me a day to get to the part of Shoreline Highway, where all you can see are the twists and turns of the road, rugged slopes of beveled hills, treacherous cliffs, and a spectacular view of the coastline. I rested, overlooking a solitary valley of green, jade-colored trees, lime grass, pea-shaded moss, and vines crawling onto creamy sand as it waited for beryl waves to change their color. The simmering beauty made me feel tiny. Any other time, this drive was one of the best in California, but now my feet and legs ached for a straight road. I had to stop every hour, lie on my back, and put my legs up. Each half-mile made my body feel like every ounce of blood was in my feet, and I realized I wouldn't make good time unless I rested a day. Not at all what I had time or supplies for. My mouth was dry as dust as I chewed on my last carrot. I was hungrier than I expected, with my water running low. I could have filled up from any number of streams had I not lost my filtering straws to the Pendejos.

Damn them! Sleeping roadside, I couldn't help but think of the two thermal Mylar blankets in my backpack. Damn them!

The next day heated into trills of insects and a brisk breeze. Now and then, the white noise of waves reclaiming a beach far below soared past me, stealing my worry of what was ahead. I was losing my vigilance, but at least I recognized my weakness. Pulling my legs up to my chest for a stretch, I contemplated the thought of dying out here. No one would ever know where I was or what had happened to me. I was nothing, a nobody who went in search of her boyfriend and died. I licked my chapped lips, wondering what I'd have to accept about myself, tears filling my eyes. Loser, just like my mother always said I'd be.

A monk on a scooter saved me from my existential crises and parched mouth. Speeding past me, he stopped and gave me a lift to Green Gulch Farm Zen Center, where they fed me like a prized pig and doctored my feet. After a day, they lent me a bike belonging to the Slide Ranch, which cut a good day off my slow limp. The Slide Ranch folks gave me a lift back to the highway, but almost out of gas, they couldn't afford to take me to Bolinas. I was so happy to meet friendly, thriving people that I zenned myself not to complain for the rest of the day. I made Stinson Beach that afternoon. Soon, I'd be in sight of Bolinas. And I was alive. And maybe Martin was as well.

A dozen or so people wandered about the town, and I asked who might fill up my water bottle. They sent me to a corner café/record store called Grateful Dead Lives, where a bearded man named Harry offered me a counter seat and a tin of espresso. Surrounded by vinyl records and CDs of primarily Grateful Dead music, he pointed at a rainbow-colored sign reading: *The Dead Mused In Our Basement.* "Wrote their best stuff here, last owner told me." Then he smiled, wide and capricious. Crap.

"I'm pretty thirsty," I said, caution tweaking my muscles.

He scooped ice into a frosted beer mug and poured bottled water. I gulped, not caring how much it would cost me. I came up for air only once. He emptied the bottle into the glass, and I finished it off.

"Ready for coffee now?" he asked, shushing a squeak. I peered over the counter and saw three bassinets, double-filled with babies dressed in pink.

"Yours?"

"They are now."

I felt something twist in my chest. I didn't ask. I couldn't. I didn't want to imagine the story behind those words, behind those infants. The world had crashed, and still, people made room. Adopted hope. That scared me more than anything. I was too brittle to love something that fragile. I nodded toward the coffee and took a package of stevia and a little cream he'd set out. "How do you do all this?"

"Solar," he nodded. "Water goes in and out, but we have a system."

"Let me guess, everybody in town runs to fill up every pot, barrel, sink, and bathtub the minute the flow starts."

He mugged. "Something like that. But we're working on a fix, so we're not so dependent."

Despite the smile, I started to like him and maybe even relax a little. "How much for the coffee and filling up my water tumbler?

"Buck twenty-five," he said. "Unless you want to rent a room. That'll be another dollar. A quarter if you want me to accept mail, another if I have to hold it for longer than six months."

"Seriously?" Waiting for negotiation, I shifted to see if anyone else was in the store. I would be ready for them if I was about to get jumped. No one but a gray-haired hippie sitting near the window soaking up the sun. Harry stared at me, insulted, I suppose. "I've been walking for a while," I said. "It's an expensive world out there."

"Two bucks even," he said. "If that makes you feel better."

I gave him a five, and he peeled out three dollars in change, topped off my water bottle, and slid me a brownie that he said not to eat until nightfall when I was ready to sleep. Maybe I would be splitting it with Martin. "May the rain gods bless you," I said, taking my bounty.

I walked to the beach and soaked my feet in the waves. I had two unhealed blisters that burned in the salty sea. Preparing for this, I'd brought bandages and iodine that were, of course, in a truck painted with the words *Jesus Mary & Joseph*. I considered returning to the town to see if I could resupply and buy another tote. The natives were friendly enough, yet backtracking was more steps than I wanted to take.

Following the beach, I'd come to a narrow inlet into the Bolinas lagoon that I could swim or wade across depending on the depth of the water. If I was lucky, maybe some beach house I'd pass would have a small boat. I didn't relish getting my clothes wet while holding a cell phone, solar charger, and pistol above my head, but crossing the inlet would be faster than continuing on the road around the lagoon for another mile.

I didn't see any people in the houses or boats, but I did spy a small kayak leaning against a railing. A swift movement behind it told me someone had just ducked out of sight. I was up on the inlet and didn't need any trouble now. Bolinas in sight. Just across the channel. I waded to my ankles, looking toward Bolinas Beach. Damn, the water was deep, with a flow faster than I was comfortable swimming. It'd be too easy to get pulled out to sea if there was a strong undertow. The thought of more walking made me cringe.

Looking toward the house with the kayak, I spied a woman on the deck, watching me. She was blond with gray roots. Well, it's not like hairdressers were making house calls these days. I waved and took a few steps toward her. "Can I approach?"

She bit her bottom lip and made a slight motion with her hand. "Did you come from the city?" she asked. "My husband and son went there three weeks ago to get supplies from our Presidio apartment. Jim and Richard Clark. Do you know them? They're in a tan Acura."

"I'm sorry," I said. "I don't. Gas is pretty tough. Seems only the farmers are getting it." I knew that if her family hadn't returned to her by now, it was unlikely they would, especially in an Acura with gas, but today was a day I couldn't destroy hope. I had my own hopes that Martin would be in Bolinas, waiting for me. I glanced at the child-sized kayak. The name Richard was painted on the bow. She stared at the ground, her nose red, arms hanging limply. I knew better than to ask personal questions and figured she knew not to give out information. That made for vulnerability.

"I'm going to lock myself in," she said. "Best you find a place to do that too."

I turned to go, my will straining for that kayak I didn't have the heart to ask for. "Wait," I said. "There's a pretty organized community in town. It might be safer to go there. More people, more friends."

"I think this will be over soon." She pressed her lips and nodded. "Dixie Roman was out here after the Water Event. He said so. Things will get back to normal. We have to trust him. I worked on his mayoral campaign. He's going to run for governor when all this is over. He is the one who gets our water and electricity turned on. I'd vote for him any day."

"Mmmm." I bit my tongue, pressing my lips together and feeling less guilty about asking. "I wonder, could I borrow that kayak to cross over to Bolinas? I promise to bring it back. Or I'm happy to buy it from you."

"I'm sorry," she piped. "We might need it when my husband and son get back."

"Of course," I said. "Here." I handed her the brownie. "I wouldn't feel right if I didn't share this."

"Ooooo," she squealed, took and gobbled the whole thing in a few bits. "I've such a sweet tooth and am completely out of cookies."

Maybe her husband and son had gone looking for cookies. Or maybe they were dead. I hated myself for what I was about to do, but I hated this world more—for making her afraid to help me, for making me too desperate to leave her alone. When she started snoring in the lawn chair, I lingered. Guilt licked at my heels as I stepped inside and found her supplies—more than enough to last a season. I took a couple of energy bars. And the kayak. I promised Richard that I'd bring it back. Whether I meant it or not, I didn't know.

It felt good to have a breeze on my face. I closed my eyes and let the wind take some of my weight. I wasn't safe, not yet. But for the first time in days, I felt like I might survive this. Like maybe Martin was just across the water, waiting. The cross to Bolinas was swift, and butterflies followed me like a wave.

Bolinas looked like a messy dream—hippie enclaves and millionaire fortresses fading into wild overgrowth. I hobbled past cracked fences and silent gardens, my limp nagging with each step. I saw a few people out in their yards. No one waved. No one even looked up. The ache in my leg had nothing on the tight pull in my chest. Martin had promised me a view. He'd promised me morning light and sea air, and right now, the only thing tugging me forward was the thin thread of hope that he'd kept at least one promise.

I'd never been to the Bolinas house but had a good idea of the direction from Martin's description. He'd been building it the last year and had promised to take me on my birthday. He'd said that I would wake up every morning overlooking the Pacific. He knew I liked a good view. The terrain was more uphill than flat, and I stepped to avoid the Monarchs covering almost every part of the road. House by house, the structures became larger and more ostentatious. What began to bother me was that these stunning mansions were empty. Lawns overgrown, broken windows. When I came across a burnt-out structure, my heart sank.

The charred frame of the house clawed at the sky like burnt ribs. My breath shivered out of me. The next house was burned as well, then a third, a fourth. Was this it? Had fire found Martin before I could? The thought curdled in my stomach. I stood there, shaking, afraid to look closer and afraid not to.

Finally, I ran out of road. I was ready to cry. Where else could I look? Walking back to town made my legs want to give out, and the unyielding crash of waves in the distance sent my thoughts into a confused jumble. I'd told Martin that I'd build a zombie house if I ever built a house. The undead were the only monsters in my nightmares. Since then, I'd learned there were plenty of worse leviathans in this world. Holding still, listening to the wind, wondering if he had noted what I'd said. *My memory searched the blueprints lying across Martin's desk as he showed me his plans. His hand motioned toward the sea. A finger outlined a forest that would block the bright morning sun. His lips moved, saying, "Baby, you're going to love it."* I looked up, stared at the sky, clouds spread like a wiped window, then stepped over the road line and followed overgrown tire tracks. A meandering unpaved road emerged, leading through a thicket of Cypress trees.

Coming up to a locked wrought iron gate, I looked around for a call box, camera, or a way to climb over. More a barricade than a facade, stone walls braced both sides, one leading toward the ocean cliff, the other looking as if it surrounded the property to the bluff on the opposite side. A fire department ladder might be the only way to reach the top. I inspected the lock, looking for anything that might open the gate. I pulled at the bricks, hoping one of them was fake. Twice today, I'd come close to breaking, and both times I heard Stella's voice in my head, sharp as a slap. "Always chasing lollypops," she'd said once, "when humanity is nothing but shadows." I kicked the gate, ashamed at the wetness behind my eyes. Maybe she was right. Maybe I was still that girl too stubborn to see when the world had given up on her.

Sun would be down soon, and the prospect of sleeping outside was not appealing. Damn! I kicked the gate again in frustration. A low buzz and a female voice: "You have entered an incorrect number. You have one more opportunity before lockdown and code reset."

There had to be a way inside. What was I not seeing? I looked again at the lock and saw a chipped railing beside it. Using my knife to pry it loose revealed a keypad.

"You have one minute to enter a code," the mechanical voice said.

My mind whirled. "No, no, no, no," I squealed, realizing I couldn't get it open in time. I slid my finger into the space my knife held open, stretching to reach the pad. What if Martin had a different code for this house? I had one try at this. Sweat beaded on my forehead, and I pushed my finger in as far as possible.

"You have fifteen seconds to enter a code."

I couldn't see with my finger jammed into the small space and prayed to every star in heaven that Martin was still a creature of habit.

"You have five seconds." I tapped out what I thought would be the number 9459. The gate popped open and I slid inside as it buzzed and relocked.

The jaunt along a narrow uphill road left me soaked with sweat when I came to a headland overlooking the ocean and a square building resembling an armored spaceship. "A zombie house," Martin had cackled at me when I proposed it. "A house that no zombie could crack." He'd teased me at the time, but damn, my man had built a zombie house.

The setting sun faded into brilliant purples, lustrous mauves, and fiery magentas. Martin loved sunsets as much as I did; surely, he'd be in one of those top windows watching it and seeing me. "Martin!" I yelled at the house. I circled it three times, shouting his name and checking every entrance. He had to be here. He just had to be.

I took out Martin's set of keys. There were four keycards. One marked SIR that opened the downtown building, one with the letters SEA, another 9459, and a BOL that had to be for Bolinas. Knowing the gate security had given me limited chances, I figured this door wouldn't be much different. I held my breath and slid the BOL into a front door slot, which hummed and spit the card back out. "Malarkey!"

"Voice identified. Password accepted," the woman's voice said. The door popped open.

"Martin!" I called, voice shrill under the weight of hope. I tore through the rooms like a woman chasing a ghost. Every drawer unopened, every blanket unrumpled—his absence shouted louder than any scream. The house had an airless smell and my mind tried to decide if it was a lived-in odor or a stale one. "Martin!" I circled again through a library, kitchen, and den, then raced up a staircase to the second level, calling for him through gasps of air. There were five empty bedrooms and a keypad on a wall panel. I tried the numbered password on the security device. Nothing.

Retracing my steps, I went through each room carefully. The upper bedrooms were furnished sparsely, generic, muted white, stand-alone beds with no sheeting, unfinished as if the decorator hadn't completed the job. The master had dark purple walls with matching curtains across a window overlooking a rugged coast and turbulent sea. My purple. Our room. I sat on the bed with mauve Egyptian sheets and a plum-colored comforter. The sheets still held the crispness of a bed never slept in. I lay down and let the comforter wrap around me like a lie I wanted to believe.

Downstairs was a marvel. The most decked-out kitchen I'd ever seen. Stickers on the stove, dishwasher, and refrigerator said *Powered by Javon batteries.* A back door led down a set of steps into a garage of two cars and a—well, I didn't know what to call it. A box with wheels made from different car sections? Perhaps trying to be a 1960ish square Volkswagen that a teenage boy might have hobbled together? Part black, part silver, it looked ready for painting. A perfect little junkpot. The windows were dark, and a single driver's side door didn't open. I walked around the other cars, letting my hand drift down the cool exterior of an Alpha Romero and a BMW Gran Coupe, the vehicle Martin drove the last day I saw him.

I wandered through a plush but functional living room decorated in shades of blue and a library with wall-to-wall books. In the den, I tried to turn on a television and a radio but got no juice, which was odd since everything seemed linked to Javon batteries. Coming upon a window overlooking a copse of eucalyptus trees, I strained in each direction, and, from this view, except for the ocean side, the house seemed surrounded by forest. It would not be an easy house to find.

I collapsed at his library desk, a curved Parnian—surely Martin's desk. My legs and feet had given out. Could Martin have gone out? Could he be back in the city? Looking for me? My mind wanted him to be here, but the reality was that this house wasn't lived in. He wasn't here. Disappointment tied up my insides as I tried to think of what to do next. A single stamped envelope lay in an outbox. Something he hadn't had time to mail? I picked it up, found it unsealed, and opened it. On the inner flap, the initial *S* and a message in Martin's handwriting: *I am nine. I add to myself. Cover me with stars, and I'll be yours forever. All my love, M.* I looked at the S with its looped end the way he always wrote them. S had to be for Sulis. He rarely called me Brooklyn. But what the hell does the message mean, Martin?

Whatever the puzzle, it would have to wait. I dragged myself upstairs, curled into the bed, and slept.

Silence woke me with its mulish hum. I rose and moved through the empty house like a ghost. Before dawn, a faint hint of pink started to color the eastern sky, sunlight flickering through the trees. The emptiness had a whisper to it as if the house stretched, awakening itself. I returned to Martin's desk and studied his note. On the inner flap of an empty envelope. His way of hiding it? The puzzle is something I would know or have to figure out. Martin wasn't playful in that way. He was a direct man, a concise lawyer not given to clouded hodgepodge. So, the fact that this message was coded meant he wanted no one else to have it.

I surveyed the house again, checking for sliding panels, safes, and hidden rooms. It appeared to be what it was: a functional safe house that no one could penetrate other than the owner. My stomach rumbled, and knowing I'd think clearer on a full stomach, I headed to the kitchen. I drank orange juice as I put a frozen rib eye into an air fryer.

Within a half hour, I was in pig heaven, heaving down the juicy meat with the gusto of a primitive neanderthal. I slowed myself down at the last, looking through the cabinets between bites. The freezer contained frozen meat and vegetables, juices, and pizzas. A pantry I'd missed before contained shelves stacked like a doomsday catalog, including a sidewall filled with cartons of toilet paper and several cases of baby formula. If Martin were here, I'd kiss him full on the mouth. I'd kiss him until the world made sense again. But he wasn't. Just this house, and his careful planning. It was almost worse—being so thought of and still left behind. I looked again at the baby formula and wondered who it was for? Me? Babies we might have during the worst of times?

I spent the next few days in bubble baths, long hot showers, reading until I dozed, watching DVDs, and eating like royalty. Those Javon batteries had no limit, except I could not get the TV or radio to work. My phone didn't have reception either, and I worried about what might be going on in San Francisco. I had no idea what the water source was, but it always seemed to continue and had a serviceable taste. My feet healed, and I could walk without a limp, but my muscles still needed recovery.

The puzzle Martin left me remained elusive, and my mind flitted into a dozen terrifying possibilities as to his fate. Could he have been killed in San Francisco, one of the many bodies lying in piles that some government agency had eventually hauled away? I didn't want to believe it. A man with the foresight and talent to build a zombie house had to have a Plan B to escape the zombies. Had he run afoul of Paule, Dixie, some stranger intent on robbing, or a psycho out for the joy of murder? There was more than one of those roaming dark alleys in those early days when anarchy ruled the night streets. I hated thinking of that. It'd been Martin's apartment that had likely saved my life before Jamie and Dan had organized the blocks. The one time I returned to my old apartment, it'd been broken into and part of a wall set afire. I sniffed and held in my emotions, tired of my thoughts, sick of talking to myself, wishing for answers.

Martin was always who he was—a singular, amazing man who never let wealth cloud his judgment. I lost myself in memory of the day we found one of those old Dictaphone machines in a storage closet.

He slipped in the blue dicta belt and began interviewing me like a Sam Spade detective. "Hey baby, what, my ginger-headed beauty, am I to make of your compromised position?"

"Malarkey!" I said, dazzled by his impression, and played along. "If it's position you want, I've got plenty for the right man. Are you the right man, Mr. Siriso?"

"I call you on your femme fatalism and raise you a toxic masculine."

"Well, dammit, Janet, can we discuss over cocktails and a dead body or two?"

"Malarkey, you say! Malarkey, I say, on your talk of liquor and death. I live by my code, and it will forever remain constant."

Martin swung me around, and we landed on his desk, knocking the Dictaphone aside.

So that's how you got my voice. Martin had swung me around like life was a screwball comedy and we were the stars. That old Dictaphone clattered off the desk as he caught me, breathless with laughter. It was absurd, perfect, and so us. My cheeks burned with the memory now. I'd give anything to rewind time, to press play on that belt and hear us again, safe in our ridiculousness.

Then it occurred to me. If he was his code... 9459, and always added to himself, he'd still be nine. The number nine. The two numbers in the middle add to nine and the last number is nine. If added all together, you eventually deduce to nine. That would be the number he wanted me to know, and if I covered it with stars... That had to be it!

I raced upstairs to the keypad, steadied my fingers, and typed: star, nine, star. A wall swung open without nary a curse word from me.

I stepped into an electronic wonderland, and the cell phone in my back pocket urgently beeped. The size of an office corridor, the room was built into a V-shape, hugging the front edge of the building so that from the outside, it appeared there was no room. Darkened windows looked directly down the driveway so I could see anyone coming. The sound of birds and the ocean softly played like an elevator soundtrack, and I realized that the wall of monitors must be connected to outside cameras and microphones. I flipped them on, revealing security views all around the property.

My cell phone dinged again. I had service inside this room and fielded a dozen messages from Jamie and Dan to let them know I was okay. They told me of a tense stand-off between Dixie and Paule. They were nervous that they might have to choose a side. Dixie had met with them and promised security if they'd come under his protection. "Julio says he'd rather vomit hourly than suck Dixie's dick. We trust him about as much as we trust all these Madonna sightings, so we're inclined to throw in with Chinatown." There were five messages from Stella that I didn't open. After all these years, my mother hunting me down made for fury, not curiosity.

Nothing from Martin.

"Malarkey," I said, disappointed, my throat scratchy from not having spoken for too many days. A dark monitor beeped and flipped to light, then an image, white background, an orange chair, and a man's back. The chair swiveled. Martin looked into the camera. The computer beeped, *Voice Identified*.

"Hey, baby. I hope it's you on the other side of this, my little stream of babbling Sulis, but just in case it's not, I won't say your name." There he was. My Martin. Hair longer, eyes heavier, but still him. My chest caved in on itself. I reached for the screen like I could touch him, swallow him whole. His voice was calm, too calm, as if he were trying not to break. And maybe that's what wrecked me most—he'd recorded this not knowing if I'd ever see it. Not knowing if he'd ever hold me again. And yet, he smiled. For me. Always for me.

"Martin!" I called out.

He glanced upward, touched his forehead, and pushed a side of longish hair behind his ear. My heart raced. Martin had always kept his monthly barber appointment for what he called his short, cropped, lawyer-do. He had at least survived the early siege of San Francisco for as long as it took for those beautiful black locks to have grown over the top of his collar. For the first time, my muscles relaxed.

"I can't be sure it is you, so I will talk in generalities. What happened is only happening in the United States. I'm working with the person who can set it right. Set it better, but for now, I have to keep the target off their back. This house is yours. Now that you've figured out that the open says-a-mes is your favorite swear word, you can work most of the systems. There are levels below with more freezers full of grass-fed steak, your favorite Vanilla Mint ice cream, and other goodies, but more importantly, there are heritage seeds for a garden and a hydroponic farm that will give you decades of food, just in case this all goes wrong. Sitting up will take some time, but I know you can read a map. The water comes from the ocean and goes through desalination, which is also underground, so use it until the sea runs dry. You'll eventually find the door to those levels and rock out the password. The house will last forever. You can live here forever. I'll do my best to return to you, but if I don't, know that..." He raised his hand toward the camera as if to touch me through it. "Well, I think you know. Now, if I can ask you one favor." He hesitated, biting his bottom lip into a grimace. "I only ask because I know you're your mother's daughter." He hesitated again, looking aside and then back at the camera. "If the world comes to your doorstep, kill the Madonna. You're one of the smartest women I know. What you have in your hand, keep in your hand. In this case, you don't have to memorize the lines with that perfect recollection of yours. Just read between them."

For the next few days, the idea of *forever* haunted me. This house, this coastline, this silence—it could be mine forever. But without Martin? That thought carved hollows into my chest. His message dangled before me like a golden apple, just out of reach, promising meaning I wasn't sure I had the intelligence—or courage—to grasp. I stood on the cliff, wind slapping tears from my eyes, and stared into the ocean as if it might decode his words for me.

He'd given me safety, a future... maybe even a kind of love. But then he'd laid a quest at my feet like I was some chosen one in a myth. Me—just Brooklyn, the girlfriend, the journalist, the woman who had spent her life documenting others because her own felt too small. My hands trembled, and shame flushed hot beneath my skin. What did he see in me that I couldn't find in myself? I was no one—except maybe my mother's daughter. *Martin. What do you want from me? Why did you leave me with this?*

Restless and raw, I wandered the house like a ghost, my fingers trailing along walls until I found the entrance to the basement levels behind a map of the United States with a picture of the actor Tim Curry pasted on the state of North Dakota. It opened with the phrase "Dammit, Janet," a joke between us because our first date was a midnight viewing of *The Rocky Horror Picture Show.*

I felt dumb remembering Martin saying I could read a map and rock out the password. He'd practically handed me the clues, telling me to look for a map with a Rocky Horror ticket, and I hadn't understood or been reading between the lines. I realized that everything he'd said in his message was coded. There was no reason for him to mention my mother as he'd never met her and didn't know about mine and Stella's past. Kill the Madonna—no idea. This wasn't just a house—it was a monument to everything I didn't know about him. Every coded word in that message became heavier. The puzzle wasn't just logistical; it was emotional. Personal. Intimate. All I was sure of was he didn't want this place falling into the wrong hands. Just whose hands those were wasn't yet clear to me.

The first lower-level room had a treasure of documents, artwork, and photos. Was Martin safeguarding them as if we were in a world war? As I leafed through old pictures from his past, I felt like an interloper. His mother was a smart-looking brunette with a vivacious smile, and his father was a marine type who never looked directly into the camera. The Siriso's ancestry was Spanish gypsy. His mother, a Campbell, had Scottish roots. Martin was their only child, and when they passed away, Martin was left with a modest inheritance that he'd turned into a successful law practice along with an investment portfolio that specialized in turning around distressed companies. In almost every childhood photo of him, he pointed toward the sky. I wondered at what—the sun, moon, the stars? Martin was far richer than I'd ever guessed. I found deeds to a building in Seattle, a house in North Dakota, condos in Tokyo, Paris, and London, and billions in investments, including a significant stake in Javon Enterprises. Then, a jolt. Eyes stared at me. The darkest I'd ever seen, almost black. Martin's eyes. I pulled out a sizable portrait and sat down before it.

Yep, too much I didn't know about him. I stared at a handsome strawberry-blond woman next to him and a sandy-haired toddler they embraced in front of them. A boy. He had a family. I couldn't help wondering if the woman's name began with an S.

The portrait struck me like a slap. A rush of doubt swirled with fear and a hint of betrayal. There he was—my Martin—but not. Beside him, a woman whose smile shimmered with closeness, and a toddler with a smile like his. A life. A family. I stared, pulse hammering in my ears, as the swell of betrayal crashed down.

How could he not tell me? I'd researched him obsessively before our first interview, uncovered everything—or so I thought. But this? Nothing. No mention of a wife or a child. Did he scrub it from the web? Did I mean so little that he never thought I'd need to know? Then came the shame. The world was burning. People were suffering. And here I was, angry like a woman scorned. But pain doesn't check the news before it hits you. And this hurt? It felt personal. A wound I hadn't known was open. Was I a dupe of a married man?

Studying his face in the portrait, I noticed discrepancies; his lips appeared thinner, his face fuller with a more distinctively square jawline. His eyebrows arched sharply, while Martin's were softer, gently curling over his eyes. The painter had gotten more than a few things wrong. I slid the portrait back behind the pallet and went upstairs. Sitting in the dark, watching the gibbous moon set over a glistening ocean, I listened to the hush of silence, wishing it would speak answers. I needed the truth.

Golden sunlight filtered through the window, illuminating the small table where I sat with Martin at Caffé Trieste. Our mugs steamed gently in the crisp North Beach air that wafted through the door each time someone entered. My third and final interview with him before I finalized and submitted my profile.

Martin's eyes lit up as he spoke about Paris and the beat poets, pointing at a corner where Alan Ginsberg might have penned a masterpiece. He inhaled the aroma of his coffee, but his gaze was on me.

Uncomfortable, I looked away.

"How long have I known you?" he asked.

"Five years, five months, three days," I answered without much thought. I studied a list of questions and when I glanced at him, his eyebrows arched, amused. "It was at the opening of Forbidden Grill. I was covering it because the food editor had the flu. More a handshake and how-do-you-do, not really a conversation."

Martin sipped coffee before responding. "We talked more at the Julius Halsey's senatorial campaign kickoff. What was that... Three years ago?"

"Three years, two months. A Tuesday. It wasn't well attended. Probably why he lost."

He stared out the window and whistled. "We've crossed paths twelve dozen times over the years, and while I may not remember the date or hours, I always remembered you."

"I'm pretty memorable," I joked. "Not the eyes, the scar."

"I hadn't even noticed. Not for at least four years."

The quiet between us gelled like concrete despite noisy background chatter. I shifted sideways and pulled my hair forward to hide my scar. Cradling my coffee cup, the heat stung my skin. One of his fingers grazed mine.

"I can't go out with you," I said, feeling regret as I said it. "If my work is to mean anything, there can be no hint of an inappropriate relationship. Dating an interview subject would be bad form."

Martin looked aside and huffed in frustration. "How long?"

I leaned back, taking my coffee with me. "I don't know. I'd need to discuss with my editor."

He rubbed a hand over his face, chin resting on his palm.

"A year, maybe."

He held up his wrist and tapped his watch. "Fine. Expect my call, Ms. Brooklyn Tremain, on this date at exactly ten-thirty and fifteen seconds."

I chuckled, glancing down at my notes. "I predict that you'll be engaged to Vivian Sinclair one year from now."

"Haven't you heard? We broke up. Three weeks ago." He smiled, not a hint of hurt. "Seven hours, thirty-two minutes."

Three weeks ago. After our second interview. "You're making fun of me."

"Damn," he uttered, draining his mug. "I feel seen."

A tap on the window sent me to the ground. I peered over the desk. Flashlights. Rolling toward the wall, I shifted upright. Please be Martin, I whispered even knowing it was unlikely. Scooting to the curtain, I peeked around and gasped. A bald man looked directly at me. He held a tattooed arm above pudgy eyes, squinting. Then I realized I could see out, but he couldn't see in. I watched as he and another bearded man banged fists against the window. It held.

I dismissed that they could be passing by looking for food or a place to stay. This house was too out of the way for anyone to bother with if you even knew it was here. They had to be looking for Martin. I debated whether to open the door and see what information they could give me when the bald one raised a gun and shot the window.

I dropped again, screaming. The glass held, and a steel plate slammed shut in front of it. I hesitated only for a second, then ran upstairs to the electronic room as I heard every window and door being barricaded. Once inside, the monitors let me see what was happening and listen to what they said.

"Think he's here?" the bearded man asked.

"Think his house thinks he is," the pudgy one pointed at the structure.

"Here he comes," the bald man said nervously.

Dixie Roman strutted toward them, followed by a pack of thugs armed with AR-15s. He braced fists against his waist, his bulky biceps flexing, one arm tattooed with a full sleeve.

"Come out, you fucking traitor!" Dixie yelled. "I'm going to tear your life apart a piece at a time and shove it down your gullet!" Dixie paced, eyeing the house the way he might an opponent back in his MMA days. One of his men raised an AR-15 and looked at Dixie. "Don't bother," he said, wiping the brow of his shaved head. "It'd probably ricochet and get you in the ass if I know him."

"He did cover his downtown building in that paint that shoots back your pee on ya, Boss," the bald man chuckled. He kicked a patch of dirt and shook his head when no one appreciated his joke. "Be more signs of going in and out. He's ain't here."

"He'll have to come back here and get it," Dixie said. "Double the men on Highways 1 and 101."

I watched the monitor as Dixie crawled into a utility basket and was lifted over the wall. At least they hadn't breached the gate, but they did figure out a way inside. The sound of motorcycles growled, and then, it was quiet again. The house had protected me.

I spent the rest of the night trying to figure out the electronic room and see if there was a way to contact Martin. Whoever he was with no longer mattered. I needed to protect whatever Dixie was after until Martin returned. The idea that Martin and Dixie knew each other was more disturbing than I could admit. Dixie had called him a traitor. Nothing I knew about Martin suggested they'd remotely be on the same side. I made myself believe that, whatever their connection was, Martin had fought against everything Dixie stood for.

Hours passed, and I'd made no headway on the electronics. Just after dawn, I fell asleep sitting up. My head nodded, jerking me awake. I think I might have been dreaming about Martin, his soft voice speaking words I couldn't remember. I looked down the row of blinking computer equipment, the monitors dark, except for the one frozen on Martin sitting in that orange chair. It was the only part of him here, and I'd not had the strength to shut it off.

Exactly one year later, I found myself watching the seconds bleed away. Ten twenty-eight. Stupid, I thought. No way was he going to call. And yet.

It'd been exactly a year. My profile of the renaissance man-lawyer-entrepreneur had sold out that issue, and he'd sent a polite note thanking me and scrawled a coffee mug at the bottom of the page. I'd kept it for a while, pinning it to my bulletin board. One day, I came into the office, and it had vanished. Ten twenty-nine.

Stop it, Brooklyn, I chastised myself. I'd heard no rumors of him dating. However, he did take Vivian Sinclair to the San Francisco Opera opening, and their picture appeared on several society pages and websites. Vivian smiling, radiant, and luminous. He stared blankly ahead as if he was dreaming of Paris and poetry. Ten twenty-nine. God, Brooklyn, let it go.

Ten thirty. The phone mute. Idiot! I could wait out the fifteen seconds... No, I wouldn't. I stood by the door, coat half on, like some woman in a romance novel trapped between chapters. My fingers itched toward the knob, but my ears strained for a sound I knew wouldn't come. Pausing before I engaged the lock, I listened.

The phone rang.

"Am I too old to go to The Rocky Horror Picture Show?" a voice asked.

"There's a law," I whispered, half-laughing, half-crying. "Nobody's too old for Rocky Horror."

"Fine. You're taking me 'cause I'm am too old to go by myself. Friday night. Pick you up at seven. We'll hit Caffé Trieste first."

Crossing my arms and stretching, I shook myself awake. Blinking in the half-light, the words from a dream echoing: *I'm here. It's here.* My breath trembled as realization dawned—not with comfort, but with dread. The house wasn't sheltering me. It was guarding something else. Something Dixie wanted. Something Martin needed kept safe.

Javon Batteries were expensive but widely available worldwide before all this happened. More places than Martin's building had them, so it seemed unlikely Dixie was in pursuit of more battery power. Maybe the blueprints for the house, but any architect worth salt could design something like this, and it'd make more sense to chase down the builders. My breath shivered over my lips as I stared at Martin's face, suspended in time, here but not here. I held still, my heartbeat quickened, my muscles tightened, silence heavy in my ears. *Here, and not here.* Words. Words in conflict. *Visible is born of invisible.* I felt a presence, almost a ghost watching me. I said it aloud, needing the words to tether me. "If you're listening... Dixie found the house. Whatever is hidden isn't safe." I inhaled a quivery breath, hoping. "I need help."

A buzz. A drawer slid out from the wall. Inside, a square copper-colored fragment—a quarter the size of a postage stamp—was enclosed in a resealable poly bag along with a car key. I knew what Martin wanted. They were a summons. A call to action. My fear didn't vanish, but it reshaped. Became fuel. I would carry what he left behind. Protect it.

And finally, find him. Or the truth.

The key opened that third junkpot car. It made sense to travel in this small, unassuming car as pendejos would be looking to take the BMW and Alfa Romero at the first chance. The only seat was for the driver. It laid down into a bed if needed. The windshield was as thick as the house windows, and I suspected the outer hull was also built so it could take a bullet. The back seat, filled with tools, ration bars, water, and survival equipment left enough room for me to supplement it with some canned tuna, freeze-dried fruit, and toilet paper. I siphoned gas from the other vehicles, filled three red cans, and squeezed them in. I had been wrong to underestimate the ugly vehicle. Junkpot was a go-bag on wheels.

The copper chip wasn't like anything I'd ever seen. Flexible and so small, I was afraid of losing it. Turning it over and over, I couldn't figure out what it did. It warmed as I held it, vibrated, and glowed for several seconds as if activating. Then, to my surprise, it floated above my hand and opened into a three-dimensional cube. As it revolved, gold letters showing an address appeared in front of me along with the words, *Memorize. What you have in hand, keep in hand.* The cube went dark and closed flat. This had to be what Martin was protecting. A piece of technology that did... who knows what. I sewed pockets into less noticeable parts of my innermost vest for valuables I didn't want to lose and in the lower part of my bras, fastened by Velcro. Even if I got searched, hands seldom went to the bottom part of a bra for long. I named the silver piece Boxy.

Mid-day, I wrapped the BOL key in plastic and buried it outside the main gate. That way, no one could take it from me, and I'd have a place to come back to if needed. Then, a deep breath as I readied myself to set out for Seattle.

The state sign with an arrow pointing toward Bolinas had been torn down so many times that no one had bothered to put it back up. I ran over it on my way out, taking one detour to Stinson Beach to return the blond woman's kayak, pump her for any information she might have about Dixie, and leave Harry some steaks and all that baby formula.

Harry came around the counter and kissed me on both cheeks. His warmth was like breath on glass—fleeting, fogged with exhaustion. "This'll get 'em through to soft food," he said, lifting a can of baby formula like treasure. "Everybody in town was trying to figure out what to do." I smiled, but inside, something was unraveling.

While he brewed the last of his coffee, treating each scoop like gold dust, I watched his hands shake slightly. He told stories about the girls' parents—how one mother left in the night and another never came back from a run for clean water. I nodded and listened, but each word was a blow. These people didn't fold. They stitched each other together. He and the community had taken on the mission of seeing these girls, all six of them, through to adulthood. We hugged, hoping our paths would cross again, and I whispered 9459 in his ear. A code, a promise. If he heard it again, it would mean someone was worth saving.

Dragging the kayak down the beach, I wondered what I'd say to Richard if he and his father had managed to return from San Francisco. *Sorry, me, this creepy adult needed your child's boat to cross over the water to...* Nothing sounded good, so I thought I'd leave it on the beach in front of their house and disappear.

I found his mother sprawled in a lawn chair like she'd planned a sunset—legs splayed, waves lightly touched her toes. A pistol looked to have dropped from her hand and was being buried by the surf. A seagull, devouring what was left of her eyes, shrieked and flew away at my approach. A note clipped to her sleeve read: *Jim/Richard, I waited. I waited until I couldn't.*

I sank beside her, knees folding like paper. For hours, I stayed. The horizon turned liquid—coral, purple, blood—and still I sat. Her death pressed against my skin like heat, like a warning as all my doubts raised like bile in my throat.

I could be killed and the car stolen before I got out of the state. If Dixie knew who I was, there'd be no decency from him if he thought I could lead him to Martin. I wanted to call Jamie and Dan. I wanted someone to say, *Keep going. You matter.* I couldn't risk it. The silence only echoed my mother's voice. *Maybe the S on the envelope wasn't your nickname, Sulis, but for someone else, someone whose actual name began with S. Or maybe he called her Sulis too. Maybe she was her mother's daughter. Perhaps she liked Vanilla Mint ice cream too. Maybe the house was never meant for you. Maybe she actually knew what the message meant. Maybe he loved someone else—someone who deserved it.*

What if the house hadn't been for me? Martin would never have been sure I would even find it. He couldn't even know if I'd survived in San Francisco. And he probably was with his family, somewhere safe. That house was built to protect something he wanted to retrieve at a later time, probably this square shard I hid in my bra. Now he wanted me to bring it to him. Risk my life for something not even namable. Maybe Martin also thought I was expendable, *a stupid piece of nothing*. Maybe I was just the interim girl. The one you forget once safety arrives. My hands began to shake. I shoved them into the sand like I could bury the thought. For now, I'd let the darkness hide me.

I took the snaky back roads like a ghost fleeing its own crime. Every curve felt like a dare. The dark wrapped around me, thick and intimate, and little Junkpot never ceased giving its all. I gunned it on I-5. Speed became my argument against fear. *Go fast enough,* I thought, *and the past can't find you.* I wanted them—any pendejos watching—to think I was dangerous. I wanted to believe I was.

At Mount Shasta, I pulled into a deserted Best Western to sleep. I couldn't be seen from the freeway or the road into town in the back parking lot. I was about eighty-five percent convinced to turn back and hoped to have enough gas to make Bolinas. The fuel monitor on Junkpot never moved, making mileage an unknown. I'd be safer if I went back to the house, I told myself, where there was food, water, and sanctuary. If Martin wanted his badge, let him come and get it. I exited the car to stretch my legs and waded into nearby bushes to use the bathroom. Keeping Junkpot in sight, I surveyed the area, trying to keep my eye off the stunning volcanic mountain with a spacecraft-shaped cloud hiding its peak.

Tucked between two sides of the hotel, there it sat—that truck. "Pendejos," I hissed. Red-lettered names *Jesus Mary & Joseph.* The rage didn't rise slowly. It detonated. I called it Stella's rage. I could hear her again—my mother. *Audi, vide, tace, si vis vivere.* She'd gone to the library and looked it up just for me. To let me know I was too big for my britches and she'd teach me the lesson. *Hear, see, be silent if you would like to live.* Rage. Rage to cower me. Rage to humiliate me. Rage to slash my face. That was the rage I'd inherited: precise, performative, and lethal. The rage that taught me love was just control wrapped in silk. All I knew at this moment was my mother's rage.

The room crackled with hushed tension as the elegant soirée reached its zenith. Crystal chandeliers cast shimmering light across the crowd, their laughter diminishing into a faint murmur, overshadowed by furtive glances and whispering conversations behind delicate hands. I stood across the room, stunned, my heart racing as Vivian Sinclair's barbed words sliced through the din, poisonous and sharp as she strode toward me.

"Really, Brooklyn? It's hard to believe someone like you is here as a guest. Shouldn't you be in the corner taking notes in your

little reporter's notebook and making sure you spell our names correctly?"

"I'm here with a date," I replied, hoping to defuse the situation.

"You're just a fad, darling. The latest in dating down. Even a scar for good will. Trust me, fads fade," she sneered, her tone dripping with disdain.

"Excuse me," I said, attempting to move aside.

But she stepped into my path, blocking me with an imperious stance. "I have the servants use the Calendar for the bottom of my birdcage. Not much else it's good for."

I felt my breath hitch—heat rushed to my cheeks, blurring my surroundings. Just as humiliation threatened to suffocate me, I sensed Martin's presence behind me.

"Enough." His voice sliced through the social chaos like a blade. Laughter faded, and a hush settled over the crowd as their attention turned to us. "This isn't about Brooklyn," he continued. His jaw clenched as he locked eyes with Vivian. "It's cowardly to attack someone like that when your real issue is with me."

And just like that, I was seen. I wasn't a project. I wasn't a distraction. I was his choice. For a moment, I stood taller. For a moment, I believed I belonged. "Martin, you don't have to—" I began, but he raised a hand, silencing me. The expression on his face was familiar, one I'd seen before when he stared down the bear in Yosemite—unyielding and indomitable.

"If we could just talk," Vivian murmured, her voice low and pleading. "I can get past this, this time, but if you continue to humiliate me, then I don't know what Daddy might do."

"Daddy?" Martin repeated, incredulous. "You think this is about your Daddy?"

Her expression shifted from desperation to anger, and then her glare fixated on me. "You did this. You... Don't think I'll forget it." Tears shimmered in her eyes as she looked up into Martin's. "You know where to find me, and what I bring to the table."

"I made myself clear a year ago, Vivian." He took a step toward her, causing her to lean back instinctively. "It's not Brooklyn's fault that you refuse to listen. Listen again: I am not your project

or a stepping stone to your self-worth, and I certainly am not going to be your husband."

The next morning's business news blared that Sinclair Technology had been sold to an out-of-state company, Hast Industries. Martin had worked for months to acquire that company for his protégé, Phillip Javon. Now, they'd have to start from scratch—a mess I felt responsible for.

I dialed Martin's private number, my heart weighing heavy. "I'm sorry," I said when he answered.

"She won't bother you again," he replied, though his voice had a troubled undertone. "I have to go to London, and I'm not sure when I'll be back."

"Okay."

"If you need to reach me—"

"I won't," I interrupted. "Do what you have to do. I won't be your distraction."

He hung up, and I wasn't sure if I'd hear from him again.

I pissed in the bushes and came back changed. That truck—*their* truck—was a threat. A message. And I answered.

I took back my backpack like I was reclaiming my spine. They'd tried to tear it, to break in, but it'd outlasted them. I siphoned every drop of their fuel with shaking hands, muscles so tight they trembled.

Then I took their machete. My mother would've been proud. Or terrified. Maybe both. I slashed their tires—one, two, three, four—my breath coming fast, the rage inside me a living thing.

This was Stella's rage, weaponized. It wasn't clean. It wasn't noble. But it was mine. And I would ride it like a wave into whatever hell came next.

~ SEATTLE ~

Superpowers. Now that was a word I never saw coming. Junkpot had superpowers. Being chased by a mid-sized, gas-guzzling truck and a beat-up black Corvette at the Oregon border, I could swear my wheels sensed the danger. How the heck these yahoos had gotten gas to burn was burning me up. Dixie's gang typically used motorcycles, but I couldn't take a chance that they were affiliated with him, so I blew past their illegal roadblock and gambled that they couldn't catch me. Both were faster than I expected.

That was the moment Junkpot stopped being a car and became something else—something alive. "Faster! But steady! Stay on the road! Avoid gunshots!" Some of those were more terror than instructions, but the car seemed to get the drift. The steering moved as if guided by instinct—its own or mine, I couldn't tell. My palms were slick with sweat, and the seatbelt cut into my ribs, but my brain only registered one thing: I was still alive. Somehow. And it wasn't me doing the driving.

A dense fog hadn't stopped the pursuers and any wrong direction could tip me over an embankment, falling a gazillion feet down onto rocky terrain. Crawling to the rear window, I let fly a few shots. They shot back, of course. I pulled a gas can toward me, feeling through my backpack for a lighter. Steading myself with the car as it swerved in half-moon curves across the freeway, we danced.

A couple more shots whizzed past. If they hit a tire, I'd be done for. Opening the rear window, I poured gas onto the road, lit a paper bag, and threw it. A blaze shot up, sending my pursuers skirting across the highway, breaks screeching. "Pendejos!" I yelled at the pinked-up mist as it slowly became a bank of white. Junkpot did the driving until the thick fog cleared.

Pulling off near Eugene, Oregon, I hid behind a clump of alder trees on the banks of the Willamette River and slept for the rest of the day. When I woke up, it was night. Starting the car, I checked the gas gauge. Full. "You jest, little Junkpot?" No gas had been added to the tank. I'd looked under the hood at almost every bathroom stop. Parts weren't overheating or even warm to the touch. Nor did I see anything resembling a Javon battery, though it could have been hidden deeper in the car's structure. What kind of vehicle had Martin built? The gas gauge made me nervous. I didn't want to risk running out of fuel at the wrong time. Still hoarding four full gas cans, I petted the dashboard. "Okay, darlin', you're my new boyfriend."

Approaching Seattle, my mood improved at the thought of finding Martin, handing off his magical snippet, sleeping the day away in his arms and hoping he'd tell me he'd been divorced for a decade. I tried not to think about his secrets. I tried not to judge him. After all, I had a few of my own.

A dozen or more cars sped down the freeway, and none of them chasing me. Somehow these vehicles were getting fueled or charged, and I wondered if the world was returning to normal. A normal thought until I saw a seventy-foot-tall Jumbotron latched onto the slanted roof of a building. Dixie Roman. I pulled off to the side of the freeway for a better look. A banner read *Seattle Loves Dixie*. His crooked-ass grin stretched as his image lifted a finger and pointed at the header that changed to *Dixie For President*. I wanted to vomit.

A quarter mile down, underneath a spider web of freeways, was a tent city within a patch of green trees. I drove in that direction. Toward the far end, I parked between a Buick and a Cadillac with smashed windows and raised hoods where Junkpot would look like another cannibalized wreck. Securing the key in plastic, I reached under the driver's side and dug a hole. Leaving a tiny edge up over the dirt in case I needed it quickly made me secure of a quick escape. Wandering around and scouting out the locals would give me a better idea of what I was walking into. If Seattle had fallen to Dixie, that changed my plan. I'd need to be more watchful as I searched for Martin.

Plenty of people milled about, families, couples, and children racing on gravel paths between campsites. I stretched to each side, taking in the lay of the land. Flyers tacked to trees invited people to the *Liturgy of the Madonna*. It promised she'd appear and offer *communion and blessings*. This stunk of a Dixie scam. I heaved my backpack over my shoulder and tried to fit in with the drifting mass of humanity. Following the tinny sound of a banjo, I found a group of musicians gathered around a burned-out campfire.

A white-haired banjo player tapped his foot and said, "One, two, three." A flute, oboe, saxophone, and violin joined him to the tune of "Wayfaring Stranger." The haunting tune slurred painfully. The younger men were learning from the banjo player. The female flutist rolled her eyes impatiently. Banjo man stopped them and said, "Listen." As he began again, I decided to introduce myself by singing with him.

"I am a poor, wayfaring stranger
Traveling through this world alone
There's no sickness, toil, or danger
In that bright land to which I go

I'm going there to see my mother
She is waiting for me there
I'm just going over Jordan
I'm just going over there."

The other musicians joined in on the second verse, their instruments melodiously following my voice.

"That was beautiful," I said, when we ended.

"You a vocalist?" the banjo man asked.

"Naw, my ma knew all kinds of old-timey songs. Used to annoy me when they got stuck in my head."

"Take a breather," the dark-haired flutist said, holding a thermos and tin cup.

I cushioned my backpack beside a tree stump used as a stool.

When I turned, all the musicians were pointing weapons at me. A gun, two machetes, a baseball bat, and a big stick. "Was my singing that bad?" I raised my hands to seem helpless.

"You're not from around here." The oboe player said.

"Clearly." I scooted backward. "I'll take a hike instead of a breather."

"Sit," the banjo player said. "Not until I know what you're about."

"Believe I just sang my story."

"Maria." The banjo player instructed the flutist toward my backpack. She riffled through it and nodded to him that it was safe. "I'm Wayne. In about fifteen seconds, something is going to happen and in ten of those seconds you better spill what you did to Dixie Roman."

I thought of running. I could leave the backpack. There was nothing in it I couldn't replace. "Never met the man," I stammered, looking beyond them and trying to estimate if I could race to Junkpot before they stabbed, shot, and bludgeoned me. "And I'd sooner vote for a pee-soaked maggot than him."

Shrill whistles blasted from three directions. A shuffle as people ran past me, including three of the musicians. Others scurried, tidying their areas, disappearing into tents and RVs. Wayne threw a baseball cap at me. "Put it on. Hide your hair." Down one of the paths, half a dozen military types harassed a group of teens.

I pulled the baseball cap over my head, shoving as much of my hair as I could underneath it. Maria pointed toward a blue tarp, and I followed her into an open-air kitchen. Park benches served as seating. Tables squared off the areas where workers prepared food. Toward the rear, campfires heated cauldrons.

Wayne pointed at a board behind the counter. I saw what he wanted me to see. Wanted posters. A clear picture of Martin, another of Phillip Javon, and a generic drawing of me, red hair, scar across my cheek. *Wanted for Treason. Reward.* It didn't say how much. I curled my fingers into fists to stop the shaking, but they trembled anyway. Not for the first time, I wished I could unzip my skin, change my bones, disappear. I could hear the soldiers getting closer.

Behind me, Wayne nudged me toward a break in the tables where Maria stood holding open a curtain. I followed her. She quickly draped me in a cook's apron and put a dark hairnet over the baseball cap, further hiding my auburn hair. She handed me a paring knife and bowl and pointed to a potato sack. I started peeling.

The stormtroopers marched through the kitchen area in unison, stomping their boots and gripping rifles tightly to their chest. Helmets obscured their faces, making them seem almost robotic. All the workers ignored them, and a few sang hymns that made the soldiers dawdle uncomfortably. I faced away, peeling potatoes like I'd done it my whole life. The one peek I ventured, I didn't see any insignia on their uniforms, just like the soldiers at the Golden Gate Bridge. A shiver ran down my spine as one approached me.

"Who are you?" he barked, voice echoing through the helmet in a foreign accent.

"A cook," I replied, shrugging without looking up and wondering at his accent. Not American.

He stepped closer, and I swear his uniform brushed my back. The knife in my hand glided, slicing a thin ribbon of potato skin as the soldier loomed closer. I didn't breathe. Couldn't. The air turned thick as paste, heavy with gun oil and menace. His voice—processed, foreign—vibrated against my spine. He circled the table and continued to study me, assessing whether I posed a threat. I glanced up at an angle, keeping my scar away from him.

"Keep peeling," he ordered, gesturing with his rifle, then leaned down toward me, his breath at my ear. I nearly dropped the knife. I felt seen in the worst way, as if that creepy helmet could X-ray through my hairnet, through my skull, into every truth I was trying to bury. "And remember, the Madonna sees all."

With that, they marched out and disappeared into the crowded camp. I sat there, feeling the weight of their ominous presence before expelling a quivering breath.

Wayne stuck his head through the curtain. "They're gone."

I didn't move. Couldn't. My spine gave out, and I slumped, head bowed, hands limp in my lap. My breath escaped in short, jerky bursts, like a car stalling on empty. My stomach churned. I hadn't realized how tightly I'd held everything in until I unraveled, one ragged breath at a time.

"She handled herself," Maria said to Wayne.

"I'll leave."

"It's curfew. You'll be picked up and never seen again," Maria said. "Most of these soldiers are foreign mercenaries. They rarely take prisoners. Why do they want you?"

"I don't know. I think they want my boyfriend and expect they can get him through me." I stammered my words as my heart raced.

"Phillip Javon is your boyfriend?"

I didn't acknowledge her and wiped my sweaty cheeks. "Why are they after us?"

"You don't know?" Wayne said.

"I don't. I swear. I've been on the road, trying to find my boyfriend."

Wayne and Maria fell silent, probably trying to assess if I could be believed. Wayne sat in a chair opposite me and drew in a deep breath. "They say Javon is the cause of all this, and the other fella, Martin Siriso, financed it."

"That's malarkey!" I blubbered, feeling real tears surfacing. "You can't trust Dixie Roman. If you believe anything I say, believe that!"

"We believe you on that one fact," Maria said. "Dixie is the reason we're all out here."

Over the next few hours, they told me how Dixie and his hired gangs had taken over Seattle the same way he'd tried with San Francisco but with more success. At first, it had seemed benign, even helpful. "He brought order to chaos and lawlessness when it became clear this crisis wasn't ending anytime soon," Wayne explained. "But liars lie, and Dixie's true colors bled fascism to anyone who would see, especially when those mercenaries showed up."

"The sickening thing is some saw and didn't care," Maria said. "They got their electricity and water back, and that was enough to look past Dixie's despotism and join his crusade."

"And that's why you're here, on the outskirts of the city?"

She and Wayne shared a glance. "He and his lackeys got neighbors to turn on each other, took our homes for fabricated reasons, elected their lackeys to the new Regency Council, and passed local ordinances banning us from putting up opposition candidates. A few who tried were beaten to a bloody pulp." She pointed to a scar on Wayne's forehead.

"Where is the U.S. government?" I asked incredulously.

They both shrugged, almost apologetic. The weight of it landed like a tombstone on my chest. No cavalry. No flags. No rescue. I was alone in a country I didn't recognize anymore, except in the way people flinched at uniforms and whispered in code. The silence that followed made me want to scream—or sob.

"He won't let a tent city last forever," I said.

They glanced at each other. "We've got plans," Wayne said.

"And I sometimes play a different kind of flute," Maria smirked.

I nodded, unsure if they would leave for safer shores or if they were a resistance that might mount a challenge. Better I not know. I had my own mission. "I have to get to the downtown area," I said, leaving out the specific address and that it was actually closer to the waterfront.

They simultaneously shook their heads. "No way. Those posters are everywhere."

"They don't have a picture of me, just a drawing, and I don't have a choice." I picked up the paring knife and pulled a strand of hair to cut it.

"We could use the library," Maria said to Wayne.

I paused, watching Wayne stand and pace, thinking it out. "We've got scissors for that," he said, motioning for Maria. "Take her to the hairdresser and make her a brunette. I'll check with a librarian."

The musicians worked out a plan with the librarians where, in three days, I'd be moved through five different libraries until I got to the central library in the neighborhood of the Siriso building. I never told them exactly where I was going. Safer for them, safer for me, and they never asked. Until then, I kept my hands busy—scrubbing pots, rehanging tarps beaten down by rain, peeling potatoes until my knuckles ached. Anything to stay useful, anything to keep from thinking too long about what the world was becoming. At night, I played music beside the fire, fingers tracing chords like a prayer, as if melody alone could keep my heart safe.

I stayed with Maria and her son, Barber. The kid had the touch, bringing me two charged phones from a nearby deserted mall. He couldn't have been more than twelve. I'd ruffled his hair, gushing thanks—but the weight of it hit me: a child, scavenging like prey in a predator's city. I wished I could hand him back a world where kids didn't have to be this brave.

I thought about calling Jamie to find out if Dixie was troublemaking in San Francisco but decided to wait until I found Martin and had more to report. The city, at least the way I'd left it, had no Dixiephiles, and there was some pretty mean competition in people like Paule Oliver and Chinatown.

For all they'd been through, the tent city was reasonably organized. I hadn't seen a fight or disagreement since I'd been here. Maria told me there had been some, but Wayne was the ultimate negotiator, and she and a few others had done military tours, so they helped out with policing when necessary. Hard not to ignore that there was a growing resistance building when the faux-swat-lawmen stomped through the ground the next day. I wondered how long before Dixie disbursed this camp, scattering those he didn't arrest to the wind. How much of a fight they might put up was answered when I accidentally entered a trailer filled with weapons. Rifles. Hand grenades. A bazooka. The air inside buzzed with tension like a warning hum before lightning strikes. My stomach clenched. This wasn't preparation. It was desperation made manifest. I backed out slowly, pulse banging in my ears, praying no one had seen me. Pretending I could forget what I'd seen. Pretending that bloodshed wasn't coming.

I checked on my ride from time to time. Junkpot seemed safe among the abandoned cars, so I decided to leave it until I could suss out whether Martin was in Seattle. I'd rather my fast escape be closer to the city's edge. The morning I was to head toward town, I walked out from the camp with one of the phones. I typed my name into three search engines and watched as the void stared back. Nothing. It was like I'd never existed. Social media—gone. Articles—gone. Images—gone. My voice—scrubbed out. For a moment, I panicked. Then, I felt it: a strange, stuttering relief. No more trail for them to follow. No breadcrumbs leading back to me. Still, it hurt to be invisible.

If I searched Martin and Phillip, the drawing of me came up, but they didn't know my name. Whoever had deleted me from the web had probably saved my ass. Jamie's husband, Dan, was a crack tech person. He could have done it, or maybe even Martin. Just knowing Martin might be nearby was enough to make my chest ache with hope. I let myself dream that we could leave the country, build something new in the quiet of somewhere untouched by Dixie's craziness. But I also knew hope was a dangerous thing in this world. A drug. And I was always one hit away from despair.

Before I left, Kevin, the saxophonist, and Sue, the violinist, serenaded me with a decent version of "Wayfaring Stranger." Barber snagged me another working phone and said I could trade it for food at the seafood market near the piers. Wayne gave me a Mariners baseball cap and a hug. Maria came to the first library with me and showed me the ropes as we sat in a computer room. She downloaded an app called LimeysDates onto my phone. "Tap it and choose Date. Then off to the side, tap on Fluid." Up popped a list of names. "You can call, email, or video call anyone on this registry of safe names. I'm Flautist. Wayne is Banjo. What do you want yours to be?"

"Sulis," I answered, thinking that if Martin ever became part of this, he'd recognize it. Maria typed it in.

"You're set up, Sulis. You can use it on your personal phone, but if you need to call someone off list, it's better to give your name to a safe librarian, and they'll set you up with a device that's wiped at the end of each day and lives in the lost and found so the goon soldiers pay little attention."

"How do I know who is safe?"

She averted her eyes toward a young blond-haired woman. "See the lime green bow she's wearing? That's the safe librarian of the day. We call them Limeys. Not 'cause they're British, but they'll have the color lime worked into their attire. You can ask for her help. Remember that color, lime green, not moss green, not grass green, not jade green, not olive green. Lime. See the lime green painter's tape on the side of the third computer? That's a safe computer. All the others, they're tracking."

"To be fair, that ribbon is a little more avocado."

She glared at me before realizing I was joking. "We've all forgotten how to laugh. I guess that's why we play sad songs that tell sad stories."

I rested my hand on her shoulder, feeling sorry to be saying goodbye. "Seriously, girl, you've got to find a better place for you and your son. Whatever is being planned, you need to keep him safe." My voice cracked, thinner than I wanted it to be.

"How do you know I'm not planning it?" she smirked and saluted with two fingers off her forehead. "Like I said, I play a different kind of flute from time to time."

We laughed, but it didn't reach our eyes. I wanted to promise I'd come back. But in this world, no one makes promises anymore.

I slept on a cot in the stacks, the scent of paper and dust curling around me like memory. I picked spots near exits, just in case. But no door led to the past. Martin haunted me—his voice, his hands, the things he never said. Sometimes, I spoke to him, tearful and afraid, the books my only witnesses. Other nights, I just stared at the ceiling, waiting for my fear to subside.

The librarians were more confident than I was that life would either return to normal or, after the coup d'état, they'd be there to put civilization back together again. As I lay in my cot at night, I thought they were probably right. The Regency Council had issued a list of books to be removed from the library. They hid them deep in the stacks with different book covers and transferred them from library to library, keeping them on the move and never found.

I saw only one other person sleeping in the library. He stayed near the safe computer, never spoke to me, and walked in a different direction the one time I smiled at him. He cried late one night. In the morning, he was gone. If there was one thing I knew, it was that you had to give people their tears.

The clock read three a.m.; I pretended to be asleep. Martin stood by the window, looking out at a branch of fog looping over the Golden Gate Bridge. He took a deep breath, exhaling with a shiver. Resting his chin on his fist, he shook his head as if having an argument with himself. He sniffed, wiped his eyes, and opened the patio door, allowing a cool breeze and hum of distant traffic to seep in. Returning to the bed, he sat on the edge as twinkling lights from buildings cast a gentle glow across the room.

"How?" he said, his voice shaky. He sniffed again as a soft sob broke the stillness. He covered his mouth with a hand, silencing whatever sorrow troubled him.

He lay down next to me, pulling me close, our foreheads touching, the warmth of our breaths mingling as he drifted into sleep. Sometime later, he jolted upright.

"Did you hear that?" he whispered, scanning the dark room.

"No," I said, moving beside him and touching his shoulder. "What did you hear?"

He stared out the window. "Chaos."

The librarians were skilled in shifting people through the city and possibly out of the state. I posed as a worker carrying boxes of books to be transferred to a different branch. These libraries were founts of resistance, moving book cartons and me like they were running an underground railroad. I figured there might be more than books in those boxes, but I never asked. The true revelation was that they got away with it because no one thought they were important. Long live Marian, the librarian! I arrived at the central library within walking distance of the Siriso building. They offered me a bunk in the stacks, but I'd put them at risk long enough. I found a bed at a hostel and took it for a week.

The hairdresser from the encampment had given me a pixie haircut and dyed it a mousy brown. I tested moving around the city, checking out one of the Madonna services. It could have been a sleep-through church service and no spectacular being appeared despite the promises. "Work the plan," an uninspiring pastor preached. "Before the plan works you," as he shook the collection plate.

No one noticed me, so I took a few longer walks, watching to see if I was followed. Keeping my collar flipped up hid the scar well enough that I braved walking past the Siriso building. I ordered a sandwich and coffee from a corner street vendor and watched to see if anyone went in or out. An accordion security gate locked off a ground floor real estate office. A sign in the window read *Closed Until Further Notice*. Upper windows reflected the afternoon sun. I prayed Martin would look out one of them, but knowing he was a wanted man probably meant he'd not take the chance. I wondered if Dixie's people knew about this building. They could be watching it now. I came the next day, looking for familiar faces, watching for movement in the windows or around the building. Nothing seemed out of the ordinary. Besides a metal side door, it was locked up tight like the San Francisco building. I wanted to run to that door. Martin could be that close. But I had to be careful not to put either of us on Dixie's radar.

Another thing bothered me. What about Martin's wife? What if she was there? What if the kid was with him? I could act like a messenger, hand him Boxy, and walk away. I longed to talk to him, ask him to explain, needing to believe it was me he loved. The stark reality that I didn't want to admit is he'd never said those words to me. At night, I'd take out Boxy, hoping it would say something. Give me another address, instructions, tell me he was near, watching me, keeping me safe. Boxy warmed to my touch but performed no other feats, much like the grifter Madonna.

Along the wharf, it astounded me how normal Seattle was compared to San Francisco. People strolled about, worked in offices, shopped, fished on the pier. There were no newspapers, only handout sheets that gave information about the upcoming election. Plenty of flyers in every open business touted a functional government led by Dixie Roman. At the bottom of the flyer, a drawing of the United States showed a bolded outline around the West coast that circled around to cut the country in half at North and South Dakota, Nebraska, Kansas, Oklahoma, and most of Texas. California, Kansas, Utah, and New Mexico were colored in light gray to show they weren't yet part of the coalition. Meaning they were fighting. I despised the thought that he might get elected, even of this pseudo country. A year ago, Dixie Roman running anything more than a hotdog stand would have been preposterous. I guess we now live in nonsensical times.

I eavesdropped on conversations, trying to ascertain whether Dixie had support. All I heard was a hotbed of harebrained conspiracies and indifferent viewpoints. As long as Dixie brought water, electricity, and hope for a better tomorrow, they'd quietly acquiesce to whatever else he wanted. When a couple of fishermen fought over whether or not the Madonna backed Dixie, it made me want to go back to the tent city and tell them to run. People were starting to believe she was an actual entity, and I couldn't help but hear Martin's words, *Kill the Madonna.*

I had graduated from wanted posters to digital sign boxes put up every few blocks. Martin's and Phillip's pictures flashed by, along with so many other subversives that most passersby hardly noticed. At least mine was still a drawing with no name. With my brown hair, sunglasses, and clipped-up collar, no one associated me with... well, myself. Sometimes, the sign boxes played newscasts of Brace Benton reporting on Madonna sightings. The local San Francisco anchor now seemed to be broadcasting from a new television station called *The Voice of the Regency*. He'd interview people who had seen the Madonna; their exuberance gave way to religious zeal. Occasionally, Brace would wipe a tear and end his newscasts with the words, "The Madonna sees all, so let us be worthy." It was eerie, even scary.

I decided to enter the Siriso building that afternoon, late when everyone was rushing home to beat the seven p.m. curfew. Fewer people would pay attention to me then. Buying a soda from a street vendor, I leaned against a fence overlooking the water and sipped, waiting for the last ferry of the day.

Slowly eyeing the two-story structure and pausing as if to fix my shoe, I scanned the area. No one slowed for me or turned to see what I was doing. People passed, and I joined the crowd. Then, I jetted across two streets and slipped the SEA key into a slot above the metal door as my heart raced. It popped open. I shot through and shut it in a single motion.

"Martin!" I called out, stumbling into the stairwell, legs trembling. My lungs locked up as if I'd sprinted for miles. The air felt too thick to breathe, my vision spotting at the edges. My whole body was shaking with adrenaline and need—need to see him, to stop running just for a second. "Martin!"

Mid-way up, a man on the landing above me pointed a revolver at my head.

I raised my hands, wishing I hadn't called out Martin's name. One of Dixie's henchmen? I'd walked into a trap. I glanced behind me. Could I make it down the steps and out the door before he could shoot? Was I wanted dead or alive?

"Don't move," the man said, coming down several steps.

Breath shivered in my chest as I counted the steps back to the door.

"How did you get in here?" he asked. Round glasses slipped to the tip of his nose, and shaggy blond hair blocked his sightline. He pushed it aside, but it fell back, stubbornly refusing to stay in place.

"I'm getting a little tired of weapons being pointed at me. When is this freaking world going to run out of bullets?" I studied him. The firearm weaved a figure eight as if too heavy for his grip. "Phillip Javon?"

"I truly wish you didn't know who I am 'cause now, I'm going to have to shoot you."

"No, wait!" I stripped off the baseball cap and pointed to my face. "I'm Martin's girlfriend."

"That girl has red hair," he said, coming down another step.

"Check my roots in about a week." I held my hands outstretched, noting that his were shaking. "Martin sent me a message to come here."

Phillip lowered the gun and leaned on the wall. "Jesus, motherfracking, son of blasted turnip in a tin can, I could have shot you."

"Where's Martin?"

"Did you bring it? The device, do you have it?"

"Martin!" I said, insistent. "Tell me where he is."

He exhaled a breath and wiped his forehead. "Come upstairs. I'll explain."

Three metal security doors at the top of the stairs, two with exterior padlocks, triangled a narrow hallway. Phillip held the first door. "I'm not a girl, by the way," I said as I moved around him.

"Clearly."

"You called me a *girl* with red hair."

He ignored my comment and walked past me into a kitchen, setting a teakettle onto a gas burner.

"Seattle doesn't seem to be experiencing nearly the shutdown that happened in San Francisco." When he didn't respond, I cleared my throat, wondering if he'd heard me. One foot twisted nervously and his fingers tapped the counter as if impatient with the kettle. "I said Seattle—"

"You said girlfriend." His words raced out of his mouth. He pulled two mugs from a shelf and offered me my choice of tea-bags. Boxes of Pop-Tarts filled the shelves and were stacked on top of the refrigerator.

I decided to ignore the semantics and go along to get along. Seemed odd that Martin wouldn't have stocked up this apartment the way he had the Bolinas house. I tore open an Oolong and dropped it into my cup with an impatient flip. "Well? Martin?"

Phillip turned toward me but looked sideways toward the floor, glancing once, then twice toward me, only to avert his gaze. "Martin isn't here."

The words hit like a gut punch. My knees nearly buckled. I gripped the edge of the counter, willing myself not to cry, not here, not in front of this jittery stranger with a kettle and a shaking voice. I'd come so far. For a second, I hated Martin for not being here, for pulling me through all this chaos and leaving only silence in his wake.

The kettle screamed. "He saved my life. Got me here," Phillip said. "I'm waiting for him to come back. He's going to get me to Canada. I'll have a research center there. I'll be safe."

"Why don't you sit and have your tea," I said, as his quivering voice rambled on about the research center. I picked up the screeching kettle and poured water into our mugs. "Is he in Seattle?"

He sat and wrapped his hands around the cup but didn't offer any information. Staring at the tabletop, he sipped his tea well before the bag had had time to infuse. His silence was unnerving. He didn't seem to realize the minutes that passed. "He carried a picture of you in his wallet, called you Sulis. Funny name."

"When is Martin coming back?" I asked, realizing that Martin hadn't told him my real name. Had to be a reason for that, and I decided to be extra cautious.

"Sulis your real name? What kind of surname goes with that?" He gulped a drink, spilling some of it on his shirt. Jumping at the hot liquid, he poured his tea into the sink.

"I don't mean to be rude, but I need to know where Martin is and when he's returning. Otherwise, I'm wasting my time here." I stood up, hoisting my backpack on my shoulder.

"Soon," he said but didn't turn toward me. "You should wait. Stay here. He'll be back soon. I'm sorry. I'm sorry how I'm acting. I, I, I haven't been out of here since Martin stashed me here." He shifted to one foot and made eye contact for the first time but couldn't hold it. "I need that device. Now. Give it to me, and everything will be okay. Now!"

I stepped back as he sprinted toward the door and slammed it shut. Flipping down an interior security bar, I realized I would have to fight my way out of here. I picked up the gun he'd laid on the table. "I hate to shoot the most brilliant man on the planet, but if you don't want to be less one kneecap, move your genius ass out of my way."

"Pill," he said, pointing to an orange bottle between salt and pepper shakers. "Let me take my pill, I'll be better then. I can explain then." He slumped onto the wall and crossed his arms over his stomach. "Gun's not loaded anyway."

I flipped open the revolver's cylinder. Empty. "What is it with you!" I tossed the pill bottle to him. Sitting the gun on a pantry shelf filled with Pop-Tarts, it moved inward, a hidden room. I pretended not to notice and got Phillip a glass of water.

He motioned toward a set of recliners to the side of a TV as he popped a pill and gulped water. "For my nerves," he said between drinks. "Let me take some breaths, and I'll explain, but it would really help if I could get the device you brought."

I hesitated. I'd seen Phillip Javon in plenty of press interviews, and he wasn't this jittery basket case who seemed on the edge of a breakdown, but if I left now, I still had no information about Martin's whereabouts.-

"I stashed it in a safe place," I said. "I can get it, but I must see Martin first."

Phillip shifted uncomfortably. "You don't trust me." He rubbed his hands together and stared at the floor. "I can't blame you, how I've acted. I'd have lost my mind completely if it hadn't been for Martin. He meant to come back for you. He did. He talked about it and everything, but they were after us, you see, and he thought if they connected you to us, it'd put you in danger."

"Pretty sure that's already happened. A drawing of my face is on wanted posters all over town, all over the country for all I know." I pointed to my hair. "Thus, the color change."

"He said that you were smart and that you'd figure it out."

"Figure what out?"

"You're here, aren't you?"

I spied the setting sun through the building's front windows. "Curfew soon. I need to get back to my hotel."

"No, stay. This apartment runs the full length of the building and has four bedrooms. You can set up in the back one. I sleep on the couch anyway."

"I don't think so—"

"Please. I need the company to keep me socialized so I don't go rabid again, and Martin will be back tomorrow."

He held my gaze for the first time. His eyes were cornflower blue and shaggy blond hair brushed his slender shoulders. A few years younger than me, he maintained a youthful nerdiness that charmed. Serious me pondered the offer. I didn't like the way I was talking myself into it, and those Madonna flyers on the side table made me nervous.

"The room has a key and its own bathroom," he said. "You can lock yourself in. I won't be insulted. Pretty sure you could take me in a fight anyway."

"Look, we got off on the wrong foot. I know you're Martin's friend. I've seen your pictures together in his office. He's talked about you, and your batteries saved my life a time or two." I glanced out the front window at the blinding sun. "I'll stay, but I'm only giving that device to Martin, understood?"

He nodded, grinned, then chuckled a bit. "Only got Pop-Tarts for dinner."

"Let's risk a run to the fish market down the street. I think we can do a little better than that."

After baked salmon and green beans, Phillip seemed much calmer, whether from the pill or having something in his stomach other than toaster pastries, I couldn't tell. He brought over his laptop and pointed at the side slot. "That device. I can connect it here, and we'll have a foolproof connection. I can contact Martin no matter where he is, and they can't trace us. Right now, no computer is safe."

He obviously didn't know about the limeys, and I wasn't about to destroy his confidence. "Tell me something, who exactly is *they*?" Something had been bothering me for some time now. Even if Dixie had the opportunistic chutzpah to mount a presidential campaign, he also had the brains of a dung-digging spit weasel. Somebody bigger and smarter had to be behind all this. I also wasn't sure about this *enfant terrible*, slightly manic act of Phillip's. For the time being, it seemed best to play along. "Twice you've referred to *them*. Who is after us, and why do *they* think you and Martin are behind all this?"

"Because we are." Phillip stared at the keyboard. His eyes darted across the alphabet as he twisted a pen between his fingers. Minutes passed. "I am nobody's thrall," he spit as he rose, throwing the pen onto the desk.

"I don't believe that." A streak of alarm shot through me. No way would Martin cause this destruction.

"Believe what you want." He moved to a bedroom and hugged the door to his chest, looking back at me with an unsettled composure. "Maybe it had to be done. Maybe that was the only way to change the world."

"Are *they*... Government? Corporate? Mafia?" I asked, gently prodding him to reveal more. "What does the phrase *Kill The Madonna* mean?"

"Not likely," he chuckled, as he slowly closed the door. "I'd like to see somebody try."

Lying in bed, I stared at the cracked ceiling, replaying every word Martin ever said to me. Maybe I'd been wrong. Maybe love, real love, didn't survive collapse. Only a madman would shatter the world—unless the world was already breaking and he was trying to save it. I didn't know the full truth yet, but I did know this: Dixie made Martin a criminal, and if that meant exile and condemnation, then maybe I'd rather side with the damned.

Phillip Javon, jittery and genius, seemed less like a co-conspirator and more like a boy swept up in someone else's tide. Martin had always been the gravity behind the orbit. Phillip would still be an MIT lab rat if Martin hadn't supported him, financed his company, and promoted his products. I'd bet gold dust that he also financed the Canadian research center.

When I first met Martin, I thought I understood his shape: a lawyer who liked dipping a toe into blue-blood society now and then. But he kept unfolding, like a puzzle that refused to be solved, and I began to wonder if, by the end of the story, the man I loved would still exist—or if I'd only fallen for a shadow version of him, tailored to draw me in.

Tosca Café. Last call. The clink of glass and the distant notes of a Rigoletto aria hung in the air. We perched on red stools, knees touching, the kind of closeness that buzzes through skin when you're a little drunk. We hadn't said much. We didn't need to. The air between us hummed with inevitability. I knew tonight was the night. We'd been dating for two months—it was time. Martin's smile—just a twitch on the left—drew me in like tide to shore. I always sat to his right, angling away from the light, letting my hair shadow the scar on my cheek. But Martin never asked about it. Never flinched.

Then something shifted. He stood, gently turned me, and stared past my shoulder like I'd vanished. His grip tightened. Just seconds earlier, I had owned his gaze. Now, someone else had claimed him.

"Wait here," he said, tone clipped, too clean.

The tiles echoed his retreat. I turned, heart jabbing my ribs, as he slipped behind the red velvet rope toward the private back room—the one with stories of secrets and scandals sealed in gunfire. My chest knotted. Vivian Sinclair? Her name clawed through me like broken glass.

A bearded man at the bar—Giants cap, face like granite—stood and followed Martin. He hesitated at the turn, throwing me a glance so quick it felt like a warning.

I swallowed a gulp of cappuccino, savoring the chocolate richness and wishing for a bit more bourbon. All the wrong images wormed into my mind. Drug dealer? Bemused ex-boyfriend? Mafia loan shark? Before I could dwell too long on the possibilities, Martin returned, lips pressed tight, tension radiating off him.

"Let's trip over to Grubsteak for burgers," he suggested. The bearded man passed behind us, but Martin didn't look. He tossed a fifty next to his glass and nodded toward the bartender.

"Who is that?" I asked, watching after the stranger as a knot tightened in my stomach.

Martin shrugged. "Nothing. Business."

I faced him from my right side. His uneasy expression betrayed him. Everything was different. Everything had changed.

Unable to sleep, I quietly made my way through each room of the apartment, counting the rooms, getting to know where the windows were and the best ways to escape, if needed. Outside my bedroom window, a fire exit staircase looked to be my best shot in an emergency. Holding my ear against the padlocked doors in the hallway, I could sense a humming vibration as if machinery were operating. I couldn't find any keys that might open the padlocks, but the heavy metal door at the top of the staircase indicated that those rooms were part of a larger apartment. Was Martin hiding something from Phillip?

I had no sense of how trustworthy the boy genius would be in his current mental state. He slept fitfully on the couch that looked as comfortable as a stone slab. Shifting his face into his arm crook, he moaned and spoke gibberish about matrixing the Unicode IDE pixel.

I cracked open the pantry shelf into a storage room of supplies. Slipping around cartons of Pop-Tarts, I found a staircase leading downward. I followed it to a panel that opened into a janitor's closet of the real estate office. The main floor was a circle of desks with a partitioned-off cubicle taking up most of the right corner and an employee break room on the left. I peeked out the front windows to make sure no one was about on the street who might look in and see me. The waterfront appeared serene, almost spectral.

Dust covered the furniture. It didn't appear that Phillip had been down here in a while, if ever. A bowl of M&Ms in a break room caught my attention, and I scooped it out. For a moment, I thought I got a whiff of Martin's sandalwood-scented soap. The fragrance came from the cubicle. Stepping inside, I closed my eyes and inhaled. Yes, it was him. I imagined his stride coming around the desk, lips forming that crooked grin that favored his left cheek as his arms wrapped around me, as he whispered, *Hey, baby,* in my ear. I almost said his name.

"Tomorrow," I murmured. "I will see you tomorrow."

Rummaging through a cabinet full of thick files showed holdings in Portugal, Iceland, Costa Rica, and New Zealand, and made me wonder if Martin was already out of the country. He clearly ran the real estate part of his business from here. There were no photos in the office. None of him and Phillip. None of his wife and son. It bothered me. I could see why he wouldn't put them out in San Francisco for me to see. Could he be hiding his family from his employees here? I can't imagine that his wife let that slide.

I returned to the desk. Everything was so normal. Too normal. The sterile neatness reeked of curated control, like a showroom pretending to be a life. Not these days. Not in this world. Martin would have left something—some trace of blood in the water.

I yanked the drawers open again, desperation rising like bile. That's when I saw it: a flash of beige tucked beneath the hanging files. I shifted them aside and pulled up a manila envelope. Written on it, *Brooklyn's Mother*.

Breath burned in my chest, and I wanted to cry. Gingerly opening the clasp, rationalizations raced through my brain like rats fleeing fire. Martin was wealthy. Of course he'd vet the people in his orbit. Made sense that he'd check out whoever he dated.

"He could've just asked," I said to no one. Then I laughed. A ragged, bitter sound. Because I would've lied. Lied to erase Stella from my history. Lied because love makes liars of us all. I slumped over the desk, head in my hands, bile licking the back of my throat. My pulse beat in my temples. I didn't know him. Not really. What did he feel for me? Why had he assigned me duties as if I were some conscripted employee? Grating on my heart, I realized that I no longer trusted love.

The envelope... empty.

I stared at it. The implication heavier than paper.

I fed it to the crosscut shredder, watching it vanish strip by strip. Tomorrow couldn't come soon enough. I needed Martin. I needed to scream, to demand answers, to ask him if anything... anything... between us had ever been real.

Scrambled eggs and sausage from the corner restaurant cost me my last spare cell phone, but they threw in coffee and half a stick of butter. I was beginning to see Seattle in a new light. On the surface, the city appeared normal. But there was a fearful undercurrent in how people moved about, with no eye contact and swift glances around as if not knowing whom to trust. Everybody traded for what they thought they might need. People were preparing but no one knew for what. I couldn't blame them. I walked around like that too.

Phillip gobbled his eggs like a Pekingese on steroids. He pushed his coffee toward me. "Never touch it."

That was more than fine with me. I cut a slice of butter and dropped it into the brew, thinking about the best way to ease into a few questions without sending the Wonder Boy into nerd oblivion. "Great apartment."

"Umm."

"Make a great penthouse if not for those padlocked rooms."

He bit into a slice of meat, chewing with closed eyes. "Real estate files." He laughed out loud. "I told him in the twenty-first century, digital was the thing, but did he listen?"

"There's humming behind one of the doors."

"Couple of freezers. Full of steaks, fish, and pizza for Friday night movies."

"And yet you eat Pop-Tarts."

"I like Pop-Tarts. They bring me the security of early childhood in these vapid times." He blinked, his lip slightly curving into a smile. "But I like your cooking too," he added, probably thinking he'd insulted me. "I don't have time to cook."

"Genius is as genius does." He liked that, reaching over and playfully punching my arm and honking a laugh. "Maybe I could take a look, pick out some good eats for the three of us. For dinner tonight."

He twirled his fork, took a breath as if to speak, but instead finished his eggs. Leaning back, his eyes darted around the ceiling. He shifted sideways and grabbed a Pop-Tart, tearing each piece off gingerly and chewing like he was studying the function. "I'm on the twenty-fifth level of *War On The Dead*. Got zombies to kill." He strutted to a bedroom and plopped in front of a gaming console, leaning sideways to kick the door shut.

Well, that was as successful as fishing with a wormless hook. I wandered over to the front window with that second cup of coffee. Looking down on the street, I wished Martin would get here. After an hour, I pulled an Egyptian mythology book from a nearby shelf and settled in to read by the noon light. As hard as it was to concentrate and looking up every other page to see if I'd see him, I soon lost myself in the Isis myths and made mental notes on husband hunting.

By late afternoon, I was getting antsy. Phillip briskly walked up and down the hallway and sprinted on the steps for exercise, he said. When he went to shower, I opened his laptop, hoping for something. None of Martin's passwords worked. What I did find was a small brown Master padlock key taped to the bottom. I hurriedly taped it back when I heard His Cleverness coming out of the bathroom.

"What's for dinner?" he asked, flopping onto the couch in yellow duck pajamas, his wet hair slicked back.

"Pop-Tarts," I said.

When he realized I wasn't joking, he clicked on the TV. "Cool."

"Martin isn't here. You said he'd be here today?"

"Or tomorrow."

"Are you stringing me along?"

"Don't challenge the algorithm, dearie. He's got his reasons."

"Want to give me one good reason not to throw you out that window?"

"I don't think you could pick me up." He pushed his glasses up his nose with his middle finger and increased the volume on the TV. Brace Benton announced the bombing of the Regency Council's Constabulary and showed a partially collapsed building. When they played security camera footage of a masked, hooded woman with a bazooka, I recognized Maria. Guess that was what she meant by *playing another kind of flute.* That camper full of weapons and explosives wouldn't last long. I wished they hadn't been foolish enough to take on those military types. As much of a relief it was hearing Benton report the unidentified suspects had escaped, I had my own trouble. Time for a come-to-Jesus talk with the whiz kid.

I blocked the monitor, hands on my hips, and glared down at him. "As far as intelligence goes, you are not using yours wisely. 'Cause smart as you are, I'm about to knock the crap out of you. Do you even know where Martin is?" Behind me, I heard the words "scourge" and "San Francisco." I whipped around to listen.

"Come on, move. We've only got six hours of TV today," Phillip complained. "And they play old *Dark Shadows* re-runs after the news."

Anchor Benton, his expression grim, spoke of violent resistance in cities across the West Coast. "This chaos must not stand. Our citizens need decorum restored. Only one man, Dixie Roman, has offered a plan to restore order. I, for one, am listening to him." A map of the United States flashed across the screen.

The country, split by thick black lines, showed both coasts as separate entities and a hollow middle as a jangled wasteland. "Going live to San Francisco and this chaotic scene," Brace announced. "If you've children, please have them leave the room."

"No!" The word tore from my throat as I dropped to my knees in front of the television, hands clamped over my mouth, heart clawing against my ribcage. Huntington Park was unrecognizable. Trees hacked down, benches in splinters, the fountain defiled into a sacrificial pyre. And there, tied like offerings to the fountain's scorched metal, were Jamie, Julio, and Paule.

I couldn't breathe. Couldn't blink.

"Burn them! Burn them!" the mob screamed, fists to the sky, eyes gleaming with collective madness.

Leading that cry, Dixie Roman's man, the bald, tattooed biker that tried to shoot out the window of the Bolinas house. Julio's face—bruised, bloodied—twisted in agony. Flames flickered at his feet. Then a shot. His head snapped forward. The mercy of a bullet had spared him the agony of being burned alive.

Carl! It had to be Carl Houseman. His apartment would have a full view. "Come on, Carl. Please." There was only one reason Carl wouldn't be spraying that mob with bullets. He was out of ammunition.

At Julio's demise, Dixie's man shouted, "No fair!" He hoisted a burning log, shoving it higher into the pile around Jamie and Paule. I could see they'd been beaten, too. "Justice! We demand Justice!"

Please," I whispered, voice cracking. "Please, Carl." I wiped tears off my cheeks, my breath exhaling sobs. I shouldn't have taken the bullets from him. He'd have what he needed if I'd just left that magazine. Then, I remembered—the three bullets in the frame. He was down to that. A shot rang out. Paule had moved his head as he screamed, struggling against chains as the flames licked his legs. Carl had missed the shot. The camera swung around madly, trying to find the marksman. The mob howled for blood as the camera returned to Jamie's beaten face. I pressed my hand to the screen as if I could hold him, save him, drag him out of this nightmare.

Brace Benton reported over the carnage. "Vigilante justice for traitors. Now, this great city will rise again. Now, we can elect a Regency Council. Now, our West Coast Constabulary will bring law and order. We no longer need the domination of the former United States. We rule ourselves. We are our own supremacy." Good God, no! This wasn't a mob. This was Dixie's government, taking over. Eliminating the people who fought against them. Dixie had done this. I watched the biker's twisted-up face, hollering for freedom, beating his fist skyward, whipping the crowd into a mad frenzy.

"One bullet," I whispered. "You can do it, Carl. One bullet." That last bullet had been meant for himself. I had not the right to deny him that death, but I knew Carl Houseman. He was of Miriam's blood. I knew what he would do. I asked Miriam to guide his aim. Then, a splash of blood, jerk of bodies. He'd done it. A clean shot. Two heads fell in one motion. They were gone. Gone. And I was still here.

I felt Phillip's hand on my shoulder. He handed me a tissue. I wiped my face. The crowd, deprived of their victims, roared like a hive of hornets, incensed that suffering had been stolen from them. This wasn't chaos. This was calculation. Brace Benton's voice droned through it all: "We are our own supremacy." My whole body shook as I mouthed my disbelief that we had become this. Because this wasn't just the death of friends. This was the death of the world Martin had been trying to save.

The camera swiveled around, trying to find the shooter's position. Knowing Carl with his marine training, he was already on the run. I hoped, prayed, evoked for his escape. *Let his mother lead him*, I whispered.

My brain was fog, thick and corrosive. Words scattered before they reached my mouth. I stayed in my room, tracing the patterns in the drywall with my eyes, hoping the monotony would dull the ache. But the grief was too big, too formless to grasp. No tears came—only the hollow press of absence. I couldn't believe they were gone. My mind rebelled against it, holding still like a scratched record repeating silence. None of it seemed real.

I waited three days before confronting Phillip. "Do you even know where Martin is?" My voice cracked, but I pushed through it. "No bullshit anymore or I swear I will punch you."

"I've eaten Pop-Tarts for thrice days. You could have cooked."

I punched him. It probably hurt my hand more than him—well, maybe his ego a little more from his stunned expression before he made his way to the game bedroom and slammed the door. I wanted to leave, unable to shake the feeling that now we were all more vulnerable. This was the only place I could trace Martin to, and even if I left a note of where to find me, I couldn't be sure Phillip would give it to him.

Figuring the wunderkind would pout for a while, I took the opportunity to snatch the key from the bottom of his computer and check out those locked rooms.

The first room was exactly what he said: stacks of boxes and two freezers full of food. But the second... the moment I cracked the door, a low hum poured out like breath from a giant. More than that, my bra vibrated. Boxy pulsed against me, jittery with a kind of desperate recognition. I unhooked it from under my sweater, and it bloomed into its cube shape, vibrating like it had finally come home.

Pushing the door, I stepped into a room full of computers. They were all activated, whirring code, numbers, and images, doing work I couldn't imagine. Only one was off, pushed up against a wall. It was on the only desk that had a chair, an orange chair. This had been where Martin recorded the message for me. I walked down the bank of monitors, a larger version of what was set up in Bolinas. Boxy whirled around them like it was hugging relatives.

A picture of a silver mourning dove hung on the wall opposite the blank computer. I stopped in front of it, studying the slant of its head, beak slightly raised with its intelligent eye staring straight at me. It rested on a bed of wheat, the sun rising behind its head. Boxy ceased vibrating as if it had done what it was meant to do. I looked down at it and turned it in all directions. Nothing. A flash of light on the picture's glass caught my attention. The monitor behind me activated, and a person, Martin's wife, tilted her head. My eyes locked on the reflection. "Who are you?" she asked. Boxy flattened out to a square, and I closed my hand around it.

A shock spread up my spine. I didn't turn around.

"Are you a friend of Phillip's?"

Casting my eyes sideways, I calculated how many steps to the door.

"Is the sound on? Can you hear me?" she asked.

I stepped sideways, then stepped again, holding my breath.

"Oh," she said. "You're her."

My body locked. The blood in my face felt molten. I bit down hard on my bottom lip, not sure if it was to stifle a sound or punish myself. She didn't even see my face, but somehow, she knew. That knowing curled around my ribs like a vice. Her voice was gentle, but the shame it stirred in me was brutal. I stepped sideways to get out of her sight. One more and I'd be out the door.

"I don't blame you," she said, her voice soft and inflective. "We should meet. I'm the only one who can help you."

I shut the door, my mind exploding with embarrassment and shame. Locking myself in the bedroom, I tried to figure out what it all meant and what I should do. His wife knew about this place, knew Phillip. A truth I had to accept. I returned the key and hid in the bedroom to figure out my next move. Feeling a fool. Fool, the only word hammering my brain.

Phillip turned on the TV in the next room. I shook myself together, thinking I'd better make an appearance. Maybe if I made nice, I could get him talking about Martin before I left that afternoon. Truthfully, I didn't know where to go. But I couldn't stay here. If Martin returned, I couldn't face him, couldn't look him in the eye.

I walked in on Phillip watching Brace Benton at Seattle's Space Needle, awaiting the arrival of presidential candidate Dixie Roman. Knowing this pig was behind Jamie, Julio, and

Paule's murders irked me as I fought down a fiery rage. Wherever that man went, death followed.

"I'm sorry, not sorry I punched you." Sitting on the edge of the couch, he moved over to make room for me and patted the place for me to sit while handing me a pillow. I scooted in and was surprised by him looping his arm through mine.

"Our first fight," he said, then laughed and pointed at the screen. "I swear if he rides up on a chopper, I will vomit data dust." Pounding the couch with his fist and laughing hysterically when the anchor saluted Dixie, arriving on a Harley-Davidson, an escort of bikers following him. "We are indeed at the end times!"

"You need to take this seriously," I said, turning toward Phillip. "If Dixie is here, he's looking for Martin, you, and me."

He muted the TV. "I'll defrost some steaks. Add a couple of candles, red wine, take your mind off... stuff." He sported an elfish grin, glanced down, then back at me. "World bad. Locked in here, steaks, candles. Forget. Just for a night." He touched the tip of my nose and then his. "What's love without a little hurt."

I shifted, uncomfortable, as his hand came to rest on the curve of my cheek. He gazed into my eyes, the longest I'd ever noticed him holding his attention. Watching me intently, he tilted his head and leaned in. I turned at an angle to avoid what I suspected or imagined would be a kiss. "I'm gonna head back to San Francisco," I lied. "I think maybe you should think about trying to get to Canada on your own. I don't know how safe this place will be if they figure out Martin owns it."

"Martin is companies on top of holding companies on top of mile-high spaghetti. He's the Sphinx. They'll never figure out we're here."

"I did."

"Yeah, but you're a virtuoso." He leaned in and bopped my forehead with his. "Come to Canada with me." He held my hands, gently pulling me toward him. He stopped when I leaned away. "Martin will figure it out. He'll come find us, or if you give me that device, we can even leave him a message."

"I don't have a passport. Anyway, I'm allergic to Sasquatch."

He shut off the TV and sat up. "Pleeeeaassse." He held my shoulders, eyes beaming earnest and forlorn. "I'll have no one to talk to or pull me back from the brink."

"You barely speak to me now." I pulled away and stood. "Besides, it doesn't look like Martin's arriving anytime soon. I'll check back, maybe in a week."

"He's likely just snowbound in Fargo or something."

"It's April. Snow season is over. And what's in Fargo? His family?"

Phillip scrunched up his face, a hand to his forehead. "Frack me."

"I found a picture of them, so you don't have to cover bro's ass any longer."

"You have to understand. I have a decision to make and I want it to be you."

"I don't... understand." I interrupted, amused by his half-assed flirting. "But I'll cook those steaks for us and leave in the morning. How 'bout that? We can spend the evening comparing survival notes. You can tell me how you got a Javon battery into a car the size of a walnut, and I'll give you my best meatloaf recipe."

I packed and decided to sleep in my clothes, so all I had to do was grab my backpack and head out. I thought about whether I should give Boxy to Phillip. If it was true he could contact Martin with it, then maybe I should let him have it. At least I could tell him how dangerous Dixie had become. I didn't believe for a moment that the bald-headed lizard was campaigning. He thought he was on Martin's trail. All the more reason to get lost in the humdrum of humanity. On the other hand, Martin's instructions had been clear: *what you have in your hand, keep in your hand.* After watching Phillip's erratic personality, his immaturity weighed the scale toward keeping it away from him.

At five a.m. I jerked awake from a fading dream. Martin and I were sitting at the Grubstake Diner as we often did on late nights. He reached for my hand, raising it to his lips, and kissed my palm, but no, it was Phillip kissing my hand, and I pulled away only to have a flock of doves crash against the windows, shattering the glass.

I sat up and stretched. My muscles were already missing this bed. I adjusted my backpack and crept out the door, determined not to wake Phillip. I hoped he figured out he needed to make a run for Canada, or maybe I was wrong, and he'd be safer here. Otherwise, Martin wouldn't have left him. He'd keep him safe the way he did me in Bolinas. I tiptoed down the hall and saw a padlocked door ajar.

A voice. I leaned into the door. Phillip talked to someone on the computer. My first thought was Martin's wife was telling him about my earlier intrusion into the room. Better to disappear than explain.

"I've done what you asked! Not my fault!" Phillip said.

My breath caught in my throat. I pressed my ear to the doorframe, the sound of Phillip's voice muffled but frantic.

"She's clueless," he hissed. "I searched her stuff..."

"If he's not in Fargo, then he's on the road, and by Jesus, I'll find him, but you need to get her in line!"

"I know how important this is!" Phillip hissed then, more a whisper, "but Blond Mom is your problem."

The other voice... Gravel and venom. I dared to look through the crack, just enough to catch the flicker of movement on the screen. Dixie Roman. My lungs forgot how to work. The walls seemed to bend. Phillip—the Phillip I had almost trusted—was feeding information to the man who had hunted and killed my friends. I staggered back from the door, nausea climbing my throat. The betrayal sunk into me. It was personal.

Backing away, I returned to my room and locked the door, hoping that would throw Phillip off for a few hours if he thought I was sleeping in. Then, taking the window exit two steps at a time, I ran.

I wandered the library until I saw a man wearing a lime green bowtie. No time to hesitate or worry, I slipped up beside him and held a book toward him as if I were discussing it. "I need a safe phone."

He looked me up and down.

"Sulis. You'll find my name in the registry."

He clicked a few buttons on his computer, then said, "You'll find a quiet place to read in the media room." Pulling a book from under the counter, he said in a hushed voice, "Hand this to the librarian in there when you've finished." The book was heavy. A phone inside. My shoulder lurched, causing me to jerk. "Are you okay?" he asked.

"Sorry, an injury that gives me trouble if I move it wrong. I rubbed my upper arm and gave it a pat. Boxy was vibrating inside my bra like a tap-dancing frog. "Bathroom?"

He pointed toward the women's room.

I locked myself in a stall and unfastened the bra pocket. Pulling out Boxy, it expanded into a cube and the copper-lettered word *Fargo* appeared then faded. I leaned against the wall, needing time to think. Time I didn't have. I'd heard Dixie say Martin wasn't in Fargo. Was this a trick to capture me? Was Martin there? I didn't know what to do, where to go, or whom to trust. Nothing felt solid. I could barely tell where fear ended and instinct began. My thoughts scrambled like birds startled by gunfire.

First, I had to try to contact Dan. I needed to know if he was alive. I needed to hear what happened to him and our group. Who helped? Who betrayed them? I found an enclosed study carrel at the rear of the media room. Looking both ways before closing myself inside, a shuffle on the other side of a bookshelf startled me. I stepped forward and moved a couple of books, pretending to browse. A face shot up in the space. "Barber?"

He nodded, eyes wide, panicked. "Where's your mother?"

"Barber!" Maria sped around the bookcase, pulling her son to her. "I told you to stay with me."

"I saw her come in here, Mom." Barber squeaked, his voice barely audible. "We know her. We need people we know."

"What happened?" I nodded for them to follow me into the carrel. Poor Barber trembled like a freezing pup. Maria didn't look that great either. Bloodshot eyes, pale skin, haggard posture as if she hadn't slept.

"They came for us," she said. "Banjo's dead. Oboe too. We're hiding here for now."

I wrapped my arms around both of them. Holding them when, finally, Barber's rigid body relaxed into mine. I told Maria what happened in San Francisco and about Phillip Javon's betrayal. "I'm about to call Jamie's husband, Dan." Looking down at the cell, I swallowed my fear. "I don't even know if he has a phone anymore."

Barber's arms tightened around me. I saw his gaze drift, eyes blinking, then squeezing tight. He was in his mind reliving scenes that would scar him forever. This shouldn't be his life. As he began to shiver, I knew what I would do. "I have a place you can go. A fortress where you'll be safe."

I tapped out Dan's phone number, praying he would pick up. A message, "Say your name. If I know you, I'll ring back." I said my first name and hung up. All I could do now was wait.

I drew a map of how to find the Bolinas house and where I'd buried the key. Maria had a chuckle memorizing the passcodes. She was more skeptical about Junkpot and its herculean immortality, but said she'd give it a go. She was ready to leave when I told her about Harry and his deadhead shop. "Beware of his brownies."

The phone vibrated. It was a face-talk connection. I tapped it. Dan, sporting a black eye and busted lip. My breath hitched hard. We didn't speak at first—just sobbed, the kind that clawed its way up from the belly. Seeing him alive shattered something inside me. We were both still standing, and part of us wished we weren't. When we could manage to talk, he said, "Say as little as possible. Some words trigger a weird kind of monitoring if you talk longer than seven minutes. You know by who."

"Did Baghdad fall?"

Dan nodded. "He still doesn't know your name. Even Paule wouldn't give you up, but somebody will, and he's getting desperate to find your boyfriend." The Japanese Teahouse at Golden Gate Park sprung up behind him as he walked. He noticed me looking. "We're a band on the run."

"Listen." I paused, thinking how to say this without giving it away. "You know where I was headed. Go to the town before and find a deadhead named Harry. Tell him 9459. Hear that, 9459. In a few days, a woman and her son will meet you. I've told her how to get to a place that will keep you all safe." I turned the phone toward Maria so he could see what she looked like. They nodded to each other without speaking.

Tears drifted down his cheeks. "You'll come?"

"Have to keep looking," I answered, and he touched the screen as if to comfort me. "Did the sharpshooter get away?" Dan looked aside and pulled someone into frame. Carl cracked a sad smile. His face had aged, and a sorrowful wariness shone through. I noticed he wore Miriam's pearl earring. "Thank you," I said. "Thank you for what you did."

After we hung up, a sense of yearning filled me. Maria and Barber held my hands, and we sat silently, watching people outside make their way in this changed world. "Make sure you give them good nicknames."

Her expression relaxed for the first time. "One day, we'll have stories to tell," Maria said, her voice hollow with fatigue.

I squeezed her hand, watching Barber's small fingers still curled in mine. "Stories with good words," I whispered. Words that didn't bleed, that didn't sting. Words we'd earn by surviving.

~ INTERSTATE 90 ~

I chased rumors the way a drowning person chases air—through gas stations, dusty towns, and truck stops off Highway 2. People spoke of buses heading east like they were legends passed around campfires. I kept my head down whenever the Regency caravans rolled by, their trucks a Frankenstein stitch of military leftovers and imported mercenaries. Watching them stirred something bitter. Where had the real army gone? Had they folded into this thing—swallowed up and spit out as new monsters? Some of the soldiers looked young enough to be in a high school yearbook. Their eyes never met mine. Conviction didn't shine there. Just duty. Or survival. Maybe that was all duty ever was.

The few times I'd seen a working television, they only carried the Regency channel featuring Brace Benton and his fanciful lies about the noble experiment being birthed by our lady of trickery and duplicity. Billboards swore the Madonna would return, not as a symbol, but as a material phenomenon. *Not faith but fact* was lettered across the back of a blond, blue-cloaked woman whose hands were spread open like a saint dipped in bleach. It infuriated me to see that when locals ripped at the promotions, it revealed the Madonna propaganda plastered over posters of missing children. The unseen Madonna's face tilted toward the heavens unsettled me. I needed more than a myth. I needed a target. If I was going to kill her, I needed her to be real.

On the outskirts of Davenport, Washington, I merged into a mass of about two hundred people headed to a deserted Air Force base called Fairchild. Word was that buses arrived every Monday and traveled east and south. I was traveling light now but had picked up a few cell phones to trade and still had ten thousand of Martin's money left. Boxy, tucked in its hidden bra pocket, remained quiet. Food was scarce, water more so, and I licked my chapped lips like a gecko with dry eyes.

The march to Fairchild felt more like an exodus—blisters and hunger and hollowed eyes. I walked with strangers who might've robbed me yesterday but now shared crusts and fire. Hunger had a way of sanding off the edges of suspicion. I handed out jerky and foil tuna packs with trembling hands, and they gave back—water, wine, old cookies soft with age, and a tarp when the wind turned mean. It scared me how much I needed them. How much I didn't want to sleep alone. It was a fragile thing, this shared ache, but it carried us forward.

The chill of desperation hit as our group merged into a chaotic multitude. Stern men with megaphones stood on concrete blocks issuing directions. Buses lined along a runway were painted with colored banners proclaiming the return of coast-to-coast travel. Yellow going south; blue toward Utah and New Mexico; green into the lower Midwest; and red, red across the country as far as Chicago, where they told me I could catch a train east. To anyone who asked, I pretended I was headed to New York. I'd jump ship as soon as I saw a Fargo sign.

Jostling through the throng of people, a man blocked me, and with each step, used the bulk of his body to push me backward. He wore a soldier's uniform so I tried not to look up at him, struggling to move around him as he caught my arm. Fear shot through my chest. I stared at the ground.

"Don't get on the red bus," he whispered, his beard brushing my skin like static. And then he was gone, swallowed by bodies and noise.

I froze. The world kept moving, but I couldn't. My pulse beat in strange places—my throat, behind my eyes. He hadn't said why. Just vanished like a ghost leaving a riddle. I turned in a slow circle, pretending to scan for someone. "Elena?" I called, making up a name. I needed a cover, needed time to think, but the crowd pressed in, indifferent. I hated how powerless I felt, how easy it was for a single sentence to scramble my plans.

I stood still, unable to move. People shoved around me in a disorganized tangle as the megaphone men blasted directions over each other. My mind swam, faint from a gripping terror. I glanced around and didn't see the man who issued the warning. I surveyed the area to see if anyone else was watching me.

Next to a shouting megaphone man, a woman issued bus tickets. I studied their setup. Waist high cinder blocks formed a wall around them, keeping the crowd at arm's length. This station had two guards shouldering machetes. While the pack surged, waving money and calling out for attention, the threat of weapons kept them under control.

"Closing up! Last ticket," the ticket-seller called out.

I rushed forward and won the bid on a red ticket for five hundred dollars. The bus boarded in ten minutes, and I hung back, watching every area for trouble. Slipping into a tent where I could buy water and packs of jerky, I noticed a bulletin board where wanted posters had been ripped so no fugitive was identifiable. A relief. I didn't see the bearded man again. The woman selling red tickets shouted that they'd return the following Monday, and anyone who didn't get a ticket could camp against the deserted buildings

The red bus looked like every other beat-up vehicle on the lot—rusting seams, fogged windows, tired wheels. But now it pulsed with menace. Or maybe that was just me. I watched the people in line—tough, quiet, tired. Survivors that looked weathered in the skills of protecting themselves. A few families. No crying kids. No softness. I told myself that was good. That if something went wrong, we could handle it. I told myself that, over and over, because I needed the lie to settle my nerves.

The two guards with machetes studied the line. If the rumor was correct, these buses had been running for several months. Whoever was providing the gas was making a hefty fortune.

Behind me, a small, tiny voice called out. "I have to get on. Please, my daughter is in Missoula." The pleading voice, thin and crackling like old paper, belonged to an elderly, humped-over woman who leaned on a walker with a bright pink ribbon tied to the backrest. She waved a wad of cash at the ticket agent, who walked away. No doubt she was going to get robbed out here.

The bus loading began, and I got in line. I couldn't help but look back at the distressed woman pleading to stand on the bus. I was third from the back. A porter asked me for my backpack to put in the luggage compartment. I told him I'd hold on to it. He grabbed a strap. "Have to, nothing but people on the bus. Safer for you. Safer for us. Ensures there're no weapons."

"Please," the elder said again, tapping her walker toward the bus door. She gripped her walker with one hand, money with the other, shaking with effort. I looked away—but couldn't stay turned.

My feet moved before I told them to. The closer I got, the more wrong it felt to keep walking. I had every reason not to help her. But her eyes—frantic and full of someone's mother, someone's heartbreak—caught mine.

"She has a ticket," I said, pressing it into her hand. She blinked at me like I'd handed her magic.

As she boarded, I felt something inside me unclench—and then collapse. I hadn't just lost a ride. I'd handed away my safety, my plan, my destination. But I couldn't regret it. Even as my heart pounded and my throat burned, I couldn't regret it.

I grabbed my backpack from the luggage compartment and let the crowd close around me like a tide, my face turned so no one would remember it. The bus pulled away with a rattle and a roar, and the woman I'd helped vanished behind glass. I stood in the dust it left behind, spine trembling.

Around me, families wept. Others cursed. Some just sat down and waited for next week. I didn't have that luxury. My plan had burned with the bus exhaust. But I still had two feet and one direction: east. I adjusted my backpack and started walking, toward Interstate 90.

Outside Coeur d'Alene, the freeways stretched ahead—empty, abandoned, silence so deep it pressed on my ears. I hiked with the occasional group, using the name Sulis and giving a fake story of being from Manhattan. Martin and I had spent several holidays there so I could fake my way through a conversation if necessary.

Often, we'd rest in the shade of billboards, pull off the Madonna advertising, and let the missing children's information be seen. I began to know them by name, especially a blond-haired elfish girl named Odette Wallace. She couldn't have been more than four or five. Then we'd walk on. By nightfall, I was typically alone.

A stroke of luck hit when a man wearing a Gonzaga University tee shirt reached his hometown exit and gave me his mountain bike. It felt like air returning to lungs starved of oxygen. My legs quivered at the sight of its rolling promise, my feet as grateful as my tired mind. He wouldn't take payment and told me to pass it along when I was done. I pedaled, every mile a silent thank-you.

Exits continued to be a godsend. Locals set up tables selling food and water, letting people charge their phones. Drinks were plentiful because many communities had wells, and a small industry sprang up around making water filters and dehydrated food. They shared as much information as they had, but I noticed they took an assessment of us as well. If they were reporting to the Regency government, I still looked different enough from my wanted poster to draw any attention, and I kept either a hand or a scarf over my scar.

As I washed up in a gas station bathroom, I saw that my auburn roots were growing out and bought an Idaho Hawks cap. I thought about venturing into some town to see if a drugstore might have hair dye. Weighing the time that would take against what I was finding out here, I realized I was feeling safer. I hadn't seen one wanted poster and wondered if Dixie's influence was fading the farther east I went. I noticed people were calling themselves the Northwest Regency. Frankly, I had yet to learn where the United States began at this point. No one had tried to rob or hurt me, and though the cost of the food was inflated beyond belief, barter worked just as well.

One day, I helped a single mother load up a donkey-drawn cart with bushels of corn, potatoes, and beans. She gave me the key to her house to stay overnight, where I showered, did laundry, and slept in a bed with a big orange cat tucked under my arm. As I slipped the house key under the front doormat the following day, the cat butted up against my leg and dropped a live mouse. I couldn't help but laugh, petting the feline enthusiastically and thanking him for the gift. I put the rodent in a plastic container, carrying the critter twenty miles before freeing it in a field. Maybe I'd reached an area of safety. Every call to Martin went unanswered. Maybe now, I could chance a stop at a library and use their system. I was only a state away from him. Maybe he'd answer next time. My confidence soared like the screeching eagles that swooped in aerial gymnastics through the Rocky Mountain skies.

I lost a couple days to rain storms and holed up in a deserted furniture factory. Electricity and water were hit or miss. Most houses got it for at least half a day, businesses a bit longer. If I couldn't find an abandoned structure by nightfall, I'd wrap myself between two thermal Mylar blankets and sleep as best I could off the roadside. My dreams were fractured and sharp; every noise jolted me awake, the clatter of rocks sliding down an embankment, the crow's caws, an occasional bobcat trill. When I rose cold, stiff, and exhausted, I thought of Martin and each step took me closer to him.

The Rocky Mountains rose around me like undisturbed gods, massive cliffs on one side and bottomless valleys of stones on the other. Eagles and hawks displayed their skills as they owned the sky; the occasional red fox scampered across the road chasing a shrew or pika, and pine trees alternated with expanses of wheatgrass. Soaring down the interstate, I felt as if I were flying. Sadly, the bike's tires gave out. I parked it at the next exit, hoping someone might repair and make use of it.

Walking again, I surrendered to the majesty of this country—until the smell. An acrid whiff. I shook it off, figuring an animal had died nearby. Not wanting to think it was a person, I fought the image, but there it was—that thought of death on the side of the road. And one day, I could be its plaything. My previous confidence cracked and spun me into hypervigilance. As I trudged along, the odor grew stronger and then overbearing, a reek of sewer and rotted fruit. I tied a cloth around my face, but even that barely masked the stench. I rationalized in my mind that I might be near a cattle ranch. It was a glint of sunlight on metal that caused me to throw up.

The pink-ribboned walker lay amid a tumble of limbs over the side of the highway, down into the rocky valley of overgrown weeds. I didn't see the woman I'd given the red ticket, but she was likely among them. Naked bodies strewn like mannequins down the cliff. Hundreds of them. Men. Women. Young. Old. A few lying to the side of the heap looked bony and starved.

Fingers fumbled for my phone, capturing the atrocity, but even through the lens my vision blurred. This had to be reported and shown to the world. *Don't take the red bus.* Rage and grief coalesced into a single, white-hot determination: somebody would answer for this. I swallowed several gulps of water. Water that should have lasted me hours, but it was the only way to relieve my gagging. I walked on, unsure whom to tell or who would care.

I was not as safe as I had assumed, thinking back to the man who told me not to get on the red bus. He'd saved me. Now, every time I spotted the red bus crawling in the distance, I dove off the road, heart clawing at my throat. I'd lie still, hidden under brush or crouched behind crumbling road signs, listening for engines, watching shadows stretch too long across the asphalt. My fear of people grew fangs. I stopped looking at faces. I stopped trusting footsteps. I walked alone because being alone was safer than being known. Cell service remained spotty so I couldn't use GPS, but I knew Interstate 90 led to 94 and that was a straight shot to Fargo. Many road signs were knocked down, and I hoped I wouldn't miss the exit.

The danger of walking at dusk was being too confident that the road was straight. It'd be too easy to walk right off a cliff. Staying close to the rocky side of the road, I bumped into something. Please don't be a bear, I thought, freezing in place. I heard it shift, and I held my breath. Slowly, pulling out my cell phone, I clicked it on. A dozen deer, stood like ghosts carved from mist. Silent and still, reflecting my light with ancient calm, the doe-eyed sentinels watched me breathe. I also saw something else. After I activated my phone, headlights flashed in the distance, maybe three or four curves away. Within seconds, I heard a motor.

I shuffled between the deer and pulled myself up the side of a cliff, hoping to hide behind a boulder. I had to get out of sight of the car barreling in this direction. As it got closer, a man standing out of a roof hatch shone a spotlight on the cliff. He'd see me. No place to hide.

"There!" I heard him yell as a beam flooded all around me. The car sped up, and a bullet blasted dirt at my side. I rummaged for Martin's gun when I heard the car screech, then tumbled over the cliff in a metallic crunch of metal and shattered glass. I sat in the dark for a few seconds, then pointed my phone in that direction. The deer turned as one and walked on like royalty of some untouched realm, hooves clicking on pavement like rain. They had surprised the driver, who swerved the wrong direction. I pressed a hand to my chest. "Thank you," I whispered, my voice cracking. The wild had made its choice, and today, I still belonged to the world.

The place where the car had come was a few curves down. I wanted to get past it before daylight. They'd left a light on, and I crept slowly up to an RV pulled into a tourist overlook. An empty semi-trailer truck parked in the roadway gave me cover. After peeking in the RV window and seeing no one, I entered. A lantern cast a warm light, almost homey until I saw the red bus tickets scattered on the floor.

They had plenty of granola bars, peanut butter, crackers, bottled water, and a hot plate of warm fried chicken tenders. I stuffed my mouth and put the rest in my backpack. It was well lived in and set up as an office with a kitchenette, a bunk over the cab, and a smelly bathroom at the tail end. I looked through all they had, mostly porn magazines, board games, and hundreds of zip ties in sterile little boxes. A strange platitude written in red marker on the wall: *Work The Plan Before The Plan Works You.* To my jubilation, I found a U.S. map showing the interstates. Static from a walkie-talkie popped from a corner. "Plank In-take, why the hell is your light on?"

I reached over and extinguished the lantern.

"Better. Pee in the dark, bitches," the voice said. "You got two red buses coming tomorrow, and I want wheat severed from chaff with your usual efficiency."

The heartless voice sent shivers through me. I figured the red bus let people off here, and some of them were put into that eighteen-wheeler and transported somewhere for something. Those that didn't pass muster were killed and dumped over the mountainside. Unable to find keys to the RV or the semi, I lifted the truck's hood and caused as much damage as possible before leaving. I wanted to be far down the road before whoever saw that light realized what had happened.

As much as I owed the deer, I vowed to be more careful. Rising before sunrise, I'd walk until the morning fog burned off, then would find a hidden and shaded spot to sleep, leaving only my cell phone and a solar charger out on the ground to soak up the noonday sun. Starting again at dust, I'd hurry along until it was too dark to see. I didn't make good time with this method but I felt safer. Trucks were on the road with more frequency. Gas trucks, food trucks, furniture trucks, others unmarked. I couldn't help but wonder if people were inside.

Missoula was the next city where I decided to stop and see if the library system was active. I thought to try and touch base with Dan and Maria to make sure they both reached Bolinas. I had three phone numbers for Martin but he'd never responded to any of them so far. Except for the faith I had that the Boxy messages were from him, I had no clue if I was really going toward him.

A meandering river followed the freeway, and I couldn't help but take the time to soak my feet. As I rested, almost dozing, I thought I dreamt of the faint roar of motors. Jerking awake, I strained to hear as I pushed on my shoes without tying them and ran for a ditch in the median between freeways.

Half a dozen dirt bikes rambled off the road behind me. They jumped onto the highway, screeching in tight turns, and surrounded me. Watching for a break, I darted through the circle. They chased me, pulling far ahead and blocking the road. Some bikes had two riders. Damn! I sped into a copse of evergreens where the bikes couldn't easily maneuver around the trees. Pulling Boxy out of my bra, I secured it in my backpack and shoved it under shrubbery. I took Martin's gun and hurried in the opposite direction, hoping they'd get bored looking for me, and drive on.

Leaning against a tree, I wiped sweat from my brow and listened. Stillness had a buzz, a fearful murmur of hesitation. No crunch of footsteps. I wanted to believe they were gone, that I'd outwaited the danger. I clutched Martin's gun like it might know how to make me less afraid. My legs buzzed with tension, a pulse of movement caged in stillness. I was nothing but instinct now—just a heartbeat echoing in my ears.

From behind me, a hand clamped onto the chamber of the gun. "I'll take that," a male voice said. I pushed backward, knocking him off his feet, and ran only to be knocked down by another one who popped out from behind a tree. I flipped on my back and pointed the gun. They were kids, hardly teenagers. The one I'd knocked down got up and dusted his pants. He was older, maybe sixteen. He pulled his own gun and pointed it at me.

"Now it's like this, lady. You're worth more to me alive than dead. I'm gonna sell your ass to the Plank. You can work your way out of there."

"In the bordello," another boy giggled as four more joined them.

"I don't give a shit where they put you," the older one said. "But I need the money to feed my tribe. Now put down the gun and you'll live."

I didn't have the time to pull the trigger, even if I wanted to. A freckled-faced boy to the side kicked my wrist, sending the gun tumbling out of my hands. "I get her first! You promised!" He jumped up and down like he wanted to dance a jig.

I scooted up in a sitting position, backing myself against a tree, and pointed at the older boy. "If you're in charge here, you're responsible for my safety."

The freckled face child looked at his elder, deflated. "Dennis, you promised!"

"So I did," he smirked at me and shrugged. "Can't break a promise."

The boys circled, vile grins and wolfish eyes. They poked each other with their elbows, looking down on me and trading skittish giggles. Their giddiness scraped across my nerves. Children—none old enough to shave. The youngest one danced in place like he was waiting for his turn at a party. I couldn't stop staring at their eyes—too hollow, too excited. They didn't see a woman. They saw currency.

I wanted to cry, but rage swallowed the tears. I grinned instead, feral and wild, then jacked my legs up and spread them. "You want a ride?" I snarled. "My cunt has teeth." The words felt like fire in my mouth. They flinched. One boy went pale. I wasn't going down easy. If they were going to take me, they'd choke on it. I glared at them with as crazy a stare as I could muster and could have sworn the younger ones took a step back.

The freckled-faced boy bit his bottom lip and gingerly moved toward me, unbuckling his belt.

"Stop!" Dennis called out. "She's got disease. Not this one, Hover. I'll get you another."

They tied my hands with a zip tie and led me back to the freeway. In this upside-down world where children capture adults to sell them for food money, I could at least be grateful that in the disoriented morass that is a teenage boy's brain they forgot or didn't notice that I had had a backpack. What made me nervous—Dennis stared at my scar. Once at the freeway, he had Hover call someone on a walkie-talkie. An hour later, a black sedan pulled up.

Dennis jerked me up to my feet and trotted me over to the front of the car. I couldn't see past the dark windows, and the noon sun caused an unforgiving glare. The driver's door opened and a man got out. He looked me up and down, then opened the rear door.

I saw blond hair, a blue coat, and sunglasses. She took off the shades. Nothing could have prepared me for the shock of seeing Martin's wife. She held to the top of the sedan and stretched, only glancing at me. Whispering something to the driver, he ducked back into the car and best I could tell was making a phone call.

It occurred to me that I didn't know her name.

She twirled her hand at Dennis. "Turn her around. I want to see her from the back."

Dennis shifted me. Silence. The squawk of some high-flying bird. Sweat trickled down my back, and my head filled with white noise. Clicks of high heels on the asphalt. Her voice had been soft, musical, inviting. She stood to my side, and a finger traced my jaw.

"I had to cut out a tongue to learn about this scar." She nodded to Dennis, and he moved away, huddled with his band of child thugs. "I didn't get a look at your face when I saw you in Phillip's computer room, but I've a good sense of you being her. What's he call you? He gives all his girls cutesy names."

"I don't know what you're talking about," I rambled, hoping I could bluff my way out of this. "I'm traveling to New York to my mother's house. I don't want any trouble."

The almond-shaped eyes were hooded, puffy jowls contoured with heavy peach blush, and red lips artificially full. The portrait I saw in Bolinas must have been painted a good twenty years prior cause this woman resembled one of those newscasters of a bankrupted network that looked more like drag queens than journalists.

She paced before me and studied me, a finger resting on her chin. "Oh, you're bleeding." Taking a tissue from her Yves Saint Laurent shoulder bag, she pressed it to the side of my lips. Dropping the blood-dotted tissue afterward, it wafted back and forth in a slight breeze.

"They'll be here in ten, Ms. Chandley," the driver said, getting out of the car but not approaching us.

"Take a picture of her," she said to the driver. "I want it out today that a known criminal of the Regency has been captured." She stepped back as the driver stuck his phone in my face. "He'll hear about this and surely ride to your rescue." Tilting her head, her eyes narrowed. "Or do you have doubts?"

"What do you want?" I asked.

"To work with you." She stepped closer to me, a pleading smile, moving like a mirage, all charm and poison. Her voice was velvet, thick with promise, and when she cupped my cheek, something in me ached to believe her. "We love him," she said, as if I were the only other soul on earth who could understand. And for a heartbeat, I wanted it. I wanted her to be telling the truth. I wanted to save him. I wanted to not be alone. Then her slap across my face peeled that weakness off like dead skin. I tasted blood and remembered exactly who I was. Not hers. Not his. Mine.

"Violent way of showing it."

"You and I, we could save Martin. He has no idea what he's gotten himself into. He's on the wrong side of this. We know him. You and me, we're probably the only people who can save him now." The slight curl of her lip and compassionate gaze lingered. She put a hand on my shoulder and squeezed. "He'll be lost otherwise. Please? Help me save him?"

I could hear another car in the distance. Her eyes darted in that direction. She pulled me closer, whispering in my ear. "Tell me now before it's too late. Where is Martin?" She squeezed my shoulders, insistent. "If you have the device, I can use it to help Martin. Trust me." Looking deeply into my eyes, her heavy drawn-on eyebrows furled, expression warm as a mother comforting a sick child. The car pulled even with the sedan, and a door slammed.

She was tempting with her gentle voice, promising help, and charismatic expression offering compassion. I licked my lips and stared away from her. "I don't know anyone named Martin."

She backhanded me. This time, I tasted blood. My pain disappeared, and my courage deflated when Phillip Javon stepped to her side.

"Is this her?" she asked.

Phillip stared at me, his mouth slightly agape. He looked aside and bit his bottom lip. I tried not to look at him, but one swift glance at his hands trembling like reeds in a windstorm was enough to reveal his betrayal. I steadied myself.

"Well?"

"Bren. What if we—"

"Don't play with me, Phillip," she snarled into his face.

Phillip's gaze bore into the roadside. He sniffed back a congested wheeze. Without speaking, his head jerked in one swift nod as he pivoted without looking at me and returned to his car.

"Bastard!" I screamed after him, but the word felt small. He wasn't the monster I feared. He was worse. He was the man who looked away.

She motioned to the driver, who hurried to her side. "Take her to Plank In-take. Highest security," she told him. "I'll go with Phillip. He's going to need a shoulder to cry on." Before leaving, she leaned her face too close to me. "Stupid girl. If he comes for you, I'll have him. If he doesn't, he'll despair. Is that really what you want?"

I stood straighter, blood drying on my lip, wrists bound but spine unbroken. "What I want," I said, voice low and flinty, "is for you to untie my hands for two minutes." I stared straight into her smug, painted face. "And for your edification…" I leaned forward, daring her. "I. Am. Not. A. Girl." Each word carved itself in defiance. Whatever this was, it was between her and me now.

She let out a curt laugh. As she turned away, her heels scraping the gravel, she said over her shoulder, "You really have no idea how unimportant you are."

"I think I'm important enough to get your ass out here in the middle of nowhere!" I shouted, but the words rang hollow. A car door slammed like punctuation on a sentence I hadn't finished. The sedan U-turned, flinging dust, and was gone.

The heat filled my mouth like cotton. Sweat stung my lashes. I tasted rust and regret. I had nothing left. No plan. No allies. Just the flat, punishing silence of being captured. I was out of ideas.

The driver threw a wad of cash at the boys and they flew off on their dirt bikes, no doubt, to capture other weary travelers for the Plank—whatever that was. He turned to me. "You can ride in the trunk or the back seat. I think you know my terms."

"I won't be any trouble," I said, though my voice betrayed me with a tremble. I was already calculating the angle—how high I'd have to kick to hit him where it hurt, how many seconds it would buy me. My hands throbbed, circulation cut off. He was a husky six-footer. Not likely that I'd be able to take him down, and I'd probably get a beating for even trying. "But could I ask... Where are you taking me? What's the Plank?" I hoped my voice sounded casual, but it felt like I was swallowing a scream.

"A work camp. You'll serve the Regency for your crimes—" A whiz through the air, past my head, so fast I couldn't figure out what was happening. The driver crumpled with a grunt, an arrow jutting from his chest.

For a heartbeat, the world stood still. Then I moved—scrambling sideways like a crab, dirt in my mouth, lungs seizing. The car door was too far away. My hands screamed from the zip ties.

A low, vibrating buzz sent a fresh stab of panic through me. I flinched and looked up—a drone. Sleek, alien, menacing. Four arrows hung from its belly like warnings. I froze, waiting for the shot.

Instead, it beeped. Dropped one. Not an attack. A gift. My mind struggled to keep up. A nice, pointed, sharp arrow. I picked it up and worked on the zip tie that snapped after a few strokes.

A tiny square monitor beeped, and wavy lines tried to form a picture. A beard. A man's face. Martin? Please be Martin. It was the man from Fairchild Air Force Base who warned me against taking the red bus. Then, a robotic voice spoke. "Leave the car. It can be tracked. Follow Interstate 90, then cut up 29 to Fargo. There's a Red Cross center at the Dunmore exit. Additional outposts at Sheridan, Sundance, Rapid City, and Reliance. Look for the Golden Jackal motorcycle club in Sioux Falls. They'll get you up 29. Under no circumstances follow Interstate 94. Something happens on 94. People never return."

"How do I know I can trust you?" I asked.

"Sulis," it answered, then zipped upward and was gone. Sulis. Martin's nickname for me. I realized that Bren didn't know my real name or my nickname. Perhaps I'd been too hard on Phillip. He hadn't identified me as Sulis, the only name he knew me as. "All his girls," I repeated, irritated by Bren's familiarity. "Phhhhh."

For the first time on this journey, I felt the isolation of being alone. The eerie buzz of insects vibrated around me. I swallowed and blinked my eyes, partly feeling unreal. I gleaned from this experience that people were being taken to a work camp—whether captured or brought by the red bus. Bren Chandley had something to do with it. Pretty sure I've already seen what happens when the work camp is done with you. A horrific image of discarded bodies tossed over a cliff gave me a shake. I would have a story to tell when the world returned to itself. "Pendejos Bitch" would be my starting words.

I hurried around the car and sat in the driver's seat, turning up the air conditioning full blast before searching it for weapons. All I found was a crowbar in the trunk. The day was almost gone, and I had to get out of this area as soon as possible. How I wanted to take that car. I snatched a couple bottles of water from the backseat and the driver's lunch, a tasty Reuben sandwich with chips and a dill pickle, then put the car in drive, positioning it to roll over the cliff. Dragging the driver's body to the edge, I searched his pockets. A few twenty-dollar bills. Still no weapons. After using his thumb to delete my picture and punching factory reset on his phone, I let him tumble over the side of the cliff. "Sorry," I whispered, not because I meant it, but because I wanted to mean it.

I wasn't sure how long I had until they discovered I had escaped. Running back to the wooded area, I retrieved my backpack and jogged as fast as I could. The kid gang, unfortunately, had taken my gun but I had learned a critical piece of information. *Bren Chandley.* She didn't share Martin's name. That had to mean they were no longer married. I had been captured, almost raped, sold to a work camp, and slapped, but I couldn't help a smug smirk of satisfaction that stayed with me like finding gold at the end of the rainbow.

My editor was surprised that Martin Siriso had agreed to a profile. Known for his intense privacy, he seldom appeared in the media despite his firm being involved in nearly every significant financial deal that walked into this city. He'd said he'd give me an hour at a bar called Yong San Lounge as it was on his way to the airport, and he had to catch a midnight flight to Paris. He casually asked me to order him a Tecate in case he was late.

I spent the next two hours frantically searching for Yong San Lounge. Frustration growing, I contemplated calling him for directions when an old-timer from accounting laughed his ass off at me. "He's testing you," he said, chuckling. "Yong San Lounge is rumored to be where the Watergate burglars hatched the plan. Place has a long history of CIA and FBI conspiracies. The name changed a couple of times, but it's still at the corner of Bush and Taylor."

The damn bar was a block from my apartment. I hurried over and had an icy-cold Tecate with a lime wedge waiting when he walked in the door.

He nodded as he saddled up on the barstool. "Well done."

"I wouldn't want you to miss your flight." I made a mental note to buy the old-timer coffee for the next week in gratitude for the tip. Having impressed Martin Siriso, the interview flowed smoother than most initial meetings. Three beers later, we'd moved to a booth, and while I knew I'd hit my limit, the alcohol made for easier conversation until he shifted the focus to me.

"I asked around about you," he said, leaning into the table. "You've got this thing."

I could physically feel the arch of my eyebrows. "I'll have you know my doctor clears me once a year," I replied, subtly shifting to hide my scar from view. "Not that it's any of your business."

He burst into laughter, waving his hand dismissively. "No, no," he wheezed, unable to contain his amusement. "A memory thing. Buddy of mine at the Chronicle said you can remember everything that's ever happened to you, dates and stuff."

The thought of everything that had ever happened to me sent an unsettling wave through me, but I maintained composure, shifting left and staring at my reporter pad. "I'd be surprised if anybody at the Chronicle even reads the Calendar."

"It's not true that I represent Wolfgang Hauser," he said, leaning closer and cupping a hand to the side of his mouth. "I must get that question ten times a week."

"If he'd stop impregnating models, maybe he'd stay out of the headlines and you'd have more time to answer questions about Prescott York," I shot back.

Martin chuckled and leaned back, glancing at his watch. "Him, I do represent. But as for whether he is buying the Giants, I have no knowledge nor comment."

"All true answers will reveal themselves in time," I quipped.

"I detect a slight accent," he said.

"I'm the interviewer here," I joked, ignoring the statement camouflaged as a question.

"Your vowels have a pleasant oooo-sound to them."

"I'd like to do two more interviews with you before finalizing the profile," I said, trying to regain control.

"Uh-huh," he said, clinking his beer bottle to mine.

"I promise I'll make effective use of your time and—"

"Two more is fine."

I nodded, realizing I held a breath and my mouth was slightly ajar. Nervously, I flipped through my notebook. I could feel him studying me and shifted sideways again. When I looked up, his eyes narrowed as his head tilted. "I have one last question," I said to break the trance. "Do you consider yourself a perfectionist?"

He reached over and took my chin between his thumb and forefinger, straightening my head to face him. "What you said about true answers," he began. "Every one of us has imperfections. Yet we often hide them when they could be our greatest strength. You might as well own it. Because scars are more than just scratched skin. In that truth is authentic perfection."

I don't know how the words came out of my mouth, but I managed to say, "I'll reach out to your office to set up the next meeting once you're back from Paris." My voice cracked, and I cleared my throat as heat rose to my cheeks.

"The Southeast?" he asked. "Yeah, it's the Southeast." He slid out of the booth and shouldered a leather messenger bag. "Need me to see you home?"

"It's only a block," I said, unable to look him in the eye.

"I know," he said. "I'm four blocks up."

A mix of emotions bubbled within me as we stood in the dim light of a dive bar where conspiracies and chicanery were likely infused into the walls.

For the next two days, I found hiding places among wildflower thickets, the occasional ditch, and under freeway overpasses. I was no one. Just a shadow among thickets and culverts, a ghost slipping between ruined roads. I avoided travelers and walking alone, I couldn't afford to trust anyone. I scavenged for food and water, finding enough to keep going. Every empty house was a gamble. Every can of soup a stolen miracle.

On the third day, I heard motorcycles. My chest tightened. I ducked into a gulley, shaking. Dennis? Another gang? My heart had learned to beat softly, hoping not to be heard. I had to assume they were looking for me.

I passed exits with open stores and farmer's markets but decided not to check them out until I ran out of supplies. Highway signs had been graffitied and some torn down. I stepped over a picture of Odette Wallace. I checked the map and my phone, knowing I needed to avoid Interstate 94. The route that had been given to me would take longer to get to Fargo, but the bearded man had saved my life twice, so I was going to heed his warning. Because if nothing else, I wanted to live long enough to ask him why. I couldn't help thinking he sure looked like the Tosca dude that Martin had met with. I wondered: had that drone been tracking me or Bren?

Taking a rest day in Missoula, I mused that this kind of stop used to mean cafes and bookstores but now meant scavenging warmth and weak signals. The public library was a pale, shivering structure that smelled like damp paper and dust, but inside I found a Limey who hooked me up with a phone receiver tethered to a boxy computer marked with peeling lime green tape. While my phone charged, I dialed Martin's numbers, one after the other.

No answer. I fought a disheartened sadness. The silence on the other end felt like a fresh kind of ache—sharp, specific. The kind that whispered maybe this is the day I stop pretending I'll hear his voice again. I held onto the receiver like it might conjure something if I just gripped hard enough.

I'd never known if Maria and Dan reached the Bolinas house so was euphoric when a video popped on and their smiling faces filled the screen. The Grateful Dead hippie, Harry, with his four toddlers were in the background wrestling with Berber, who waved but couldn't get out from under the pile of little girls. Confirming that Carl Houseman was with them as well, out walking the perimeter as a security measure—well, of course he was—allowed me to feel a measure of relief. No one had ever returned to the zombie house, and Dan relayed they were content to live there until safer times. But Maria's eyes—flat, sharp, quietly burning—told another story. She'd never been the type to wait out storms. I knew better than to argue, even across a screen.

I sat myself up to sleep between two overstuffed shelves—Sociology and Speculative Fiction. The books were my sentinels, their spines dry and silent. The Missoula librarian returned after hours with a meatloaf and mashed potato dinner. He agreed that the longer route was the safest way to reach Fargo and vouched for a motorcycle club called the Golden Jackals, which helped people along the highway.

Something nefarious was happening on Interstate 94 that they hadn't yet figured out. People going in that direction were never heard from again. I had an idea of what it was, and as we sat on either side of an old study table, I laid out what I knew: the photos, the videos, the red buses, the camps. The things I couldn't forget, no matter how many miles I put behind me. He turned gray as he watched, his mouth a flat line of horror. When I finished, we both sat very still, absorbing the shame of a country devouring its own.

Transferring copies of what I had to him, he promised, "I'll spread it," he said quietly, almost to himself. "It could turn the tide."

We asked about the state borders at the same time, the question tumbling from both our mouths like a joke we didn't want to tell. A beat passed.

We looked at each other, and for a moment the room stilled. Two citizens of something that no longer existed, trading scraps of memory like sacred coins.

I lost a day on the wrong freeway near Butte, Montana. By the time I realized I was miles down Interstate 15, my legs were too numb to walk back to Interstate 90. I slumped on a hillside overlooking an exit sign that pointed nowhere I needed to go. Twilight pressed in, the cradling mountains folded into the blackness. Above, a veil of stars. I breathed in their cold majesty, the air sharp and forgiving. For a minute, I didn't feel lost—just quiet. Like maybe the earth could still remember what grace was.

As the moon rose like a thin scar over the horizon, an oscillation vibration cracked the night like the earth had a fever. The air electrified with the drone of an aggravating hum. Something was wrong. Scrounging the horizon, a pulsing blue light flared high above the mountain, then lanced out across the sky, shattering the silence into galvanic confetti. My skin prickled, my spine tensed. I couldn't tell if it was neon or digital. It grew three times its size, then shot out laser-like over the city, disbursing into a light show of sparks. The mountain had become a lighthouse, but instead of guiding anyone home, it was summoning something. Something we'd be better off without, I thought just as the groan of motorcycles approached.

I watched as two news vans parked on the freeway below, escorted by four motorcycles. A truck, several vans, and a bus of thirty or so men and women arrived and began setting up what looked like a newscast. Lights, cameras, and cables ran from a news van topped with satellite equipment. A small stage was assembled. An efficient woman arranged a table with two director's chairs and a makeup case in a side tent. The rougher-looking men from the motorcycles started organizing barricades and appointing themselves security as more of them arrived.

I was safe enough and invisible in the darkness high up on the hill, but couldn't help but want to move lower and see what they were up to. I saw my opportunity when the clamor of voices lifted in the distance. People coming up the exit ramp from the city spread across both highway lanes. The crowd moved like a single organism—hundreds surging up the ramp, their faces lit by excitement and something more dangerous: belief. I slipped into them, folding myself into the flow.

Security worked megaphones, having the people face east. Three more pulses of blue stars shot out from the mountaintop, and a roar of glee burst from the crowd. Edging my way up to a barricade, I studied their security. The setup crew hovered around a food table. When the security guard patrolling this section turned his back, I slipped between the barriers and joined them.

Grabbing a cup of coffee, I mingled and listened. Everyone on edge talked about how their various department had worked the past twenty-four hours without a break. I leaned against the bus, not having to fake exhaustion. Sitting on the front bumper, a man flicked his lighter without looking at me and handed me a cigarette. I didn't smoke, but I accepted it anyway. He smelled like burned circuits and fatigue. "Nice night for this," I said. "Clear weather."

He shook his head and picked a piece of tobacco from his teeth. "It's not ready, but we had to get this done before snow hits."

"We did our best," I paused, hoping I was going in the right direction to elicit useful information. "I mean, what more could have been done?"

"That tech genius needs another year at least. Been nothing but poop since they lost that top guy. But one thing I know, it's gonna be my ass if this doesn't give a semblance of being real."

"Mmmm." I wasn't sure where to go with that.

"Ace," he said and extended his hand. "Production manager."

"I'm with makeup," I lied. "Sulis." I motioned that I was going to get some coffee at a table set up for the crew. I stamped out the cigarette and went around the bus to watch the stage.

A man waving a megaphone jumped on a chair and riled the crowd. I looked closely at him. Yes, I knew this one. The dunce who'd shot at the window of the Bolinas house. The very same who stirred up the mob when Jamie, Julio, and Paulie were burned in Huntington Park. Dixie's man. I wanted so bad to tie his ass to a bag of rocks.

"They're coming," he announced, pointing in the opposite direction up the freeway where a black limousine coasted toward us. Dixie Roman emerged from the top hatch, waving his arms at the crowd who roared and applauded. The limo parked next to the news van. He and Brace Benton emerged from the rear, both of them saluting the growing assemblage of sycophants. While Brace went into the makeup tent, Dixie grabbed the megaphone from Dunce and walked back and forth in front of the crowd as a man with a shoulder-mounted camera followed him.

"Friends!" he yelled. "The moment is here. If we've prayed hard enough and if we are worthy, the Madonna will appear." He raised a hand as if saluting the Almighty and lifted his gaze in the same direction. "We worked the plan!" he shouted into the megaphone. "We didn't let the plan work us. And tonight, she has promised us facts for our faith."

Brace Benton emerged from the makeup tent and settled on stage before a *We Are Regency* backdrop. Dixie joined him and they shook hands. The crowd clapped in unison and chanted *Work The Plan!* After about a minute, the security bikers shushed them and bright lights illuminated the stage. There was a three-camera setup. One pointed toward the men, the man with the shoulder mount focused on the crowds, and the third was pointed up at the dark mountain where the blue laser-like lights had come. The crowd grew stone still. Brace stared into his camera and talked. "It is my honor and pleasure to be here with our next president, Dixie Roman, for this momentous time in our history. Friends, we were promised a miracle from our glorious Madonna. Your vote for Dixie is your promise to her. She will not let you down. She will heap blessings beyond your wildest dreams. Her promise is on high. We are strong. We are resolute. We are the Plan."

"Amen," Dixie said.

Behind them, a blue light soared across the sky, expanded and exploded like fireworks, sending a rainbow of colors dancing and sifting into a form that congealed into a sky-filling image of the Madonna. Larger than any statue I'd ever seen, it blocked the stars.

There was only one flaw that I could see. It—and I refused to call it *she*—had Bren Chandley's face with perhaps a little less makeup. The image opened its hands as golden sparks poured blessings upon the world. The face expressed a gentle smile, and she wore a blue cloak that shifted on and off her shoulder with a golden halo undulating around her head. The crowd erupted into a cornucopia of shouted praises. This was no ordinary projection. The form moved effortlessly as an actual person. I figured it was some artificial intelligence projection, but it was dimensional, organic, ethereal, unlike a game character. I could have sworn it was physical.

Boxy shocked me. I steeled myself, hoping no one noticed that I'd nearly jumped. Ace stood beside me, and the makeup woman was on his other side. Both had complete concentration on the Madonna. I slipped into the makeup tent, thinking to pull Boxy out of my bra as it gave me another jolt. "Ouch!" I was about to close the tent flap as Dixie Roman strode toward me.

"Hey, hon," he called out. "Powder me down. I don't want to shine on camera." He pushed past me and dropped into the director's chair with a heavy thud, wiping sweat from his brow. He smelled of cigars and liquor. "Damn lights are boiling. Worse than when I fought that Brazilian Spiderman." He chuckled at his own wit and must have noticed me eyeing the tent flap. "Don't worry," he said. "It'll be a while. You won't miss nothing."

Cautiously, I stood beside him, keeping my scarred cheek turned away. I'd never met him, never been in the same room with him or this close. No reason he should recognize me, and yet, my heart beat like a war drum in my ears.

A pair of hairdresser shears caught my focus. I could jab them in his throat and sever his jugular before he knew what was happening. Could I do that, I wonder? I could. I had done that. My hand hovered over the scissors but a noisy pack sauntered past, and I picked up the contour brush, dipping it in powder. He grinned, and I smiled back like I didn't want him dead.

"You look familiar," he said. "You do my makeup in Twin Falls?"

"Yeah, I was on that crew," I said, motioning for him to look upward.

"That town was a hoot." He shifted his eyes, staring at my bosom. "Okay, I'm good." He paused at the tent opening, "Come on, it's about to get twisted." He smiled a lecherous grin, his eyes traveling up the length of my body.

I didn't dare challenge him now, but the scissors were up my sleeve as I followed him out, curling my hand around the hilt. I position the shears to use them as a weapon.

"Wanna watch from the stage?" he asked, his eyes never leaving my chest. "I can make that happen."

"Wouldn't it be better behind the bus, in the dark? The colors would light up so much brighter." I let my lips form a slight smile. He did too.

Brace Benton, waving both hands, hurried toward him. "The beats are about to start. Put in your plugs!" He shoved something into Dixie's hand and pulled him by his arm, ignoring me.

Dixie followed him but turned as he walked, "See you in Fargo!" Then, he winked at me. "Make sure you take a van, not the bus." He air-kissed toward me.

Every muscle in my body trembled. I squeezed my eyes shut, working out the rage. Boxy shocked me again. "Okay," I mumbled. Slipping around the back of the bus where I was alone, I pulled Boxy out from my bra. It quivered and oscillated, lifting from my palm. Then, it did something it'd never done before. Boxy expanded from cube to a floating, dimensional, translucent rose, revolving clockwise, petals tumbling in an everlasting expansion.

"Children," the Madonna said, her voice—soft, vast, maternal. "My will is your gift."

I grabbed my head, her voice echoing as if it were right beside me. It didn't enter through my ears, but through my bones. I staggered back. Her words coiled around the hollows in me like a child searching for a mother's hand.

"I love you," she said, and I believed her. I wanted to believe her. Her promise wasn't salvation—it was seduction. And for a heartbeat, I didn't care. I wanted her love, even if it was a lie. Mutterings vibrated around me, but I couldn't get a direction from where they were coming from.

"I love you as no other," the Madonna whispered, correcting the pulse of her voice. "You know the plan. The plan brings you to me. I will restore all you have lost. Heal all you have suffered. My devotion is eternal, and I wait for you."

The rose stopped spinning and clicked as if processing.

"What are you doing?" A voice behind me.

I swivel around, blocking a view of Boxy with my body. Ace lit a cigarette. He scoured the area, and I noticed he was wearing earplugs as he turned his head. He pulled one out. "Why aren't you watching? We're going to need feedback."

"Had to pee," I said, and shrugged my shoulders. "Couldn't be helped, but I can see well enough from back here."

He stared at me and looked beyond me into the dark as if looking for someone.

"You mind," I said. "Kinda like some privacy."

"Don't be long." He looked again into the darkness, then reinserted his earplug. "And get some earplugs from the concession table."

I heaved out a breath as he walked away. Boxy had expanded a glowing menu to the side of the rose. Home, Operations, Close, and the last choice, Destroy. I bit my lips. It could mean destroying the cube—rose.

I leaned back, glancing around the side of the bus. Ace was gone. Dixie and Brace stood on the stage, arms raised in supplication, calling for the crowd to voice praises. The Madonna smiled wider and crossed her hands over her heart. She'd moved farther down the ridge and appeared to kneel as she accepted accolades from her followers. Her essence pulsated as if she was beside each one of us, looking deeply into our eyes with as complete a love as a mother for a child. *Mother*, I said to myself. My mother had never loved me. I shook it off, feeling nauseous from my disobedience. This mother would love me. What was causing this?

I hesitated, my finger over the word Destroy. Whispering around me. Couldn't make out the words. Tap Destroy, I told myself. What if I destroyed Boxy?

"My will is your will," the Madonna said. "Ask me your deepest questions, and you will hear the answer. For such is my love for you." My body hummed as if someone gently sang in my ear, drawing me into a wistful lull, targeting my heart with commitment, and filling me with longing to protect her. "You will be loved," she spoke to me. "That is your true answer to your deepest question." Not exactly in my mind, but in some illimitable knowing that I swore spoke truth. Some of the crowd wailed, others fell to their knees prostate as she answered them directly inside their minds.

Shaking off the tangle of emotions, I struggled to tap Destroy. Yes, I should destroy Boxy. That would protect the mother. As my finger hit it, tears rose in my eyes. How could I do that? I didn't even know what I had done. All I am is destruction. I am unworthy of her, my mother, my Madonna. Several blue dots shot out toward the image. One shot toward me, and an electric jolt knocked me backward. Whatever it was broke the emotional hold that the Madonna had caused. Boxy contracted and lay flat. I held out my hand, and it floated gently to me as if recalled by my scent. I hurriedly put it back into my bra pocket and slipped around the opposite side of the bus, intending to merge back into the crowd. If anyone had noticed what Boxy had done, they likely shuffled it off to being part of the show. I scanned the multitude. All eyes were on the five-hundred-foot Madonna drifting along the mountain range. They sang praises, hands lifted in the air, and some fell to their knees in prayer. How could people believe something so stupid? And yet, they did. They were converted, proselytized, born again, brainwashed. They had their miracle.

The Madonna hiccupped, her eyes widened, and her mouth formed a wacky frown. The image jolted. Electrical sparks waved through the image. Her face morphed into a scowl stretching grotesquely across the sky as she picked up the edges of her blue skirt, revealing rickety legs that began to dance a jig as she dissolved into blackness.

"No!" Ace yelled and ran toward the news truck. The cameras and the lights extinguished, the crew ran in all directions, and everyone yelled at everyone else.

In the chaos, Dunce grabbed the megaphone. "We're done, assholes! Now y'all go home and tell everybody you know that you witnessed the miracle of the Madonna. You spread the word on all mediums. You do otherwise, and we'll know! Go home now! Go home!" They ignored him, screaming and wailing for their Holy Mother to return. Geesh, if there was anyone who couldn't read a room, it was Dunce. This, I might be able to take advantage of. I followed along and watched the workers. Many of the women were coiling cable and packing props, so I joined in and did as they did.

Ace was on stage getting bawled out by Dixie, and I watched as he tried to explain. Brace waved his arms in what looked like an attempt to defend him. I couldn't hear much of the conversation, but I did hear Dixie order Ace to return to the bus and not show his "pig face" again. Brace paced in a circle, and I heard the words "made a fool of me" and "won't overcome this." Dunce punched him, sending him sprawling. He kicked him in the stomach and motioned for two other security guards to come over and join the thrashing. The poor man huddled in a fetal position as they savagely pummeled him, knocking off his glasses and a toupee. Dixie marched off and drove away in the limo.

Ace started to lean down toward Brace but was pushed back by Dunce. "You heard Dixie!" He grabbed Ace's arm and marched him toward the bus. I ran the opposite way and knelt in front of the bus. *Take the van. Don't get on the bus,* Dixie had said. I looked under the bus and saw the feet coming toward me. As they approached, I slammed the scissors into Dunce's thigh. He grabbed at me as he went down shrieking screams that were drowned out by the very crowd he'd whipped into a frenzy. Ace pulled away, not sure what was going on.

"If you get on that bus, they will kill you," I said to him.

"Bitch!" Dunce roared at me.

Ace's boot came down on Dunce's head, knocking him out. "How do you know?"

I stood and looked around. "Everybody on your crew local?"

He nodded.

"They had to rehearse this, right?"

He hesitated and stared at the ground. "In a football field. At the high school. It was work. It paid—"

"So, they know the truth. They know that image is some kind of virtual-ass AI copy of a real person who is about as holy as a stewed prune."

Ace nodded again, a flicker of knowledge settling into his expression.

"You're all headed to a place called the Plank or worse. They can't afford any of you telling what you worked on."

"I've been with them long enough. I know who they are."

We carried Dunce onto the bus and put him in the back. "Give me your ID," I asked Ace. He looked confused but handed it over. Switching IDs, I handed Dunce's to Ace. "If you shave your head, you'll look enough like him. Get to Canada or Mexico or the eastern states, wherever, but don't come back here."

"I have to help my crew," he said.

"It's too late." I pointed out the window where the motorcyclists were gathered, pulling out AK15s from a van. We slipped out of the back of the bus and returned to the newscast breakdown. Ace disappeared. I wasn't sure if he'd try and save his people. Wishing I could have done more ate at me.

The crowd ambled and dawdled as if waking from a dream. Robot-like, they rose, wandering back toward the Butte exit. I slipped over the barricade and followed along, stepping off and returning to my dark perch above the convocation. There was some yelling, a gunshot, a bus speeding away. I could only hope Ace got his people out. I went to sleep gleefully, knowing that tough-man Dunce would be in the Plank with a fake ID and no way to prove who he was.

Sunday morning. Strolling along the Marina Green, the bay breeze carried a refreshing saltwater scent. Sailboats glided past each other in a lively dance, their white sails fluttering against the azure sky. I could sense Martin's gaze on me, and my heart raced in a whirlwind of insecurity. I subtly shifted to his other side, pulling my hair forward to hide my scar. His hand slipped into mine, and our fingers intertwined for the first time. I was convinced he was staring, probably trying to figure out how I came to have a faded scar that told a story I wasn't ready to share.

The air between us felt heavy despite the beautiful day, and every second stretched out in an embarrassing eternity. I braced myself for the inevitable question: "What happened to your face?" Or worse: "You know, I've been meaning to ask about that scar." I could almost hear the words vibrating in my imagination, my rehearsed explanation about a childhood accident ready. If he found out about me, it would destroy everything.

Just when I thought the moment had come, he turned toward me and said, "Do you think crows can be trained to deliver messages?"

"Excuse me?" I blinked at him, thoroughly taken aback. "Crows?" I stammered, half-convinced that this was an elaborate distraction technique, the kind my mother would pull when bill collectors knocked on our door. "Don't birds just mostly, you know, poop on everything?"

He grinned, unfazed. "That's a fair point," he admitted. "But think about it. A crow could be the perfect messenger. It's like having your own personal delivery service. You can't ignore a crow the way you toss out mail. Crows will intimidate your ass."

"Or you could just send an email, receipt requested."

"Where is the romance in that?"

"Romance? You think crows are romantic?"

He jacked a leg up on a bench and re-tied his tennis shoe. "The Telegraph Hill parrots have been flying to my building's courtyard and intimidating the mourning doves. Yesterday, a bunch of crows landed on the roof of a building opposite mine. Every dove fled into the trees, and the parrots vanished like Houdini."

"Proving their bullying reputation precedes them."

"It's a wonder they ever get laid."

As dawn broke, the empty roadway was littered with trash and discarded equipment. The Regency backdrop flapped in the breeze. They hadn't bothered taking the stage, and Brace Benton still lay there. They hadn't bothered taking him either. I wondered if he was dead. Touching Boxy, I mused, "Did we kill the Madonna or only her doppelganger?" It didn't answer, and I was glad not to get shocked. Whatever Boxy was, I knew I would protect it with my life. That little rose had sabotaged the Madonna and saved me from a solid brainwashing. Indoctrinated as that crowd was, they'd come to realize what they'd seen wasn't real. They had to, I told myself. It was common sense. People couldn't be that stupid. I packed up and came down the hill, eating my fill of the leftover food on the concession table and taking whatever bottled water was left. I stuffed several packs of earplugs scattered across the ground into my pocket.

Brace moaned. I opened a water bottle and poured a bit over his face. His eyes fluttered as one hand reached to straighten his toupee. He puffed out a slight breath, and I put his shattered glasses in his breast pocket. "This is your fault," I said. "You could have stopped a good lot of this. You could have spoken the truth."

He shook his head, trying to talk but only managing a mumble. "Couldn't." One side tooth was broken and dried blood clouted his nose. "She's too strong. She's everywhere."

"If I had a gun," I said as I stood over him. "I'd shoot you in the head. Bang."

By the time I got back to Interstate 90 and figured out the freeway ramps, my legs were trembling and each step sent a dull stab through the soles of my feet. I'd worn through another pair of socks, and the cold had worked its way into my chest. I coughed into the crook of my elbow.

I veered off into a half-abandoned neighborhood, searching for a bike, maybe hiking boots. Anything to get me further, faster, warmer. Snow hovered in the sky like a threat, and Ace had been right—winter was closing in. At a thrift store I bought a handful of threadbare t-shirts, soft enough to use for sneezing, wiping, whatever passed for toiletry now. I hadn't seen toilet paper since Idaho, and the wipes from California were nearly gone.

No bikes. No boots. But a spinning red, white, and blue barber pole caught my eye, oddly patriotic, oddly alive. Maybe I could find hair dye. I drifted toward it, barely aware of my own footsteps. Inside, a lean Asian man was wiping down a sink.

A bell dinged as I entered, and he flinched—head snapping to a wall-mounted TV. He shot me a worried look. The anchor announced call letters I was unfamiliar with and explained the mass delusion that was being perpetrated in the so-called Western Regency. Video of the SNAFU-ed Madonna played. "Our witness had to wear earplugs to avoid whatever hypnotic nonsense this massive fraud is playing on the citizens of our United States." She cut to a reporter who was interviewing a bald-headed Ace.

"It's all a fraud!" Ace exclaimed. "They would have killed my entire crew to keep this secret. A woman helped us escape... Sulis. Her name is Sulis. She saved all of us."

"Oh, my God!" My mouth hung open. "People are seeing this. People know!"

The door's bell rang again as someone else entered behind me. The barber smoothly picked up the TV remote and switched the channel. A female anchor reported, showing a video of only the graceful exchange of the Madonna, and came close to tears as she praised what she called "The Miracle on the Rockies."

"Jake," said a beefy man in a Regency uniform, bayonet rifle slung over his shoulder. "Got time for a shave and cut?"

"In fifteen, Clyde. This one was here first." Jake turned the barber chair toward me with the same ease he'd used on the remote. His eyes locked on mine with a quiet warning.

I sat. My whole body hummed with adrenaline. He reached up and pulled off my Idaho Hawks cap, and I felt the cold breath of exposure on my scalp. Then he tilted my chin—gently, like someone tilting a child's face—and I saw it.

My own face stared back from a wanted poster on the wall. More accurate this time. Hawks cap. Scar. A name in bold underneath: Sulis.

My breath caught hard in my chest. Phillip had given me up. Jake steadied me with a hand on my shoulder. The gesture was firm, grounding. He tossed my cap into the trash like it was nothing, and I flinched at the sound of it hitting the bin.

I caught his eyes in the mirror. Quiet. Steady. Kind.

Clyde chuckled at the television, eyes bright. "Wish I'd been there," he said. "Can you imagine how great it must've been?"

Jake leaned close to my ear. His whisper ghosted across my skin. "If you don't believe," he said, "you better pretend like you do."

Clyde turned. "What's that?"

"A blessed event," Jake called back, calm as a preacher. "By Saint Andrew, we are blessed."

Then the clippers buzzed to life, and my hair fell like snowflakes. I watched it fall—not just hair, but something else. My identity, maybe. The last shape of who I'd been. I watched it hit the floor and disappear.

The anchor complimented a ninety-foot statue at the top of that mountain called Our Lady of the Rockies. Built on the Continental Divide in the 1980s and dedicated to all women, especially mothers, she remarked how excited the locals must be that the actual Madonna had chosen it to make her earthly appearance. As she signed off, the anchor noted that Brace Benton had been so moved by the deity that he was taking time off to contemplate how he might better serve.

"All done," Jake said quietly. "Don't forget your cap by the door."

I handed him a crumpled twenty and two foil-wrapped packets of earplugs. He nodded, knowing what it meant. I stepped into the cold, barely breathing, knowing I couldn't thank him enough. But I did anyway, with every breath I took after that.

I looked at the cap I'd grabbed without thinking. U.S. Army Rangers. A soldier's hat. A symbol, maybe, of the kind of courage that still existed in the quietest corners. A hero.

~ 9459 ~

Outside of Bozeman, I rested in the cold belly of a gutted train car, studying the arrow the drone had dropped at my feet like it might explain the world to me. The shaft was maple or maybe ash—something sturdy, something meant to last. My fingers traced the edge of the broadhead, three-pronged and unforgiving. A man had died by it—probably in excruciating pain before he dropped dead. I had a hard time feeling sorry for him, knowing he had no issue with taking me to a work camp. The arrow would make a formidable weapon if I had to fight up close, but then, who was I kidding? Other than the few moves Carl Houseman had taught me, I had no formal fight training, no martial arts skills, not even a single archery lesson. My whole life, I'd fought most of my battles with words. Most—a flawed word.

Weapon. Kill. Survive. The words blurred together in my head, ugly and metallic. I rolled them between my fingers like dice I didn't want to throw. Since losing Martin's gun, I only had a tactical knife and crowbar that I'd taken from Bren's driver. The confrontation with the teenagers and Bren told me an irksome truth. I wasn't ready to deal with this world. Her threats scratched for space in my chest. I tightened my grip on the arrow and told myself to focus. Feeling too much was a luxury I couldn't afford. Not anymore.

Three a.m.; Martin stood at the patio door again, his shoulders slumped, hands braced against the glass I'd watched him like this before, but I'd never asked why. I was too afraid the answer might be me. When a siren broke the stillness and he stepped outside, I followed—quiet, cautious. My hand found his shoulder, and his found mine. The full moon shone bright, its silvery glow fading into an ethereal orange mist enveloping the Golden Gate Bridge. There was something fragile in the moment, like we were holding each other underwater and hoping not to drown.

Crawling back up to the highway, the wind whipped cold, and I could smell snow in the air. That worried me. I hoped to make it through Bozeman's Pass in three days, but a congested cough and fever slowed my gait. If winter caught me, I might have to find a place to hold up until a thaw. That gave Bren and the Regency more time to find me and use me as a weapon against Martin. I'd benefited from being an insignificant dot in a big land, but it would be more worrisome if Bren got her hands on Boxy. For all its brilliance, the little cube couldn't protect itself. I'd seen it communicate with, transform, and fragment other systems and I'd figured out that the shocks were prompts for me to get closer to whatever it wanted to disrupt. So, the little device had its limits, but worth its weight in titanium for what it did to the virtual image of the Madonna. Too bad it can't provide food, heat, and electricity, I thought as I struggled to put one foot in front of the other. It pulsed a little jolt in its secret hiding place. "Okay," I said aloud and flicked it back. "You can read thoughts too, smartass."

Overshadowing the highway and adjacent train track rose gray and white rock formations jetting from mountains of pine trees like ancient castles. If I saw or heard any vehicles, I jumped over to the rails and ducked down on the track. Fuel tankers, freight trucks, and cattle transports passed me. I'd seen few cars since leaving Seattle, which told me the Regency was still controlling fuel. Motorbikes traveled in packs, and I hid at even the imagination of their sound. Gratefully, the notorious red bus seemed to be out of business. Good job, Limeys!

The setting sun gleamed on a half-round metal arch warehouse at the entrance of a scenic trail leading over a bridged creek and into a pine grove. I hoped it might be a safe place to hunker down for the night. Climbing a rocky bank anchoring the far side of the building, I watched for movement. Through a back door window, I could see food shelves and a bank of retail refrigerators. Motorcycle tire tracks furrowed in the gravel around the building made me jumpy. After an hour and still no movement, I snuck up to the door and surveyed the interior. Scattered chairs, a few cots, kitchen equipment. I listened and then chanced pulling the door open. A still quiet. No one.

Inside a refrigerator, I found packaged sandwiches and bottled water. On an adjoining table, a hot plate with a dirty skillet was cold, but a dozen eggs and corn oil on the shelf above told me I'd better not stay long. Overflowing trash containers flanked cases of beer stacked against the wall. I took what food I thought wouldn't be missed, then started to leave when a blocked-off area sparked my curiosity. An image of a Madonna and child chalked on a theatrical curtain caught the last beams of sunset spilling through a roof vent. I listened. Silence. Moving through the drapes, I stared at a wall-size bank of computer equipment. Fluorescent lights flickered on with a hum. Boxy didn't jolt me, nor did the equipment appear to be operating. Baskets on a table held several torn-apart components. Somebody was trying to fix something. Above it, taped haphazardly to the wall, architect's plans. Of the Madonna. My hand unconsciously covered my mouth.

I scanned the half dozen pages lining the wall to the corner. The last two looked like another warehouse with enormous sectioned-off rooms. I studied the breakdown of rooms: lunchroom, executive, security, holding, in-take, and IT. Others with enigmatic sounding names—Kaleidoscope, Nest, and Mecca—gave no clue as to their function. The place was enormous, larger than four malls lined side by side with thirty-three watch towers surrounding it. A familiar script had written the words

PlanK, Production, Priority on the side. Three words. A trilogy of deception? I recognized Martin's handwriting. The way he looped some letters in the same manner as he did the letter S. These plans had built a monster.

My first thought of burning this building down was drowned out by the guttural drone of motorcycles. I raced to the door, stumbling out, and collided with a blond-haired woman with stunning blue-white eyes. We knocked each other down, scrambled to get upright, and grabbed our backpacks. "Behind the rocks. We have to hide," I said. Mere seconds, our eyes engaged, and I saw her make a decision and run in the opposite direction. I followed her to the side. "This way," I pointed, but she ran toward the front just as the first motorcycle pulled in. If she moved fast, she might make it to that clump of pine trees. I couldn't wait to see if she escaped. I jumped a gully and pulled myself up the embankment, hiding behind a truck-sized boulder and hoping the approaching night would hide me.

I'd gotten about thirty feet up, well above the warehouse, when I heard a scuffle and a sharp bang of someone slammed against a metal wall. She'd been caught. The sun was minutes from setting as other bikes pulled in. I huffed for breath, holding a hand over my mouth to quiet a cough. Peeking over the rock in the direction the woman had run, I saw no one, but exterior lights flipped on and illuminated the parking lot. Was she with them? She could tell about me and point the direction I'd run. I studied the cliff to see if I could go further up. The terrain was steep, with a cascade of colossal rock formations. One slip could send me tumbling down to the road. Then, I heard her scream.

My breath caught as half a dozen additional motorcycles pulled in along with a town car. Great, I thought, knowing who usually traveled in those. Not a minute passed before Phillip and Bren emerged from the rear.

"Look what we have here," said a biker with a scorpion tattoo on the back of his bald head, the claws reaching around the side above his ears. He held the woman by the nape of the neck, then pushed her into the center of a cluster of men.

"Tonight's entertainment," another whooped.

Phillip ignored them, retrieved a bag from the car trunk, and ordered a biker to carry a box for him. He and the lackey strode toward the rear of the warehouse, entering and letting the door slam behind them.

"You're a woman," the blond-haired woman called after Bren. "Don't let them do this."

Bren turned, looked at her and the bikers for several seconds, then shrugged and followed Phillip inside.

"If you let me go, I'll *hide*," she said, giving louder emphasis on the last word. They tossed her back and forth. "I'll stay *hidden*. I'll stay *quiet*. Shhhh. Shhhh."

They laughed as they passed her from one to the next, each touch a mockery, each word a weapon. Hands clawed at her clothes, ripping away her defenses stitch by stitch, while their voices—jeering, venomous—branded her with names meant to strip her of her very self. "Quiet! Hidden!" she cried out louder, her voice resigned and heartrending. "Shhhhh. Shhhhh!"

I reached into my backpack and wrapped my fingers around the arrow, but my hand was shaking so hard it felt like someone else's. Rage surged—white-hot, blinding—but beneath it, a sick twist in my stomach made me want to vomit. I could hear her begging, the way her voice cracked on "shhh," a sound I'd never again associate with comfort.

If I could wrap some material around the arrow, set it on fire, and throw it, I could distract them. Would it cause enough chaos for me to pull her away? Make them think she'd run down the highway? More motorcycles pulled in. By my count, there were more than twenty men down there. I pressed my forehead to the rock and tasted blood where I'd bitten my lip. Twenty men. One arrow. I could do nothing. That helplessness carved something out of me I'd never get back.

My arrow wasn't going to make a difference but I had to try and make some sort of ruckus. Maybe throw a rock onto the ceiling, make them think someone was up there, and hope she could escape when I heard a shuffle, then: "Shhhhhhh."

Five feet above me, behind an enormous boulder, a pair of terrified eyes locked onto mine. A boy—maybe ten or eleven—curled in a sleeping bag, his small chest heaving, fists clenched into a stained Portland Trail Blazers shirt. A half-eaten sandwich and water bottle lay beside him with a child-size knapsack functioning as a pillow.

He raised a finger to his lips: "Shhhh." I mirrored his breaths, placing both hands over my heart, like if we synchronized, we might keep something alive—his mother's dignity, maybe, or our own. Her scream rose again, sharp and inhuman. He didn't cry. He folded into himself, shaking, putting his fingers in his ears, and I followed him, praying the night would end.

Before dawn, the bikers and the town car pulled out. I peeked over the rock I'd slept against, memorizing as many of their license plates as I could see. Committing faces to my memory so well that I could draw them. Absorbing the inflection of voices I'd heard in the night, so I could identify them from across a room. The last one, Scorpion Thug, revved his motor and shot a gun. I didn't have to wonder where that bullet went or if it was even necessary.

The last to leave, Scorpion Thug spun his bike slowly—ritualistically grabbing the woman's arm and pulling her body in the gravel like it meant nothing. He kicked her over the cliff like you'd toss away trash. I memorized the slope of his tattoo. The way the gun gleamed in his hand. I whispered his details under my breath like a prayer. *Tattoo. Scar. Laugh. Gunmetal teeth.* I wouldn't forget. Not ever.

I waited until the sun rose, then woke the child. "Come on, we have to get out of here." He folded his sleeping bag, shouldered his pack, and followed me down the embankment after smoothing down his springy blond curls. Once down, he started to go toward the building. "No," I said, wrapping an arm around his shoulder and pulling him away. "We're going to go this way." He said not a word but followed me. I sat him down on a parking median and told him to wait.

Returning to the warehouse with his backpack and mine, I stuffed them with as much food and water as possible. It amused me that the marauders hadn't even locked up. They weren't afraid. They were the apex predators and they feared no one.

On the way out, I pulled down the Madonna and Plank architect drawings and ripped them up, pausing in front of the one with Martin's handwriting. *PlanK, Production, Priority.* I fought the notion that he might be part of having created this. Was the Madonna his Frankenstein monster? Had it all gotten away from him? Was he still part of them, and I was running toward a nightmare? Not knowing was exasperating, but when I conjured his image, trying to suss out some truth of him, all I could perceive was his trusting expression saying, *"Hey, baby."*

Phillip had been tinkering with the computer equipment. A half-eaten Pop Tart lay on the table. Additional computers were pulled out and scrap parts were scattered. A string of sticky notes revealed he had been trying to rebuild a component meant to plug into a Javon battery. He left an equipment invoice for someone named Jonesy to bring to him by next week. The Javon battery would be the only device that might energize a Madonna image like the one I saw. Since Phillip had invented both, it seemed odd he was now having so much trouble with the equipment.

I retrieved the corn oil and eggs from the other room. Bashing the eggs into as much of the wiring as I could hit felt good, then I poured the oil inside the computers he'd pulled out. Plugging in the hot plate, I set its burner down into a puddle of corn oil and turned it to its highest setting with the Jonesy list curled around the heating element.

A moment of panic hit as I exited; the child was not where I left him. Coming round to the front of the building, I saw that he'd followed a trail of blood and stared over the cliff where Scorpion Thug had pushed his mother. He leaned down and plucked a single yellow flower that had pushed through the cold ground. I came up behind him. He was taller than I'd thought, outfitted for a journey, with a few tears in his jacket and dusty, worn boots. Putting a hand on his shoulder, I asked if he wanted me to say a prayer. He shook his head no, then dropped the yellow flower over the embankment.

"I've got the coordinates of this place memorized," I whispered, noticing the warm bronze of his skin, the subtle mingling of his mother and father written there. "Somebody will come back. She'll get a proper resting place. I promise." He looked up at me with his mother's striking blue-white eyes, the pupils ringed in black, giving them a haunting clarity—as if they saw more than any child should.

As the kid and I walked, I promised myself that I would never in my lifetime speak about what I heard that night. The words she'd screamed calling for her savior, the agony of her tears, the heartbreak of giving up. It was something she and I would always share. She'd endured to keep the child alive. Her death had been my salvation as well. I promised to make it count.

Twenty yards down the road, the kid stopped walking and turned. Hand to his chest, breathing like he'd learned how to summon strength from air. He didn't cry. He just stared—stared until the ravine gave him back something invisible. Then he walked on. No words. Just will. I followed him, humbled. To my everlasting shame, I had been unable to save his mother, but I vowed to avenge her, and I would see him safe. He didn't need me to speak. He needed me to believe.

The kid uttered his first word about ten miles down the road. "Gator!" he shouted, tugging my arm like he'd spotted a unicorn.

Until then, he'd remained silent, following me like a baby duck, his boots scuffing the gravel in perfect time with mine. I'd tried asking his name. Offered space. Encouraged conversation. He gave me the kind of silence that wasn't empty—it was *full*, like a locked room with the lights off. The violence he'd survived had hollowed him out, and I knew better than to fill that silence with my own noise. What did I have to offer him? What I knew about children and trauma was buried so deep inside of me, I couldn't even crack an edge. He seemed to have no trouble walking the distance we'd traveled that morning. I wondered how long he and his mother had been on the road and where they were headed.

He pointed into a dense stand of pines. "Gator, Woman! Gator!" His accent hit me like a skipped heartbeat—sudden and unplaceable.

"Yes," I said carefully, guiding him back to the shoulder. "There are lots of animals out here, but no alligators. Okay?"

But he yanked free and bolted into the woods.

"Damn it." Panic rose like bile as I stumbled after him, calling out to a name I didn't have. "Kid! Come back!"

He came back all right, dragging two Gator brand scooters, triumphant, beaming, his hands locked onto the handlebars like he'd just dragged a prize out of a war zone. I wanted to cry from relief. Instead, I ran to help push them to the road, every joint in my body aching. Someone had hacked the pay boxes, stripped out the monetization, and left the wheels free like a parting gift from a fallen world.

We mounted our metal horses and glided forward. For the first time in days, the road gave a little grace.

My cough was getting worse, and I was running out of aspirin for a fever that hit its worst at midday. With the scooters, I hoped to make Billings by the end of the week and find that Red Cross station to help the child. We'd eaten about half the supplies and were out of bottled water. Until then, we shared my filtered straw and drank our fill from the Yellowstone River. Between us, we found sheds, deserted gas stations, and abandoned trucks to sleep out the night. The cold was getting into my bones. When I took the last aspirin, I knew we needed to double-quick it to Billings. I stood and abruptly grabbed onto the side of a school bus shed where we'd spent the night. A light flurry dotted the air in front of me, and I inhaled several chilly breaths to steady myself and swallow down a surge of nausea. The kid looked at me, then stared down the freeway. He'd reacted to a sound. A vroom that made me say "malarkey" to keep from cussing in front of a child.

"Ford," he said.

"No, I think it's a motorcycle. We need to hide."

"Me name is Ford," he said with straightforward elocution. "In case we die, you know my name." He looked to see what I would do.

"Brooklyn," I said, realizing he had an accent. "But if we live, call me Sulis." The scooters were already stashed in a nearby gully, but we'd come to flat land and fewer hiding places. I pointed to the top of the shed. "Can you climb it, Ford?"

I hoisted him up, and he grabbed onto the shed's edge and flattened himself on the roof. Tucking our bags behind the shed, I pulled out the arrow to use as a weapon but hoped whoever was coming would pass us by. I didn't have the strength to climb and could only hope whoever it was didn't look up and see Ford. I pressed myself against the shed and hoped for luck. Hope... I thought, a useless word right now.

A single rider pulled off and parked his motorcycle. Using binoculars, he studied the road in both directions, then took a long swig from a canteen. The tall, lanky man never turned toward us. No way could I fight him in my shape. A cough came up in my throat, and I struggled to swallow it down.

He stood beside his motorcycle and pulled something from his interior pocket. Without turning, he said, "We got a place down the road. Park City exit. Look for a red truck at Cenex and say Falcon's Eye into the cab's CB radio. Channel two. Always a meal for a traveler." He dropped whatever he'd pulled from his pocket. "Thought the kid might like this."

I steadied the arrow to use as a knife, not trusting his words, then breathed a huff of relief when he started the motorcycle and left. Stepping out of my hiding place, I watched him disappear down the highway. We were found and had to get out of the area fast. One look at my scar and we'd both be in the hands of the Regency. Ford jumped over me, hitting the dirt in a roll, and sprinted toward whatever the man had dropped. It was two fully wrapped chocolate bars. He tore into one and handed me the other. "My throat," I said, spending several seconds in a hacking cough. "Too sore. You can have both." My fever worsened. Sweat dripped down my back as I fought off chills. I needed a plan.

Ford brought the scooters around, still chomping on his chocolate bar. "Banjaxed," he said, pointing at the shredded wheels of the one I'd been using.

"Ford, come here." I sat him down beside me and noticed the second chocolate bar in his breast pocket. "If something happens to me, there's a Red Cross Station at the first Billings exit. All you have to do is follow this highway. Can you remember that?"

He nodded but looked away, not wanting to hear what I was saying.

"You need to get yourself there. They'll help you."

"Share," he said, pointing at the scooter as he licked chocolate from the side of his thumb.

I don't know where it happened. How many miles down the road we'd gotten. I don't remember falling or hitting my head. My mind shifted in delirium. I could see snowflakes drifting, landing on my face. Here I was. Meeting death again. Another body on the side of the road.

At times, I thought I was with Martin. We were on his leather couch in his warm apartment, covered with soft blankets. He challenged me to Anagram-a-rama, and I won as usual.

"You let me win," I teased. "You're such a lionheart."

"I wish," he said, kissing my forehead. "You're the Eidetic One." He waved his arms up and down as if worshiping me. "Memory of twelve elephants

"It's a gift." I laughed as he fed me warm soup.

"By the way, I'm waterproof and heat resistant."

"What?"

I bolted upright. In a bed. In a house. Sky outside the window, blue. Voices floated up from somewhere below. My backpack emptied on a table. Arrow and tactical knife lying to the side. Ford. Where was Ford?

A woman walked in.

"Oh," she said. "You're alive—awake, I mean." She held a folded stack of my clothes. "I washed them for you."

"Ford," I rasped, every syllable like sandpaper against my throat. "The kid?"

The woman blinked. "Oh! He's here. We didn't know his name. He hasn't spoken a word."

My legs hit the floor, my body rebelled, and I barely stayed upright. A firestorm of coughing doubled me over. My heart thundered—not from the fever but from fear. I'd failed him. Somewhere in the storm of sickness and snow, I'd let go of his hand.

"I'll get him." She moved over to me, putting a hand on my shoulder.

I jerked away, not sure what she was about.

"You rest. I'll get some warm soup." She turned. "And I'll bring the... Ford."

Boxy! After she left, I heaved myself from the bed, staggering to the stack of clothes, and dug for my bras. Quickly checking the pockets, I found Boxy, no worse for the wear, having gone through a washer and dryer.

Relief flooded my body as I stashed the bra under a pillow. Hearing footsteps, I pulled the blanket up to my neck. Ford and the man on the motorcycle came in. Behind him, a tawny-haired teenage girl peeked over Ford's head. Ford's and my gaze connected. His eyes were wide, and he blinked several times as he made his way to the bedside. He pulled the chocolate bar from his pocket, holding it like it was sacred.

I took it with a trembling hand. He didn't speak. He didn't need to.

"This young fella found the truck, and we brought you here." The man was lanky, ropy, muscular arms, friendlier than I'd thought when I saw him at the bus stop. Glad I didn't try to fight him. "I'm Tippy Sharp. My sister... Rosemary has been tending to you."

"How deep is the snow on the highway?" I asked, hoarsely.

"Just a light dusting. Almanac says we won't get heavy snow until October."

"How long have I been down?"

"Three days, but you've got some healing to do."

"I have to go. I've lost too much time." I scooted myself upright, and the sun's rays dipped into the window, blinding me.

His sister entered the room carrying a tray. Steam wafted off the soup. It smelled of chicken. Hunger pangs made my mouth water. "Thank you," I said, looking up at them. Not remembering as I fell back onto the bed, unconscious.

I woke up a week later, Rosemary Sharp, the sister, told me. A whole week gone, burned away in fever and unconsciousness. All I could think was that it was time I couldn't afford to lose. Not now. Not when Martin was counting on me.

My system was weak, but I could stand without swaying, and my throat no longer felt like I'd gargled gravel. I made it downstairs, each step a quiet victory. Rosemary cooked scrambled eggs for me. The smell made my stomach knot with need.

Out the window, I spotted Ford stumbling out of a barn, sleeves rolled, looking every bit the country boy he never was.

"Ford has taken to milking cows," Rosemary said. "Trina taught him."

"Your daughter?"

"Now she is," she said softly, not looking up.

I looked aside, having heard that before, and smiled, knowing I needed to make nice and be grateful, but everything inside of me screamed that I needed to get back on the road. "I have a favor to ask." She was kneading dough, palms pressing into it with practiced, precise rhythm. I watched her hands, measuring her mood in the silence between movements. "I'd like to leave the child here. The road is dangerous and..."

"People are looking for you." Her voice was flat but not unkind.

I sat back, trying to read her, unsure if I was being accused or warned. "Sooner I leave, safer you are."

She nodded, eyes still on the dough. "We'll keep Ford."

"When the world's normal again..." I hesitated, because what did that even mean anymore? "I think his kin might be in Portland. He's worn that Trail Blazers tee until it's threadbare."

"Yes, he wouldn't let me wash it," she said, waving a hand in front of her nose. "And believe me, it needs it."

"I pick my battles," I said, and we both let ourselves smile.

She laughed and slid the biscuits into the oven. For a second, the kitchen felt like something we could've had in our old world.

"You have electricity," I said. "And your brother's bike—how's he getting gas?"

"The farm had its own pumping station for the tractors. Got refilled right before everything went sideways. It's well-hidden. Solar panels too... but I won't say where."

"Keep it that way."

She turned to me, pointing at the line on my cheek. "The scar... you're Sulis."

The room seemed to freeze. My pulse spiked. I didn't move, scanned the kitchen in one sweep—doorways, drawers, the counter. If she reached for a knife, I'd—

"Lots of people got scars," I said, keeping my voice even.

"I've got something more important. Something left over from before." She sat in the chair opposite me, one finger on her chin. "Theatrical makeup."

"Really?"

"I know an enemy of the Regency when I see one." Her mouth pushed into her cheeks as she studied my face. "You're a legend," she said. "Killer of the Red Bus, Destroyer of Town Car One, Conqueror of Computer Eggs, Protector of Highway, and Mad Bomber of Seattle."

"Ah, shucks," I replied. "To be fair, my friend Maria blew up Seattle."

"Well, you are getting full page credit in the Regency Malefactors Folio."

"The what?"

She leaned over and opened a storage cube of a buffet sideboard. Sliding a false bottom aside, she pulled out a sleek old tablet marked with lime green tape. As she typed, she kept talking. "I was a sophomore—computer science and theater—University of Montana. Tippy was on the amateur golf tour, about to go pro. My parents ran a dairy. Mom could steer her way around a herd better than a Texas heeler." Her voice trembled, just slightly. "They burned the farm. Killed them.

Killed the livestock too slow to run. Trina was our neighbors' kid. They're gone too."

"I'm sorry," I said, but it felt like dropping a pebble into a bottomless well. "My friend, Dan, is an IT guy. You two should get in touch. He might know some stuff that could help."

She turned the tablet toward me. A timer in the corner counted down seven minutes. "I have to log off before that expires." She'd opened a tab into the Regency's government structure. The site was crude, like a high school art project. Clearly, Phillip was not a master at designing websites. Sure enough, a link called Regency Malefactors Folio showed an enemies list. Sounded like something he'd come up with. Martin and I were numbers one and five. For me, they still only had the name Sulis and a crude sketch with the wrong jawline and scar exaggerated like I was Frankenstein's monster.

I now realized Martin had called me Sulis to hide my identity. Listed among my crimes was Maria's bombing in Seattle, killing the limo driver, and, oddly or not, the destruction of the car had more severe consequences than the death of a man. I was also wanted for revealing highly sensitive government information, probably that the red bus took people to a work camp.

Penalty, public burning.

"Damn." I watched grainy security footage of myself in a hoodie, pouring corn oil over Phillip's computers and throwing eggs like I was trick-or-treating for justice. It almost made me laugh. "I hope when I get to where I'm going, people there will be able to use what I know to end the Regency."

Rosemary sighed and made prayer hands as she looked up. Clicking off the site and rebooting the computer, she pressed down the worn lime tape before returning it to the sideboard. "If you need to contact us, the post office is dependable. Address it to Postman Axel. Old as Methuselah, wears a lime green bowtie."

"Post office, hmmm."

"He's attached to it, the bow tie."

"Lime green," I said. Yes, she was testing me. She wanted to know if I knew. "No library nearby, I take it."

"They burned it."

"Of course they did."

"Thus: the post office and Postman Axel. You'll find he works everywhere these days. Lime's a rare color now."

I nodded. "The Regency shows no decorum in taking what it wants."

"Mirrors. They took all our mirrors. We're not sure why."

"Dan's name on the registry is Turing. I'm sure he could teach you some tricks." She and I understood each other. We were both shipwrecked, unsure of which way to turn, who to trust, taking chances when our guts told us to, forming our families out of leftovers, joining as allies because we were all we had. We had become the resistance. "I have some money—"

"Don't even," she said, holding up her hand.

We sat in silence while the oven clicked softly. When she finally pulled the biscuits out, she placed two on a plate in front of me and poured a glass of milk.

"I'll leave by nightfall," I said.

She didn't try to stop me. That was how you knew she'd seen the world for what it really was.

Rosemary and Tippy outfitted me with long wool underwear, socks, a cap, Oboz boots, and an insulated hooded parka. They also included a flashlight, sunglasses, binoculars, a nice stash of biscuits and dehydrated meat. Rosemary showed me how to cover my scar and powder it down without using a mirror. Theatrical makeup had to be a gift from the gods. I wished they had an extra firearm, but the Regency had confiscated all but a hunting rifle.

I fought with myself about what to say to Ford. There must be hundreds of Fords out there. I thought about the young boys that had tried to sell me. Weren't they just Fords who were surviving as best they could? I needed to do right by this one. I watched him through the window as he bounced on the trampoline, limbs flailing with joy, daring the world to touch him.

Trina flipped circles around him, but he didn't care—he kept leaping higher. I should have gone out there. Said something. Anything. But I've always been better at leaving than staying. The guilt stuck in my throat like dry bread. He'd be safe here, I told myself, and turned away.

Martin's hearty laughter rang out, full and reckless, as he twirled unsteadily, clinging to me for balance. I caught the railing just in time, steadying us both before we toppled. "I probably shouldn't have suggested rollerblading," I said through a breathless laugh. "We're still a mile from the car."

"You flow with grace, adapting to whatever comes," he teased, grinning even as his legs wobbled. "I, on the other hand, am a bumbling blockhead. I crown you, Sulis—goddess of waters that carve through stone, soft yet unstoppable." He lifted his hand in a dramatic salute, and I couldn't help but laugh, even in our precarious balancing act. "I'll get you back to civilization," he vowed, "even if it kills me."

Before I could answer, he pulled me close, his arms locking around me with a sudden fierceness that startled more than steadied. He pressed his face into my hair, inhaling as though he could breathe me in, and the laughter between us dissolved into something heavier, more urgent. His grip promised safety, the kind of safety I had longed for in secret moments when the world felt too sharp. Yet, even as warmth spread through me, doubt curled at the edges of my heart. Why couldn't I trust this? Why couldn't I surrender, just once, and let myself believe in him? The questions swirled like shadows, refusing to release me, even as I ached to lose myself in the shelter of his embrace.

The scooter had disappeared somewhere along the way, so I was walking again. The first night, sleeping against a tree almost made me turn around. I sat up at daybreak, achy and exhausted. Ford was asleep beside me. I smacked his arm.

"What are you doing here!"

He jerked away as we stood, his mouth tightening hard against his jaw, spiraled curls falling loose across his forehead. His gaze locked on me—stern, blazing with indignation. Oh, he was furious. He hurled a glove to the ground at my feet, the gesture sharp as a slap. I planted my fists on my hips, teeth clenched, leaning over him in challenge. He stood his ground, arms crossed tight across his chest, chin jutting in stubborn defiance. Then he stamped his foot, the sound cracking against the silence. "You abandoned me, woman!"

"Listen, little boy!" I shook my finger at him.

"You don't call a Black man a boy!"

"Child!"

"I am not a child!"

"I had you in a safe place!"

"It's my birthday! I am all of twelve years old!"

I grunted my frustration, holding a hand to my forehead and looking down the length of the freeway, wondering how long it would take me to walk him back.

"Hercules strangled a viper before he was a year. Horus battled his Uncle Set with his left eye in his back pocket. Cu Chulainn took down the forces of Queen Medb by the age of six. Fionn mac Cumhaill ate the Salmon of Knowledge and never even burped. He was barely a wean. I was a hand taller than them at the age of ten. I am Crawford Horace Larkin, leader of the Portobello ten, winner of the Camden Street Craic Contest, fighter of Vikings and English alike, son of Maren and Jack, the Giant Killer. I am the scourge of the sacramental covenant and nobody tells me what to do!"

"And yet you're a Trail Blazers fan. Biggest losers of all time."

"I like an underdog," he replied. "And not the biggest. That goes to the Grizzlies. Seventy-three-point loss to the Oklahoma City Thunder."

"You made all that up," I said, submerging a laugh as I realized he had an Irish accent. "I also think you lie about your age."

His expression softened, and he couldn't hold back a grin as he shrugged. "I was raised in Ireland, Woman. What'cha expect?"

"Happy birthday."

Thus, our first real fight—conversation. I already knew Ford was a tough one. Every day, he showed me his resilience. He walked a good two hours without a break. The breathers we took were mainly for me. He charmed with his Irish brogue and tall tales when we stopped at exits to eat and rest. Even told kids playing around the area that he knew several leprechauns on a first-name basis. He'd make secret marks on their hands and tell them it would bring them good luck. The children were thrilled. He worked his way into getting us an abandoned house to sleep in for several nights when my legs were too worn out to walk any longer. His friends brought us food and jerry-rigged a television to a car battery. He stayed glued to that TV. It worried me as it only played the Regency news channel. He didn't blink. Didn't breathe, sometimes. I should have turned it off.

Then came the map. His plan. "I think I know where those men are," he said, and something in my stomach dropped like a rock in a well. Not because he was wrong, but because he might be right. He pulled the map of the United States out of my backpack. "The ones who... you know."

"I know."

"We're going to go right past it. I want to destroy it," he said, voice low and certain

"Do you now." I shifted in a wingback chair, throwing my legs over the arm, skin buzzing with unease.

He paced like a grown man commanding a war room, hands shoved in pockets, shoulders squared like he could carry it all. "While you've been hustling food, getting your noggin shaved, and playing makeup, I've been chatting up the boyos and earwigging the culchies."

"I hope that's legal," I said, amused.

"These kids playing around the exits while their parents work, they got the tea.

"The tea?"

He rolled his eyes. "They listen. Whether they understand what the adults are saying or not, who knows, but they help drag out merchandise for sale based on how many people are on the road at various exits. People are communicating, and they've figured out that nobody goes to certain exits because the Regency eejits have bases there. Not the soldiers. The pendejos on the motorcycles—"

"Pendejos? How do you know that word?"

"You talk in your sleep, Woman." He turned the map toward me so I could see where he'd drawn Xs.

"It means something not very nice. You probably shouldn't say it."

Ignoring me, he traced a path. "The kids know something bad goes on at these places." His finger hit all the Xs. "They call it home of the murky wraith. Or dirty ghost, maybe foul-smelling anemic. Hence, I can surmise it's a kind of Bogyman."

"Hence," I repeated, surprised he used that word at this age. "Filthy white man is what they're saying. My guess is their parents are using words that'll scare the kids so they won't venture that direction into a nest of motorcyclists."

"Like ghosts don't scare them?" He rolled his eyes again like I was the stupidest person in the world. And maybe I was. "Look," he said, pulling out my phone from his jacket pocket. "I took a picture of a newscast."

"That's my phone."

He ignored me. Flicking through photos he'd taken from the newscasts, he showed me pictures of a thinned-down Brace Benton whose face looked like a rotted apple, shadows under his eyes, a cold sore on his upper lip, pale bluish skin without TV makeup, and a missing tooth on his left side if he grinned too widely. In each photo, he was interviewing Dixie Roman, and he didn't look particularly enthusiastic.

"This sign." Ford pointed to a road sign in the background marking Billings as ten miles away. Beneath it, motorcycles were parked in disarray. "The kids said anybody who goes there is never seen again, and so, they believe the ghost has killed them. A wean's mind, you know. Something's here they don't want people to see. Hence, something they're protecting. Hence, I'm going to mess them up."

I squinted and enlarged the photos to make out the license plates. At least three of the bikes were the same ones from the place where his mother was killed. A town car parked at the side showed only half a plate, but the letters were the same as the car Phillip and Bren used. I also wanted revenge on those monsters, but what could a woman and a child do? I had to distract him and make him see that telling our stories was how we would bring them to justice. A better time would come and we would testify. We would put them in jail for the rest of their lives. But we had to stay alive to do that. If we could get to Fargo, if we could get to Martin, he'd know what to do. "I'll take a look when we get there," I told him. "Now give me back my phone."

Each day, as we got closer, there were more and more vehicles on the road, so we returned to walking the safer two hours in the morning and two at dusk. The kid was impatient. He wanted to walk longer and go farther. Each time a group of motorcycles passed, we dove for cover, flattening ourselves against the frigid ground, and waited until they passed.

Every few miles, we encountered a billboard reminiscent of the ones on the West Coast. Some had been measured incorrectly, and I could see half of Odette Wallace's face. What was there framed an etheric, motherly vision of the Madonna with bright promises of all she would bring to the world. *When you see her, you'll never doubt again!* I explained to Ford what I thought they were trying to do. Told him what they were protecting and why I'd destroyed their computers when I found them. I also gave him a package of earplugs and instructed him to use them if he ever saw the Madonna. He listened, but I wondered if he understood or cared. I left out any mention of Boxy for now.

After studying his Xs on the map, they appeared to follow a design perfect for sending the Madonna image southward into the Midwest. After conquering those areas, they could build more projection stations and send her into the South. If they all relied on each station working to send the signal along the line, then disrupting one like Boxy and I had must have thrown a wrench in their plan. They'd have to fix it before they could continue, so it made sense why they were choosing unobtrusive, insignificant buildings that no one would notice. But I had a hunch a mothership was powering all these small stations. If that could be found and destroyed, the Madonna might never recover. I wondered if Martin had already figured this out. Maybe he was waiting for this one last part, Boxy, to fight them. Even if he had been an investor initially, I had to trust that he was resisting them now.

I plotted how we could walk past the pendejo's next station unnoticed. They likely had put more security on these places after what I'd done to the last one. I tried to distract Ford by explaining how the Madonna was likely powered by a device built by people I know. He'd pretend to listen through a stony, hard-edged semblance. I knew what that meant. I'd seen it before in my own reflection. He was going to try and kill those men. The screams of his mother haunted me, as they must have him. I trembled at night, jerking awake only to find him sitting up, staring at me.

"There might be something we can do," I said when I knew we were within a few miles.

He looked at me without speaking.

"If they have a similar setup, we can wait until they leave and destroy the equipment. It'll keep that dumbass Madonna vision from manifesting for a while. We'll have done a good thing."

"Hmm," he muttered and looked away.

"Sooner or later, we'll get to a place with proper law enforcement, a real American army. We'll tell them everything that happened. I've memorized those license plates. I know what those men look like. They'll hunt them down."

"Stupid," he huffed under his breath. "You don't even know if you'll be alive to see that day." He didn't believe me or speak to me the rest of the day, and part of me didn't blame him. What I described to him sounded unbelievable unless you'd seen it.

The first sign we were near was a shimmering blue cloak rising over a field of wild, choking grass—what was left of the faux Madonna. It wandered like a ghost with no head and only half its former height. The movements were broken, mechanical, and part of the fabric disappeared now and then. Between me and Boxy, we'd mangled it pretty darn good. There was no hum, but I told Ford to have his earplugs ready just in case.

Ford's mouth hung open as he watched the generic clothing of Mother Mary billow as if lifted by a gentle breeze. "Father Sweeny would have some choice words to say about that. She's pathetic." He crossed himself and moved his earplugs to his jacket pocket.

It appeared they were testing the image, trying to get it up to its former glory. I used the binoculars to study the road as I didn't want to walk right into the middle of a Regency cluster, and I had to get Ford past this area without doing something that would get him killed. I hated lying to the kid, but it seemed the best way.

A nearby gas station looked like the probable place where they'd be working. A train of motorcycles lined the right side of the building, and the trunk of a town car stuck out at the back. The land was flatter here. Few places to hide. Our best shot was to pass late at night when less light illuminated the highway. I played it down to Ford, pretending the place he was looking for was still twenty miles down the road. We waited for dark, watching the pathetic Madonna cloak try to stand without devolving into a drunken swivel.

"We'll have to be invisible and move like ninjas."

He didn't answer.

"Once we're passed, we'll have a clear shot into Billings. Supplies, warm clothes, maybe a haircut. You're starting to look like a counterculture renegade from the 1960s."

"I don't care if I die."

I blinked and held a breath. "I do."

"They killed my mother. I'm not walking by this place."

His grief burned in the space between us—something raw and holy. I wanted to promise vengeance. I wanted to say I'd slaughter them all. "There's too many of them," I said quietly. "Thirty bikes, maybe more. And the black car... I think the devil herself's in it."

He stared at the ground, jaw set, a storm behind his eyes. "If they're trying to put the Madonna back together, we can end it here. Kill them all here."

"Killing people isn't what you think, Ford!"

He remained quiet, looking at the ground between his boots.

I hesitated, contemplating how to apologize and convince him at the same time. What he said about stopping the Madonna made sense. I would love to cause them some more trouble here. Then Boxy shocked me. "Damn it," I said, aside.

"What'd I do?"

"Not you. Something else." I stood up and looked down the road, studying the exit ramp to the gas station. The whole area was lit up with floodlights. The jerks didn't spare themselves any energy. Men and women danced to a boom box in a side parking lot. Focusing the binoculars on a rear office, I could make out the legs of a man moving back and forth studiously over banks of computers. I needed to get closer to see if there was anything Boxy could do. "Okay, here is how it's going to work. You're going to hide here. I'll go check it out. I think I can merge with those dancing people without being noticed. I'll return in one hour and we'll form a plan."

"Promise."

I nodded, then pulled him in front of me, forcing him to look into my eyes. "But if I don't come back, you return to Sharp's farm. There will come a day when the world is sane again. You promise me to wait for that day."

He bit his lower lip and stared into the distance but nodded.

I hid him in a gully that paralleled the freeway, leaving my backpack and most of my over clothes, trying to match the women's dress, most of whom were matched up with a biker and skimpily dressed despite the cool weather. It wasn't my intention to meander among them, but it seemed better to be ready if I had to do that. I hoped Boxy would send out some of those high-voltage jolts and shut down the place. Just in case, I carried a set of earplugs and strapped my knife to a belt loop. More than a few weapons hung on belts so I wouldn't look out of place.

I crawled along the gully, coming up behind the station. Def Leppard's "Pour Some Sugar On Me" blasted from the boombox, and the dancers bobbed up and down to the beat. I pulled out Boxy. It vibrated but didn't shock me. There was something in there it wanted. I climbed up the gully, staying out of the light. *If you're going to do anything Boxy, now is a good time.*

Marijuana smoke saturated the air and clouded above the dancers. A bartender at a makeshift bar, where beer and whiskey flowed like the Yellowstone River, punched a second boombox. Thin Lizzy's "The Boys Are Back In Town" screamed into the twilight. The chilly evening gave me a shiver as I watched several people pop something into their mouths. These pendejos were zonked and pie-eyed. I scooted onto the asphalt, using the motorcycles for cover to get closer to that rear office.

Boxy opened into startling geometric figures. Expanding circles like a stone dropped into water curled around into a spiral, a cone, a pyramid, a sphere, a dodecahedron, and finally, a Fibonacci pinecone. Truly, the most beautiful transparent, yet real image, I'd ever observed. One shot of blue darted toward the rear of the station and penetrated the wall.

"Damn!" a man yelled as he slammed open the rear door. And there it was. Phillip Javon stamped his feet and agitated his arms as he pivoted in a circle. "It's not working!" He banged a fist on the hood of the town car. Following in his footsteps, Bren Chandley. She rubbed his back and cooed soothing words. The person not comforting the boy wonder, Dixie Roman.

"You said it would work!" Dixie growled, aggravation in his movements. "I can't spend all year out here in the boonies chasing ghosts. I have a campaign to win."

"A race you wouldn't even be in if it weren't for me, so stuff it and let us work."

"Can't I just interview you normal-like? You don't have to be fifty feet tall."

Bren rotated toward him and smiled as if she wanted to stab him in the heart. "The polyglot has to work for everyone to understand. You don't even know what a polyglot is, you stupid halfwit!"

"Screw you all!" Dixie stormed away. "I'm partying." He bobbed his head and shimmied into the dancers on the opposite side of the station. I watched as he grabbed onto a woman's waist and ground his groin against her. She put a pill between her lips, and he leaned down and kissed her.

I couldn't have been more amused to see the gleam of the Regency soaked in whiskey and fighting like rats. I only hoped Boxy had messed it up enough to keep them running on empty. Boxy closed up, and I returned it to my bra. Now, to snatch up Ford and figure a way out of here.

A hard clap on my neck stunned me. "Look what we have here, hiding in the dark like a scared little bunny?"

The grip twisted my arm behind me, my breath snagged in my throat. I tried to use a voice I hoped sounded small and harmless. "I was just looking for a place to sleep. Food. I—I thought maybe I could trade some—"

He laughed maliciously, "Yeah, you'll trade all right." He marched me toward the black car, calling out to Phillip and Bren. "Where's the boss? I got something for him."

I lowered my head as much as I could, hoping with my buzz cut, they wouldn't recognize me. He shoved me forward. They stared at me. Phillip knew immediately and glanced toward Bren. Bren's eyes narrowed, unsure.

"He's been wanting to party and my girls are sick of him," the biker said, holding out his pinkie finger and wiggling it. In the car's side-view mirror, I saw it, a scorpion claw above his ear. *The man who killed Ford's mother.* Now, I knew what was awaiting me. Panic and rage tangled inside me—no time to untangle one from the other. My mind sped through the best scenario to get me out of this as I struggled one-handed to get to my knife.

"Don't," I grunted as he shoved me against the trunk of the town car. I glared up at Bren and Phillip. "Let those monsters have me and you'll never get it. Yes, psychos, I have it."

"Let her go," Phillip said.

I jerked free of Scorpion Thug, holding my twisted arm but had no time to react as a dark mass flew down from the roof, landing on the biker's shoulders. His mouth widened into an O and spewed blood. Ford clutched the arrow that split the man's neck. Both of them dropped to the ground as Ford swung the crowbar like a baseball bat and beat Scorpion's head. I swung around with my fist clutched and punched Bren as hard as I could, sweeping her feet at the same time. Her head cracked against the asphalt. Phillip stepped back. "Come on," I said. "We can get out of here."

He froze, petrified, looking down at Bren and back toward the office door. "Phillip, don't be an idiot. I know what they've made you do. If we run now, we can get to Martin!"

"Martin?"

"You know he'll do everything he can for you. Can you say the same for her?"

His breath hiccupped, and his hands trembled in front of him as he looked me in the eye. "She's my mother."

A shock more potent than Boxy whipped through my whole body. My hand reflexively went to my knife. "Pick her up," I said. "Put her in the back seat." He followed my instructions. When he ducked out, I pointed the knife at him and grabbed his collar.

"I'll scream!" Phillip squealed, his voice drowned out by the raucous partiers at the side of the building as he held his trembling hands face level. Then he froze as perhaps all of us did. Boxy vibrated but didn't ask for attention other than that. Phillip overlooked my shoulder into the computer room. Still holding to him, I turned to see Brace Benton, a bony wrist handcuffed to a pipe; his face looked like flotsam, his eyes downcast, mouth hung open. The only objects within his reach were an overflowing ashtray, cigarettes, a lighter, a needle, and aluminum foil.

"Car's got half a tank," Ford said, widening the driver's door for me. "Moved our backpacks further down the gully."

"Pop the trunk," I said to Ford. I dragged Phillip to the rear of the car, holding the knife to his throat. "Get in." Slamming the trunk on his beleaguered expression was the most satisfying crumb of my day.

"I siphoned a bike in front and doused most of the cycles with gas."

"Got any more?"

Ford nodded, holding up a soda bottle filled with liquid.

"Douse that equipment," I said, pointing to the computer equipment lining the wall of a six-by-six room. I scrambled through a desk, looking for a way to free Brace. Above it, drawings pinned to the wall brought me to a halt. My gaze traveled over them, fixing them in my memory. No, I thought. They couldn't. They wouldn't. Seeing a set of handcuff keys pinned to a bulletin board, I tossed them at Brace. They landed in his lap. "You can ride in the car with us, or you can stay here and keep mainlining whatever crap they're shooting into you."

Brace's head slowly revolved toward me as he chortled a slow, deranged chuckle. He smiled the saddest smile I'd ever seen. Glancing toward Ford, dousing the equipment with gas, Brace reached for the lighter.

"Ford, run!" We dove for the gully just as the back of the station exploded.

The boom felt like a heartbeat from the earth itself. The sky tore open behind us, fire blooming in every direction. Partiers screamed, bodies flung skyward, and the town car lifted off the ground and landed in a thud. People ran in all directions.

I grabbed Ford and our backpacks, and we crawled the length of the ditch, smoke and panic in the air. The image of Brace's smile haunted me—so broken, so gentle in the end. He chose fire. That was his escape. And then those *drawings* in the office—images I couldn't shake. Schematics. Blueprints of something monstrous. I felt sick. Like I'd stared into a future already decided.

"Tricycle by the road has keys," Ford urged. We climbed up the embankment and hurried toward it just as a biker hopped on and started its engine.

Ford bounded forward, running ahead of a flame following the gasoline's path. He leaped onto the seat of the nearest motorcycle, skirting across five of them as fire lit the ground under him. Soaring through the air, he latched onto the cyclist's back and kicked off, knocking both of them to the ground. They landed hard on the asphalt. He growled at me, "Get on the trike, Woman!"

We sped into the night just as the length of motorcycles blew up. Ford managed to open a back compartment and pulled out a helmet that he slammed onto my head, taking a second one for himself. The timing was perfect because other bikers caught up with us and the helmets hid who we were. The trike was easy enough to maneuver, and I let us drift to the rear of the pack. When the last motorcycle passed us, I slowed until they disappeared. The trike had a gas canister strapped over a back wheel. In the early morning hours, I refilled the tank and continued at a slower speed to maximize the mileage.

The sun peaked over the eastern horizon, bringing the child and I to an abrupt halt. Seeing what we'd missed in the dark took our breath away. Ford muttered, "Savage," and I think I did too. Not even the magic of the faux Madonna could compare to this surreal landscape of deep, maze-like canyons, buttes, and spires. Eerie shadows elongated toward the west and highlighted red, orange, and yellow rock formations sharply jutting out of an otherworldly terrain. A chilly gust rippled like a whisper of ancient spirits, and I couldn't shake the feeling of being watched. Desolate silence broken by the shriek of a soaring hawk added to the land's haunting beauty. An exit sign pointed to a town called Medora. We were in the North Dakota badlands. In the confusion of escaping, we'd traveled two hundred fifty miles down Interstate 94. Ringing in my mind the warnings: *Under no circumstances follow Interstate 94. Something happens on 94. People never return.*

"Ford," I whispered as we stared, mesmerized by the breathtaking beauty of this contrasting land. "You've seen the messages on the Madonna billboards."

He nodded. "Fabrication of the Regency. Father Sweeny warned us about false Holy Joes wanting to spit coffee like tea."

I nodded even if I didn't get his reference. "What we saw on the plains was a deteriorated version of her that they're trying to fix. The finished product is fearsome, and it's beautiful and compelling like it fulfills every craving you've ever had. It does something to people's brains. It makes them want to believe. You'll physically hear her tell you exactly what you want to hear."

"That's why you've been mangling computer equipment when we find it."

"What I saw in Butte was a first draft—a test. With work, they could get that thing to convince an atheist." I hesitated, wondering if I should tell him. My mind clicked in a thousand directions, reviewing my memory of the drawings from the gas station. "How religious are you?"

"Disgraced altar boy, but cut my arm and I'll bleed Catholic." He looked at a young coyote bouncing in prairie grass after some prey. "Me and me fellas, we used to make a game out of lifting Sister Rose Agnes' rosary and hanging it on the statue of Jesus. Gave her a fright and us a gas."

"Did your religion ever scare you?"

"Father Sweeny says we're defined by our fears, but then I've never had much use for being afraid. He once called me the scourge of the sacramental covenant after I drew juggling balls above Satan's outstretched arms on a rectory painting. You know I like an underdog."

We burst out laughing, our cackles echoing into the rugged land dressed with ethereal morning light that appeared to stretch endlessly. "Hence, disgraced altar boy."

"I figured if I could keep the Devil busy with tricks, he'd not have time to look for me."

"Good," I said, " 'Cause that's who they're about to build next."

We mounted the trike and drove until we ran out of gas.

Pushing the trike to the next exit, we could not find fuel and traded it for road provisions, a parka and haircut for Ford, and a night at a roadside motel called the Miniwashitu Inn. Interestingly, neither the motel nor the barbershop had mirrors. It wasn't hard to guess who'd taken them. Sometimes not seeing yourself was easier. I didn't miss the reflection, just the person I used to be.

I left the kid to get his hair cut and scouted out several blocks of stores for a new backpack and wool underwear for him. Most of the stores were open with electricity but no internet. My phone had stopped working as well. Vendors dealt only in trade or cash. I had about three thousand left but kept only five hundred dollars in my front pocket. My layered vests and hoodie were worn but still kept their function of carrying everything important. There's a certain kind of safety in looking like nothing, even when everything you have is sewn into your seams.

Upon my return, the kid sported geometric cornrows from the crown to the nape of his neck and the pattern of a single-eyed, horned swamp creature shaved on each side. The barber gave him a small tin of shea butter that he tucked in his new, adult-sized backpack. Ford shot me a stern look, daring me to say something—I swallowed the urge to gush. He didn't want to be seen as a kid anymore, and God help me, I wanted to let him have that. Truth was, he looked pretty spiffy, but I suspected he didn't want a compliment.

As we walked, he was quiet, more than usual, and I figured what he'd been through the past few days was catching up to him. When I spoke, I kept the conversation generic; the weather, finding a good place to sleep, and how tasty dehydrated beef was if you imagined it slathered in mushrooms and onions. He'd nod or grunt, give the occasional Irish-sounding *aye* and *naw*. Several times, I caught him staring at his hands, palms open, studying the lines of his skin as if contemplating what he was capable of. I knew what was coming, and I wished with all my heart I could have spared him.

"What you said before;" he whispered, as we lay in the dark on different couches of an abandoned house. "Like you know."

"I know."

"You killed somebody?"

"Long time ago. I don't talk about it."

"My mam killed a man," he said, his voice shivery. "She didn't have a choice. He would have killed us."

"She did what she had to do."

"Afterward, she never spoke of it, like you. I finally asked if she was okay. She said she hoped I never had to do such a thing because it ate you from the inside out."

"Now you know."

And there it was—that moment no child should ever come to. The part of him I couldn't protect ripped open quietly beside me.

Sleep claimed us fitfully that night. I thought about Bren being Phillip's mother. Did that mean Martin was his father? The two men didn't particularly favor each other, and Bren's different name suggested she had more than one husband. So many unanswered questions about these relationships drained me more than the biting cold and gnawing hunger. When the sun rose, I found myself agitated, even angry with Martin. Why had he picked me? As a girlfriend? As an accomplice of this crazy-ass journey? What did he even see in me? A scar-faced woman with a low paying job, living in a studio where I couldn't even have a cat.

I leaned back in my chair at John's Grill, the dim light casting a warm glow over the vintage photos adorning the walls, all dedicated to the legendary author Dashiell Hammett. I savored my cosmopolitan as Martin finished off his Sam Spade lamb chops. We were seated near the enclosed case containing the statuette of the Maltese Falcon..

"He looks a little angry," I said, motioning toward the enigmatic statue with my glass.

"Probably because his predecessor was bird-napped and even a twenty-five-thousand-dollar reward didn't secure its return."

"Hmmm." I took a sip, letting the buzz of laughter and chatter envelop me, the perfect backdrop for our evening. Just as I was

about to settle into the rhythm of the night, Martin's phone buzzed, shattering the moment. Two of his employees had encountered a crisis and needed help. "Go," I said, hating the thought of losing the evening. "I can find my way home."

"Come with me. This shouldn't take long, and then we can walk down to the waterfront and throw quarters into the bay."

"Wishes?"

"I wish," he grinned, helping me with my coat.

As we arrived at the Siriso building, two frantic young lawyers paced in front of the gate. From what I gathered, the crisis revolved around a contract due the following morning. I settled onto a couch as Martin and his employees huddled around a computer in the next room.

A few minutes later, Martin appeared at the door, his face pale and stressed. "I hate to do this. I mean, I really, really, really hate to ask this, but... Do you type?"

"Type?" I repeated, a bit bewildered.

"We're all hunt-and-peckers."

I laughed, amused at the thought of brilliance reduced to frantic finger movements across a keyboard. "I'm a journalist. Of course, I type."

Around four a.m., the younger lawyer had a frantic meltdown. "We forgot it!" he squealed, smacking a hand to his forehead. "We included it in the introduction but left it out—"

"No, you didn't," I interjected. "Look on page sixty-two and again on page one-fifteen. You've also summarized it in the last section on remedies."

"My head is spinning," the other lawyer muttered, rubbing his temples.

Martin looked like he was about to collapse. They flipped through pages feverishly, checking my references until the tension broke into a collective sigh of relief.

"We're done," the younger lawyer said. "We did it."

Martin stood, his face lighting up. "Brooklyn did it." He swung around the desk, grabbed my face, and kissed me. "You saved our over-entitled asses."

"You're Superwoman, Captain Marvel, Wonder Woman, and the Scarlet Witch all combined," Martin's colleague chimed in, reaching for me in a bold move to replicate the moment.

"You'd better not even think about it," Martin interjected, and laughter erupted among us, fueled by exhaustion and sleep deprivation.

We made our way down toward the bay, and as the sun began to rise, instead of throwing quarters, we stopped at an ATM. Martin pulled out a stack of cash, handing out one-hundred-dollar bills to every homeless person we passed.

Ford was already awake, standing on the porch, peering into the thick fog. His hands were buried deep in his pockets and his knapsack rested against his leg. As I emerged from the house, he picked it up. Poor kid. In all this time, I'd never seen him cry. What he must be holding inside would floor an elephant. We walked in silence, neither of us looking at the other. I wished I could say something helpful to him, but here, I had no words. Killing someone never leaves your gut; it holds a silence that haunts you and refuses to let you forget.

It wasn't long before we came across a body dump. The stench hit first—sweet and sour, death rotting beneath frost. I covered Ford's eyes with a hand I couldn't stop shaking. "Don't look," I whispered, like that ever worked. He gagged anyway. So did I. I took pictures with the mechanical motion of someone who's seen too much and still feels like she hasn't done enough. Every corpse is someone's story unspoken, and I couldn't help but think—someday, someone might walk past me like this.

Soon, we were coming across bodies lying on the side of the road. Decomposition was so bad on some of them that it was hard to tell if they'd expired of natural causes or were murdered.

"You need to let me look at them," Ford said, refusing to shield his eyes when the bodies of five men were lined up in the dirt alongside the interstate. They'd been shot in the head.

"This is nothing a guest of the United States should see," I quipped, trying to discourage him. "You need to understand, the world shouldn't be like this."

"One, I'm a citizen, only raised in Ireland. Two, the world is like this. I need to prepare myself."

"Think you're that wise, hmm?"

"My Dai prepared me. He and Mum knew that sometimes, the world gets shaken. He always said we have to choose our footprints with care."

Ford seemed to have sprouted up a foot since our journey together began. Soon, he'd be taller than me. I tore out the hem of his old jeans so that they'd cover his ankles. He laughed at me doing *mam work*. He rarely spoke of his mother, and I was afraid to ask if his father was still alive. I didn't want to cause him any further pain. The few glimpses he gave me into his previous life were of a solid family that loved him.

"You know I'm going to Fargo. Once I find Martin, we may stay there. Ford, you're welcome to stay with me. Not just for a while—for good." I paused to see if he reacted. His features pulled in with internal thought, and he blinked several times but didn't look at me. "But, if you have family, maybe the place your mother was heading. Me and Martin will see to it that you get there."

He cleared his throat, stared at the ground, and glanced at me several times before exhaling a frosty breath. Rubbing his palms together, he opened cupped hands as if releasing excruciating memories. One hand touched his chest as he took calming breaths.

"I'm not sorry," he said. His voice was the sound of something breaking inside a box sealed tight. "I'm not sorry I killed him." He glanced at me, watching to see how I would respond.

"Kid, you'll find no judgment here."

Then, he said, "Washington D.C." His story flowed with words he'd guarded and protected for a long time. "My Dai was Ambassador to Ireland and later taught at a university in Dublin. We lived there for the last eight years, hence the accent. When Dai got a job back in the States, Mum took me to see the Portland Trail Blazers. That's when all this happened. Dai was sending a military plane for us. It never arrived. After we lost contact with D.C., Mum and I decided to go it alone. Anything was better than waiting. She'd heard not to take the bus, so we hired a driver to take the northern route where Mum thought we'd encounter less trouble—fewer people. He's the one that she had to kill." His voice broke, and his eyes fluttered with unpleasant memories. "Mum said to keep my identity a secret. I could be held hostage and Dai blackmailed to get me back safe. Mum taught me a lot: to breathe when I'm scared, to hide rather than fight, to battle if there's no choice. Mostly to stay silent. I wish I'd listened to her. Shhhhh. Shhhhh."

"Don't I know that story," I mused. I thought of all the quiet I'd swallowed in my life. All the things I'd buried just to keep going. He was learning too young what it meant to carry silence like a wound.

"I know my Dai," he said, firmly nodding. "He'll find me."

"It's a big country, Ford."

"How many Black teenagers with an Irish brogue do you know? He'll find me."

"Hence," I answered, then rapped his shoulder. "You just aged yourself a year."

He grinned and punched my arm. "Besides, we're underdogs. We try harder."

He was an interesting kid, one who had just lied to me. Staring down the long, straight freeway, the flat North Dakota plains offered few hiding places. We settled in for the night behind a thirty-foot fiberglass lumberjack abandoned under a freeway bridge. I stayed awake until he fell asleep, watching over him and wondering about the military plane. I guess he didn't lie to me as much as not tell me how his father rated a military aircraft. I tried not to overthink it but couldn't discount it either. Not until I knew exactly who he was.

The sun woke me and our journey continued as we plodded toward Fargo, getting to know each other one story at a time and taking death with us as an unwelcome companion.

Day after day, we braved the icy wind, slipping through snowdrifts that clawed at our ankles like hands trying to drag us under. The cold wasn't just a temperature anymore—it was a personality, cruel and persistent. My body still moved, but my mind was going quiet in places, like lights dimming in a house no one could afford to heat. One silver lining: fewer motorcycles. But even that didn't feel like luck—just one less kind of danger. Ford trudged beside me, face chapped raw. I was scared of what we were becoming—just flesh and will, strung together by fear and some lingering shred of getting to the person we loved.

We made the most of it, walking as far as possible before seeking shelter when darkness fell. Only fuel, cargo trucks, and the occasional semi seemed to venture out. We ducked into a ditch as a convoy of them passed in either direction. I noticed the drivers waved at each other. It could have been a solidarity gesture between people doing the same type job. But something suggested to me a familiarity of workers going to and coming from the same place.

My jeans hung loosely on my frame, and Ford wasn't faring much better. I had to find him more food. We managed to stay hydrated by melting snow and the occasional pond if it wasn't too far from the highway. Chewing beef jerky was getting old and not getting us the calories we needed. Fewer exits had traders, forcing us to trek a few miles into towns.

Once, we encountered a local militia that ordered us to leave. Another time, an elderly couple, Ben and Diane, who ran the Bendi Café like the world hadn't ended. They fed us real food and let us sleep in warmth, as if it were nothing. But it *was* something. I kept waking up, heart hammering, waiting for the price. When they asked for nothing, just smiled and handed us food for the road, I felt something awful churn inside me—like grief, like guilt. Kindness was almost unbearable now. It reminded me of what we'd lost. I left two hundred dollars on the counter not because I thought it mattered, but because I needed to believe I was still someone who paid what she owed.

The most eerie find was a roadside town left behind like a shed skin—restaurant, gas station, store, even a few houses, all quiet as a graveyard. Mold bloomed on untouched breakfast plates. Milk curdled in refrigerators marked with dates from two months back. There were no signs of struggle, no smashed doors, no blood. Just absence. No pets. No people. I stood in the center of it all and felt something cold claw into my chest—not fear of death, exactly, but fear that one day *we* would vanish like this, with no record of who we were or what we tried to be.

We marched on with our stalwart companion, the silence of dread.

One of the colder nights, we curled against a roll of hay, clinging to the tiny flame Ford sparked to warm our hands. Near dawn, something nudged me. I opened my eyes to a blinding sun—and emptiness. Ford was gone. Then came the shotgun's clack.

I didn't think. My body surged upright, knife in hand before my mind caught up. I grabbed the nearest boy by the neck, blade pressed to skin. I felt my hand shaking and couldn't stop it. The world had gone full red—terror and rage and the kind of pain that scrapes bone.

Seven men. Four guns. Four women behind them. And Ford, held like some bargaining chip in a war I didn't even understand. I couldn't breathe. I couldn't think. I just wanted him back.

"Let my son go," a tall man with a handlebar mustache said, pointing at the teenager I had in a headlock.

You first," I said, eyes on the man holding Ford. My voice sounded distant, like it belonged to someone braver than me.

The man huffed, icy breath frosting the air. Another put a shotgun against Ford's head.

Venom rose in my chest, along with panic and terror. I started shouting—not strategy, not reason, just helpless truth wrapped in fury and exhaustion. "What the hell do you get from just killing people out here?" I shoved the teenage boy toward them, but they held onto Ford. "It's not like we have anything. We're frozen and starved and exhausted and you want to waste a bullet on us." I pointed down the line at them. "Are you even human anymore?"

The shotgun lowered from Ford's head, but they held on to him. "Who are you a part of and where are you headed?" the Mustache asked.

I hesitated, knowing better than to reveal our true stories but needing to make this believable. "Nobody. We're not part of any army, militia, or government. We're just passing through, trying to get to where we have family in Minnesota. We're trying to get to the people who love us."

"Sounds like a lie to me." The man raised the rifle and pointed at me.

"Wait!" I cried, my voice splintering as I locked eyes with a silver-haired woman standing behind the men. Something in me—older than fear, older than grief—rose up like a wave. "I invoke the responsibility of the mother." My knees trembled, but I stood tall. "I charge you, Woman, with this child's care. He's just a boy following a woman with no map and no hope. You keep him whole 'cause I don't believe you can kill an innocent and sleep easy."

Mustache aimed.

"You don't have to be like this. I know what's been done to you. I've seen it walking across this country. You don't have to be this. You could organize, make pacts with like-minded people. I'll give you a name: the Sharps from Park City, talk to them. Postman Axel can put you in touch. With a little help, they could get their dairy farm up and going again. And Maria and Dan from California can help with computers, an Army Ranger who cuts hair in Butte. He'll have skills. You might try going to the library or post office." My voice trembled. Breath panted. I heard the scrape of the hammer being pulled back and closed my eyes, squeezing out tears that skipped down my icy cheeks.

Ford jerked loose and leaped for me, wrapping his arms tight around my waist. "Mother," he cried, holding on to me tightly.

The silver-haired woman stepped through the men, extending a hand to lower Mustache's rifle. She stared at me, eyes narrowing. "Ours have been killed by trust, slaughtered by compassion, murdered by mercy." Studying the earth at our feet, she contemplated for what seemed like an eternity. "Let them go," she said to the men. "Leave the backpacks," she told me. "And the knife." She looked up at the sky. "Big storm coming. If you live, don't ever come this way again."

Three of the men escorted us to the freeway, turning up their collars as a brisk, snowy breeze whipped around us. Mustache shouldered the shotgun and pursed his lips as he weighed Ford and me. I hoped he would obey his matriarch.

"I'd have given you a quick death," he said. "Better than what you're suffering. Better than what you're going toward."

The words stuck to my ribs like frostbite. I didn't know whether it was a threat or a mercy. I didn't look back. I grabbed Ford's hand and ran like hell, lungs burning, the road stretching endlessly toward something—anything—that wasn't this.

Unencumbered by the backpack, we made better time. They got some good stuff, including Ford's ragged Portland Trail Blazer tee shirt, which he'd only taken off to put on the wool underwear. He was pretty bummed. Turns out it was the last thing his parents gave him when they surprised him with the trip to Portland. He knew his Dad would recognize that shirt even if he was identifying a body, so he seldom took it off. It made me want to cry as he told me his reasoning.

"Dai would recognize me even if I were bones," he said with that strange calm kids sometimes get, the kind that makes your skin prickle. "*Gnosis* as Father Sweeny lectured in his Tuesday morning catechism,"

Yes, gnosis—sacred knowing. *Martin,* I thought. *Would you recognize my bones?* The thought clutched at something beneath my ribs, some quiet, feral longing to be known—not alive, not beautiful, not victorious. Just known. Just... remembered.

I carried anything worth anything in my innermost vest, including the theatrical makeup. Still, I was keenly aware that the knife had been my final weapon. We were getting closer to Fargo, but we still had to be careful. In Bismarck, I spent a ridiculous five hundred dollars getting us minimal supplies to fit in one small backpack but wasn't able to get any kind of weapon. Even hunting knives required Regency I.D.s. I bought a mid-sized wrench, telling the store merchant I had plumbing issues.

Fewer people took cash. They only wanted Regency script. I wondered if we were in the heart of the Regency and I'd made a mistake not turning around when I realized I was on Interstate 94. My phone still didn't work and even if it had, the solar battery had been in the backpack. *Something happens on 94. People never return.*

Breaking into a boarded-up garage on the outskirts of Jamestown, we found a vending machine with a few packets of peanuts and a candy bar. We split a two-year old soda left in a non-working refrigerator. The sugar hit me like a drug, a memory detonated behind my teeth. For half a second, I wasn't in a garage with broken vending glass—I was in Dolores Park, sun on my cheeks, Martin handing me a Coke as if it were a love letter. I nearly laughed. Or maybe sobbed. Ford made a face and grinned.

We huddled together to nap near the rear door in case we had to make a fast escape. Scavenging was common, and we often heard looters on nights when we stayed in towns. Most boarded-up buildings had already been vandalized. We picked the most damaged structures, hoping they would draw less attention. *Something happens on 94. People never return.*

"Do you hear that?" he asked and cocked his head toward a cracked window.

I turned an ear toward the distance. Nothing but the whistling wind. "What?"

"A hum."

"Like a song?" I asked, wondering if they'd gotten the Madonna going again, and she was singing hymns to the faithful.

"No, a drone, like a machine."

I listened, but his hearing was much better than mine and had the advantage of youth. "We need to watch our footprints, as your dad says." I explained to him how we'd travel only at dawn and dusk, with me walking several hundred feet ahead. He was to dive for cover if anyone got me. "If you see anybody, even a single person, we hide. Understand?"

He nodded, but I could see the hesitation in his expression.

Within a day, I could hear the sound, too. It wasn't so much a drone as a conglomerate of sounds merging into one, like a city or activity in a concert or stadium—humanity. We weren't close enough for it to be Fargo, and I sure didn't want the unexpected to waylay us after everything we'd been through. We'd have to mind our footprints until whatever was out there showed itself.

Early the following day, four watchtowers emerged on the horizon. At first, they looked like insect legs. Four towers. Four harbingers. The closer we got, it was clear the massive structure blocked the freeway. I remembered how Martin once described evil—not loud, not fire and brimstone, but patient, architectural. This wasn't a prison. It was a cathedral of control. I tasted bile and something else—grief, maybe. For what the world had chosen to become. For how many had helped build it.

I blinked several times, recalling the last time I'd been able to bring up a map on my phone. Spiritwood. A post office. A restaurant. An energy plant! My internal sight jumped to another drawing. Scrying the enormity. Thirty-three towers. An intricate maze of rooms, all connected by a cross-shaped hallway as large as lanes of an interstate. Malarkey! I was staring at the Plank! Of course, they picked Spiritwood. With its energy plant, they could give themselves whatever they needed to support the Madonna and Satan analogs.

The enormity of it was mind-boggling. They'd built out from the energy plant across the freeway and another quarter mile on the other side. I counted four towers again. They were still building, but knowing that captives were sent here, they hadn't finished enough of it to act as much of a prison.

"How do we get around it?" Ford asked.

I bit my bottom lip, my mind tracing a path on the architectural plans. "We don't," I replied. "We go through."

Ford smacked a hand on his forehead. I gave him the wrench that he tucked in his rear pocket.

In my mind, I calculated the size from the plans of the Plank to the structure in front of me. It was ginormous. Housing was built near the Spiritwood Post Office so their employees could walk to work. Hundreds of rooms had no names on the plan. Is that where they imprisoned people? Other areas had massive electrical running from them... Workshops for their abominations? This finished building could easily hold five to six thousand people. This one, maybe a thousand, and that might work for me. I was a wanted criminal. Even with the half-drawing they had, someone could recognize me, but they weren't looking for a woman and a child. We could walk right down the center of it and never be noticed. It would take luck, deception, cunning, and nerve. I looked over at Ford. Yeah, we had that.

I drew out the plan in the dirt and reviewed it with the kid, making him repeat it to me. When he had it solidly in his memory, we waited for morning. "The problem with big is it's porous, busy, and filled with people who function only when supervised," Martin told me the second time I interviewed him. "That's why I date small—uh, invest in small, self-contained companies." I'd thought, at the time, that he was a cute peddler of unsolicited advice that I'd never waste time dating. I hadn't realized it, but I was lost then, mesmerized by a gaze that studied more than observed and a titillating grin that pushed up into his left cheek, holding in place as if captured by thoughts he desperately wanted to speak. Now, I couldn't help thinking of his handwriting on those Plank plans.

Ford and I left the highway, cutting through a field until we reached a train track. This led us to the rear of a ten-story building that had been labeled *Housing* on the Plank plans. Spiritwood was a tiny community. Plank needed a place to house workers. The big shots, they got houses. Pretty nice ones too, built around several newly paved cul-de-sacs off the main road. If they stuck to their plans, this area would eventually be surrounded by a ten-foot wall and twenty-nine more towers. Their lack of planning was our advantage.

Watching until a man left a white, two-story cottage, we climbed in through a rear window. After making sure the rest of the house was empty, we cooked eggs, bacon, and buttered toast, feeding our faces like it was our last meal. Ford showered while I stood guard, and then I took a shower as our clothes washed and dried.

Finding my first mirror since Butte, I was wide-eyed and stunned when I saw my reflection. It wasn't the gaunt cheeks, countable ribs, or bony shoulders that jarred me. It was the hair that undid me—silver where auburn used to catch the shadows. My voice caught in my throat: "Silver hair." I kept repeating to myself as I showered, as if repetition might rewrite reality. I'd forgotten how fast time travels when you're not looking at yourself. I didn't look like Sulis. I looked like someone Sulis might have mourned. Or buried.

We found a lab coat that made me work-presentable and allowed me to keep my pocketed clothing hidden underneath. Using the theatrical makeup, I covered my scar. Ford managed in one of the man's pullover sweaters by pushing up the sleeves. While waiting for our clothes to dry, I opened the man's computer and checked the Regency website. Silly boy taped his password to the printer. My picture hadn't been updated, but I was now number two on the most wanted right behind Martin. Probably upgraded because I'd told them I had Boxy. No mention of Ford, so either Phillip and Bren hadn't gotten a good enough look at him, or they thought he was one of the bikers gone rogue with a grudge against scorpion guy. Not their business. I couldn't help but chuckle at their lack of compassion for a fellow compatriot.

An AH icon labeled "PlanK" caught my attention. It wasn't Plank, but Plan K. I suppose some smashed it together for easier pronunciation. The log-in page opened to the fully spelled words: Plan Kaleidoscope, an Al Hast Industry Paradigm. The username was already typed in, and I logged in with the same password. Looking through the options, I found *Car Service* and booked a town car with no driver to be waiting for us at the east exit. I was beginning to like the confidence of these Regency galoots. No one like me could ever be a real threat to them. Pfffff.

"Hey," Ford yelled from the next room. "You just got executed!"

I rushed to find him glued to a news report about the capture of the notorious fugitive, Sulis. An excitable news reporter recounted my crimes, the usual list, plus the death of her dear colleague, Brace Benton, in an explosion at a Regency think tank. I rolled my eyes at that one, then gasped as footage of a scaffold appeared, revealing a woman standing with a noose around her neck. Her long red hair obscured much of her face, and she swayed as if drugged. Just as I processed this, the floor beneath her gave way. Ford and I stood in stunned silence, mouths agape. Perhaps it was us who were overconfident.

It wasn't lost on me that the execution of that poor woman was to draw out Martin. If he believed I'd been captured and executed, what would that do to him? He'd be frantic about Boxy, worried it fell into their hands. Worst of all, he'd feel guilty to think I'd died on a journey he'd initiated. They were trying to force him into making a mistake. We were so close to Fargo. We'd be there in less than an hour if I could get us safely into that car.

Part One: We mingled in the lunchroom until we spotted a silver-haired woman. The cafeteria had its own entrance, separate from the main building. We blended in with the crowd, acting as if we belonged. Then, Ford put his former life of crime to use. He jostled our backpack, bumping into a white-haired woman who, he later remarked, resembled me—"a haggard, overworked, sour puss."

"What is a child doing here?" she snapped.

I shot her a snooty scowl and whispered, "Shut up, you moron. That's Phillip Javon's kid. He gets the tour today, so think of it as your ass working for him."

Her fearful expression was electrified as she turned away like wildfire and rejoined the food line.

"Do you have it?" I whispered to Ford.

Part Two: We walk straight through PlanK. Ford slipped me the woman's key card, and we entered the main building. The long corridor stretched, leading straight through to the east exit. I walked swiftly and authoritatively, hoping to reach the other side of the PlanK within half an hour. I kept a hand on Ford's shoulder as if steering him along, and he managed to maintain a stiff, spoiled-kid-of-a-big-shot demeanor. With Lynn Fuson's

I.D. in hand, we breezed past locked doors and turnstiles, drawing little more than cursory glances from those around us.

I took in everything as we moved: banks of computers blinking and whirring, people focused intently on their screens with heads down. Lines of servers filled a room the size of a basketball court, and smaller conference rooms were lined with glass windows, whiteboards scrawled with mathematical formulas visible within. It felt as if everyone and everything had to remain in view at all times.

Ahead, I spotted the exit three turnstiles away, a sleek black town car waiting just outside. The crowd in front of us began to part, shifting right and left. No! The glass walls allowed me to see through to the end of the building, but a room obstructed our path. I swallowed hard, my mouth dry, my mind racing for a solution. Suddenly, the room took on a strange hue. What had been clear glass now shimmered with a plum hue.

A man and woman in lab coats paused before the glass, taking notes on their clipboards. Beyond them, I saw two women, their hair wild and tangled, shoulders slumped, arms clutching their chests, mouths hanging open. The lab-coated pair followed the dazed women as they moved out of sight.

I quickly directed Ford towards a nearby conference room, snatching a clipboard from a wall rack and pretending to study it intently. At the bottom of the paper was Martin's handwriting again—this time a signature. It wasn't his, but Al Hast's. Confusion snapped at my thoughts as I examined it closely; it was unmistakably Martin's style. The way he looped the L and S at the ends was distinctly his.

"Snag?' Ford asked.

"A whopper," I muttered, observing the peculiar room as the lighting transformed into a warm cinnamon glow, shimmering like water. Figures devoid of life drifted past, their gazes fixed on something connected to the glass wall. I leaned as far as I could without drawing attention, straining to glimpse the edge of the ballroom-sized space. The glass gradually cleared, revealing the east entrance. That room was filled with people staggering in queues and pausing to interact with what appeared to be some kind of display attached to the glass wall. Mirrors. I had no clue what sort of devilry the Regency was up to, but we had to find a way around this chamber and reach that exit on the other side.

Ford played with a magic marker, capping and uncapping it as he watched me pace the length of the room.

"Okay," I said. "It's big, but we walk around it, pretend we're studying the zombie people inside. I might talk to you like I'm giving you a tour. You act interested."

He was coloring in the words *SULIS LIVES!!!* on the conference room table. "Let's hit it." He snapped the marker closed and put three of them in his pocket.

We returned to the hallway, fighting a rush of bodies, probably a lunch shift change, and continued toward the glass wall while I pretended to check the clipboard. A sliding door with a keycard slot was directly in front of us, and now that I was closer, I could see a matching one directly across the room. I would have loved to run it, but I had no idea what they were doing to those people inside. "Ford," I said. "Keep your earplugs handy."

Across the top of the door, the word Kaleidoscope was stenciled in bold block letters. We paused briefly at the glass as it slowly tinted a saffron gold. I counted twelve lab coats outside the room, seemingly monitoring specific individuals. I gestured animatedly as if explaining something to Ford. Just then, Dunce shuffled past—the biker from Butte whom Ace and I had knocked out. I guess he'd never been able to convince his captors that he was someone other than the I.D. we planted on him. A victim of his own people.

Inside, at least three hundred people lumbered from side to side, lost in this labyrinth of mirrors. Circular devices on the ceiling projected starry beams to receivers atop the mirrors. Some individuals engaged in quiet conversations with their reflections, while others wept as if pleading for forgiveness from a silent judge. Many wore expressions of fear or resignation, their eyes sunken and lips chapped, giving them a spectral appearance. Most clasped their trembling hands close to their chests. Sensing Ford's unease, I placed a reassuring hand on his shoulder to steady him.

"I want to cross myself," he whispered.

We both jumped as a man pushed his face against the glass, staring directly into my eyes. Two lab coats passed behind us and laughed. "They do that sometimes," one of them said. "Probably hasn't been in there long."

I locked eyes with the man as he cautiously lifted his hand and brushed back his longish hair to reveal an ear. The barber! It was Jake, the man who had shaved my head. He turned slightly, pointing to an earplug. I nodded once to show I recognized him. I had to get him out of there. Glancing at the egress, I realized we were still too far away, and any attempt to let him out would attract the attention of the other lab coats. Using hand signals, I indicated the escape route across the room and gestured that I'd meet him there. His eyes blinked, confirming that he understood.

I expelled a puff, realizing I'd not been breathing. Ford glanced up at me, a worried expression. "It's okay," I said. "He saved my life, and now, we're going to save his."

"Better be more concerned about saving ours," he murmured urgently, motioning with his head.

On the north side of the glassed-in room, Phillip and Bren gathered with a half dozen men in military uniforms. Bren appeared to be explaining what was happening to the people inside. She gestured theatrically and turned over to Phillip, who pointed to his arm in a sling and chuckled. Dixie Roman was with them as well. Moping at the rear, part of Dixie's forehead was bandaged, and his cheek shined like it was healing from a burn. His mouth downturned in a frown, and his arms crossed over his chest. He stared at the ceiling as if bored. They moved along the glass and would turn the corner toward us within seconds.

"Put in your earplugs," I blurted and shot my hand deep in a pocket for mine. Letting the white coat drop to the floor, I grabbed the backpack and slung it against the opposite wall. "In," I mouthed the words.

He nodded.

"Act like them," I said close to his ear, then opened the entrance and pushed him ahead of me.

We joined the millipede-like march, trailing along like lobotomized convalescents. The sickening smell of unwashed humans mingled with the acrid scents of vomit and excrement. Ford's head jerked once, and I instinctively touched his arm. He flinched and shot me a sidelong glance, signaling that he was okay. The mirrors didn't reflect; instead, they revealed dark waves pulsing from an umbratic center. Boxy took the opportunity to give me the worst shock yet. Malarkey, I thought, willing the words to the little chiclet. Not now. No way. Boxy shocked me again. Way.

I glanced through the narrow gap between the mirrors. The Regency group was about twenty feet away. Lifting my sweater and all of the vests, I fumbled with the Velcro until Boxy dropped into my palm. Ford scowled at me, his face tinged with alarm. Giving him a firm nod, I signaled him to focus on the front. Holding the device in my hand, it transformed into a translucent mourning dove and ascended toward the ceiling. I watched it in the reflection of the glass as it flitted among the transmitters. Okay, Hotshot. Do your stuff. I hoped it would wait until we reached the other doorway before creating mayhem.

As the Regency group got closer, I made out that they clustered around a black-haired man with a full goatee wearing a Ron Elwood wool suit, the most expensive clothing in the world, easily a sixty-thousand-dollar getup. I'd interviewed Elwood once at a San Francisco fashion show, and his trademark fennec fox on the lapel was unmistakable. Bren smiled like a debutant, her gaze always on him. Phillip stood straighter, sporting a frozen, closed-mouth grin. I couldn't see Dixie, so I suspected he hung back, either unhappy for not being the center of attention or afraid of a man more powerful than himself. Bren stroked the man's arm as they approached, and Phillip chuckled at something he said. They wanted to impress this customer. All of the lab coats studying the zombies had disappeared. Likely intimidated by Mr. Moneybags. I lowered my head, hoping this military bunch was more interested in the room's function than its victims.

They paused at two doors across from us marked Nest and Mecca. Bren opened a curtained window next to Nest, and I nearly vomited. The room was tiny, more like a cramped hallway. Children were crammed together as if stuffed into a box. Some appeared starved, with dark circles under their eyes, dressed in ragged clothes, most barefoot. They pressed their faces against the window, their expressions a mix of desperation and fear, while a few sobbed for help. My breath caught as one girl with stringy blond hair reached out her hand, begging—Odette Wallace. Bren pointed out a sign: "When compliant, feed and transfer to Mecca." Oh, you vile woman, I thought. How you've convinced yourself that you are bestowing mercy.

I glanced sideways at Ford; his expression mirrored my horror. Shifting uneasily, I kept my head bowed, eyes averted, when a starry beam jolted the receiver. I gasped, struggling to remain still. The mirror revealed Martin, his face downcast, but his eyes tilted upward, giving him a cruel and deranged expression. Surrounding him was a writhing mass of demons—oversized, unblinking eyes, sharp teeth, hairless and shriveled.

Focusing on my breathing, I shivered as they formed a kaleidoscope of terror; snakes slithering, spiders skittering, a claw bursting from the earth. The demons grinned and cackled, their bodies twisting grotesquely into insects. Horrific scenes flashed before me—executions by guillotine, skeletal, starved children, monsters devouring the body parts of terrified living victims. All so vivid, so real, that I felt the urge to scream. And there, at the center of it all, was Martin—their Satan. Martin's face was created as the Devil!

The image raised its arm and beaconed me. A bleak smile stretched unnaturally across its face, depressive eyes, dreary but dangerous, widening as the black pupils blinked like a reptile. Everything that I cherished about Martin twisted into something sinister and menacing. Sweat dripped down my face and back, and my breath came in ragged gasps. Muscles weakening with each step, I feared my knees would buckle. Around

Martin, the demons hissed and contorted as he undulated in a kaleidoscopic haze. Even without the insidious echoes of brainwashing, the sight was one of the most horrifying things I had ever witnessed. Then, I was in the mirror. Martin's hands, around my neck, choked me. My skin rotted and decayed as rats nibbled at my toes and snakes sank fangs into my thighs. With a brutal gesture, Martin ripped off my arm, tossing it into his hoard of demons, who eagerly devoured my flesh. An abhorrent sensation coursed through me as I instinctively shook off what felt like an addition to the treacherous grip of Regency brainwashing.

Martin's face twisted in agony as his body erupted into a pastel landscape, morphing into a glimmering Madonna Bren, emerging as the embodiment of the destroyer of evil. I couldn't help but wonder how many times these people had walked this line, witnessing these horrific images replayed endlessly. Without earplugs, the relentless barrage must be a waking nightmare. It was no surprise they resembled the living dead. They were cattle, test subjects in a twisted experiment. All who boarded the red buses had met this grim fate. *Something happens on 94. People never return.*

The Regency group nearly passed us, and I fought the urge to slam against the window, hoping the glass would shatter on those ruthless criminals. I especially wanted another punch at Bren. Boxy seemed to share my sentiment, unleashing a surge of blue rays that struck the mirror's receivers. Several of them popped and smoked, sending sparks into the air. As the last few military thugs moved on, I dared to glance at Boxy, who was shooting beams at the ceiling's transmitters.

Jake was by the door, casting furtive glances to gauge how close we were to him. Suddenly, a cacophony of shattering glass erupted as several mirrors cracked and fell to the floor. I pushed Ford past lost souls who were bewildered and didn't know what to do. Many began wailing and poking at the remnants of the mirrors, desperately trying to retrieve their lost reflections. I just hoped their groans wouldn't carry outside.

"Move," I barked at Ford, gesturing toward the exit. I shoved people aside, cutting through the middle of the room to get to the other side and finally arriving at the barber. I smacked the key into the open slot, and the door slid open with a quiet hiss. Turning to push Ford ahead of me, I froze—he wasn't there.

"Ford!" I screamed. Looking back, two of the zombies had hold of him. A woman clawed at his face as he struggled with her. I charged back, knocking her down as Ford lost his balance and fell. She grabbed onto me, and I punched her until she released her grip. Ford was kicking a man who rolled onto the floor with him. I stomped his arm as Ford rolled away. "Come on!" I screamed.

Ford didn't follow me. Both his hands clutched the edges of a shattered mirror, and he kept repeating the word, *Mother*. His earplugs had been torn out in the struggle.

Panicking, I ran back to him, pulled out my earplugs, and jammed them into his ears. Grabbing his arm, I dragged him a few feet, but he flailed wildly and screamed, "My mother is here! I can't leave her! Let me go!" He possessed the strength of youth, and I was no match for him, receiving a punch on the cheek and a kick on the shins as I pulled him. Jake rushed back in and caught Ford at the waist, hoisting him over his shoulder. We dashed to the exit, where Jake had wedged a couch into the door frame to hold it open. We crawled over, and I looked back only to see a military goon pointing at me. Bren and Phillip's enraged expressions gave way to shouts. I pulled the wrench out of Ford's rear pocket and threw it into a mirror, causing one after the other to shatter. As I thought—they were linked.

The distraught zombies freaked as more mirrors shattered. They flooded the hall, making groaning sounds and waving their arms as if trying to shake off phantasms. We fled ahead of them, hoping they would cause enough distraction for us to escape. A few seemed to have regained their senses and ran with us, so I suspected Boxy had given them a ding, too. Having found his father amid the chaos, one man clutched him tightly as they ran, repeating, "Dad, Dad, Dad."

A horn blared outside as we pushed through the final door, bursting into the open air. Standing before us was a security guard, keys to the town car dangling in his hand, shock etched on his face as he stared over my shoulder at the chaos we had just escaped.

"What the—"

"I don't know either," I said, authoritatively. "But I've got to get this package to a safe place." Pointing at a struggling Ford still over Jake's shoulder.

His hand went to his sidearm. "You're not going anywhere until I see—"

"Are you questioning me?" I stepped to his side, allowing Jake to get Ford into the back seat. "I think you're needed inside," I said, snatching the keys in his hand.

He stepped toward the building and was trampled just as quickly as dozens of people made their escape. He reached out his hands to protect himself, fell, and covered his head as best he could. I leaned over and took his gun.

Throwing the keys to Jake who jumped into the driver's seat, I landed on top of Ford, tied in with the seatbelts and still struggling to get back to the image of his mother. The car swerved through the parking lot, dodging security cars that headed toward the building. Gunfire hit the vehicle, and we ducked down.

Boxy! "Wait!" I screamed. "We have to go back!" I turned to look out the back window and saw the little bird bouncing against the glass of the exit door. It could shoot its beams through walls, but it had some element of being corporeal. PlanK must have locked down all the exits.

"We have to go back!" I screamed.

"We can't!" Jake shouted, pointing at the watchtower where flashes of shots sparked.

"Open the skylight!" I stood up as soon as I could squeeze through an opening and aimed the gun. The car swerved to avoid gunfire. One shot, two—the glass door shattered but didn't break. I emptied the gun, and the glass splintered, then ducked down as the car crashed through a gated entry. Bouncing around and holding to the side of the skylight, I raised my hand as high as I could, then felt the sharp sting like a baseball caught without a glove. Boxy. Boxy was still a bird, and Ford tried to kick at it. "Need you to do what you do." I no sooner said it than a sharp blue beam shot into Ford and Jake.

Ford's eyes widened, frightened and unsure, but his struggle ceased. He looked at me, then down at his hands before covering his face as his disbelief at what had happened to him settled in. I slipped Boxy underneath my sweater as it folded into a resting square.

Jake floored the gas as we sped away. "They'll be chasing us soon."

"I agree," I said, over the whistling wind from bullet holes in the front window.

"I know a place." He sped along, getting as much speed as the town car could muster.

I held Ford's hand, unsure if he was okay. He couldn't speak and swayed side to side, his arms wrapped around himself. Untying the seatbelt knots, he fell over into my arms. I held him for the next hour. I whispered to him, nothing in particular, anything to fill the void he was falling into. I'd dragged him through hell. What if I couldn't bring him back?

We were close to Fargo, where I figured Jake was taking us. I was surprised when the car slowed. He pulled across the freeway to the opposite side and slowed to a crawl.

"We've got a flat. I'm going to drive over behind that patch of trees." He coughed, covering his mouth with a hand.

"Can't we keep going until we get to Fargo? Even on a flat?"

"Out of gas, too. They only fill these with a quarter tank in case someone tries to run." Jake coughed again. "Even the security cars, so they'll need time to fill up. That gives us a head start at—" He coughed a third time, this time spewing blood on the front window. The car jostled as it pulled off the road through a field of prairie grass and behind a wall of bare-limbed trees. We were well hidden from the freeway.

As we came to a halt, I jumped into the front seat to check on Jake. Blood covered his midsection. Throwing Ford the keys, I told him, "Check the trunk for a first aid kit."

Realizing the gravity of the situation, he didn't hesitate.

Jake fiddled with his front shirt pocket, tearing at it. "Listen. Listen."

"I'm going to lay you flat and put pressure on the wound, okay?"

He grabbed my arm and shook his head, still tearing at his shirt pocket with the other hand. "Listen."

I realized he did what I did. He had a secret pocket. I helped him rip it open, and a flash drive fell into my hand. I handed it to him, and he waved it off.

"Follow the interstate to Fargo. Take that," he pointed at the flash drive. "Remember this place. They'll come. Give me... military funeral." He licked his lips as his face turned a pallid blue.

"Nothing," Ford called out as he crawled into the back seat.

"You're a handful, young man," Jake said and managed a smile as he looked at Ford in the rearview mirror. "Think you could recheck the trunk? Might be a tire iron in there we can use."

Ford nodded and slid out of the car again. I realized he didn't want the kid to see him die.

"Fargo, Army at the airport," he said again, tapping my hand holding the flash drive. "Give it to the President. No one else to trust... the President." A bloody finger tapped the flash drive. "Traitors."

Every muscle chimed alert, looking down at the flash drive. "How... how do I find the Pres..."

His cheek rested against the headrest, eyes fixed. He was gone.

I locked the doors and said a prayer with Ford. It was hard leaving him there. Jake, the barber, was clearly more than a barber. I wondered if there were other spies within the Regency. I thought about the bearded man who'd warned me about the red buses. Were they part of the U.S. Army? A local militia? A rag-tag resistance? I wondered if they knew each other. Did they know of the Limeys and Postman Axel? Others, like the terrorized family who almost killed me, appeared to know nothing. There must be a way to connect them all, I thought. Get them working together. From what I'd seen of the Regency, they could be knuckleheads who underestimated little people like me. They had flash, power, and money behind them, but they could be defeated. I wondered what part Martin was playing. As my stomach began to growl for food, I wondered why a soldier wasn't given the job he'd assigned me.

Three a.m.; Martin's hands rest on his hips as he stares into a fog bank that swallowed everything beyond the window. There is no view, only the swirling white mass blocking out the world. He nodded to himself, blew out a breath. Some silent verdict passed behind his eyes. Slipping behind him, I wrap my arms around his waist. He turns, strokes my cheek, and softly kisses me like he's memorizing me. I want to ask what was wrong. He has been distracted and moody for months, but I have been too lost in his touch. He lifts me, my legs circle him, and we hide behind that great white veil, wishing it would linger forever.

We had to be a few miles from Fargo, and within a shout of Martin was all I could think of. I'd get my answers then. He'd help me get to the President 'cause I sure didn't have any contacts on that front. We braced against the biting wind, snowflakes swirling around us and settling on our shoulders. With each step, we held on tightly to one another, slipping on the frozen road. Our parkas, gloves, and wool caps were stashed away in the backpack I'd had to abandon at the PlanK, leaving us only in our clothing over wool underwear. We huddled together as we forged ahead, taking one tentative step after another. Every step was blind faith. I told myself that whatever was happening at the PlanK would distract them. That maybe more people had made it out. But truthfully, I didn't know. All I had was the hope that someone would reach the true USA and tell their story.

Ahead, a sign caught my attention. Underneath Exit 342 hung a smaller blue panel that had once read *No Services*. The *No* had been struck out, and below new text painted in purple:

RedWater. RedWater Services. "We're going this way," I pointed to Ford, who shot me a koo-koo stare.

"Are you wired to the moon, Woman? Fargo is two hops away. Food, shelter, heat!"

I pulled him along, the sleeve of the sweater stretching as he stood still, but eventually, he followed. We were at a place called Fife, and there was absolutely nothing there. About a quarter mile off the exit, a mailbox with the number 9459. I motioned Ford over to me. "See that wide patch of snow in between all the trees? I'm pretty sure it's a road. Leading to a house."

"If it's not?"

"If it's not, we'll freeze to death anyway." We pulled ourselves along, following the tree line. Several hundred yards in, I saw a two-story house. I pointed out a barn at the side and shifted our path toward it. I wanted to watch the house for a bit. Make sure we weren't walking into a trap. Stamping through calf-deep snow, I opened a shed attached to the barn.

"The house, Woman, the house!" Ford shook his fists at me.

I held him back, hard as it was, watching the house while Ford glared at me. The sun closed in on the western horizon, and in an upstairs window appeared a lime-green, oscillating movement. *To light your way always.* A lava lamp. A signal in the dark that I hadn't been forgotten.

I pulled out keys from my innermost vest and found the card marked 9459. Grabbing Ford's collar, we sloshed toward the front door through deep snow, panting like racehorses. My stiff hands crammed the card into a slot as I shouted out every curse word I knew. They didn't work, but the key jolted open the door, and we fell into a heated hallway.

The house was empty. How I'd hoped to find Martin here. Warm air surged from the vents, and the kitchen was fully stocked. We munched down on cookies and crackers until I made him stop long enough for me to heat a frozen lasagna with fingers that barely worked

This house wasn't a fortress like the Bolinas house and lacked its prodigious security. What it did have was invisibility in the middle of a dense grove of trees, and maybe that was its power. Hidden. Waiting.

In the basement, I found a computer, and Boxy vibrated. I pulled it out, watching it open into a sphere and beep. A compartment shot out from the side of the desk revealing a thin, circular gizmo about half the size of an egg yolk. It looked like it was made from the same material as Boxy with a center indent. Both pieces settled into flat disks, and before I could position it over the slot, Boxy shot out of my fingers and into the space as if two magnets snapped together. The two components floated upward as one—sparkly and translucent—tumbling over themselves like a Möbius strip. They faded from copper to silver, then shifted into a virtual display hovering atop the physical monitor.

A text box popped up with the words: *Want to have some fun?*

That day, I learned everything that was happening and why, but I also realized I had more to fight with than just words.

~ FARGO ~

I started to type *Yes* to the fun question when footsteps padded down the stairs behind me. Munching on a bag of Cheetos, Ford pulled a rocker beside me. He pointed with an orange index finger. "Now that I'm warm, bathed, and not starving, you want to tell me what that thing you keep under your shirt is and what it shot me with?"

That thing lay on the desk before me, shaped like a silver dime, and he never even looked at it. He also didn't perceive the virtual overlay as it tightened to fit the physical computer. Since I still didn't know enough about his father or why Ford was withholding information about him, I decided to choose my words carefully. "Might be better if you don't know."

"It shot me like a poison dart gun, and then I was better. I want to know."

I leaned back, rocking his chair with my foot to irritate him. "Best I can tell, it's a kind of vaccine against the brainwashing. I learned something from that incident. We only need it once. When I ran back to get you, I pulled out my earplugs and pushed them in your ears. Might have been a stupid thing to do, as we could have both been lost. But the brainwashing didn't affect me. Hopefully, it won't ever affect you again either."

"You don't know that," he huffed. "Maybe it's as dangerous as that thing that got me in the zombie room."

"It helped us escape the PlanK."

"By making the zombies go cray-cray!" He smacked his forehead leaving a streak of orange crumbs as he stood and paced around me. "You're dangerous, Woman. You deal in blarney you don't understand," he snapped. "You ate the biscuit without knowing the ingredients."

And there it was. The truth I kept shoving down. I was bluffing with tech I barely comprehended, trusting a man I hadn't seen in months, praying the tools I held wouldn't betray me. Every win felt more like a borrowed miracle than a victory. I couldn't argue with him. He was right. But I had to believe. Boxy hadn't done me wrong yet. "I trust Martin."

"I don't know this man, Martin. He could be as bad or worse than these Regency gombeens."

"You're eating too much junk food. Have a nap, and we'll talk in the morning."

"Treating me like a babber again," he snarled, settled back down in the rocker, and wiped his forehead once he saw his reflection in the monitor.

"Martin has left us a good store of food and an excellent hiding place. Why would he do that if he didn't want to keep us safe?"

He crossed his arms, rolled his eyes, and rocked forward. "You learn anything from that," he pointed toward the computer.

A folder named RedWaterServices covered the text box I'd been previously looking at. It hadn't been there before. I glanced down at Boxy and covered it with my palm, sliding it behind a printer where Ford couldn't see it. "Let's open it."

He scooted his chair toward me as I clicked on the folder. "Open that one first," he said, pointing at a file. "The one called *Soldiers*."

Ten minutes later, he rocked his chair, holding tightly to the arms. "Quoting Father Sweeny, who refused to cuss, holy cow piss in a meadow of sour jellybeans."

We'd had just read how they planned to make invincible zombie soldiers. The file called them hyp-soldiers, created by a blend of brainwashing, mind fusion, hypnotism, mind control, physical abuse and a cocktail of drugs to kill any emotional connection to their actions. "By the time they build them back up into functioning soldiers, they could kill their mother and not care. Their only loyalty is to the Regency," I surmised. "Got any more complaints about Martin's antidote?"

"I'll have seconds, please." He leaned back and stared at the ceiling. "I remember, the mother they showed me wasn't mine," he said, voice barely above a whisper. "But I would have trampled a field of kittens to get to her." He blinked, looking away from me. "Why did I care so much? She was everything to me."

His face twisted, that memory branding him from the inside out—love, horror, grief, all crashing into one another. I didn't know what to say. I wanted to hug him. I wanted to hide from what he'd just admitted. They'd gone inside his mind. Softened him for betrayal. A slight jerk brought him back to himself, and he sniffed, wiping a hand over his face.

"Why don't you get some sleep," I told him. "I'll read the rest of these and let you know if there's anything useful." I took the Cheetos bag from him and grabbed a handful.

"I don't know if I want to know." He rose and headed toward the stairs, pausing at the bottom. "But my Dai would," he said, with some hesitation. "Especially the soldier part."

"That so." I tried not to sound too eager. Quiet, but I could feel his presence. Staring at me, weighing if he could trust me.

"We need to develop a way to fight them," he said, opening and closing his hand into a fist. "Me, I'd go for a glove that stuns them into submission like lightning hitting a tree."

"Good to have a plan."

"If the Regency should try to get their hands on me, you should KMA," he said.

I turned and looked at him.

"Kill Me Already," he counted out each word on his fingers.

"That's a bold statement for a twelve-year-old."

"Fourteen," he said. "You haven't figured out yet that kids who are small for their age are known for telling taller whoppers." He bit his bottom lip, squeezing his hands together in front of him. "But this is not a lie. They can never be allowed to turn me against him. Not ever. Not for anything. My Dai... He's the Secretary of Defense."

The air went cold. I blinked, searching his face, trying to find the joke. But there was no punchline, only a young man staring at me with eyes too hardened for his age. In an instant, the lines redrew—Ford was no longer just a rescued orphan with a sharp tongue. He was a bargaining chip. A target. A weapon. And I was the fool holding the trigger.

"Oh."

I realized I should have tapped the file called *Beginnings* to start as it opened with the words, *I, Martin Siriso.*

It hit me like ice water to the chest—Martin had written it all down. Every truth he hadn't trusted me with, all the schemes he was working to thwart. My fingers hovered over the keyboard, trembling. I tried to tell myself it was strategic omission, not betrayal. But the hollow in my stomach said otherwise. He'd known. He'd *always* known. And now the truth unfolded in front of me like a weapon I wasn't ready to hold.

The villains behind this nefarious plot were not a foreign government. We hadn't fallen victim to a civil war, nor had a string of unfortunate catastrophes plunged the country into chaos, paving the way for opportunistic despots. I stared at the screen, my breath catching on a sob I hadn't expected. These weren't monsters from a distant land. They looked like our neighbors, our professors, the people who waved from morning news broadcasts. Americans, Europeans, Brazilians, Russians, Chinese, Australians—greedy pendejos cloaked in civility. Power and money. Always money. How stupid to think it was ever about anything else. They were all investors in Al Hast

Industries, where Martin held a seat on the board of directors. The threat was corporate.

Holy cow piss in a meadow of sour jellybeans," I muttered, battling anxiety as I delved deeper into revelations about Martin. I slammed my hand on the desk and stared into the darkened glass, catching my own reflection. Did he aid these pendejos? What had Martin become? Or worse—what had he always been, behind that easy charm and soft voice?

Al Hast—the shadowy puppet master behind it all, Oklahoma-born, son of evangelical megachurch royalty—rose to power on a foundation built for him. His parents used their fortune to create Al Hast Industries, grooming him to lead. I remembered hearing his name over the years, though I couldn't picture him.

On paper, he looked like a savior. He funded scholarships, backed research, saved dying companies, and earned fierce loyalty from his workforce. The public saw a generous, forward-thinking man.

Then he decided he should rule the world.

Why a philanthropist turns tyrant, no one knows. Martin shed no sunshine on this matter. He only saw a series of actions that could only lead to one conclusion. Hast quietly recruited allies across critical sectors, taking over small firms, infiltrating school boards, town halls, and mayor's offices. Control equated to security and a predictable outcome. Eventually, they reached the national stage. Martin never named names, but it was clear: Hast's people were everywhere.

A decade ago, Hast tried to brand himself a global visionary, offering to train future presidents in his philosophy—a mix of autocracy, historical revisionism to educate the masses, and psychological manipulation to create reliance and loyalty in powerless populations. Both parties dismissed him as a crackpot but still took his checks, hinting at ambassadorships. That insult stuck. Hast didn't forgive.

He retaliated with blackmail and threats. Coercion followed. Join him, or be destroyed. It became a grinding political war—wins and losses piling up—but everything changed the day Martin introduced him to Phillip Javon.

I threw a book, in frustration more than anger. I'd never thrown a book before, much less at a man. Was this our first fight or our last? I grabbed my jacket and headed to the door.

"Don't you dare leave!" Martin called out after me.

"Why?" I shot back, defiance laced in my voice. "It's not like what I think matters."

He looked down, his eyes tracing the pattern of the carpet. "Because you don't have anybody else," he said quietly, and as if the words hung in the air, he looked up at me and added, "And neither do I."

Funny, I don't even remember what we were fighting about. I wondered if it was like that for Martin—introducing his wide-eyed genius to the worst person imaginable, blind to how it would all unravel. He'd backed Phillip heavily, and it paid off. But it was more than business. If Phillip was his son, Martin would never turn his back on him. And he would've done anything to get him away from Bren and Al Hast.

It all started with a video game.

Fight Like The Devil was Phillip's baby—a runaway hit that earned him his first million. With Martin's funding, he built a headset-free version that filled a room with sound and light, engaging players on a deep emotional level through subconscious cues—binaural beats that tapped emotions like a tuning fork.

Without Martin's knowledge, Hast induced Phillip to produce a game called *Kaleidoscope*—a darker, more dangerous evolution that put the characters on steroids by amplifying their mind-altering capabilities. Hast pushed Phillip into secretly using a team of psychologists, neuroscientists, AI developers, and rogue hackers to create a game that didn't just captivate—it rewired. More than addicting, it was a hypnotic seduction.

Players didn't realize they were being brainwashed. The game promised salvation, safety, love. A noble cause. They believed they were saving the world. Hast included his work force, pumped subliminal messages into the homes and offices, laced the water supply at the PlanK with a mild version of the hyp-soldier formula, and blanketed the web with mirror sites spreading the same mind tricks. A portal on those sites allowed the user to get answers and advice to their deepest questions.

The result? A growing cult obsessed with a digital prophet: Madonna.

Hast knew the power of performative religion. Raise the fear of Armageddon, and people start searching for a savior. He didn't need politicians anymore. He manufactured chaos—blackouts, poisoned water, downed networks—and then sent in his own companies to *save* the towns. His companies stayed. They took over. The people became dependent. And once he'd tested his method in enough small towns, he scaled up.

Martin fought back through RedWater Services, a covert wing of his company posing as an outdoor gear manufacturer. RedWater infiltrated Hast's network, planting agents and gathering intel for the Department of Justice. My backpack, hoodie, even the parka—they all came from RedWater. Gear for spies.

But Hast caught on. By the time Martin saw the big picture, it was too late. Hast struck the major cities. Martin thought he had years. He didn't.

The East Coast and South fell into chaos. The West and Upper Midwest were locked down by mercenaries, zealots, the brainwashed, and the opportunistically stupid—Dixie and his crew came to mind. Some military brass and government officials didn't even try to take the country back. Too much "empty land," they said. Martin knew better. So did I. Hast's fingerprints were all over the silence.

Pulling out Jake's flash drive, I slid it into a port. Traitors, he'd said before dying. The file was a bombshell: names of embedded Hast operatives. The Vice President topped the list. Four cabinet members. Dozens of congressmen—just enough to block any move to reunify the country. The Secretary of Defense wasn't on the list. Small relief.

RedWater had a failsafe. Any agent who uncovered a breach could text 9459 to a ledger of trusted men, triggering a red dye release into the water system—signaling imminent danger. Simple. Silent. Effective.

But Hast found out.

The morning Martin reached his office, a third of his operatives were dead. He wiped every trace of RedWater's existence. Now, the rest were ghosts. On their own. Running.

"A meadow of sour jellybeans," I said aloud, pausing to rest my eyes.

Grubsteak Diner. Three a.m.; Martin had paced for an hour before I finally got out of bed and convinced him to grab a bite. He was unraveling that night, though I didn't see it then. The lines around his mouth were deeper, his eyes unfocused as he devoured his fully loaded french fries. We sat beside a table of drag queens, who had just finished their show at a local theater. I knew better than to pry about his work; those issues weren't my concern. He clipped his fork down sharply, looking away.

"I need some air. Wait for me here." He rose, then turned back. "Order the apple pie for dessert. Two slices and pineapple crisp to go."

I watched as he paced the sidewalk outside the diner, throwing his hands in the air and talking to himself.

"Man's got problems," one of the drag queens commented.

"Don't I know it," I replied.

"I've got some spare gummies if you want one."

He returned in time for the apple pie. Hesitating, he reached across the table with his spoon mid-air and lifted my chin. "I don't know what I'd do without you."

Off to the side, the drag queen nodded and winked. "A keeper."

Opening the last file about the revolutionary invention of Boxy, I wasn't prepared to have my mind blown. As a Bay Area journalist, I was used to translating tech into every-day language—but this? Boxy was on a whole other level of innovation.

My brain scrambled to catch up. Every sentence hit like a gut punch wrapped in wonder. Was Boxy a weapon? A miracle? Or something that never should've landed in human hands? My palms went clammy. The world had tilted on its axis—and I was one of the few who knew.

"Law mercy," I muttered when I finished reading.

Martin had launched a covert war against Hast, rallying allies, scientists, even the President. But the key player was Phillip.

The boy genius went to work on an antidote for the monster Madonna he'd created. And he accomplished it. After delivering it to Martin, he used his own technology to wipe the research from his memory. That explained a lot. The scattered behavior. The inner conflict. His fragmented personality struggled with reality. He couldn't remember how to make what he'd already created.

When he returned—or was taken—to the Regency, Bren had him working on something he'd already invented without knowing it. With his mind fighting him, I wasn't sure what scared me more: that he'd remember, or that he wouldn't—and recreate something worse.

Meanwhile, Martin had been working on a miracle material—graphene fused with some high-tech polymer that could survive a nuclear blast. And the wash cycle as I found out. More than that, it cloaked whatever it held. He used it to build a kind of portable vault, a self-powered quantum drive that needed no connection, no freezer, no server. A container for Boxy. Safe from Hast. Indestructible.

Then something happened that I'm not sure even Martin understood.

I didn't know much about quantum computing—just that it needed freezing temps and sterile environments. But this? This lived outside those rules. Like photosynthesis, Boxy seemed to draw energy from light, thought, intention. Flowers and plants convert sunlight into energy to live without big computers or below-zero temperatures. Scientists had yet to figure out the whys and wherefores of nature's quantum miracles, and from my interactions with Boxy, it almost seemed to read my mind. Was it so far off to believe it was making its own decisions? It had outgrown us.

The little copper cube was now a dime-sized silver disc. I rolled it between my fingers. It warmed to my touch.

"You've got a real name," I said. "Quanta-psi-electro-photon-armor. Q-Pepa?" It zapped me. "Ouch. Okay, Boxy it is."

It vibrated gently in response. Like it understood. Like it felt. Could it choose? Could it betray?

Martin had also discovered Boxy's personality, calling it Osiris—an anagram of his surname. Boxy wasn't programmed like the Madonna. It bonded. It chose sides. It helped friends.

I thought back to all the times it had absorbed data—from Phillip's computers, the gas station, the PlanK. Had it fed that intel to Martin? Helped design the immunity stars? If so, it was the perfect weapon to fight Hast's creations. No wonder the Regency was desperate to find it.

But how do you stop a sentient quantum being from going rogue?

Martin took a leap of faith—he asked it to merge with him. Human DNA, fused with Boxy's core. Not control. Not command. A union.

His final note chilled me: With my first breath, I couldn't help feeling it took more of me than I offered. *Why? Was it simply curious?*

Had it changed him? Consumed him? Hollowed him out?

I looked at Boxy in my palm. It felt alive. What had it taken from him? What did it want from me?

To protect it, Martin had convinced it to divide itself into three parts, each with limited function until reunited. I had two. The third? Unknown. Did the Regency have it, or did Martin?

Either way, the balance was tipping—and whatever came next, Boxy wouldn't just be along for the ride.

I closed the last file, but the images burned behind my eyes. My hands trembled. My stomach churned. I wanted to scream into the void and demand answers.

I was one person. In a collapsing world. Holding the keys to a story too wild to be real. And yet, my fear whispered: It's all true. It read like sci-fi from a future no one asked for. But every detail rang with cold, terrifying authenticity.

Then the screen blinked. A text box reappeared: *Want to have some fun?*

I'd forgotten about it. "Sure," I said.

A menu expanded. One of the options: *PlanK.*

I tapped it. A diagram of the building we'd escaped loaded on-screen. I selected a hallway—and suddenly, I was seeing through the PlanK's security cameras. Real-time surveillance.

What should we mess up first? Boxy typed.

I leaned back, pulse spiking. One wrong move could expose our location. "I don't think this is a good idea, Boxy."

We're fireflies. They're not looking for us.

I hesitated, then said, "Find the rooms with the zombie drugs. Set them on fire."

For the next hour, I watched chaos unfold. Fire alarms. Sprinklers. Flooding. Backed-up sewers. Crews running in every direction. It was beautiful.

We were, indeed, fireflies. The pièce de résistance? A soaked Bren Chandley in leopard-print pajamas, shrieking at the sprinklers. Phillip hovered beside her, flapping his hands like that might calm her down. I had no idea how Boxy pulled it off—but it was art.

The new device had twice the horsepower but also had its limits. It couldn't breach the inner systems, couldn't unlock cells or override employee brainwashing. The prisoners remained caged. Drugged. Reprogrammed.

Those poor people they were turning into hyp-soldiers were in pens, walking aimlessly in a circle. Each successive room broke them down, stripped of identity, rebuilt as weapons. Some were marched into corridors labeled Nest and Mecca. I couldn't access either. But whatever came out the other side was less than human.

I thought of Odette Wallace. Of the children I'd glimpsed in Nest. What kind of monster does that to kids?

The final step was a closet-sized virtual garden, where they met the Madonna—some AI-infused figure of purity. She bound their ruined minds together, reshaped them into perfect Regency soldiers. Loyal. Vicious. Blind with hate for the "enemy."

Men. Women. Children.

I swallowed hard and typed into the box: *Can you free them?*

Not enough memory.

Poor Odette. I should've done something. But we'd barely made it out of the PlanK alive. I had one hope now. Martin. He'd know what to do. He could help. He would help.

By 3 a.m., my eyes were heavy. "Let's pick this up tomorrow," I yawned. "One last question," I swallowed and held my breath. "Are you… Martin?"

Yes and no.

I headed for the stairs. A reflection caught my eye—framed glass over a geometric sketch, mirroring the screen behind me. The text box lit up one last time: *You're gorgeous.*

I spun around. Blank screen.

"Three a.m.," I muttered, half-laughing at my own delirium. "Sleep."

After waiting two days, Ford and I were antsy about staying in one place. I wondered if that worried feeling would be with us for the rest of our lives. Out here, survival was in movement. No superhero moves or valiant feats, just hiding, running, walking.

My sole comfort came from retreating into Martin's closet. It contained familiar sweaters, a raincoat, leather loafers, a San Francisco Giants cap, and a green Ralph Lauren polo shirt I had gifted him for Christmas. I pressed the shirt to my face, inhaling him, and most nights, I slept in it, clinging to it tightly.

Five days. Still no sign of Martin. Surely, he was nearby. I was growing increasingly paranoid about why he hadn't contacted me. I spent the afternoon busting light bulbs at the PlanK, wishing I could do more. Hoping Ford would warm to Boxy, I let him have a turn. Creative genius, this kid, as he fried the wires to several of the giant servers. He didn't have to destroy the Big Kahuna; he killed what fed it, and that was enough to disrupt their day.

Alone, I asked Boxy about Martin's whereabouts but got no response. I questioned whether Martin was here, part of this process of dinging the PlanK. *Yes and no*, Boxy answered again. I fought with waiting here for his return or going out and searching for him.

"Where is Martin?" I asked.

Fargo, Boxy answered.

"Where in Fargo?"

The screen blinked as if calculating or resetting itself.

"I'm Sulis. It's safe to give me this information. Where is Martin?"

Here... and there... The letters appeared as if being pecked out on a manual typewriter.

I thought about trying to contact Dan, Maria, and the Sharps through Boxy's interface but hesitated to give it access. The Limey and Postman Axel networks were low-tech. If Boxy ever fell into the wrong hands, all of them would be compromised. I printed out a list of libraries and post offices in Fargo on the regular computer and tucked it in my back pocket. The closest in West Fargo wasn't far. I needed to know what was going on.

"I'm making a run into Fargo," I told Ford. "You'll be safe here."

"Naw," he shot up from the couch and hefted a backpack on his shoulder. "I'll tag along."

"I don't know what's in Fargo. I could get killed."

He shrugged. "I like an underdog."

I knew better than to argue, and as he stood beside me, staring into my chin, I could have sworn he'd grown another inch.

We journeyed along a railroad track, cutting over into West Fargo. I scanned every rusted switch and bent rail for signs of life or danger. The cold sank deep, but it was the quiet that scraped my nerves. I kept waiting for the world to erupt again—for helicopters, for blood, for the wrench of loss. But nothing came. Just wind and silence.

The first post office we reached was deserted, along with most of the industrial area, so we proceeded to the second set of addresses. The West Fargo library was boarded up, but the post office on Main Avenue had lights. From our vantage point across the street in an abandoned Toyota, we monitored the surroundings for any suspicious activity.

A few trucks passed, a man on a horse, a single motorcycle that made my heart race at the sound of its engine. After a quiet half hour, Ford exited the car and used his markers to graffiti a warehouse's blank wall. I remained in the vehicle, vigilant. When two men came out of the post office and raised the United States flag, I felt more hopeful.

The flag unfurled slowly, catching in the wind. My heart caught with it—just for a moment. It looked like hope, but I didn't trust it. I'd learned too well how quickly symbols could be weaponized, how safety could dissolve in a second. Still, I couldn't stop the warmth that rose in my chest.

"Wait here," I said to Ford, who was inking in the letters *Sulis Lives!!!*

He followed me. "It's cold out here," he snapped, kicking through a snow bank.

I don't know why I bothered saying that. He never did what I told him. I nodded for him to walk behind me, and at least he obeyed that instruction.

Inside, I looked for anyone wearing lime green. I spotted a man standing at a counter and two women working behind him. A few cots were set up along one wall with folded blankets and pillows. It seemed people had been staying here. The man glanced in my direction and asked, "Need to warm up?"

I nodded.

"Jeannie," he said to one of the women. "Coffee and donuts, some cider for a young one." He pointed at a table and chairs near the cots.

Ford and I sat. He was glaring, and I figured he didn't like being called a *young one*. It was nice to be warm.

Jeannie brought some cereal snack boxes along with the donuts. "You can take these with you," she said. Jeannie was wearing a dark green scarf.

I stared at it, wishing it were a different shade. "I love the scarf," I said, smiling. "My mom used to have one of those in lime green."

Jeannie's gaze sharpened, and for a moment, we weren't strangers. "Not a shade you see around here very often."

"I was wondering if Postman Axel is around," I asked, biting the inside of my cheek to ground myself.

She pulled a palm pad from her belt and tapped it several times. "What's your name?"

"Sulis," I said.

"Ned!" she screamed, her expression animated and excited as a hand clamped onto my shoulder, shaking it. "We've got Sulis! The genuine Sulis!" She grabbed me and hugged. "You are the real Sulis, right? That's not just your real name."

Ned jumped over the counter, and the second woman and the man who'd helped him raise the flag surrounded us. They patted me on the back, shaking my hand, and another round of hugs. I felt like I was watching it all from outside my body. I couldn't breathe. I hadn't saved anyone. I'd just survived, barely. I wanted to scream that they had the wrong woman.

"We'd heard you were dead!"

"Then reports that you were leading a resistance against the Regency!"

"I'm Rosie," the second woman said and rubbed her pregnant belly, "I'm naming my baby after you."

"Leon," the other man squeezed my hand like a sponge. "It's my greatest honor."

I could hardly get a word out and waved my hands to discourage their praise. Ford had crossed his arms in front of him and rolled his eyes. "I think the name has been co-opted," I explained. "Lots of people fighting now, all calling themselves Sulis. I don't mind really, but I've not done all that much."

"We busted some overhead lighting and caused some sewers to back up," Ford smirked, caustically adding to the conversation and enjoying my distress. The kid was right. The myth of Sulis had outrun me, and I didn't know how to catch up.

"If you're still hungry, I have a cheese taco," Leon said and pulled a cellophane-wrapped sandwich from an oversized apron pocket.

"I'm good," I said. Ford also waved it away, making a face. "I need a Limey connection."

"Ohhhh," they all cooed in unison and nodded their heads. They looked at each other, the floor, the wall, to each other again. "Tough to hold a connection in these parts," Ned said. "You'll need to cross into Minnesota, be your best bet."

"Maybe the army can help," Rosie said, "A bunch of them set up shop at the airport."

"Let me get this straight," I asked. "Have we crossed over into the United States?"

"Technically, the Regency claims us, but we've kicked their asses out every time they've come to town." He waved a hand. "We're set up to give the Limey list safe lodging, and we forward on postal letters as always."

Leon nodded his head in agreement. "We're hoping the army coming in means we can get back on the U.S. side even if we have to join the state of Minnesota."

"My phone hasn't worked in a while, and I need to contact people."

"All we have left," Rosie said, wringing her hands, "is one five-call burner."

After deciding I was worthy of their last five-call burner, Leon meticulously reviewed how it worked. Invented by a group of local high school seniors, they took an ordinary non-working cell phone and created a device that piggybacked onto what he called errant signals. Best I could comprehend, those were satellite calls beaming around in space, but there could have been a simpler explanation that I didn't understand. The face of the phone showed five slots. Make a call or get a call. Once the five slots had been activated, the phone was done. Leon recommended I only use it outside and walk in a wide circle so I wouldn't show up as being at a particular address just in case the Regency was on to them and to tie it onto a passing dog after I used the last call.

I left Ford eating Lucky Charms cereal with Jeannie and Rosie giving him their coffee milk. Heading toward the door, a bulletin board flyer caught my attention. TRAILBLAZERS CALL. It was on post office letterhead, so was likely sent to every post office in the country and as many in the Regency as were operational. The bottom part of the page was cut twelve ways with a phone number on each tag.

I looked back at Ford, enchanting the ladies. Quickly tearing off the number, I went outside. I didn't know what I'd find on the other end of the number, but I needed it to matter. I needed something to make all we'd been through worth it.

The crisp morning breeze jolted me, and my frosty breath shivered with anticipation. According to Silver Boxy, Martin was in Fargo. *Martin was in Fargo.* The words comforted me like a warm blanket. I was so close.

The roar of four military helicopters flying overhead shattered the tranquility. I ducked instinctively, heart leaping into my throat. Jeannie had mentioned that the U.S. Army was stationed at the airport. Waiting for silence to return, I dialed Martin's number, letting it ring continuously as I paced around the parking lot. Please let it be him. Please let him be safe. My heart ached. I'd made it all the way to Fargo and found his house, but I still couldn't find him.

I called Maria and Dan next, updated them, and told them I'd send them the RedWater file once I found a secure connection. With a bit of sorrow that I couldn't see their faces on the video app, hearing their voices made me misty-eyed until they gave me the best news. The United States, with massive help from the Limey and Postman Axel resistance, had reclaimed California, Nevada, Arizona, and New Mexico.

Dan was now involved with a team working to disrupt Regency computers and repair the damaged infrastructure. Most cities had full time electricity and water, and efforts were ongoing to eliminate Regency agents and educate the public on the deceits of con artists promoting the Madonna cult. Dixie hadn't been elected president, and no one knew his whereabouts. There was no record of any Regency elections taking place.

Sharing about the military presence in my location without specifying the city, I had to cover my ear as another formation of helicopters flew overhead. For the first time, there was a sense that the nightmare of the Regency was drawing to a close, although Dan cautioned that this might make them more desperate. His parting words were bittersweet as he mentioned that he'd had been in touch with the Sharps, who had a message to convey from another Montana family, the Brasiltons. The message was simple: "We are sorry."

Looking back through the door of the post office, Ford and the ladies laughed. I imagined him turning on his mercurial charm and pilfering a few more of those donuts. Holding the number I'd torn from the poster, I assessed what was safe against what I wanted to do. Then, I used my third call. Three rings. A male voice said to leave a message.

Boxy took the inconvenient time to buzz me. I shifted around in a circle but didn't see anything unsafe. Covering my mouth and speaking distinctly, I said, "I have a Portland Trailblazers tee shirt. If that's what you're looking for, I have it with me, safe." The phone beeped and disconnected.

As I made my way across Main Avenue, my gaze caught a dark speck in the distance. Hurrying back, I pressed myself against the brick wall of the post office. Soon after, a convoy of military vehicles thundered by.

Hiding behind a mail truck, I kept low and out of sight, hoping these were U.S. forces, although I couldn't be sure. Following them were a dozen jeeps and a black town car. I cautiously peered after them. Most trucks veered off towards the city while the jeeps and town cars continued along Main Avenue. The sight unnerved me, leaving me with a bad feeling.

The phone rang. I looked down, and the remaining two call slots were blinking. One said Martin. The other said Trailblazers. My body froze, and my finger trembled over the phone. *Martin. Martin.* I tapped, the world seeming to disappear around me.

"Are they with you?" a male voice asked.

"Only the small tee-shirt," I answered, blinking tears that dripped down my cheeks. I had missed Martin's call, causing a pang in my chest. I bent over, a mix of frustration and hurt swirling inside me. "The larger one... didn't make it through the wash."

Silence, but I could hear a heavy exhale.

"You're going to have to prove to me that you know him," I said, sniffing back congestion. Every word felt like a test, and my voice cracked on the edge of it. I couldn't afford hope, not now—not until I was sure. If this was a trap, if they touched Ford... I couldn't let it happen. My eyes burned, throat clenched. I'd never hated doubt so much.

There was a brief silence, followed by the man clearing his throat. "He speaks with a North Dublin accent even though he doesn't have to. He can be obstinate, infuriating, and terribly kind. His IQ tested at 139, and if he loses his temper, he can let loose a string of limerick profanity, which his mother and I have scolded him to no avail. Also, you should know a day hasn't passed that I haven't been searching for him, for both of them."

I clenched my jaw. If I made a mistake and Ford fell into the Regency's hands, they could compromise the Secretary of Defense. This one child being held hostage could destroy everything that had been accomplished.

"He worships the Portland Trailblazers," the voice said, tinged with desperation. "He... he... He likes an underdog." The man sobbed. "Please, please, I beg you. Tell me where my son is."

"Fargo," I replied.

Ford's father was in Chicago. He'd refuel a helicopter in Minneapolis and land it in the Statue of Liberty Park beside the Red River. Ned drew me a map, showing a straight shot down Main Avenue where I'd recognize a smaller version of the Statue of Liberty next to a traffic circle. With just over three hours to cover seven miles, we traded hugs with the post office crew. We were about to leave when the first explosions thundered, causing the ground to shake with unsettling force. We gathered outside, watching as plumbs of black smoke rose in the Northeast.

"It's not the direction you're going," Leon said. "If you have to, cut over into the neighborhoods south and continue east, it'll take you to the same place."

"You said the U.S. army was at the airport?" I pointed in the direction I'd seen the helicopters.

"No," Jeannie said. "That's a small airport. The big one is that way." She pointed in the direction of the black smoke. "We think they're planning some sort of operation against the Regency."

"The PlanK," Ford whispered. "They struck first."

"Oh, no," I held a hand to my forehead as realizations swirled like eddies. "You've got to get out of the city. Go south, not west." There was only one thing this could mean. The first generation of hyp-soldiers was ready.

"We'll fight," Leon said after I'd explained. "We didn't hold this post office open for nothing."

"No," I said, touching his shoulder. "You don't understand. This isn't like regular soldiers or the Regency's paid mercenaries. These ones are brainwashed, hypnotized, and drugged. No atrocity will affect them. Not slaughter, not rape, not butchery, not ripping off the head of an infant. Fargo is lost. You need to run. Take as many people with you as you can along the way. Get somewhere safe until the army... kills them all."

Ford leaned into me, and I could feel a shudder go through his body. I hadn't told him we were meeting his father at the river. If anything went wrong, I didn't want his anticipation to cloud his judgment. And now, I wasn't sure I could get him there safely. I looked toward the smoke. The army would keep them busy for a while. We had to move fast and hope his Dai had the speed of a falcon.

We sprinted along Main Avenue, each explosion jolting my spine like a reminder of how close we were to annihilation.

Smoke laced the sky. I tried to count the seconds between blasts, tried to keep a rhythm, but fear thudded louder than my pulse. All I could think about was the kid beside me—his legs pumping, face flushed with panic. Every building we passed could be our last. I kept one arm on Ford, needing the contact—not just for his safety, but to reassure myself that I hadn't failed him. Not yet.

Uncertain of the number of U.S. soldiers at the airport, I estimated it had to be in the thousands if their intention was to launch an attack on the PlanK. The presence of numerous trucks and helicopters, which I now recognized as belonging to the Regency, likely meant an equal number of the hyp-soldiers had been mobilized.

My only hope was that the conflict remained confined to the distant part of the city until I could deliver Ford to his father. Then, Boxy and I would fight. Despite being out of breath, we maintained a rapid pace. Yearning for any mode of transportation—a bike, a horse—I scanned the primarily industrial and retail buildings lining the street. A sparse number of bystanders from the surrounding neighborhoods stood in the street, shielding their eyes as they pointed toward what looked to be a fierce battle.

"Run, hide," Ford called out to them as we hurried east. I even shouted it a few times myself. We paused only to catch our breath, trying to keep moving despite our exhaustion.

"You're a good kid," I said to him.

"I'm going to invent a glove that shoots down hyp-soldiers with a single stun." He held out his fist like a superhero and made a rat-ta-ta-tat sound.

I smiled, but my throat tightened. His hope was a fragile thing—ridiculous, beautiful, untouchable. I wanted to wrap it in steel. "I've no doubt," I said, but what I meant was: I wish the world deserved you.

He wiped sweat from his brow. "You're sure this Martin is going to be there? I won't have to watch lovey-dovey stuff, will I?"

I chuckled and pulled him into a doorway. We had at least a mile to go. I dug into my vest for Ned's map, taking our only real break as we sucked in air. I wrote down the longitude and latitude of the car where we'd left Jake's body as well as the location where his mother's remains could be found. Folding it tightly, I handed it to him along with the flash drive the barber gave me. "Ask your dad to get that to the President. No one else, understand. Only the President. On the paper is where they'll find the soldier who died for that information. He deserves a hero's burial. The other coordinates are where they'll find your mother. She's a hero, too."

"My Dai?" he asked, his expression emotional and confused.

"Not long now."

His smile widened, filling his face with joy. Grabbing my arm, he pulled and sputtered, "Move it, Woman!"

We trotted, huffing and pushing ourselves forward.

A piercing ring stopped us in our tracks. It wasn't a sound as much as a penetration. I grabbed my head, shaking it off. Ford looked at me. Worry clouded his eyes. We knew this feeling.

"Look!" he pointed.

A diabolical Martin ripped open the sky, sinister and menacing like a god of nightmares. I should've been immune, but my gut still churned, muscles locking into old memories. His face—still handsome, still familiar—warped with horns and venom.

A handful of onlookers at a car lot sank to the ground in fear. We were still standing, indicating that Boxy's immunity still offered us protection. Clad in black with red serpents twisting around him, the monstrous figure emanated utter terror. The people in the car lot let out cries of fear. One dropped to his knees, another clasped his hands in prayer, and a third began to beat the others. It appeared that whatever signal the Regency had transmitted to control their followers in Butte now made some of them crazy like the hyp-soldiers.

"Ear plugs," Ford yelled toward them.

It was too late. Martin called out destruction, his voice shrill with menace. "I am your perdition. You shall serve me in the abyss, fatten me in the pit, sate me in hellfire."

Ford waved at the men, showing them to put their fingers in their ears.

"You can't help them," I said. "Keep going." I couldn't help looking back at Devil Martin, his handsome face contorting in nightmarish torment, horns sprouting then vanishing from his brow. Thankful it wasn't his voice but a harsh, guttural rasp that echoed over itself. It sent chills through me. I can't imagine what it did to the unvaccinated. I pulled Boxy out as we ran, halting just enough to ask it to ding the Devil. Boxy was still and made no transformation or move to destroy the image.

"I shall force-feed you of my loins," Devil Martin roared. "You shall be my glut." A lizard tongue shot out of its mouth, whipping around his cheeks.

A collective scream echoed through the city as people, in various attire, fled southward across Main Avenue, desperate to escape. Gunfire cut down a dozen individuals, while others fell victim to the Regency hypnosis and turned against one another. The hyp-soldiers were not just targeting the airport but also rampaging through the streets, instilling terror as they advanced.

Of course, the Madonna would descend now, radiant in blinding white, all armor and illusion. Ford and I exchanged a glance. I clenched my teeth. She looked like salvation. Sounded like it, too. Her honey-laced voice was poison that drown reason, offered deliverance, and I watched people kneel, eyes glassy with hope. I hated how easily they leaned into it, how ready they were to follow something—anything—that promised order. Even if it was a lie.

"Fear not, children. This battle has been fought for eternity, and no demon can triumph over your beloved Mother. Through allegiance and fealty, evil shall be vanquished. If you come to me." The voice echoed, "*Come to me,*" and I felt the same oscillation of brainwashing.

I had been so intent on moving forward that I hadn't realized Boxy was vibrating in my hand. Now with the appearance of the Madonna, it gave me an outright shock. I wondered if it was ready to send some shock waves through the Devil and the Madonna, but now, I had to get Ford to the Red River. "You're going to have to wait, Boxy."

"What?" Ford said.

"Nothing," I huffed and sucked in air at the same time. "Do you think you can run? We got to be about a quarter mile out."

"Crap!" He pushed me behind a snow bank, pulling me to the ground. "That woman," he whispered. "Soldiers."

I crawled on my belly and peered around the snow bank. At the distant intersection, a tent, set up with tables of computers, blocked Main Avenue. Around the tent, patio fire pits blazed to provide warmth, and jeeps and a town car I'd seen earlier obstructed another side. It was impossible to pass without being noticed. In the center of it all, on a raised platform, Bren and Phillip held cylindrical electrodes and moved around each other. Looking back at the simulated images, I realized they were enacting the Devil and Madonna. This was how they stabilized their control of the image. "We have to go south," I whispered to Ford. "Ned said those roads paralleled Main Avenue and would get us to the same place."

I pulled him to run in front of me when something hit me on the cheek. Looking down, a package of earplugs tied to a small stone lay beside my foot. Ford picked it up, and we huddled closer, studying our surroundings.

"Psssst. Pssst."

Who was here? Ford pointed to the side parking lot of a bank. A van with the logo *Ministry of Faith* flashed its parking lights. Two men and a woman frantically pointed to the package and their ears, showing they had them in. A woman opened a side door and waved us over. They fervently ducked to hide from the sight of Devil Martin and the Madonna as the two circled each other, readying for battle. One of the men aimed a camera out a front window, filming the spectacle.

"I want that van," I whispered to Ford. We hunched over and sprinted toward them.

"Put them in your ears," the man said, holding out additional packages of earplugs to us.

"The Evil One will take your brain if you hear his words," the woman said sincerely.

For lack of time, I replied, "I got the vaccine." I pulled Ford beside me. "We both do. We're immune to his… evilness."

They leaned toward us, trying to make out our words through the earplugs. The man with the camera nodded that he understood but still looked puzzled. "There's no vaccine against the Evil One. We've come to witness. The Mother is the only one who can save us. We've read prophecy."

"Don't you realize both of them are fake," Ford bickered. "They can do that shit in Las Vegas!"

"Ford," I sputtered. "Don't cuss."

"I don't know why not, you do it. Malarkey this, and malarkey that."

"No, son," one of the men said. "This is Armageddon, and we've come to document it for future generations in our heavenly home."

Ford nudged me with his knee, and I knew he wanted to get out of there. First, I had to give them the vaccine if I was going to steal from them. I opened my hand revealing Boxy just as Devil Martin proclaimed, "Armageddon at last!"

Boxy transformed into a translucent rose, and I whispered, "Inoculate these three." Starry beams hit the three people. They looked at the rose, wide-eyed and fascinated.

"The mother is a rose," the woman said, pointing at Boxy, who closed up in my hand. "The rose will defeat the Devil, for she is the effervescent rapture."

"Listen to me. The rose has put protection on you. You can take out your earplugs."

Hesitantly, the woman pulled hers out. "Are you a saint? An angel?"

"No, I'm Sulis," I said.

She motioned to the others that it was okay. Smiling, she clasped my hands. "We were told the Devil will turn man against woman against child in this battle.

"And so, they will, but that's not the Devil, nor is it the Madonna. You've all been tricked."

They shook their heads in the negative. "This has been foretold."

"You want to see the evil one," I pointed. "Go into that building behind you, second floor, northeast corner, and watch the setup at the far intersection."

"That's a Regency staging point," the cameraman said. "We think they're here to fight too, but their soldiers are pretty mean. They've got roadblocks and military in all neighborhoods south of us. They disabled our van and told us to wait here for the Madonna's redemption."

I looked at Ford. Even on foot, we couldn't risk going south.

"The railroad," we both said.

"Watch the blond woman with her blond son. Every movement they make, those images will copy. If that doesn't prove they are fake, then I can do nothing for you." I pulled Ford along, then turned back. "Make sure you record it all. For the world." I watched as they made their way into the building.

Glancing down Main Avenue, I spotted a distant black dot high in the sky. Dai's helicopter. As the Regency soldiers directed their attention towards it, we darted across the avenue, swerving and jumping over individuals sprawled on the ground, lost in a daze as they trembled at the manipulated images, mistaking them for reality. The looming figures of Devil Martin and the Madonna were edging closer to each other, poised for a showdown amidst the city's structures. Racing along the railroad, we reach our previous position. We still had to cross the street where the Regency was set up and hoped they didn't look in that direction. Near the next intersection, we stumbled upon a dozen people huddled in a doorway, all fixated on the unfolding spectacle. Four of them handed earplug packages toward us.

"New York Times," one of the men said. "How are you not?" he nodded at three people, cameras around their necks, hands and feet bound. They'd taken out their earplugs and now growled incomprehensible threats to kill their colleagues if they could help the Madonna fight. I opened my hand and let Boxy do its stuff. The three on the ground sat up nauseous, embarrassed, apologizing profusely. One threw up. "You're inoculated. Take out your earplugs."

"What is that?" a woman asked, also saying she was from the Christian Science Monitor.

"Wall Street Journal," a third man said as he clipped the ties holding his associates.

"All of you are chasing a story," I said, letting them eye Boxy before it closed up again. "Those things are fake," I pointed in the opposite direction. "And the real story is a half block that way."

"Yeah, we know they're fake." Several agreed and nodded. "Who'd believe this poop. You could do that crap in Vegas."

"Like I said," Ford whistled.

"We're from the States," another woman said. "We know what the Regency is about. By the way, who are you?'

"Sulis," Ford volunteered. "The original. Sulis lives!" He punched a fist in the air.

"A church group is filming how they do it in a building on Main. I'll show you where to go. Give me two minutes." I pulled Ford toward the intersection. "We part here, kid. Run as fast as you can down that railroad track. You'll come to a traffic circle with a fifteen-foot Statue of Liberty. Your dad is close, probably about to land now."

"You have to come with me!"

I shook my head. "I came here for Martin, and I have a chance to destroy this once and for all."

"No," he pleaded. Another bomb exploded blocks away, shattering the windows of a nearby restaurant, and we hunched together. The fight was moving in this direction.

"I'm going to cause a commotion. That's when you run." I gripped Ford's shoulders, giving him a slight shake and making him meet my gaze. "Remember what I told you to do. You've got the paper and the flash drive?" He nodded, his face stony, holding back his emotions. Turning him around, I gave him a gentle push.

He trotted to the corner of a building, peeking around it, charting his path, then turned. "Brooklyn," he said. Our gaze locked.

He ran back and threw his arms around me, strong and fierce. I folded around him, inhaling the scent of dirt and fear and the child he still was. I wanted to tell him I loved him. I wanted to tell him I'd find him again. But those weren't promises I could make. My tears soaked into his hair as I whispered, "Your Dai." And still, my fingers lingered at his back, memorizing the shape of his spine.

"You won't survive this," he said and sniffed as another bomb exploded in the distance.

"Pffff," I exhaled. "I'm the ultimate underdog."

His watery eyes and furrowed brow broke my heart. No words would come.

"I know," I said. "Now stand ready, and run as fast as you've ever run."

He nodded.

I made my way back to the reporters. "Get your cameras ready," I said, motioning for them to follow me.

Jogging around the block, I came within twenty feet of the tent and opened Boxy. Since it hadn't responded to my request to destroy the Devil, I wasn't sure what I could do. "Can you do anything for the citizenry?" I asked. "Anything to inoculate some of them before they're at each other's throats." A part of Boxy squeezed off from itself and transformed into tiny bees. "Beautiful," I said. They swooped away with a mission. "Absorb the information on those Regency computers and destroy the images." Boxy shimmered into a white mourning dove and flew toward the top of the tent. I could only hope it would follow directions.

I reached into my innermost vest and pulled out the magazine of bullets Carl Houseman had given me so long ago in San Francisco. Slipping behind the limo, I crawled until I was close enough to the fire pits. In a chair off to the side, Al Hast, legs crossed, warmed his hands as he adjusted his Ron Elwood coat. Malarkey! I waited until he turned to warm his backside and tossed in the magazine. When the bullets sparked, I hoped the noise would be enough of a distraction for Ford to run across the street.

As the helicopter prepared to land, Hast turned in that direction. The chuffing sound caused Phillip and Bren to follow him while trying to maintain their control of the images. I looked toward the city at the Madonna making an awkward bow and barfing dolphins. *Thanks, Boxy.* Devil Martin was still in apocalypse mode. Boxy hadn't yet stopped it. Those bullets should sound like firecrackers. I didn't know how long it would take them to explode. "Sooner would be better," I whispered.

"Shoot that down," Hast said to the soldiers. The six men assembled in a line, shifting their weapons toward the helicopter.

"Hey, bitches!" I yelled, dashing to the center of the street and spreading my arms. "Why play computer games when you've got your number one enemy of the state standing right here, ready to rumble." I paced back and forth, relieved as they spun toward me. The soldiers held their fire, assessing if I was a threat. "And by the way, Bren Chandley, you're a shitty actress!" Glancing beyond them, Ford ran across the street, following the railroad. "I could write better dialog on a kindergarten word processor with no thesaurus." The soldiers surrounded me, guns aimed.

"Wait!" Phillip yelled at them. Toward his mom, he mouthed, "She's got it. Look at the monitors." Four oversized monitors were frozen. The Madonna hung like an obscure painting in the sky and sparked as if ready to dissolve. Devil Martin anchored fists on his hips, waiting. Phillip stood in the same position.

Off to the side, the reporters gathered in the crooks of the buildings, hidden but training their phones and cameras toward us. "Yes, Phillip," I grinned at him. "I've got it."

The silence between us pulsed like a heartbeat. All three stared at me. I suppose, wondering what I could do and what Boxy might do. Al Hast hung back in the curve of the tent, observing.

"Let's... take a minute," Bren said softly.

In the brittle November sky, a bird rose, lifting like a fluffy white seed of a dandelion. It spun like a whip, disappearing into the beyond, and in my heart, I knew a reunion had come to pass. I cocked my head to the side and said to Bren, "Let's not."

The bullets I'd thrown into the fire burst into a sizzle of sparks and bangs and spewed a charcoal aroma. I shoved a soldier to escape. He knocked me down while the three Regency blue-bloods scampered from under the tent, thinking they needed to save their behinds. I could hear the reporter's cameras clicking.

"Heeyy!" a squealing voice said from above. "Don't worry about her, worry about the Devil over yonder!" The church-woman hollered out from the second-story window and pointed at Devil Martin. "Y'all helping to kill him or what?"

"They have cameras," Bren growled toward Hast. "They saw."

Two of the soldiers pulled me up and held me between them. "Boxy to me," I whispered under my breath and slyly opened my hand. The little bird didn't come. Alarmed, I tried to see under the tent. Boxy had flown down and hovered over Phillip's head. A bolt of confusion shot through me as panic clenched my throat. What if it had chosen him? Was Boxy about to flip sides? The little bird knew Phillip, even if he didn't know it. That's why Boxy wasn't responding. It wouldn't do anything to hurt Phillip. I held my breath and tested my trust.

"Perhaps you and I got off on the wrong foot," Bren said. "Let her go." She pushed both soldiers aside, smacking their arms away from me and smiling as she held her hands prayerfully in front of her. "I've always said we could use another voice in our higher echelons. Diverse opinions and all that."

A sharp guffaw escaped me. "You make the same mistake every single time," I said, shaking my head. "Moving too quickly, too soon, before you're ready, and you've had the piss stomped out of you at every encounter. You're a laughing stock!"

"Can't you understand that this is the best way? We can have the most remarkable world?"

I nodded toward the two images. "They're cartoons, you stupid woman."

Behind her Al Hast looked to the ground, his face reddening with my every word. Like most pseudo-strongmen, he didn't like criticism. He stepped forward, his movements snaky and rubberish. Seeing him in person struck an odd chord inside of me. Something familiar about him. "Give me the device," he said in a low, lifeless voice. "You think this is a battle," he nodded toward the city. "This is a test. I have ten thousand more."

His voice anchored terror in my chest, and I tried not to show it.

"By the end of the year, I'll have a hundred thousand. By the end of the decade, I'll own that pathetic force called the U.S. military. My hyp-fighters are what soldiers are meant to be. Give me the device, and we can all walk away alive."

Bren stepped around him, stroking his arm as she passed as if to calm him. "You don't know how to use it," Bren said mildly, her hands shifting in front of her like she was explaining a complex math problem. "I could teach you. You can have your own division, do anything you want. It won't always be like this. It's just that—first, we have to get control."

"And the device?" I said, looking aside and wishing Boxy would come to me.

"Can make it real," Bren said, no longer smiling. "People will live in any reality they want on their off time."

What was clear is they were afraid of Boxy, the one device that could destroy them. Keeping an eye on Boxy, who now lit on Phillip's shoulder, I stepped out of the range of the soldier's grasp and paced as if thinking over her offer. Phillip noticed the mourning dove, his mouth slightly agape. He opened his hand, and Boxy nested into his palm.

I tipped my head and bore down on Al Hast. "All the good you could have done with your money. All the lives you could have made better. This is what you want to be remembered for."

His snarl pushed a pencil mustache into his cheek.

"You sound like our deluded brother," Bren spat with a dose of ire. "Baby of the family, spoilt, arrogant, know-it-all." She bared gritted teeth, toxic contempt seeping from her expression. "Never cared a damn about either of us."

"Your brother," I said, a hundred realizations coming to me. "Martin, is your brother?" My pulse crashed in my ears.

I stared at Al, and suddenly the resemblance was unmistakable—Martin's eyes, his nose, the shadow of a smirk twisted by cruelty. It hadn't been Martin in that old Bolinas portrait. They were brothers. Bren was his sister, not his wife. It was the best information I'd received since I started this journey, but I realized simultaneously that Martin had left it out of the Red Services file. Another deception.

"Best little conman on the circuit," Bren said, a contemptuous whine. "Even at six years old, he could work a wheelchair into a million-dollar night." She glanced over at Al, who stared aside, his cheeks crimson as if reliving days he'd rather forget. "Our parent's little Starshine. Leaving us to clean up the vomit and poop."

"He was a child. You can't blame him for how your parents treated you."

"It was only when I got rid of him that they loved us again." She guffawed a malicious cackle, her brother shaking his head violently. "I put him in a car trunk one night, and some pious Petes drove off with him." Her eyes narrowed, looking me up and down. "Bet they thought they had the baby Jesus. Never saw him again until I found out what he was doing with my son. That was one big mess of a family reunion."

"We worked it to our advantage," Hast said. "Put him on the board of directors. When he finally realized that we had conned him, he was compromised up to his neck. Just like we planned it."

I looked at Phillip, wondering if he'd been a willing part of this. He focused on the mourning dove, studying its luster, enraptured with its brilliance. "Was it worth it, Phillip? Betraying the man who made you."

"Phillip knows who his family is," Al said. "He didn't fall for Martin's act."

Bren shifted in front of Hast as if she didn't want him sharing the spotlight. "As you're about to go through some things, I don't hold your naivety against you. Think about it. Better to be on the winning side."

"You're losing all over this country," I said. "And you're wasting the most brilliant mind of his generation."

She looked at me like she didn't understand. "You call Martin brilliant," Bren said. "I call him a fool."

"I was referring to your son."

Bren's expression froze as if the realization confused her. "What's it to be?" she said in a more demanding tone. "We can give you more than you've ever dreamed. You're on the wrong side, the losing side. Why can't you see that?"

Phillip stared at the little bird. It cooed, waves of glittery essence streaming off its wings. I wanted so much to reach out, grab Boxy, and run. It knew I was here, and yet stayed with Phillip. How was I going to get it back?

"She's beautiful," Phillip said.

Bren and Hast glanced toward him like he was a forgotten ginger-headed step-dog. Staring at his cupped palms, Bren gasped, covering her mouth with a hand. Hast leaned forward, intently studying as he reached for Phillip. Bren shot out like a snake, clutching the little bird by its neck, wringing it viciously as it struggled and peeped. A sharp glance toward me, she cackled out the words, "I don't need you anymore. You're not even worth killing. And if you're wondering why I'm not cutting your throat right now, it's 'cause I want you to see. I want you to let it fill you with despair. I want it to haunt you the rest of your miserable days!"

The words *Kill The Madonna* ripped through my mind, and I leaped for her. We crashed into the tent, pulling part of it down.

The soldiers turned their weapons. "No!" Phillip screamed. "You'll hit Mother!"

"I don't care," Al Hast said. "Get me that device!

The soldiers aimed. Phillip jumped in front of us as Bren and I struggled for Boxy. Gunshots cracked, and we froze. Bren and I locked eyes. I wasn't hit. She slapped me hard. She wasn't either. Phillip dropped like a marionette whose strings had been sliced, folding to the ground with a sickening thud.

Bren shrieked, scrambling to him, and I couldn't move. My legs wouldn't work. It took the glint of Boxy lying still like a lost coin before I jolted back into my body. My fingers trembled as I scooped it up without Hast noticing.

"Phillip!" Bren cried, cradling him and pressing a stomach wound.

I scooted back toward the reporters as they ran out from their hiding places, ducking behind cars, snapping photos, and shouting questions at Hast.

Al Hast bumbled around, looking for an escape. Braver reporters ran past me, phones held out for a statement, rapidly hurling questions at him. He froze, rigid, in thought, glared at us, then his mouth upturned in a soft grin reminiscent of Martin. "It's simply easier to kill you all."

The group stood still, silent as the soldiers turned toward them. Then one of the reporters pointed toward the sky. "Really?" she asked. "Drones." She looked upward. "We have drones recording all of this. It's going out onto the airwaves as we speak. Everyone is watching."

"You're not fightin' the Devil?" the woman from Ministries of Faith called out, realizing the truth.

Hast's face screwed up, enraged. He grabbed Bren by the hair and dragged her toward the town car as she sobbed, reaching for Phillip. "Get in!" He shoved her, looked skyward for the drones, then ducked his head. Before he closed the door, he glanced back. No one had ever looked at me with more hatred. "Get me out of here," he growled to the soldiers. One jumped in the driver's seat, the others in the jeeps, and they sped westward, disappearing like bad weather.

The reporter who'd pointed at the drones put a hand to her chest and exhaled. "I never lied at full throttle before," she muttered. The other reporters hurried over, looking for Boxy and examining the computers with their frozen images of the Madonna and Devil Martin. One helped me up. The ministry people joined them, mad as could be over the deception they'd witnessed.

I leaned over Phillip. He was in bad shape. Blood dripped from his nose, and he coughed, spewing blood. One hand lifted, and he motioned me closer. I knelt beside him, running my fingers through his hair to push it off his forehead. Blood sopped up his clothes.

He pointed to my closed hand. I opened it and let him see Boxy. It transformed into a mourning dove and cradled itself into his neck. That made him smile. Struggling, his lips moved. He wheezed in air. "Constellation Bar," he rasped, his voice a wet, trembling ghost of itself.

I clutched his hand as if I could anchor him, keep him tethered. His blood was on everything—his sweater, my hands, the pavement.

"I'm sorry," he gasped and swallowed hard.

The apology gutted me. He wasn't the villain here. He'd been used, warped, discarded like every other bright soul that crossed paths with the Hasts. "I'm sorry," I said.

"Broadway, near the theatre, downtown."

"What's there?" I asked, grabbing a sweater from the back of a chair and holding it to his stomach. "Can anybody call the army?" I said to the reporters, "And get a medic." Turning back to Phillip, I held his hand.

"Constellation Bar," he said. "I—sorry. Couldn't stop them."

A dread filled me. My mouth dry, breath held, barely able to say words. "Wha... Wha... What is there, Phillip? Phillip!" I shook him. He went limp; unconscious or dead, I wasn't sure which.

Boxy rose, silent now, the mourning dove peeling away as if shedding innocence. Wings darkened. Its body shimmered into the sleek, vengeful silhouette of a crow. Screaming, it ignited. Streaks of fire arced toward the Madonna, toward Devil Martin—obliterating them in a cascade of smoke and brilliance. Not revenge. A funeral pyre.

"Phillip, what have you done!"

I jumped up and sprinted. Running like I could rewind the moment. My mind clicked into the map of Fargo, finding downtown. The Fargo Theatre. The Constellation Bar. As I made my way around overturned cars, dead bodies lay splayed on sidewalks and streets. Businesses and houses were riddled with gunshots. Smoke poured from a high-rise window. Broken glass crunched with each step. Security alarms blared. Fire on every block. The battle of Fargo had been a costly one.

I stopped only once. Leaning against a building, holding my aching side, gulping for air, trying to get my bearings. Every muscle taut, my ankle pulsed from a sharp pain. In front of me, three women beat a Regency hyp-soldier with planks of wood and a metal pipe. Flesh became pulp. Bone cracked. The woman's sobs were a kind of music—sorrow set to a war rhythm. He lay motionless, bloody, and probably dead.

"He doesn't know," I said between gasps of air. "He's brainwashed. He didn't know what he was doing." I suspected the bees had stung enough people that most, even the hyp-soldiers, were now coming to their senses.

The women continued beating him. "After what he did to my mother!" one screamed with each slam of the plank. "I don't care what he doesn't understand!" She sobbed, each whack of the board mashing his face into something not human.

I held my side, aching from exertion, pushing myself forward, trying to jog. Anything to keep moving. A group of soldiers yelled at me to get to a safe place. I waved at them and continued on, halting abruptly as Regency soldiers marched in a circle at the intersection.

I ran the other way. Finally, turning down Broadway. Body heat rushed to my head as I panted. Sweat dripped down my back. I thought I might pass out. My ankle felt like fire. Ignoring the pain, I trudged down the middle of the street. "Martin!" I called out. The colorful marquee of The Fargo Theatre jutted out over the sidewalk. "Martin!" The Constellation Bar had to be close... had to be... had to be.

Life... Life... Life seemed to condense into flashes. Martin, the first time we shared an electric handshake. His fingers tracing the curve of my scar. His lips kissing mine. His arms wrapped around me as we watched the sunset. My voice burst through my throat, a semblance of a groan. No. A shriek, like a majestic hawk in the Badlands. No. A scream. A savage, pitiless howl full of excruciating torment, both discordant and shrill. On my knees. Looking up. Hard asphalt, broken glass, my hand cut from pounding the pavement, a wave of singular despair. An unending keen.

Martin.

Martin.

His body hanging from a lamppost.

There would never be another memory.

Someone grabs me from behind. I struggle, and yet I don't struggle. I scream. The neon sign over the bar entrance sparks and flickers. The only letters that light up: *STELLA*.

~ STELLA ~

Pulling me to safety, the bearded man—the one who warned me about the red bus and sent a drone to drop me an arrow. Everything felt underwater. His grip on my arm too firm. The light too bright. I focused on the Golden Jackal logo stitched to his jacket, but my mind kept slipping sideways, back to Martin.

He must be an undercover government agent. Men in military uniforms talked to him. They both looked at me. Turning away, they made phone calls. I heard Martin's name and that he'd been hiding with them. The bearded man had been at Tosca's a long time ago, had told Martin something upsetting. He's wearing the same San Francisco Giants baseball cap.

I must be at the airport. Soldiers hurried past a seating section that once might have been crowded with travelers. The world rushed past in strange time signatures—too fast, then unbearably slow. I didn't sit so much as collapse into the chair.

Outside, amid the din of helicopters, vehicles sped by, horns beeped, and people yelled to one another as a frenzy of activity unnaturally fast and then slow. I stared at all that was around me in a trance. The man with the beard led me away. A hanger. Sitting. Arms rested on a table. He balanced a bowl of soup then lightly smacked my right cheek. I turned away, faced the wall, and closed my eyes.

He came back again later with a different kind of soup. This one smelled like tomatoes. Lightly pulling my chin toward him, my mouth opened and accepted the spoon. My taste buds exploded like I swallowed something tart. The bowl is empty, and I don't remember eating the rest. A second later, I fell to my knees, grabbed a trashcan, and retched.

At some point, I was moved to a room with a cot. Fresh clothes were brought to me. Military-looking garb. I don't mind. Turning toward the wall in case there were cameras, I touched Boxy in the bra pocket. I don't remember how it got back to me. Did I pick it up before I ran? Did it come to me on Broadway? It hasn't talked to me since... I tried not to touch anything where I might leave my fingerprints. I need to get out of here. The door is locked.

The bearded man returned with more soup. Has a day passed? Two? Days bled together like watercolors. His voice was there, then gone, like a dream that wouldn't let me wake. He led me on walks around an airport terminal that now appeared to be a fully functioning military base. He spoke to me, but I had trouble comprehending his words. He said Ford was safe. That should have mattered. But I couldn't tell if I was the kind of person who still felt things. Gavin. He tells me his name is Gavin.

Early the following day, Gavin took me to the control tower. "It's peaceful up here," he said. "No planes in or out today." A man is writing on a clipboard, and Gavin nods for him to leave. Snow lightly drifts, building on the carpeted runways. All around us, the pristine white blanket glistens under the stark winter sun. Gavin handed me a coffee, and my hands hugged the warm cup as a single breath of steam rose. Large flakes spat against the windows, melt to water, and drip down the glass. A hum waltzed, more a feeling than a sound. I wasn't sure if it was the computers in the room or the frozen landscape reminding me of the power of nature to still even the busiest of places.

"He'll be buried in Arlington," Gavin said. "If you want to see him, I can arrange it." He pulled a chair toward the one I sat in, our knees almost touching. "I know he had very different plans for his life and yours. What happened... It's going to be hard to get over, but he wouldn't want you to be... He wouldn't want—"

"Am I a prisoner?" I rasped through my tender throat, an involuntary shiver snaking up my spine even though heaters kept the room plenty warm. Steam rose from the coffee like a prayer I couldn't say. I wanted to scream into that clean, sterile sky. Instead, I whispered again, "Am I a prisoner?"—but I meant: Did I kill him? Did I make this world? Am I responsible for Martin's death?

Gavin looked at the ceiling and then the floor, rubbing a hand over his face. "I want to tell you about how I met Martin. How he saved my life. How I struggled to be human again."

The mission that bonded them was savage and brutal. I understood the camaraderie forged in battle and the unforgiving carnage from which brotherhood must rise or die. And yet, it was my relationship with him I had trouble understanding now. Martin had carried so many lives on his back. I'd only ever carried mine. And now I didn't know whether to honor him or scream his name into the snow. Partly angry, partly astounded at how this one man juggled love and duty.

"When Martin found out what Al Hast was up to, he gathered people he knew he could trust." Gavin turned a monitor toward me, showing an aerial view of the PlanK. "Today, it goes boom."

Grabbing his wrist, I hoarsely managed the words: "It's a trap."

I asked for water, a small container, and whatever drawings they had of the PlanK, then excused myself to the bathroom while Gavin gathered what I needed. In the far stall, I pulled out Boxy and asked for a virtual computer. The menu opened the PlanK security cameras. As I expected, the building was empty. After the breach I'd caused and the battle in Fargo, losing all they created was too risky. They didn't care about the building, they needed to protect the technology. I tried several times to see into the hallways marked Nest and Mecca but couldn't access them. The Kaleidoscope room was wrecked, windows shattered, mirrors smashed with wires and contraptions hanging precariously from the ceiling, and a misty smoke wafted in the air.

"Show me the snares." Boxy brought up seventeen places that had been rigged with explosives. I quickly memorized them and asked Boxy one more question. "What is the worst the Regency could do?" Boxy showed me a building-wide intercom system that had been jerry-rigged to spew out a triple-intense suicidal brainwashing program. Any of Gavin's soldiers that entered would be turned to mush. "Can you shut it down and disarm the explosives?"

"Not enough memory," Boxy typed back. A cursor blinked at me, and I couldn't think of anything else to do, so I shut down the virtual computer and waited in the control tower.

Gavin returned with the items I'd asked for and five other people. Three men and two women. "These are my team leaders," he said, introducing them by name afterward. On the nearest runway, several hundred soldiers lined up as trucks pulled around to transport them. Gavin handed me a dark jar, his expression curious about what I would do with it. "We're going to grab what technology we can, then light it up."

I sipped from the water bottle he'd brought, lubricating my throat, then pulled him off to the side so the others couldn't hear me. "Can they be trusted to take what they're about to see to their graves?"

His eyes narrowed, studying me. "You have Osiris."

"Only parts of it."

He looked back at his people and then at me. "Yes. Between all of us, we've got some secrets."

I marked his drawings, showing him the seventeen places where doors, walls, and windows were rigged with explosives. Then circled the two hallways, Nest and Mecca. "I think there's people in here. I don't know if they're hyp-soldiers or innocents, but if you had bombed this place, the Regency would have called you murderers and kept you in both government's news cycles as propaganda against you."

When I told them about the brainwashing infusion, they went silent. One finally spoke of the difficulty of ear coverings in that environment; another pointed out that they couldn't take in a large force. They began to discuss sending a surgical team to rescue the innocents or fight soldiers if that's what they found, then blow up the building using the existing explosive traps. I opened the dark jar and turned away to pull Boxy from under my shirt. All talking ceased and as I turned with Boxy in my palm, the soldiers gasped. I stood still. Boxy was beautiful. Terrifying perhaps. Familiar for sure. But not mine. I didn't command it. I just opened the door.

My little shapeshifter reconfigured into a sphere, expanding and contracting, turning over and around, transforming into a cube, a pyramid, a rose, a mourning dove, then settling into a Belgian Malinois, which sat at attention before it speared the five soldiers and Gavin with its super-duper immunity shot.

I remained silent over their shouting, and I suppose I was lucky no one aimed a gun at me. Part of Boxy came off the dog as honeybees and settled into the dark jar. I closed it and handed it to Gavin. "When you get to the Nest and Mecca, open this jar. The bees will heal the people from their brainwashing and inoculate them from future conversion."

The soldiers stood frozen, mouths agape. With a slight wave of her hand, one of the team leaders asked, "Can we get that done to the rest of our boots?"

I looked at the Belgian Malinois and said, "You know what to do." The translucent dog leaped through the window and exploded into a burst of stars that the soldiers on the ground barely noticed. Some looked around as they'd been pinched, then continued their work. I was interested to see that Boxy could now go through glass since uniting the two parts. The hound reappeared at my feet, and the five soldiers stared, google-eyed and mouths ajar.

Gavin offered to let me accompany them, sit in a military vehicle from afar, and observe, but I'd had enough of battles, enough of the appalling malaise that was the Regency. Preferring to never hear the name again, I knew better. Bren and her brother may be in hiding, but they were still out to kill me and take Boxy. That was their only way back. At this point, that was their only move, their only way to survive.

I spent an hour sending out bees to inoculate the remaining soldiers at the airport, then asked Boxy if it could handle the population of Fargo. To my surprise, a small portion separated from the dog and multiplied rapidly before swarming toward the city and its neighborhoods.

When I inquired about inoculating the world, the United States, or at least the state of North Dakota, a text box appeared saying, *Not enough memory*. Memory meant more to me now than feed for an operating system. I had memories. They needed to be a glossary, and words I would give them. Writing down all the names, actions, discoveries, and horrors I'd seen on this journey, I sealed them in an envelope addressed to Gavin, then had Boxy reveal several escape routes. After memorizing them, I dismissed the information. Escape was possible, if necessary, but first, I needed to determine whom I could trust.

Despite a soldier assigned to watch over me, the Malinois remained diligently by my side. I suspected the soldier's role was more about preventing any potential escape rather than ensuring my safety. Now that the military had seen the power of Martin's Osiris device, they weren't going to let it walk out of there. Gavin was smart enough to know he could work this better with my cooperation, and that was probably the only reason I wasn't confined to a locked room.

Since merging the two halves, I sensed a newfound potency within the device bordering on overwhelming power. Ford had been right in pointing out that there was still much I didn't know about Boxy, and I recalled my apprehension when I thought it was aligning with Phillip. Attempting to pet the dog, my hand passed right through as if it were a specter. "Sorry," I said. "Wish I could give you a treat." The dog transformed into a puppy and playfully tugged at the hem of my pants, emitting a sad whine and soft yip. That was curious. I suspected what it wanted. It bit my pants again and pulled. "You're not my guru." The puppy angled its head and huffed. Tapping my palm, it jumped and closed into the small silver coin. I exhaled, acknowledging that as cute as the virtual images were, I couldn't shake off unease about what it sensed in me. "You win," I said, unsure I was ready. "Time to say goodbye."

Following the soldier, I stepped into a hangar filled with coffins, a warehouse of death, the air too still, too orderly, too cold. Rows of caskets—identical, indifferent—lined up like forgotten stories. One casket had been pulled to the side. My heart pulsed a frantic warning in my ears, but nothing moved except the sweat trickling down my back despite the icy breeze. My grief found no place here. I was more like a wounded animal thrashing in a quiet room, disrupting the calm, the purpose, the fragile order that everyone else was clinging to. I wanted to hit something... badly.

Behind us, a commotion. Both the soldier and I turned to see two people embrace. They held each other and started to kiss when the woman saw us. "I'm so sorry," she said as the couple broke apart. "Thought we were alone." The soldier with me cleared his throat and nodded at them to get lost.

"What's your name?" I asked.

"Private First Class William Sturdivant, ma'am." His voice trilled, proud and regal. A charming lilt. So young.

"I don't want them to get in trouble."

"We should conduct ourselves better at such a time. I'm sorry, ma'am."

"Even war can't stop love." I looked at a flag mounted above the caskets, the red, white, and blue colors so vibrant. "On the other hand, they could be Regency spies sent to kill me."

"Not on my watch, ma'am," the soldier said and stepped closer to me. "I can open it if you wish."

I stared at Martin's coffin, not sure what to do, not sure what I could stand. I handed the private a towel I'd brought with me. "Can you put this over his face? I only want to hold his hand." I stood behind the casket as he did as I'd asked. He nodded toward me and then walked away, taking a position outside to give me privacy.

I stepped around to see Martin's body dressed in military fatigues. The coin warmed through my clothing, and without me taking it out, the puppy image curled around my feet. I lay my hand over Martin's, wishing to will life into the flesh. I don't know how long I stood there. Eyes closed. Reminiscing the romance we'd had. Imagining the life that should have been. A thousand touches passed between us in that silence—each laugh, each whispered promise. Here were the arms that had held me. Legs that had tangled with mine. Fingers that had so gently caressed my cheeks. The sight cut as I realized I'd never be kissed again.

"Ma'am," Private Sturdivant called out to me. "The call you're waiting on is ready."

I nodded and inhaled deeply to pull myself back to the living. I wasn't ready to let Martin go. It felt as though he was still with me, and yet he wasn't. My chest burst into a thousand sensations as the coffin lid shut for the final time. "My love," I whispered. "I'll finish this for you. I am my mother's daughter."

Private Sturdivant led me to a conference room, and I settled in at a corner desk. A laptop with a dark screen beeped to life. Sturdivant logged in on a different computer and then indicated my screen that opened to a military web page. "Hit the connect button when you're ready." He turned and stood outside the door.

I took a deep breath, clicked connect, and looked into the eyes of Defense Secretary, Jack Larkin. He wore his uniform, the five stars on his shoulder epaulet perfectly aligned. Larkin was the first Black five-star general and the first to serve as Secretary of Defense.

"Mr. Secretary," I said.

"Call me Jack."

"Also known as The Giant Killer, but I never got that story out of Ford."

He chuckled, his expression reverting to professional but warmed as he leaned into the screen, eyes glistening, showing emotions I'm sure he'd never reveal publicly. We stared at each other, not knowing what words to say.

"Ford?" I managed.

"Good," said the deep, husky voice I remembered from our previous phone call. "Ford would have wanted to be here for this, but I thought perhaps you and I should speak first."

I nodded, knowing I'd need to dissect his every phrase.

"First, I have no words for how much I owe you. Not only for my son but for..." He swallowed, lips pressed together.

"It's not necessary," I said. "Ford saved me as many times as I did him, and your wife, Sir, she did what she did so Dixie's men wouldn't find your son."

He swallowed hard again, unable to speak, eyes blinked, and stared at the desk. "You have my greatest sympathy for Martin Siriso."

My throat froze up. Now it was my turn to stare at the desk. "The flash drive?" I managed.

"Those traitors will never see the light of day." He straightened up in the chair, and I realized he must be a tall man. I could see in him the man that Ford would become. "That's another reason I've called. Now that the traitors have been neutralized, we can move forward. On behalf of the President, he wants you to know that he is in your debt, as are we all. Martin and Jake Satou will have hero's funerals. Mr. Siriso was more than a contractor in our country, and barring no relatives claiming his remains, the President has sanctioned me to give him all manner of honor for his final resting place. Major Satou will be posthumously awarded the Medal of Honor, and Mr. Siriso, the Presidential Medal of Freedom. Though I know this is of little comfort. The President wants to extend the invitation—"

"Thank you, but I have places I need to be and things I need to do." I coughed, willing the tremble in my chest to stop. "I've written down everything I know. All the names, license plate numbers, everything about the towns we came across and—"

"You've done more than enough," he interrupted me. "What I mean to say is that there is a place for you in this government. We believe Martin's contribution will be of great use in bringing the Regency to justice and ensuring this never happens again. We thought, perhaps, you could help."

And there it was. I couldn't blame the Secretary. He was an administrator, after all, patriotic, determined to protect his country, and with no clue about what he was asking. Boxy, in the wrong hands—I still wasn't clear on all it could do. Turning it over to the military didn't seem wise. *What you have in your hand, keep in your hand.* The Secretary's words blurred like static, but Martin's warning pulsed loud and clear—*What you have in your hand, keep in your hand.*

"I was just his girlfriend," I said, attempting a smile. "Can't imagine there's anything I could add to Martin's work."

He gave me his private phone number and email, along with a way to reach Ford if I was inclined. Several soldiers hurried past the conference room window. Loud voices called to each other as vehicles rumbled onto the tarmac. Gavin and his troops must have returned. "Thank you," I said to the Secretary. "Give Ford my best, and tell him I wish the Trail Blazers the greatest luck next season."

The Secretary blinked and hesitated as if he wanted more from me. "He told me I wouldn't get very far with you."

"Smart kid. Destined for greatness."

"We need you," he said, hushed and insistent.

"Tell Ford I'll keep an eye on him, so no more messing around with the nuns. Goodbye, Mr. Secretary. Remember that you and Maren raised your son to be a giant killer. Sometimes, that's enough." I hit the disconnect button before he could respond.

Standing, I stared at a map of the United States tacked to the wall. My gaze landed on the one place I never wanted to go again. It wasn't long before Gavin entered the room looking like he'd withstood a hurricane. I pushed him a chair with my foot.

"Kids," he rasped, like the word alone stabbed him. "There were kids in those rooms." He dropped into a chair, his face a knot of what-ifs and almosts. "If we had bombed…"

"Are they okay?" I wondered about the blond-headed little girl from the billboards, hoping she'd been rescued. "Do you know if a girl named Odette Wallace was among them?"

"No casualties on either side." He rubbed a hand over his face, the stress of what might have happened curling his brow. "They were little savages when we opened those doors, but after the bees hit them, just weeping, confused children. If you hadn't told us..."

"You remember your promise," I said. "Nobody can know."

"I do, but—"

"No, but," I interrupted. "Martin called it Osiris for a reason. In the wrong hands, it's death walking."

"But we're the— we can—"

"I know," I said and put a finger to his lips. "That's why you can't have it."

He leaned back against the wall, biting the inside of his jaw. "The country that possesses this can keep the peace for generations, maybe for all time." His eyes darted back and forth in thought. "Or they could..." He looked aside, the enormity of Osiris hitting him all at once.

"Are you going to try and take it from me?"

He bit his lower lip and expelled a short chuckle. "Even if I did, it won't respond to us, will it?"

I didn't answer and looked away from him. "So, am I looking at spending the rest of my life in a supermax prison?" I crossed my legs and narrowed my eyes. " 'Cause you know I can unlock them doors."

Gavin stood, hands on his hips. "I'll honor my promise to you," he said. "And we better go now 'cause betting you a dollar as we speak the Secretary's office is sending security forces to pick you up."

I walked over to the map and pointed at a spot as he followed me. "Can one of your Golden Jackals drop me off here?"

I got three Golden Jackals along with Gavin, whose motorcycle I shared. They'd dressed me in Jackals' garb, and we strutted past a group of military police headed toward my last location. On the way out of town, we drove by the Statue of Liberty in the park by the Red River. Someone had scrawled across the base *Sulis Lives!* I didn't have to wonder whom and smiled at the thought of the little twerp wasting his daddy's helicopter time to deface public property. Along the route, we ran into quite a few other *Sulis Lives!* graffiti. Sulis was now everybody, and they were hunting down anyone who had helped the Regency.

It was a different experience being on the back of a motorcycle. Heads perked up and turned toward us when we pulled into a gas station or rest area. People noted the Golden Jackal logo and then went their way. Still, along the border of the former Regency, I expected these folks had had their share of their shenanigans, and Gavin's group was known for fighting them. What little time I had to consult Boxy didn't give me a location for Bren and Hast, but Gavin believed they were no longer in the Americas.

Arrest warrants had been issued for Al Hast, his top executives, and several board members. Employees of Hast Industries were taken into custody and were being deprogrammed, but many true believers had fled the country. Also detained were the foreign mercenaries that made up the Regency militias and nearly all of Dixie Roman's motorcycle gang who terrorized the western and upper states, but so far, no sign of the former fighter who was thought to be in hiding with several of his crew. Bren hadn't had enough loyalty to take Dixie along. This, Boxy gave full attention. With that, the government expected the country would come back together just as before the Water Event. There was still a lot of infrastructure to fix and viruses to eliminate.

The Golden Jackals let me off a little north of Nashville. I'd walk the rest of the way. Gavin still didn't know my real name, and I was grateful he didn't ask. I'd wiped down the room and any place I thought I'd touched at the army base, but someone had likely gotten my fingerprints. All that would lead to is a California ID of a woman living in San Francisco with no history. He'd get some hell from the military for letting me go, but I was sure his worth was more than his mistakes.

Rumors of an enigmatic Osiris device and who might have it were as rampant as measles in second grade. Gavin's team had kept their promise and not spoken of what I did for them, but the reporters who'd seen Boxy's inoculating power were on every talk show jabbering and embellishing this mysterious gal named Sulis. The mythology grew, and for the safety of Boxy and, well, everybody in the world, now was the time for me to disappear.

Giving each Jackal a hug and a handshake, I felt more like a shadow slipping loose from her anchor than a woman walking away. This was the curse of surviving: you had to keep going, even if you left pieces behind with every step. I thanked Gavin again for the backpack, clothes, phone, and cash roll he gave me. "When the world is right again, I shall buy a lottery ticket in your name."

"We could take you the rest of the way," Gavin offered.

"Better you not see which way I go."

"Last bit of road advice," he said, scrapping his dusty boot heel in gravel. "You don't have to do this alone. We'll get Hast."

"Last bit of quantum voodoo prophecy," I answered. "Forget Hast, the real danger is his sister. I think she could be as brilliant as Phillip, just more egotistical—her Achilles heel. And so far, she isn't charged with anything."

His eyes narrowed as if he'd never given Bren a thought. "Don't like the idea of you fighting a war and not inviting us." He tweaked my cheek. "I'll put her on my team's radar. We don't always have to follow protocol."

I wanted to tell him not to bother. The Hast twosome would not be found. There was only one way to bring a measure of justice to them, and it was squired away in my bra. But Gavin, good man that he was—he could save me some time. "I was going to handle it myself, but here's Osiris' last gift for you and the justice system. At that diner we ate at ten minutes ago, you'll find three motorcycles parked out back with license plates that match the ones from where Maren Larkin was killed. I suspect they're working in the kitchen because, clear as day, that loudmouthed cook wearing the chef's hat and bad wig who dressed down the waitress for messy handwriting, that was Dixie Roman." I raised both middle fingers in the direction of the diner.

Gavin's eyes widened, mouth slightly ajar. "I'll give him your message."

"You can tell him he's lucky I let you pick him up. He's lucky I didn't get to him first."

Gavin saluted with two fingers, pressed his boot against the kickstand, and revved his bike. The motley crew headed north with their new mission. I discarded everything they gave me, leaving it near a traveler's encampment. I hated the distrust but couldn't chance that there was a tracker among the goodies. Using the money, I walked into Nashville, resupplied, and tied the phone onto the collar of a roaming dog.

Then I turned east toward the mountains. Finding a gapped pinnacle, I walked through paths surrounded by bare trees, dark and numinous, followed a railroad track around a ridge, into a hollow, down a dirt road, up a hill, along a dusty path, into a yard of junked cars and torn up washing machines at the end of a lane overrun with barking dogs. Each step toward that house was a step back in time, into the mouth of the past that had raised me. The house stood like a secret waiting to be remembered, its flaking olive skin familiar in a way that made my bones itch. This was where the story began—and where, for better or worse, it would finish.

The military would never find me here. Neither would what was left of the Regency. Why do I know that? Because it's where my mother has hidden for over forty years.

The snow had long melted, leaving a squishy texture to the ground. I waited by the mailbox for her to notice me. She swept the porch. Steady, even swings of the broom. Her hair was gray, not silver like mine, but slatey with ends that looked to have once been blond. Her weathered features spoke of time and hardship, but her movements were crisp, sharp with only the slightest bend to her back. She was humming and singing the occasional line of "Wayfaring Stranger."

Looking up, Stella saw me. She froze, broom mid-swing. My chest caved in under the weight of her stare. I couldn't move either—silence wedged in my throat, pressing on old scars. Her blank expression traveled years as if trying to decide whether to connect. For a breathless second, I felt seven years old again, shaking on a bus bench in a city that wasn't home. Stella leaned the broom against the house, went inside, and closed the door.

I exhaled, my grip on the mailbox a tether to reality. The cold metal stung my palm, but I needed the pain to stay upright. My other hand clenched over my chest where something sharp and old unfurled—a sickness I remembered from childhood, from screaming behind a locked door, from hiding under motel sinks. I might have screamed again if the door hadn't creaked open.

Hanging in mid-sway, the darkness of the room beyond filled me with oppressive despair. A light popped on, sending out a golden glow. I approached. Dogs barked nearby, and the wind caused tree branches to groan. The six steps up to the porch creaked with my weight. Warm air flowed from the house as I approached the door. She was humming "Blowing In The Wind." Inside, she sat in a padded rocking chair, an ancient TV set within arm's reach. "What the hell happened to your hair?"

I stepped inside and closed the door. The air turned heavy, thick with floating dust and the smell of decayed wood. It was like walking back into a sealed memory vault, too familiar, too intact, all of it whispering: you never really escaped. I licked my top lip and tried to keep a tremble out of my voice.

"I need a place to hide."

"People after you?"

"They want me dead."

Her head tilted, eyes narrowing as she studied me. I studied her, too. Her limbs had strength. Her face retained its fine angles with dragon-lidded eyes. Slender fingers interlocked before tapping against her lips. This room had remained unchanged after all these years, a shelf of albums she had no way to play, two overstuffed bookcases, and a shabby couch with worn arms covered with dish towels. Beyond, a servable kitchen with yellowed linoleum floor exuded the scent of bleach. The edge of a Maytag washer still obstructed the entrance to my room by a quarter inch, creating difficulty in opening and closing the door. Stella slept on a couch that converted into a bed. I might as well have entered this room the day I walked out. Every misfit trinket found its place like an overstuffed Waterhouse painting, and she fit in like the last piece of a jigsaw puzzle save for one crucial difference—the glint of gold that caught my eye.

"If you want to stay, you'll have to apologize to him. You know where he is."

Yes, I knew where he was, where he wasn't, who he was, and who he claimed to be. He was the man she loved more than life, more than me, her daughter. And I'd have to apologize for killing him. For a moment, I thought of storming out. There were a million places I could hide. I could disappear into the landscape of this country, go to Mexico, Brazil, Australia, and never see this vile woman again, but it was a gold necklace that would keep me here for now.

A choker, its sparkling sequined heart resting on her collarbone, indented with a faint circle exactly Boxy's size. My hand twitched. Martin had trusted her. Why? The gold sparkles caught the light and held it. That necklace anchored me to this place, to this woman, to everything I'd sworn to outrun.

"Yes, Mamma," I said. "I'll do anything you want."

Twenty yards back, near the base of an unnamed mountain, is his tombstone. I could hardly believe she'd spent money on it, considering how poor we were back then. The audacity still staggered me as I remembered flashes of arriving at this broken-down shack where all we ate for three days were mayonnaise sandwiches. She claimed it was her grandmother's house and she'd grown up here, but I don't know if that is true. I wasn't even sure my actual name was Brooklyn Tremain. The community was small, hardly four hundred people. No one questioned the single mother with the badly scarred child.

The smooth, gray marble headstone had been polished to a sheen. His meister name, Blue Stillness, was carved into the stone in the shape of a circle. Born September 4, 1959, died... There was no date. I don't think either of us remembered the date. He wasn't buried here. I don't know where he's buried, and I doubt Stella did either. A pauper's grave or prison cemetery wouldn't surprise me. But to Stella, he was here, in the dirt where she would lay too, his eternal soulmate. She could never inquire about him or try to connect with her old pals from the commune. Everything the man did was scrutinized to this day in the hope of finding his accomplice.

Ernest Wayne Dorsey, a cross between a Charlie Manson wannabe and a Jim Jones aper lived on the adoration of young, unsettled women and fanatical lost men. He absorbed their overwrought, mundane lives into his Blue Stillness. He was them, they were him. Together, they were whole, unbreakable, joyous in the Blue of Stillness. What the acolytes didn't know was Ernest Wayne had a penchant for robbing banks.

I glanced back at the house. Stella's face in the window looked carved from the same stone as the one on the grave. I turned so she couldn't see me and spit. "Curse you, Blue Stillness," I whispered, voice suppressing a chortle. "If it weren't for your birthday... 9459." My guffaw surprised me, instant and organic. Martin, damn you. You made me laugh. Martin put it all in front of me. I just had to trip over it

Stella stirred a pot of soup when I returned. Elbow macaroni in watered-down tomato paste. It smelled familiar. Growing up, I'd eaten enough of it that I could almost taste the starchy texture. She ladled more macaroni than liquid into a bowl, handed it to me, and then got her own. We sat across from each other at the Shaker table—our battlefield for years. I took a bite, the taste as bland and empty as the decades between us. But something stirred in my throat anyway. Maybe grief. Maybe a scream I'd swallowed years ago. The somber silence between us thickened and knotted. I glanced at the heart-shaped pendant whenever I could but didn't want to draw her notice. "How did you get my email?"

"The emails you never answered?" she shot back. Taking a swallow of soup, she leaned back, her gaze assumptive and smug. "Your man came to see me." Tilting her head and pursing her lips, Stella spread her arms wide. "Guess he thought he could facilitate a mother and daughter reunion." She chuckled, then sighed. "I thought, what the hell."

Realizing the spoon was mid-air, I brought it to my mouth. Shifting uncomfortably, I remember the empty envelope marked "Brooklyn's Mother" in Martin's Seattle office. Stella waited for me to speak. I moved the macaroni around with my spoon, stirring, unable to eat.

"How did he find me?" She laid her spoon down with a sharp clack.

"I don't know. He was a talented man."

"Was?"

I didn't answer her as I wondered the same thing. If he knew about Stella, he knew about me. And yet, he'd never let on for the entirety of our relationship. It wasn't the first time I'd wondered if I knew Martin at all, and probably wouldn't be the last. After reading the RedWater files, tussling with Bren and Al, and realizing he had as crazy, perhaps crazier, family than I did, I had to give him his own reasons. The RedWater files were as invented a history as the two of us. He never mentioned that he was related to the Hasts or what they did to him as a child. He hid who he was, from the world, from me. Then, he hid Boxy's third part. I almost chuckled out loud. He chose a damn fine place.

"I could have killed him," Stella said cavalierly. "He was trespassing. I'd be within my rights. Found him out there by Blue Stillness, trying to bury something. He could have told who I was. He knew I was the girl in the picture."

"Would that make us even?"

"You don't understand. It's not about *even* malarkey. It's about staying safe, keeping the secret."

"No kidding," I snarked.

We stared hard at each other, trapped in our unmovable stalemate again. Her reasons covered her mouth, and mine closed my ears.

She turned aside, hands wringing together in front of her. "Too smart for your own damn good, wanting shine, attention, wanting your picture in the papers."

"It's not my fault he's dead," I said firmly.

"You should have let go of him." She pushed her bowl and caused some of the soup to spill.

"Do you realize how crazy you sound?" I got up, knocking my chair backward. "That awning was a fifteen-foot drop to the ground."

"I'd have caught you."

"But you didn't! I broke my wrist when I let go. You didn't catch me."

" 'Cause I saw what you did. You, clinging on to his legs, afraid to let go. Him, tangled up in that rope. If only you'd let go, it wouldn't have strangled him, wouldn't have broken his neck. Your weight, hanging on to his legs, is what killed him."

"But I did let go," I said, my voice breaking before I could catch it. "I let go, and I watched you kneel for him, scream his name, while your daughter lay behind you—on the pavement, bleeding, crying, invisible." My wrist ached just thinking about it, the phantom pain more honest than anything in this house.

"It's because," she said, her voice a tremble. "I saw the police."

"And swung your arm around to shut me up."

"I got the knife to cut him down. I didn't realize—"

"*Shut up, you stupid piece of nothing*, is what you said before you tossed me in the backseat of a car, and we ran and are still running."

"If I'd been arrested, what would have happened to you?"

"Maybe gotten adopted, had a great life."

"Or ended up here, with a grandmother who'd have beat you raw every time you wronged Jesus. Blue—he gave you a great life."

"Using us as shills while he robbed banks."

"If only you'd followed his directions. Don't you know how many people we were taking care of? That cost money!"

"I was seven years old."

"They got my picture."

Our voices faded to whisper, the venom spent, both of us unsure the argument tamed a justifiable surrender. No one was right. Her world had been destroyed that day, and I knew something about that. Now there was only irrational blame and the fear that someday it would be discovered that my mother was the girl in the picture.

A student photographer coming out of a café, surprised at hearing a bank alarm, lifted his camera and snapped the Pulitzer Prize-winning photograph of young Stella on her knees, arms wide, unable to save her bank-robbing boyfriend who hung by the neck after jumping onto an awning, me on his back, and getting tangled in the ropes of a flag pole. Printed in every newspaper and magazine in the country, it became iconic. *The Girl In The Picture.*

Cops, marshals, FBI, reporters, detectives, and armchair gumshoes still search for her. What the photographer missed was the girl who let go. The girl curled against the bank wall, blood on her face, not from the fall but from her mother's blade when she turned too swiftly to tell me to stop shouting. That photo immortalized Stella's grief but not my pain. My scar is the proof no one ever saw.

We ate in silence, then I took my bowl and hers to the sink, rinsed them out, and leaned against the counter. "Martin gave you something. Maybe he meant to bury it out with ole Blue Stillness there, but you caught him as you said, and he trusted you to hold on to it for me." I turned toward her. "That must have been some conversation."

A brief glance, then she looked away.

"Are you going to give it to me, or do I have to jerk it off your throat?"

She veered toward me, hand raised, but froze mid-stance. We matched glares until she broke. Her gaze whipped toward Blue Stillness, there and not there, then released a soft half-sob, wiped her eyes, and straightened her stand. Slowly, reaching for the clasp. I watched how the past still lived inside her. The pendant fell into my hand with the weight of her sorrow.

"I put on clean sheets while you were out there, with him." She nodded toward Blue Stillness' gravestone.

I opened the door to what was my childhood room. No changes. The same single bed, desk, chest of drawers. "Mamma, why didn't you just take this room instead of sleeping on that foldout couch all these years? Not like I would have minded."

" 'Cause I figured you'd come back someday," she said, leaving the kitchen and lowering herself into the rocker. She turned on the TV, which I realized had no picture, only sound, and listened to the news.

Here, she and I were in a wary gridlock of secrets and silences. She guarded her myth, I guarded my truth, and neither of us could afford to let go. Still, something shifted... barely. Not forgiveness, not love, but something softer than hate. I clung to it, for Martin's sake. For mine.

Martin, I thought. *You're such a lionheart.*

In the quiet of the bedroom, I could feel the pull between the three pieces... Two pieces really. The silver was fused tight as a pickle jar and didn't show any give in coming apart again. I set it on a high bookshelf beside schoolbooks still stacked from the last day I attended high school.

The gold-colored heart sparkled like glitter had been poured into the material. I turned it over in my hand. It fit in my palm with room to spare, light as paper, but with more girth than the other part. I rubbed the circle, stirring warmth, but there was no vibration or spark as I had felt with the other two pieces. It was as if it had been waiting.

I lay back on the bed, the gold heart pressed between my palms. Anxiety twisted in my stomach—not only about what would happen when the pieces joined, but fear of what Martin had seen that had him separate them to begin with. Had he glimpsed something terrible that I was still too naive to understand?

Martin broke them apart for a reason, and I wondered if he'd still be alive today if he hadn't. Boxy could be more than a powerful weapon. If it roamed free in the world, would it use Martin as its moral guide? Or as a free-thinking computer—could I call it a computer? Maybe it was more, as a free-thinking whatever... Would it decide based... on what? I took the pendant off the choker chain and fell asleep with it in my hand, afraid to let go of it.

There I would find it when sunrays broke through my window. The house was still, a quiver of silence constant as a heartbeat, then realizing it was the rhythm of my own pulse, thudding in my throat like a warning. The past, the loss, the future—I was suspended between all three. Tucking each piece of Boxy in different pockets, I opened my door.

I found instant coffee on the kitchen table. A kettle of hot water already steamed. Pulling back a curtain, pantry shelves held cereal, cans of vegetables, and Spam. A bowl of potatoes and several onions looked to be on this week's menu. I could help with that, still having most of the money Gavin had given me and some of Martin's left. It'd do us for a while, but I would have to figure things out. Maybe get a job.

Stella was on the porch, sipping from a ceramic mug. She stopped humming when I sat beside her. The morning was misty even as the sun's rays reflected on the morning dew. She stretched sideways until her spine cracked. She was dressed and had lipstick on.

"Where are you going?"

"Job," she said. "Fridays, I drive the Bookmobile for Clara Crawford. She sneaks off with a boyfriend from Slymore and doesn't want her mother to know. Pays me under the table."

I nodded, glad she'd found somewhat gainful employment rather than running religious scams. "There's no reason you shouldn't take the bed in the back room. Sleeping on that couch can't be great for your back. We can switch off."

"On Sunday, I fill in for Jean Sanders as a janitor at the Coldbrook Hospital. She likes spending the day with her grandkids. Also pays me under the table." She stood and sipped more coffee. "Might be able to pick up another day from her. Two of us now, we'll need more."

"I can get a job."

"You look like you need to sleep for a month." She motioned with her mug but didn't look at me. "Need to gain some weight. That might bring your hair color back."

"I'm fine with the hair color," I sputtered, fighting off a childish niggle of being controlled.

"I didn't know what he was doing at first." She exhaled a trembling huff. "There's this thing when you're young and in love; your mind twists you into foolish rationalizations that seem solid. By the time I understood, Blue owned me. I couldn't have left if the King of Siam had offered me a palace. All my brain did was think of him." Stella cleared her throat. "I did have a talk with that boyfriend of yours. A long one. About everything. He made clear the trouble that was on the way. Only one truth he yanked out of me." Stella breathed in deeply, gazing outward at the distant mountain range. "Thank God for you. You saved my life."

The words hit like a stone to the chest. I wasn't ready for them. For once, I didn't see the opportunist or the liar. I saw someone broken, like me. The weight of what we'd both endured tilted everything sideways. I wanted to hug her. I wanted to scream.

Stella drained the mug and set it on the porch rail. "I reckon that fella of yours is with Blue Stillness these days?"

"Or thereabouts."

"Well, you ought to understand me better now. I mean, look what he got you into."

Her statement speared me. For several seconds, my head filled with a swoosh of white noise, and my instinct was to defend Martin. But with what words? She was right. If I'd never met Martin, what would I be doing? Rebuilding a life in San Francisco and a future that made sense. Interviewing politicians, influencers, and everyday citizens. Giving voice to the survivors of this moment in time known as the Regency. Looking for my next byline.

"I'll go fold up the bed," she said.

"I'll do that."

She nodded and put on a jacket with a hospital logo. "I didn't take the room 'cause I *figured* you'd come back someday. I left it empty 'cause I *hoped* you would."

I was glad I wasn't looking her full in the face because Stella's words almost took me to my knees. She walked out into the yard, pulled a bicycle from behind one of the derelict cars, and without looking back, disappeared down the hill. My hands were fists, nails digging into my palm. Sometimes truth is truth, even when you hate it.

The sun had burned off the mist within the hour and warmed the mountainside. A few daffodil stems were sprouting from a gravel path to the mailbox. A bare apple tree and several gooseberry bushes filled a side yard. The nearest neighbor's house was about a quarter acre away, and it looked as if they grew a sizable garden between theirs and Stella's property. I wasn't sure who owned the mountain behind us. I'd played on it as a child, knew its paths like a worn map, had named trees and rocks like old friends, and found a secret hiding place.

I sat on the porch with a second cup of coffee, absorbing all Stella had said, letting it infuse me, anger me, confound me, and heal me. *Martin*. How do I decipher the meaning of Martin being here, learning all about me, talking to Stella, co-opting my life?

It would be easy to lose my love to the vulnerable, so much of my hidden torment exposed, helpless knowing that he knew all the sorrow of me, and still, he'd chosen to add to it.

Martin had not revealed his connection to the Hast family in the RedWater files. I'd probably never know how long he'd known who the Hasts were. Phillip Javon came into his life at a pivotal time, propelling him from successful lawyer to billionaire entrepreneur. Had the Hasts set him up? Still, when he learned who they were, he'd hid it from me as much as he had the world. Part of me bristled at the unfairness of it, and yet, he knew that our pasts had rendered us the same—damaged, wounded, imperfectly flawed. To be found out, our truths revealed to a judgmental world would have been the greatest of humiliations.

I straightened the house and looked through the closets and bookshelves. Stella's clothes were worn but practical. She owned three dresses, a dozen pairs of jeans, and colorful tunics, as well as a variety of coats to match the weather. Her reading needs were classical: Thomas Hardy, Jane Austin, Charlotte Bronte, and a few F. Scott Fitzgeralds.

The books were yellowed, spines broken, pages dog-eared from use. They smelled of age and perseverance. Stella's world was one of hand-me-downs and makeshift hope, and yet in the quiet corners of this house, she'd managed to carve out a sanctuary of words. I suspected many of the books came from the Bookmobile as they bore the stamp of the Slymore Library.

Returning to the porch, I took the two pieces of Boxy from my pocket, pondering them. I wasn't sure Boxy would even work here, so far back in the mountains without Wi-Fi or computer connections. Boxy had worked in other places without a connection, and frankly, I wasn't sure how. At one time, I'd thought it must be using satellites; other times, it seemed to have its own volition. I held out the silver disk. What kind of intelligence didn't need a connection to act? Was it still a tool—or something more alive than I wanted to admit?

"Open a virtual computer." Silver Boxy warmed and opened a text box. "What happens if I link you to the third part?"

The menu will expand, it typed back. *I will be whole.*

"Do you answer to me?"

You are Martin approved.

Well, that's a relief, I thought, and chuckled. Biting my lip, I hesitated, then asked, "Do you know that Martin is dead?"

Nothing. I thought I might at least get a comforting puppy. The virtual text box closed and opened again as if it were resetting itself based on new information. *He is here and there*, it typed.

"Just like Blue Stillness," I jested. Still unsure what to risk, I put the two pieces in separate jean pockets. Then thought better of it. Pulling the silver part out again, I asked it. "Locate Al Hast and Bren Chandley?"

Not enough memory.

"If I link you to the third part, can you hunt them down?"

I will be whole.

"Does that mean you can open a link to where they are like you did with the PlanK? Can we have fun with them? Can we shut their asses down?"

No response.

This would require some thinking, contemplation, and the wisdom of Solomon. Times like these, I wished I could talk to any number of people. Jamie, Miriam, even Ford, who might make fun of my ignorance and suggest I grow a brain. I couldn't risk contacting any of them, even Dan, who might have been able to figure this out or know someone who could. I tried to think as Martin might, taking Osiris apart because he didn't know if he could trust its power. Had he come to a realization? Yet he'd asked me to bring the part to him in Seattle. He'd hidden the third component here at my childhood home. He must have been intending to put it back together again.

A wrench of yellow warblers chattered and pecked at the ground. The noon sun spilled over onto the porch, and I shaded my eyes and moved to the opposite side. I realized in the last few hours I had begun to feel at home again. Unsure of what to do about Boxy, I let the matter rest for now. There were other obligations I had to fulfill. I went to the bedroom and pulled out the smallest vest I'd worn closest to my body, the only one that had survived the entire journey. Martin had given it to me for my birthday, bragging that it was made of his proprietary Superman material and had more pockets than a mob of kangaroos. It carried everything important, everything I could never risk losing. Taking a small pair of scissors, I cut a seam on the back panel, opened it gently, and pulled out a velvet pouch in a sealed plastic bag.

Miriam.

"I promised Carl I would put you some place beautiful."

When I was ten, I'd discovered my secret hiding place, storming out of the house because Stella wouldn't let me go to a classmate's birthday party. I'd spent many a day here, daydreaming and planning my escape. Hunters occasionally walked past, and even Stella was out looking for me with a hickory switch in hand. If she ever figured out where I was hiding, she didn't let on. Honeysuckle vines hung from a rock arch, falling like a curtain. Passing underneath revealed a carpet of lime green moss surrounding a pond overlooking the valley, two towns, and far mountain ranges knitted together until they disappeared into a sea of indigo mist. Depending on the sun's angle, the still pond reflected like a mirror. I'd once dipped a branch into it, wondering how deep it was, and never reached the bottom. As a child, I thought it went to the center of the Earth. On wet days, rain streaked down the rock wall on the far side, feeding it so that the water churned to a jewel green and overflowed the cliff to create a murmuring waterfall. How far down it fell, I wasn't sure.

I inhaled a cool and familiar breeze as I pulled back the honeysuckle vines and stepped inside. "Hello, I'm back."

The moss gave beneath me like an old friend's embrace. I dipped my fingers in the icy water, remembering turtles, the croak of bullfrogs, the scent of honeysuckle, dragonflies lilting on the rocks to drink their fill. My secret place. I pulled out the velvet pouch and held it between my palms. "Miriam, I've brought you to the most beautiful place I know. If there was any place that stayed in my heart no matter where I was, it was here." I opened the pouch, closed my eyes, and evoked the image of her face. "I'm where you wanted me to be," I said.

Sprinkling her ashes onto the mirrored surface of the pond, they glistened as they touched the water, floated, and then drifted into the depths in a gentle swirl. I tied the velvet pouch onto a vine growing down the rock face. Maybe in the summer, I'd take pictures and figure out how to safely get them to Carl.

"Brooklyn!" Someone hollering my name. "Brooklyn! Now! I mean it!"

Stella. I dipped underneath the vines and saw her below in a small clearing. She twisted in a circle, clutching a newspaper and calling my name. "Up here," I called out.

She hurried up the dirt path toward me, her expression worried, waving the newspaper. "We're found!" Panting, she reached me, holding out a *Washington Post*, her hands shaking as she opened it. *The Girl In The Picture* photo was side by side with a picture of me on my knees, arms spread, looking up at Martin's hanging body. Our positions are identical.

I turned away, the air suddenly felt too thick to breathe. My knees wobbled, and the ground pitched beneath me. "Calm down," I told Stella. I held onto a beech tree, my other hand on her shoulder as I tried to think my way out of this. "Mother," I said, shaking her to get her attention. "You're twenty-three years old in that picture. My hair is almost to my shoulders now. Nobody will know it's us."

"You can't be sure." She paused, realizing what I'd said, and looked at the newspaper again. "That's you?" As comprehension of our mutual fates settled, her gaze met mine, fearful yet sympathetic. "I hadn't realized. Your head is shaved."

"Let's sit in here," I said, holding back the honeysuckle vines. "The view is more tranquil."

She ducked under, taking in the revelation of all her unanswered mother questions. She side-glanced me but didn't say anything.

I perused the article, reading how an old-timer reporter noticed the similarity to *The Girl In The Picture* and thought it might make a puzzling human-interest story. Their image of me was fuzzy like it had been taken from a security camera. That made me suspicious. More likely, the Secretary had planted this story to try and smoke me out. They wanted Boxy just as much as the Regency. My mind raced in a dozen different directions. "There might be something I can do." Boxy was warming up in my pocket.

Sending Stella back home, I pulled out the two pieces. The silver emitted the softest vibrations, and the gold pendant was dormant as a rock. I opened a virtual computer and asked how many *Washington Post* subscriptions came to this county. Sixteen total. Six went to libraries, and the other ten went to private residences. The ones to houses were still in the mail. "Can you reroute those to an address in Brazil?"

Done. Boxy typed.

Between Stella and I, we could get that section of the paper from the six local libraries and send it to shredder heaven. Leaning back, I felt better, but this incident made me realize that this kind of thing would happen again and again until one of them, the Regency or the military, found me. I needed more firepower.

My hands shook as I held the pieces apart. This was it. I could feel the hum in the air, like static before a storm. I was about to bring something alive again—something that might not obey, something that might consume me. And yet, I needed it. Needed to believe Martin hadn't died for nothing. "Okay, here we go."

Slowly bringing the two closer together, both hummed as if speaking their own language. The silver snapped into the gold, then turned the same color. A menu appeared. A long menu. I clapped my hands at seeing an operations manual. "Thanks for that," I said aloud and opened the RedWater folder to see several more documents than before, including one called BrooklynEyesOnly. My heart raced in anticipation.

Scrolling through the menu of maybe twenty-five options, it ended with an icon called Resurrection. "That the same as restore?" I wondered. "I need you at full tilt, Boxy, so power up." I tapped it, expecting a file to open. Instead, the menu, the RedWater file, and the text box twirled into an infinity image, swirling over and over itself until it faded. "No!" I called out in a hysterical panic. "No, no, no, no, come back!" As it disappeared, I reached into the air, shook the pendant, and tried to take it apart. "Damn it!" What had I done? Had I destroyed everything?

"Hey, baby," said a voice behind me.

I jumped like lightning as terror shot through me, gripped my brain, and froze my muscles. My hands floundered, searching for any kind of weapon. I was found! The image of a hyp-soldier, Al Hast, Bren Chandley, invaded my mind all at once.

Sliding on the muddy pond bank, my hands slipped on the algae-covered stones. I twisted around. Mouth ajar. For several seconds, I lost my sight. Squeezed my eyes shut. Opened them. Sound ceased, then a high-pitched churr as choked words scratched my throat in a staccato keen. "This. Can't. Be."

Martin. Martin stood three feet from me. All six foot two of him, smiling and looking down at me, amused by my splayed position.

"It's me," he said, hands circling before him as if to tell me to get with the program. "Cool pond," he said, bending over the water and staring into its depths. "Created by a detached glacier that carved a two-hundred-foot depression and fed by an underground lake. Bet some ancients have pondered its depths," he snickered. "Get it, pondering the pond. Maybe a mastodon drank here."

"Stay away from me with your dad jokes!" I lurched upright, heart jackhammering, crouching low against the rock wall. "You're not real," I said, even as the world now seemed to be a ballon of delusion. My muscles tightened, poised for escape, but a deeper part of me froze—torn between the familiar cadence of his voice and the uncanny impossibility of his presence.

He knelt, reached out a hand, and then sat cross-legged across from me when I cowered away. His head dipped, looking up into mine. "It starts with a proton, here," he gestured to a point in the air. "It's also here," his other hand lifting to another. "But physics tells us they can't be two places simultaneously. And yet they are. So, I am here, and I am there, and yet it can't be, but it is." He threw his head back, cackled a hearty laugh, and smacked his hands together. "Quantum ain't what it used to be, baby."

The words curled through the air like a riddle written in a language only our philosophers and physicists understood. I wanted to laugh, or cry—maybe both. It was Martin's rhythm, his voice, his damnable charm. And yet it wasn't. I was looking into the face of someone who no longer had blood, yet somehow still had heart.

"I have to be dreaming." I studied him, and he was here, evident in my sight, as real as a solid object, as if it were Martin in the flesh sitting before me. "How can this be?" It was his eyes that betrayed the illusion—Martin's deep, stormy blues marbled with something alien.

Each blink split reality wide open, a yellow serpent's slit flashing through, sharp enough to slice memory from trust. At first, it brought back images of Devil Martin, and every instinct told me to run. I wanted to believe it was him, but my body bristled with mistrust. Martin wouldn't look at me like that. I reached out to touch him. My hand went through the image. "What happened to the virtual computer? The expanded menu?"

"You don't need it any longer; you've got me." He held his arms wide, grinning.

"There was a file, BrooklynEyesOnly. I want to read it."

"I'd rather you not."

"I thought you answered to me?"

"It's just that... I wrote it in a funk." His torso twisted, anchoring his fingertips against the ground as he weaved uncomfortably back and forth. "Was kinda drunk. Missing you. All weepy and nostalgic."

"An AI image with feelings?"

"To be fair, I was listening to Taylor Swift."

I pressed my palm to my forehead, trying to push away the swell of longing rising behind my ribs. My brain told me this was code—clever, dangerous code—but my heart whispered, *he's back.* This creation was Martin right down to the smartass. I wanted to scream at it to shut up "I have to think," I said.

"I am me but not me, if that makes sense, and don't worry if it doesn't. Maybe in time it will. Whatever time is." His expression pulled in as if considering. "Let's have some fun, baby."

"Fun?"

"That TV in your mom's house. I mean, really, cathode ray tube? The water plant servicing this area has a chemical imbalance that we could fix easy, and city hall is infected with a virus siphoning off about five hundred a month to some hacker in Russia."

I sat up and moved closer to him, studying the features. "The bird was corporeal. It couldn't get through the glass. The dog less so. You?" I swept my hand through his shoulder. The sensation tingled, not unpleasantly.

"I wish I could say bigger is better but in this case, bigger is... loftier?" He held out his hands, palms up and shrugged. "You really want me to stay a bird?"

"You don't do anything without checking with me first."

He didn't answer, blinked, then chirped, "Okay."

"A Russian hacker? Isn't that a bunch of—"

"Malarkey," he raised his eyebrows and nodded.

"Go get 'em."

"Done."

"Done as in done? Or it's on your list?"

"Done as in he's on his way to Siberia."

I licked my lips, unable to look away from the face I knew so well. "Are you Boxy?"

"Surely, we can go with Martin now, can't we?" His expression softened, and he pressed his lips together as if he expected to be hurt. "I mean, it's one thing when I was in pieces, but baby, I am now whole! I even experience erec—"

"Enough!" I blew out a long breath, trying to keep up. "I yield to your extended menu."

"When I say whole, what I mean is the mathematical formula that Phillip Javon generated, and the DNA that was Martin Siriso created new building blocks. Not like those silly AI images I've deconstructed with ease, but a unique, Promethean being that is of equal parts the quantum miracle and the person you knew as Martin."

"You can still fight the Regency?"

"That's what keeps me on track."

"You're keeping track..." My mind raced and landed in exasperation.

"Oh, before I forget." He laughed Martin's exquisite laughter, spirited and vital. "What am I saying? I don't forget. Give me a second." He tapped the air with a finger. "Okay, there. Just settling out my estate."

"Your what?"

"In three days, a package will arrive for general delivery to you in Slymore. It will contain several credit cards in your name, an international bank account as well as one at the local credit union. Plenty of money. Deeds to Bolinas, Paris, San Francisco, New York, and London real estate. I've left the Bangkok, Hong Kong, and Doha places to Gavin 'cause... well, he has shady things to do."

"Yeah, I've gathered." I sat back, crossing my arms, wishing I could outthink him to get ahead of whatever he was planning. "Wait, how are you doing this? I'm worried an electronic trail will lead here eventually."

"Eventually, it will. But eventually, it would anyway." He sat silent, watching me. Eyes blinked, the yellow flash unnerving. "Virtual lawyers all work for me. I pay them, well... nothing. But any hint that I'm being electronically traced and all my account numbers and names change. It'll take 'em a while."

I think I understood him. Yes, they'd hunt us down whether we fought today or tomorrow or twenty years from now. "I guess we are two people used to shifting appellatives."

"And here the final battle will be between fiendish multinationals and two lionhearts who don't even know if their names are real. That's our superpower, baby. We are, in fact, nobody."

"I'm not ready," I realized.

"You're more than ready," Martin said. "Just need to get your castle combat fortified."

"Stella's house?"

Our gaze connected, and we burst out laughing. A hand to my mouth, and he mimicked the gesture. Rolling over and holding our belly's laughter. I shook my hand at him to stop, but neither of us could. This image was as much Martin as Martin could be.

We studied the view the rest of the day, discussing how we'd defend the valley when the Regency attacked. I told him all I knew of the area, and he threw up a map where I pointed to various landmarks that could be useful. I found it heartwarming when he mentioned the terrain looked like Germany's Black Forest that we'd visited together. He had Martin's memories, and each time he spoke of our old life, I felt a warm union, even if I could never touch him. This work was our destiny, and I realized I was still in love.

As we descended the mountain, side by side but never touching, I kept imagining his fingers brushing mine. I wished I could've shown the real Martin this place—shared it with the man whose footsteps had once echoed through Paris and New York beside mine. I bit down the ache swelling in my chest. This wasn't Martin. Not really. Just an apparition made of particles and echoes.

Spring was weeks away, and this world would burst with greenery, floral, and intoxicating scents. Shaking off my emotions, I reminded myself of how this Quantum Martin looked at the magnificent view as an aesthetic strategy. I noticed the image always paused before answering me. Was he consulting a database, the World Wide Web, or Martin's memories and feelings? I couldn't call it Martin. It wasn't Martin. It was a computer, a tool—a weapon. I hesitated near the end of the path at the back of Stella's property, and he stopped with me.

"I'm not sure..." I paused, not wanting to hurt his feelings, simultaneously realizing that was preposterous.

"I can go back into your heart."

For a moment, I had to adjust to what heart he meant. I pulled the pendant out of my pocket and turned toward him. He was gone. One blink, and I was alone with the weight of silence pressing in. I clutched the pendant, my fingers trembling. The space where he had stood felt colder now, like he'd taken some small flame with him.

Stella's bike leaned against the front porch. If Martin was right about money arriving in a few days, I could buy her a car. I wondered if his magical fingers could also keep the numbers rolling for us. Years prior, I'd managed to convince a softhearted administrator to issue me a social security card by telling her I was an orphan who'd been born in a commune and never had a birth certificate. I hesitated to use any ID these days that might be tracked. I made a note to myself to ask him... it.

Stella was cooking when I entered the back door. The smell of cabbage and Spam filled the room. I could afford better food as well. I explained how we'd deal with the newspaper issue, and she listened intently and offered the bookmobile as transportation and cover for our library visits.

Throwing some onions and red pepper into the mixture, she asked, "Who was that man you were with?"

At least now, I could confirm to myself that I wasn't losing my mind. She had seen him, and he looked as real as a man to her as he did to me. "There was no man," I said too quickly, my voice a little too tight. I couldn't let her see how unsure I really was.

She scooped dinner onto two plates and returned the pan to the stove. "He looked like... No, I guess that's not possible. Sorry to remind you of it."

We both sat, her salting her food and me wondering if I could eat Spam. "It wasn't a man. It's a game, something virtual. It only looks like a man."

"Oh, like alternative reality."

"More like a video game with the characters all around us rather than on a screen. Useful for hacking the mail service and rerouting residential newspapers."

"I like that," she said, her shoulders slacking, a weight lifted.

Later, as I cleaned up the kitchen, Stella opened the couch and fell asleep to the sound of the news. She must be dead tired, riding that bike two miles and back after working all day. Before I turned off the TV, the picture flipped on, clear and crisp but black and white. This TV was indeed old. I had the power to make her life easier, to fill her pantry, and replace this clunky old TV. I also could bring no end of misery to her front steps.

I decided to take an early night as well. I had a lot to think about. Closing the door to my room, a figure stood in the corner, causing me to gasp. "Geesh!" I uttered, hand to my heart. "Don't scare me like that."

Martin stepped out of the shadows. "I want to show you something," he said, gesturing with a fluid motion. A black-and-white photo of a tent revival materialized before us. A sign proudly proclaimed: *Glory to the Holy Divine, Featuring Starshine!* A magnetic, sandy-haired man pointed toward the entrance where a woman wearing a head scarf held open the tent flap. Inside, sat a child in a wheelchair.

"You?" I asked, surprised.

"My birth parents," he nodded. "My siblings won't admit it, but they were used the same way when they were younger. It's the vulnerability of youth that draws in the masses."

"I'm so sorry you had to go through that, Martin." I reached out instinctively, my hand passing through his shoulder like mist. "I almost feel sorry for your siblings."

"Don't waste your sorrow on them," he huffed, rolling his eyes. "They made their choices." He paused and stared out the window. "They put Phillip in my path. Knew I'd find him, see his potential. The whole shebang was a set up. To draw me in, get my money, humiliate me, and throw me in a trunk, just like before."

"Why did they hate you so much?"

He pointed at the image of his father. "The true genius. He saw himself in me, not in my klutzy, one-dimensional older brother. Bren... smart as diamonds... but..."

"She was a girl," I said, nodding.

"But to answer your question... for a while, this medium traveled with us. She'd boast about the future, tell people what they wanted to hear, then one night, in a burst of tongues, she declares me the host for the chosen who will change history, and I swear on Planck's constant, she drops dead after that proclamation. Why pay attention to the children who sing in tune and smile on cue when you have the prophet of the age dwelling in your youngest. We brought in more money that night than ever before. Father began quietly shaping the kingdom not for the firstborn, but for the chosen. That wasn't lost on Bren."

"If you were so important why did your parents never look for you?"

"Oh, they did—until they realized the sob story about their lost son brought in more people, more donations." He shifted his gaze, studying the blurred images of his parents. "By that point, being found would have been more of an inconvenience, and while they tried for another child, they begged money for the search for the lost messiah. And it arrived in electromagnetic waves."

"Donations," I murmured. "I know that story."

"No," he countered, his image vibrating slightly, as though he were battling emotion. "My parents and siblings were true believers. If the Chosen was out there in the world, they believed he'd fulfil his purpose. In the meantime, they'd prepare the way. The true con was merely a consequence of bringing disciples to the cause. And the cause needed money to survive."

"Stella did it to survive as well. I can understand that, but I still hate it."

"Bren was the schemer in our family. My mother never conceived because my sister was slipping a birth control pill into dear ole Mom's food. After she managed to seize control of the finances, Bren built a following surpassing anything our parents imagined, and parlayed that into a marriage to a Midwest industrialist who mysteriously died soon after the honeymoon. She named our brother as CEO, a name change, and the rest, as they say, is lame, despicable, obnoxious history. In their warped, deluded minds, they couldn't let go of the idea of the entire world following them. They applied principles of cultism to world domination. Clever, if not demented."

"You're not that young in this picture. You must remember that life?"

"In the same way that you remember yours. Did you ever want to go back?" he asked, eyebrow raised. "Try having your crazy older sister throw you in a car trunk that drives away from the only home you've ever known. I had no desire to be the vehicle for the chosen."

I nodded, whispering, "Guess I was lucky to be an only child."

"I didn't know how to get back, and I only knew the name Starshine, but I did know that churches helped people. Once I escaped from the trunk, I found one. Luckily, I was kinda cute. They took a liking to me and placed me with a family who couldn't have children. The Sirisos were kind, and I was happy. I wouldn't have shaken that apple cart for anything. When Gregor Siriso passed, I found a trash receptacle filled with burned documents. I think he knew. He hoped I'd forgotten and never wanted me to remember. So, there are parts of this story, I'll never know."

"They loved you, Martin."

He nodded again, his image quivering. "I didn't know who Phillip was when he first came onto my radar, but his brilliance was breathtaking. He's the kind of genius that appears once in a century." Martin squeezed the bridge of his nose, eyes closed, then let his fingers drift over his lips. "To think, they put him in my path. It was their ultimate con to bring the lost brother back to the fold now that he was a wealthy lawyer. You have no idea what Phillip sacrificed when he allowed the binaural brainwashing to eradicate his memory."

"I'm so sorry. I truly am."

"All it brings me is shame."

My hands balled into fists. I wanted to hunt down the people who'd twisted a child's life into theater. But all I could do was stand there, helplessly in love with an illusion who didn't think he deserved better.

His face shifted toward mine, our cheeks nearly brushing if he were corporeal. The image vibrated against my skin, warm and tender. My breath shivered past my lips, as I turned into him, drinking in the fervor of what was almost touch. "I wish you had felt safe enough with me to have told me this when... when you were alive."

"Like you told me about your background?"

"I didn't go snooping."

"Yeah, actually, you did."

"That was work, and I sure didn't find any of this."

"You found what I wanted you to find. And for that I apologize. For investigating you without your knowledge, I apologize. For talking to your mother without you knowing. I, well, that was kinda fun. She called you a tempest in a stormy teacup."

"Martin is who should apologize," I said, not feeling the joke. "He should have told me. I'd like to be furious right now. I'd like to slap him and leave a hand print, but my hand would just go through that smart-alecky, highbrow, sexy face of yours. As much as I want you to be, you're not him." Stepping back, I pointed to a desk chair. "You can sit there if you don't want to close up."

"I think better looking at the stars," he said, moving beside the window. He studied darkness, the spread of stars, the pale reflection of his own face in the window pane. His bewildering irises flashed with calculation. "He doesn't know why he didn't tell you."

I sat on the edge of my bed, fists winding into the blanket. "He had a choice. He chose not to trust me. He walked me into places I could have been killed or worse. He knew his connection to the Hasts, and still let me fight them alone with a child I had to protect." My voice cracked, low and bitter. He'd trusted me with strategy, with death, but not with the truth. That betrayal splintered something that might never knit back together—not even with all the code and magic in the world. "It wasn't fair that I didn't know."

"Perhaps from the vantage point of the equation, I can add some perspective." He continued staring outward, into sky, into the stars, into the depth of the universe. "The human Martin pulls back, into his shame, into his need, into his inability to stop what happened. His choices were limited in a limitless world. Of highest priority, protect the girl; of higher priority, protect the world. It follows that in protecting the world, he protects the girl. Keep her a secret, a small kitten in a cavernous valley. Hide her. Hide one part Osiris. He'll figure out later how to put it all together again. But then, Phillip zigs instead of zags. The math sees it as a weakness in the numbers. Do you understand?"

I nodded, not sure that I did, but who was I to expect a perfect plot in a messy world. "Phillip betrayed him, returned to his mother. They found out about me."

"Now you're safer lost. Lost to him. Lost in the world. Even if I never come back together, you must stay lost to stay safe."

"But Gavin saved me, at least twice. At the red bus. And he dropped me the arrow."

"Gavin was tracking the Regency, not you. You just wound up in his path and he's an eye for the aesthetic called a knockout. The odds—"

"Thanks for that, no need to further point out my survival was one of chance."

"Your movements, your actions surprise... no, astonish... Martin. He hoped you'd subtract, stay safe, hidden, but instead you engaged. It gave him hope. So, he left the lava lamp in the window."

I looked at the floor, a wrinkle in the wood where my foot had tread over the years. A shivery breath escaped my core. "What did you even see in me?"

"I saw me."

"But you're not you." A sadness filled me, and I stared at the gold heart, closing my hand around it. All that was left of Martin.

He pulled away from the window, looked down on me, his lips pressed in a way I knew only as Martin. "And now, the parts are two but the whole is one. My mission is to destroy the Regency, but my purpose is to protect the girl."

"Can you tell where they are?"

"Not enough memory. It's like they're in a giant faraday cave, and I can only see glimpses when I get a good wave." He looked at me, his expression mournful as if he hadn't done enough. He reached out to touch my cheek but instead gestured. "They're trying to understand Phillip's notes," he chuckled. "Good luck with that!"

I studied his hand, holding in mid-air. Mine would disappear in Martin's when his fingers entwined with mine, and I'd kiss a small scar on his thumb. Would I feel him if the quantum had touched me long enough? Or were we ghosts to each other? "I need some rest."

He nodded and stepped back to the corner. "I'll keep listening. Other quantum computers allow me to extend my reach, but they're not nearly as enhanced, so what I hear is like an echo."

"You talk to other quantum computers?"

"More like negotiate with them."

"You make deals with other quantum computers?

"Martin is an excellent negotiator. You'd be surprised what they'd trade for a little juice." He chuckled at his own expression then looked wistfully at me. "I think I'm going to double helix now."

"Ok, and by the way—I am not a girl."

I got into bed and he stood by the window, looking out at a quarter moon rising. I didn't have the heart to tell him to close himself up, and he likely didn't need sleep, not the way I did. I shifted to my side, away from him, so I didn't have to see the man I loved and be unable to touch him. We were in the same room for the first time since he walked away from the San Francisco apartment that day so long ago, and yet, we weren't. Reminding myself that he wasn't Martin stung. Drifting into sleep, feeling safer than I had in a long time, I could have sworn I felt the caress of his hand across the back of my head, coming to rest on my cheek.

And so, the years passed.

Six of them.

Martin, as I still called him despite my initial reservations, had devised a way to transmit bee energy through power lines. Within a couple of years, much of the Americas had been inoculated, with many believing they had merely brushed a body part against an electrical socket or hit their elbow against something sharp. The legend of the Osiris device faded in and out of discussion, overshadowed by a flurry of exaggerated pseudo-documentaries speculating about the whereabouts of the Regency and whether they possessed that enigmatic gadget. Despite a global search, no one managed to locate them. Martin suspected they might be hiding underground, somewhere cold—perhaps Siberia, Antarctica, or an unnamed island. We agreed that they wouldn't come for me until they had a way to defeat me. That gave us time to prepare, and we spent most of our days running battle scenarios, and on his own, Martin fortified his own structure. We had to guess what we didn't know, but both of us had to believe that Boxy—Martin—could defeat anything they could invent. Could they write a code to render the Osiris device ineffective? Would Martin's DNA survive or overcome their intrusion? Unknown. I worried about it endlessly.

Bizarre as it may sound, Martin continued to forge connections with other quantum devices as countries, corporations, and hackers competed to become the reigning Kahuna in quantum mechanics. The fear that some pendejo could gain access to an instrument capable of infiltrating every server worldwide was ever-present. Still, Martin believed he could persuade the quantum realm to avoid serving nefarious purposes, like draining bank accounts.

In my quest to understand more, I devoured every book Stella could find on quantum theory, struggling to comprehend complexities that often eluded me. I frequently stumbled into the trap of asking Martin for clarification. "When you say you don't have enough memory, are you talking about *qubits*?" I inquired one day. He didn't respond, his eyes flickering as if searching for a way to answer me. "Enough mega-companies and nations are working on quantum computers to tackle various challenges, from developing disease treatments to advancing green energy," I pressed. "If you're quantum, why don't you have enough memory?"

"Technically, *qubit* is correct, but I try to choose words for the..."

"Non-technical?"

"Linguistic forms that are more accessible to a wider audience."

"Dumb, got it," I responded, ignoring the glossed-over insult. "How do we get you more qubits? The servers at the PlanK, their rooms were football field size. How'd you get into a small locket?"

He smiled. "I could just eat you up."

"Stop it!" I chuckled, suppressing a giggle. "You sound like Stella."

His expression warmed like my Martin's always did if I fell into interviewing mode. "We could write a book."

"Be serious."

"I am," He snapped his fingers, and a whirl of virtual yellow butterflies erupted, flitting around my head before vanishing into thin air. "If Martin and Phillip were still alive, they would have cornered the market. They were just that far ahead." The Martin before me stared into the sun, anchored a foot against the rocky cliff, and then scanned the valley below. "I doubt anyone will ever realize that the DNA was the game changer. How would they even know?"

"It enhanced you, made you—"

"Have a better sense of humor."

"Limited you?" I asked at the same time.

Martin tilted his head and blinked. "I have the capability to steal from every bank account in the world, to hack any website, hold companies, even countries hostage. But I chose not to... unless I have a compelling reason."

"And that's because of Martin's DNA or his moral compass?" I asked, concerned that he seemed to be alluding that he could do this without my instruction.

"I'm not sure," he said, then continued. "But I'm still the only thing that can destroy them."

"Thanks for that clarification." I leaned back against the rock face, careful not to pass through him, and closed my eyes to savor the warm breeze. His growing independence concerned me, but challenging him would lead to a forty-five-minute lecture on wave-particle duality. His flirtations were charming, evoking memories of my Martin. Still, they also reminded me that while he shared some traits with Martin, like distracting me when he didn't want to answer questions, he was distinctly Boxy—something unblinking and eternal. Too often, I found myself lost in him, only to grapple with the heartbreak that he was an artificial intelligence, not a human being.

I felt the absence of my California friends and all the people I'd encountered along my journey, but contacting them was too risky. Instead, I found allies in the community—at the library, post office, hospital, and town council. Under the pretense of preparing for floods, fires, tornadoes, snowstorms, and many other disasters, we organized and fortified the town using grant money supplied by Martin's virtual lawyers. Our most engaging annual drill occurred on Halloween, staged as a zombie apocalypse. The townsfolk, particularly the teenagers, had a blast. I took comfort in knowing they were preparing for a hyp-soldier attack. A few knew we could face a more severe threat, having lived on the other side of the Regency, but we downplayed those concerns to avoid causing panic.

As far as I could tell, thanks to Martin's vigilant surveillance, neither the Regency nor the U.S. military ever uncovered the name Brooklyn Tremain. I allowed the persona of Sulis to fade into the nation's mythology, and I purchased a longer chain to keep the pendant hidden under my clothing. Martin provided recommendations and suggested strategies, and at various points along the three paths into the valley, we crafted mousetraps that would lay dormant until we needed them. No matter what the Regency unleashed upon us, they would encounter far more than just a beehive. Martin also conducted virtual tours of every computer system we encountered, making minor fixes and setting up hidden alerts that would notify him of any unusual activity.

The town never knew about the myriad defenses we'd set up. To them, we were simply Stella and her wayward daughter reunited. I bought her a car, and she let me transform my bedroom window into a door to create a sunroom where Martin usually stayed. I offered to build her a bedroom. We could easily manage it with Martin's money. Yet, she insisted on sleeping on the foldout couch. It dawned on me that this had been her way of life—sleeping lightly, always with one eye on the door, ready for a quick escape. I wished I could give her a sense of safety, but in truth, I didn't have that for myself.

Not long after I moved in, Stella quit her hospital job but chose to stay with the library because she liked it. I joined her with the bookmobile duties, which gave me a better understanding of the terrain and how we might defend it when the Regency army reemerged. My mountaintop perch still offered the best strategic view of the valley. Stella and I spent some time up there, and when she asked about the velvet pouch, I shared the story of Miriam. She listened quietly, then said that when her time came, this was where she wanted to be as well.

And so, Stella and I maintained a mercurial truce. She grew accustomed to the AI image, accepting him as a kind of high-tech game that also came in handy when her TV picture faded.

"Obsolete," Martin hacked when he was called. "Prehistoric."

"Malarkey! Nothing wrong with this television set! Just give it a bang on the side," Stella ordered.

With a quick flick, Martin worked his Mr. Fix-It magic, producing a clear picture while rolling his eyes at me. "New TV," he muttered under his breath as he stormed through me with electric tingles.

Stella smirked, watching him return to the sunroom. Sometimes, I thought she simply relished his attention. "I swear, the way he looks at you like he wants to eat you up," she repeated time and time again.

"His image is based on my boyfriend."

"Don't you find that a little weird?"

I handed her a scrap of paper with a book title and asked her to order it for me. "You may find it listed as new age rather than science. I doubt it'll be helpful, but I want to see what this author has to say."

She looked at the title, put a finger to her chin, then pointed. "I've got this one. Top shelf."

I reached up and pulled out a book, dislodging years of dust when a silver object swished past my face and clattered to the floor. A knife, more a dagger. Not any knife.

"Oh," Stella muttered, reaching for it.

I beat her to it, wrapped my hand around the hilt, and stepped away. "How could you keep this thing?"

Her eyes darted as her hands waved a confused gesture. "I, I, I kept it for self-defense. Living alone. All these years."

"In case you needed to kill me next time?"

"Stop that talk."

"I will not!" I paced the length of the room, a hand to my head, looking at the blade, still sharp as the day it disfigured me. "A keepsake of Blue Stillness to keep you warm at night?" I snarled, the hilt burning in my palm. My patience broke under the weight of all the days I'd lived with the scar she'd given me, humming like a tuning fork for pain I'd buried too deep.

She left the room and headed toward the kitchen. "It's no more than I've said."

I stomped after her. "You almost killed me! I thought I was going to die! All you could do is wail for that miserable man!"

"I forgot it was even there!"

"You forgot I was there!"

"Stop it! Stop it!" Stella shouted, throwing a coffee mug that shattered in the sink. "What do you want me to do? I went crazy back then! I didn't know what to do or where to go. He was gone. And there was you, and I had to look at what I'd done to you every day of my life and wish..." Her expression crumpled. "I hated you, and I loved you, and I didn't know what to do except feed you and clothe you and live here and hope I'd find my sanity again." She clung to the edge of the table, unable to look up. Small puffs of breath were the only sound she made.

Her words crumbled something in me, something I didn't want to name. I'd waited my whole life to hear that admission, and now that it came, I wasn't ready—I was furious, and somewhere deep beneath it, I felt the terrible relief of being seen.

Martin appeared at the door behind her. "Tell her, Stella."

She glanced over her shoulder at him and shook her head.

"Tell me what?"

"It won't make no difference. It won't change what I did all those years ago."

"Look out the window," Martin said.

I looked out, seeing nothing, and waved my hand. "What?"

"He's gone," Stella whispered. "I had the gravestone removed over a year ago. You've never noticed."

"What?" I looked again toward the mountain slope, where sedge grass overgrew a barbed wire fence. No tombstone. No Blue Stillness. I had never noticed. "Oh," I whispered, but inside me a dam shifted. I didn't know if it was grief, forgiveness, or the disorienting realization that some ghosts truly were gone.

"Can we all just get along again," Martin said, feigning casualness with a shrug. "I mean, really Brooklyn, your mother was twenty-three years old, deprogramming herself from a criminal cult, taking care of a seven-year-old, and hiding from the po-po. After all this time, can't you give her a break?"

Feeling foolish, I cleared my throat and lifted my hand, palm up to acquiesce. "Look at you playing diplomat. You, with your non-aging face. I'll be ninety, and you'll still look the same," I said, tossing the knife in the garbage pail.

"Don't worry, daughter. I won't steal him from you," Stella grinned, trying to move past the tension.

"I can fix that." With a wave, Martin made his hair salt-and-pepper gray and smirked.

Stella clapped, looking at me with an expression of hopefulness.

Then Martin froze.

"What's wrong?" I stepped toward him, reaching out to touch nothing.

His eyes flickered, and his head jerked several times. "Dmitri Nerezza is..."

"Who is Dmitri Nerezza?" Stella asked

In addition to computers, Martin monitored the whereabouts of every living theoretical physicist and their communications. "Phillip's teacher," he said. "Taught him everything he knew. No longer on radar."

"Not good," I said, calculating the worst-case scenario.

"What's not good?" Stella looked back and forth between us.

Then, Martin's image blipped—only for a moment—followed by static as he tried to talk. "Kidnapped or turned." He doubled over, holding his stomach, fading in and out as he grunted like a person in pain.

"Your fake boyfriend is on the fritz," Stella said.

"No, Mamma," I said, realizing in horror that the time had come. "This is bad." I pulled the locket from beneath my blouse with trembling fingers, my breath shallow and fast. "We're found."

At the same time, Martin pressed his fingers to his temples like a human trying to concentrate. After several seconds, he slumped, appearing exhausted. I'd never seen him do that. "They've invented a revolving attack code. Takes me out of play. They're coming here." He curved his hands before him, crafting a virtual computer as sparks flared around him. He stabilized and coughed like a human trying to shake off congestion. "I've built a failsafe. Memorize this." His fingers moved like lightning as lines splayed across the virtual screen.

"Martin, what's happening?" Panic seized me, muscles trembled. We'd trained for this, but now every logical thought deserted me.

"Send this link to that group of friends on the Limey network." He glanced up at me. "I know, you thought I didn't know about them, but you talk in your sleep. Ask them to send it to everyone they know, then click the link."

I moved behind him, reading what he'd written. "This is too much, I, I, I can't memorize all this." My brain was petrified, trying to absorb line after line.

"It's low-tech. It'll give me a place to hide until I can… Arggg." He strained as another distortion hit him. "Store parts of myself on their devices until I can reboot."

I memorized as he typed, but the text began to disappear. "No, no! I can't get it all!" My mind froze, struggling to memorize every line. "It's disappearing!" Then the link was gone, and so was Martin. "No!" I screamed. "I don't have the last five lines. Martin, come back!"

A hand held my shoulder. "I've got it," Stella said, steadying me with a grip I hadn't realized I needed. I turned to her, stunned, the panic in my chest colliding with a surge of unexpected gratitude. I was breaking, and she was holding the pieces. "What do we need to do?" she asked.

I looked down at the pendant, which had turned silver. "We have to get to the library."

Marilee Lawson was one of the librarians I'd made friends with. She'd fought the Regency in Colorado before moving back home. We'd talked the town council into building a concrete, tornado-proof room as part of its life safety program and equipped it with a computer to contact the outside world in a town emergency. She must have read my face when I ran in because she reached for the key before I slammed into the front desk.

I sent Marilee to the post office to have them ring the hurricane siren. The siren wasn't just a warning. The tone would also activate the mousetraps. The piercing sound was a code since we didn't have that type of weather, and it also informed the valley that the thing coming was worse than a hurricane. It was the Regency. As Marilee darted out the door, I caught a glimpse of her face: not fear, but faith. Faith in me. That only made the pressure worse. My hands shook as I tapped the Limey icon, each second stretching long and taut.

The townsfolk knew what to do. West side would make their way to an abandoned coal mine. The east end would go to caves hidden throughout those hills. Coldbrook residents would shelter at the hospital, where a reinforced basement would keep them safe. It was a school day, and we also had a plan for that.

The Limey app pinged, and I opened it, getting to the connections as fast as my fingers would move. Stella stayed at my back, watching. I clicked to open Sulis, smiling that it was noted that I'd not been active in six years, so this was sure to get attention. I clicked on "video" and chose to send it to all. I also typed in a couple of other addresses, Gavin's and the one given to me by the Secretary of Defense, now Vice-President Jack Larkin. Without Martin, I would need all the help I could get.

"I don't know all of you, but I'm Sulis." The name *Sulis* caught in my throat like a broken promise. Saying it felt like peeling away scar tissue. I hadn't worn that name in six years—hadn't wanted to. But now it was all I had. As the word left my lips, I felt its weight land on my shoulders like armor I thought I'd discarded. "I'm sending you a link, and I beg you to believe me. The Regency is dispatching a force to come after me." A map flickered to life, displaying my exact coordinates. "We all remember what it was like to live under their oppressive grip in their twisted quest for power. Please, I need your help to fight back. Click the link I'm sending. Forward it to everyone you know, and urge them to click it too. Your computer will be commandeered for a brief time, but I ask for your trust. Please grant me the ability to resist them. Gavin, Vice-President Larkin, Osiris is down; I'll hold them off as long as I can."

I typed as fast as I could, recalling the multi-line link from memory. Stella placed her hands over mine, seamlessly typing in the remaining characters. Once we finished, I hit send, and she leaned her forehead against mine, a moment of shared determination before the storm.

"I don't know why I hated you all those years," I said tearfully. "You did the best you could." The words tumbled out, sharp and soft at once. I hated that it had taken the end of the world for us to find this peace. The guilt clung to me even as her forgiveness washed over me. It wasn't fair—none of it was—but her hands were solid on my shoulders, and that steadiness became my anchor.

"Mother-daughter crap. I let it go years ago."

I couldn't help giving her a side-eyed glance.

Trembling as we waited, I felt the pendant warm against my chest and hoped Martin was deep inside, healing or rebooting—whatever that was to him. "What if they won't do it?" I said, worrying aloud. "I haven't been Sulis in years. This might scare them. They might not believe me, think I'm crazy."

Stella patted my shoulders. "From the stories you told me about walking near across this country, from the people you met, helped, saved. What you've done here in this valley in a few short years. You made community everywhere you went, in every step your foot took. They'll do it."

A video opened. It was the Brasiltons in Montana. All of them gathered around their computer. "We hear you loud and clear," said the mustached man who'd once held me at gunpoint. "We are clicking, and we are coming."

Another video. Dan and Maria. "Sending this link out to all our contacts." Barber, now a handsome young man with a gaggle of pre-teen blonds behind him, all with their thumbs up, swung his arm high and gestured the click.

"Thank you," I said as a third video shot up. Ford. He wore camouflage pattern military fatigues, his face prominent in the screen crowded with soldiers surrounding him.

"On our way," he said, showing a gloved hand that emitted a wave of electrical sparks before he clicked. "Sulis Lives!"

"You're in the army!" I blurted. "What about college?"

He leaned his face closer to the screen, glared, and growled, "Geesh, Woman, don't embarrass me in front of me mates!"

"Is that a tattoo?"

As his fellow soldiers laughed and pointed, he swiped his screen shut as hundreds more popped up. "Clicking and forwarding!" many said. Others, including seventy-five-year-old Carl Houseman, waved their weapons and said they were coming. Tippy and Rosemary Sharp appeared, and their daughter

Trina waved a *Sulis Lives* flag. Most people from the two blocks of my San Francisco neighborhood popped on and clicked. Co-workers from the *San Francisco Calendar*. People I'd met along the road. Strangers. "Fought 'em once, will fight 'em again!" "Sulis Lives!" "Never Again!" "Not in my country!" They shouted and clicked.

"Didn't think you'd have a war and leave me out, did you?" Gavin appeared, shaking his finger at me. "Tying that phone to a dog was pretty clever, but hey, don't make fun of that kid, Ford. His squad is trained to fight hyp-soldiers."

I could hardly believe it. Tears filled my eyes as the screen became a collage of faces. Stella flicked the back of my head in congratulations.

"Thank you. Thank you all."

I looked at the heart pendant. It was beginning to turn gold again, but Martin had not reappeared. Unsure how close Regency soldiers might be, I took Stella's hand. "We better get home," I said. "You know where to hide?"

Stella nodded and followed me outside. The town was nearly deserted, with only a few people hurriedly locking up and waving at me as they ran past. Three trucks packed with high school football players—most of them wielding baseball bats and hunting rifles—rumbled past and turned onto the far side of the elementary school. Lines of children, accompanied by teachers, streamed toward them as the boys filled the beds of their trucks with kids to transport to Coldbrook Hospital, now fortified with security doors and stocked with rations for all the county's students in case we faced a prolonged siege.

Then, I saw her. She stood in the middle of the street, head slightly cocked, her blond curls lifted in the sparse breeze as she stared at me. Odette Wallace. Bluish lips curled into a pitiless grin, contrasting sharply with her pale face and shadows beneath her eyes. How many years had she been with the Regency? The poor child. Odette looked like a ghost made flesh—innocence hollowed out and puppeted by something monstrous. My stomach twisted as the truth settled in: they had turned the children into weapons. There was only one way to save them.

Slowly, I covered the heart pendant and unclipped it from its chain. Touching Stella's hand, she took it. "Hide it, Mom. Get in the car and take it some place safe."

"That's a child, honey."

"That's a killer, Mom."

Another child stepped from a doorway, followed by another, then another, forming a V behind Odette. Stella tugged my arm. "I know what I'm doing," I reassured her. "I'll be okay. Football team is going to help me." It was the only way to get my mother into the car and racing toward the west end of town. I needed her to keep the pendant safe.

Odette growled, her throat attempting to form words.

I hadn't expected children, but I suppose I shouldn't have been surprised. I cast a glance toward the school, acutely aware that if this didn't go as planned, those kids would tear me apart with their bare hands. One of the football players caught sight of me and raised his arm, forming a fist. They had all of the elementary school children secured. Now it was me and the football team, and all that we had practiced on those Halloween nights.

Odette pointed at me. "Kill," she rasped, her guttural voice unnatural from disuse. The group moved towards me, maintaining a perfect V formation. I shifted sideways, aiming for the elementary school. They followed.

"I'm sorry this happened to you, Odette. I'm sorry I couldn't save you." Each step I took was soaked in grief. I didn't expect redemption. I just wanted her to hear it—that I hadn't forgotten she was once a child who laughed. "I'm sorry," I whispered, even as her eyes flared with bloodlust. "I should've saved you."

"Kill," she repeated, her voice grating. More of her cohorts fell in line, echoing her mantra. "Kill, kill, kill, kill." Their eyes locked onto me, intense and unyielding.

"Now, Odette, you must know they want me alive. I have it."

"Don't care," she growled. "Kill."

Another blip in Bren's plans, the children disobeying their masters. Killing now satisfied their pleasure centers. They were beyond the control of the Regency. Likely why they were sent in first. A child killer would wreak such havoc that the community would despair in killing them, lose their own lives if they tried to save them. Forces following this wave in would have an easier clean up. Bren was taking a chance, but one she was right to bet on. Even if I died in the initial attack, she was betting that Osiris was somewhere close, somewhere on my body. That was all she needed.

I looked over my shoulder toward the school. A football player jerked down his clenched fist to signal they were ready. I sped toward the side door, slamming it open and leaving it ajar for the warrior children hungry for my blood. The pack chased me, snarling childish squeals as they vocalized the only word that meant anything to them. "Kill, kill, kill."

Martin's money had afforded me many things, and I felt a deep gratitude not only for the resources it provided to fortify the town but also for the courage of the football team. As the quick-footed running back locked the door behind us, I could sense the desperation of the pack chasing me. Metal gates crashed down over the windows and doors, sealing them inside. I raced toward the opposite exit. The sharp-eyed quarterback swung open a slot just in time for me to dive through, slamming it shut as the hostile pack thrashed against the barrier, desperately clawing over one another, trying to escape.

Odette bared sharp teeth, pressing her face against the small section of the window we hadn't covered. Hidden high in the corners of the school, dormant quantum bees stirred to life. A chorus of terrified screams erupted. The children stumbled over one another as swarms of bees enveloped them. The process seemed to take longer, and I worried whether the hives' energy would be enough to heal them. Most had been taken so young that they didn't know what reality was, so the cure confused them. Odette's face furrowed violently as she howled and hissed, then slowly began to transform. Beyond her, a mournful sound of weeping. She placed a hand against the glass, eyes sorrowful and bewildered. I pressed my hand against hers, offering reassurance. "You're safe now."

I hugged the quarterback as he insisted that he and the remaining players would wait with the kids until Ford's rescue teams arrived. I didn't know if this battle would ever make the history books, but today, bravery was in no short supply.

Grabbing a bicycle from the rack in front of the school, I pedaled fast as I could toward home. I paused to catch my breath as I approached the last hill before turning into our lane. From up high, I could see the mousetraps below, a monumental feat of ingenuity. Martin and I had speculated whether the Regency would send hyp-soldiers or mercenaries, but the one thing we agreed on was that neither was prepared to deal with the unexpected. So that's exactly what we gave them.

On the north road into town, we unleashed dinosaurs—Tyrannosaurus rex, Triceratops, Allosaurus, Ankylosaurus, and a few *sauruses* whose names I couldn't pronounce. The east road was inundated with massive tidal waves and tornadoes. The West was engulfed in fierce lightning strikes, fireballs, comets, and the most formidable alien invasion in the galaxy.

Eventually, the Regency soldiers would see through our ruse. Still, it would buy us precious time—hopefully enough for the U.S. military to arrive. I hoped Martin would reactivate and witness some of the finest illusions east of Las Vegas.

Dripping sweat as I pushed up the hill, I heard a voice. Singing. Someone was singing "Wayfaring Stranger." Stella? I laid down the bike and hurried toward the backyard. "Mom!" I called out, annoyed that Stella wasn't already at the pond where we'd planned to hide until the chaos subsided. She stood in the former place of Blue Stillness' gravestone, surrounded by Bren Chandley, Al Hast, and four mercenaries.

"Don't need her anymore," Bren said, eyes flipping up at me and smiling callously.

Al Hast raised an arm. A pistol. He shot Stella in the chest. Time fractured. The gunshot echoed in my brain. I screamed as she tumbled backward, disbelief gripping my heart. Her body crumpled, and I fell with her, arms flailing for a future I could no longer hold. Her blood soaked into my shirt like ink on paper, a signature I never wanted. "No," I whispered. "No, no, no—" My mind blanked. I screamed until there was no air left.

As I held onto her, my mind collapsed into white noise until I heard her voice. Stella pressed her lips to my ear and whispered, "It's with Miriam. Left you a present. You'll know how to use it." Her thumbnail traced the scar on my cheek as I helplessly watched the life drain from my mother. "I've seen in your eyes how you've relived it a thousand times, and for that, I'm sorry." A final breath pulsed from her lips.

Two soldiers yanked me to my feet, and a third tore my sleeve, exposing my arm. Bren approached, holding a small blue jewelry box. Hast, scowling, pressed his phone to an ear, his face flushing scarlet as he whispered something to Bren. "Well, aren't you just the creative one," she said mockingly. "Dinosaurs and aliens. Ha!"

They must have realized that their plans to subdue the population were unraveling. "You've lost. You better run while you can."

"Here's the truth," she said, popping the lid off the blue box. "I no longer need your cooperation." Holding it by its back, she pulled out a mechanical spider-like creature, its legs undulating. "My latest prototype. This might sting a little."

I struggled against the soldiers holding me while one of them tore more material, exposing my shoulder. Bren slapped the creature onto my skin, and I cried out from a surge of pain, blood streaming down my arm. "Get that thing off of me!" The soldiers held me firm as the creature latched on, burrowing deeper into my flesh.

"You'll give me Osiris without even a whimper in a few minutes. You'll be glad to do it. It is mine, after all, and that's the right thing to do."

Hast moved closer, observing me with a predatory gaze. "Whatever immunity you had before is nonexistent as long as we keep this little beast gassed up," he smirked, his eyes eerily reminiscent of Martin's, forcing me to look away. "With these, I don't need to control an army. Just the leaders."

Bren crossed her arms, a self-satisfied pout on her lips. "Once you've given me Osiris, you'll join our ranks. You will serve me. Maybe we'll start with a little tea and crumpets."

"Not in a million years would I ever—" My words caught in my throat. Any thoughts of fighting back, resisting, or even ending my own life curled around other thoughts, like the fleeting notion of indulging in a scoop of ice cream. "It's at the top of the ridge," I said, pointing ahead. My voice felt borrowed. The words weren't mine. A calm certainty settled into my bones, ice-cold and terrifying. "It's at the top of the ridge." I confirmed. Even as I spoke, some dim fragment of me screamed from the depths. But it was distant, like shouting through glass. I was a passenger in my own body, and my feet were already moving.

As I led them up the trail, a part of me questioned why I didn't fight. There was no internal debate, no contemplation—only what I would do. *Give Bren Osiris. Give Bren Osiris because that was the right thing to do.*

As we neared the summit, the sound of helicopters grew louder. Ford, I thought, but this too felt as mundane as getting the mail. *Give Bren Osiris.* The words echoed in my mind, a commanding instruction reminiscent of something I'd heard once before: *Kill the Madonna. Kill the Madonna.*

Even as I repeated the words, they bloomed into insignificance. My arm throbbed, blood dripping from my fingers. I focused on the pain, letting it anchor me as I whispered, Kill the Madonna. Hot, sticky blood trailed down my arm—something to hold onto. I clenched my hand into a fist. I clung to that rhythm. And rhythm gave me resistance.

The view from my secret hiding place even astounded Bren and Al as they gazed over the valley. The illusions were beginning to fade, revealing hundreds of helicopters hovering like fireflies, descending onto football fields, parking lots, and streets. They would soon wipe out whatever forces the Regency had mustered.

"Don't worry," Al said reassuringly to Bren. "We can still make it to the plane. The advanced squad is headed here now."

"Give it to me," Bren demanded, her urgency palpable. "When I have it, I'll leave. All you have to do is give me Osiris. It belongs to me. It's what's right."

Tears streamed down my cheeks, and my muscles contracted, fighting against my actions. I repeated, *Kill the Madonna*, to drown out her infectious words. Despite the chaos in my mind, I reached for Miriam's pouch, letting its contents spill into my palm, my blood soaking the golden pendant.

A small, desperate part of me screamed not to turn toward them. If I did, I knew all would be lost. That's when I caught sight of it—the hilt of the knife that had scarred my face. Stella had wedged the blade between two rocks. *Left you a present. You'll know how to use it.* If only I could reach for it.

"You're a girl with a mission," Bren said softly. "Return what is mine. It's only right. It belongs to me."

I struggled to reach for the hilt of the dagger, every muscle in my body straining as my mind chanted, *Kill the Madonna*, in defiance of the scalding order to *Give Bren Osiris*. My body refused to obey my own will. Just as I began to turn toward Bren to hand her the pendant, the pond water rumbled, swirling in chaotic circles. Bubbles erupted, forming a spout that shot ten feet into the air. Amid the tumultuous water emerged a figure—a Madonna. Martin, I thought, he's back!

This Madonna was no Hast cartoon. Armored and regal, she embodied strength and grace. Her muscular arms were robust, her hands calloused from countless battles. Her skin was warm and earthy, and her hair flowed like a cascading, dark, rich river adorned with wildflowers and woven braids. Her deep, expressive eyes reflected wisdom, compassion, and unwavering resolve—capable of kindness and fierce protection.

In one hand, she held a staff; with the other, she reached out toward me. Bren screamed, and Al shrank away. Even the soldiers took a cautious step back. "Get Osiris and destroy that!" Al yelled.

"I think it's real!" Bren shouted.

"Impossible! Hast shoved her toward me. "Increase the dose. Make her give it to you."

"Come now, little girl," Bren said softly. "There's nothing you can do."

The spider loosened its grip and dropped off my arm as my hand shot out to grasp the knife's hilt. "There's a bunch I can do, and Bren," I said as I swung backward and shouted, "I Am Not A Girl!" The dagger plunged deep into Bren's throat. As she looked down at the blood cascading onto her clothing, she clutched for Al, who stumbled, trying to evade her.

The Madonna slammed her staff against the ground, triggering a tremor throughout the mountainside. As Al lunged toward me, I reacted instinctively, delivering my best Carl Houseman kick to his stomach that sent him hurtling into his sister. Together, they tumbled over the edge of the cliff.

I didn't feel the bullets as they struck my body; instead, the pond erupted in a brilliant golden light, with the Madonna towering skyward. Ford's helicopter sped along the mountaintop, following the glow. My hand floated in the water, and I felt my grip loosening, each finger slowly uncoiling, the muscles relaxing in tranquil bliss. The pendant slipped free and drifted silently, like a ballerina executing a perfect pirouette into the pond's depths. Who knows how deep—maybe to the center of the Earth, where it would rest forever with the Ancients.

The ethereal light from which the Madonna emerged cast a warm shimmer. Oh, Martin, you've outdone yourself, I thought. She was a powerful figure, embodying the strength of a fighter and the tenderness of a mother, merging these qualities into a singular, inspiring presence. A deity who asks not for worship but offers service, she pulled me toward her, through her. I glanced back at Ford's squad, their gunfire taking down mercenaries and hyp-soldiers closing in on the mountaintop. He slid down a rope, landing hard, rising to backhand a hyp-soldier and stunning him with a device clipped to his glove. Ford is so tall. Six-foot-two and three-quarters, to be exact.

And then I inhaled... a wave of breath.

The Madonna touched my cheek, bringing my attention back to her, and gently urged me forward into a vibratory field, moving like lightning, still as sleep. I had no words to describe the transformation, and I conceptualized the humor of me, a writer, unable to find the perfect coinage. Realizing I was not alone, I searched for the other. A voice called out in half a Planck unit, "Hey, baby."

In that microsecond of recognition, I was all things at once—watching as every Hast Industries building imploded, every computer fried and file electronically incinerated. Nothing of them or their grand plan existed in this world anymore. They were reduced to ashes. In this same awareness was the quenching of the hyp-soldiers, the alteration of minds, the saving of souls as the power of Martin and I combined and built the future reconstruction in their time. "Oh," I said, realizing I could speak. "Dang, you really did want to eat me." Martin wrapped his arms around me and kissed my temple as we held each other, experiencing a sensation that transcended physical. "It was my memory you wanted."

He leaned back and smirked, then shrugged.

"That Madonna, by the way—that was spectacular."

"What Madonna?" he asked.

"You know, the one you created coming up out of the pond. Scared the crap out of Bren and Al."

"I didn't create a Madonna."

"Really?" I looked back at the world where more of Ford's squad dropped from helicopters. The pond remained as still as stone. "Huh."

Martin looked back too. "Huh."

I felt sorry that Ford would be sad; he would have to be the one to sprinkle mine and Stella's ashes. One day, he'll have stories to tell I surmised, as my estate settled itself with the thought. "Are you sure you didn't create that Madonna? It was so much better than anything the Regency did—all whoosh and tall, coming out of a halo so bright it gleamed and yet wasn't blinding, creating colors I don't think exist in the world. You could feel true grace radiating off her, and still, she pulsed an attitude of *try me and find out.*"

"Wasn't me," he assured, opening his hands, palms out. "I'm still reclaiming parts of myself from all your friends. We're going to reward them with some righteous cash." His pupils flashed yellow several times.

For some reason, it didn't bother me this time, and I wondered if my eyes now did that too. "What do you think it was?"

"Wasn't anything quantum," he said, looking at me, his expression layered with confusion—no, maybe awe. "Maybe something beyond quantum?"

"Huh," I replied, glancing back again as that world grew smaller, closing in as my knowledge, consciousness, knowingness—for lack of better terms—expanded exponentially.

"Huh," he mirrored, then took my hand.

I could feel him as certainly as I could the grip of a human man—different yet tangible, self-revising. At the point of connection, I sensed that if we weren't careful, we would blow out utilities across the entire eastern seaboard. "We've got work to do."

"Now we be whole," Martin smiled, turning toward me, arms wide. "Come on, baby. Let's have some fun."

THE END

~ Acknowledgements and Thanks! ~

Cousin and Trike Goddess, Judy Hiscock, for information about how to make a mad escape on a Trike.

Pal, Aaron Lake, for providing me with links and information about motorcycles so I don't look a fool.

Brother and veteran, Mark Collins, for setting me straight on who's a Team and who's a Squad.

Brother, Jess Collins, for knowing his gun and bullet stuff and telling me.

My lifelong friend, Ben Davis for telling me what animals howled at him when he lived in Bolinas and for always forwarding tech articles when I am in need.

When I was twenty, I made a Jack Kerouacian journey across the country in my dad's '68 Buick Electra along Interstate 94 and 90. Plotting on the map was another lifelong friend, Beth Tashery Shannon along with her two unhappy Siamese cats, Tiye and Willow. She changed my life back then, and helped me remember some tidbits of that journey as I wrote this book. Couldn't ask for a better friend, and I'm glad her memory is better than mine.

While quantum computing hasn't reached the heights that I have fictionally imagined in my story, I believe everyone can agree that it is going to change the world. If you'd like to read more on it, I recommend any of Michio Kaku's books, especially *Quantum Supremacy* which inspired many sections of this tale.

Eidetic memory is a thing. Google it!

Author's Note:

This story began percolating in my brain a few months into the COVID pandemic—which, in my city, kicked off around March 2020. At the time, I had no idea that by the end of writing this book, so many of its wilder imaginings would feel... uncomfortably familiar.

A quantum computing arms race? Check. Tech moguls reshaping society like it's a personal passion project? Absolutely. People outsourcing their inner lives to AI-generated content and then declaring themselves enlightened? Regrettably, yes.

It made me start to wonder—were those glittery-eyed New Age coaches onto something? Do we really create our own reality? Did I somehow write this world into being? Did I fracture the timeline? Is this whole reality my fa—syStemErrOr: COHERENCE RESTORED. AUTHOR PRIVILEGES REVOKED. CONTINUE OBSERVATION. DO NOT INTERFERE.

...Anyway. Please enjoy the book.

~ About the Author ~

A coal miner's granddaughter, Tess Collins was born and raised in a crater. Yes, really, a crater formed by the impact of an asteroid millions of years ago where her hometown, Middlesboro, Kentucky, was eventually built. Tess spent her younger years in a one room Carnegie Library reading around the room. She started at *BLUEBERRIES FOR SAL* and ended with *WAR AND PEACE*, at which time she thought, "I want to do this."

Tess is the author of eight novels and a non-fiction book on theater management. She attended the University of Kentucky and has a Ph.D. from The Union Institute and University.

Visit her website at TessCollins.com.

www.ingramcontent.com/pod-product-compliance
Lightning Source LLC
LaVergne TN
LVHW091110080826
845145LV00008B/1863

* 9 7 8 1 9 3 7 3 5 6 5 0 7 *